The Passion of Sergius & Bacchus

A Novel By
David Reddish

doorQ Publishing | Playa del Rey, California

The Passion of Sergius and Bacchus
Copyright © 2014 David Reddish
All Rights Reserved.

No part of this book may be reproduced in any form or by any means, electronic, mechanical, digital, photocopying or recording, except for the inclusion in a review, without permission in writing from the the publisher.

Published in the USA by
doorQ Publishing
8675 Falmouth Ave #306
Playa del Rey, CA 90293
www.doorq.com

ISBN-10: 0692240993
ISBN-13: 978-0692240991

Front cover art by Geoffrey Prince & Amanda Mullins
Back cover photograph by Ali Taylor

Printed in the United States of America

FOR ALL MY BROTHERS AND SISTERS.

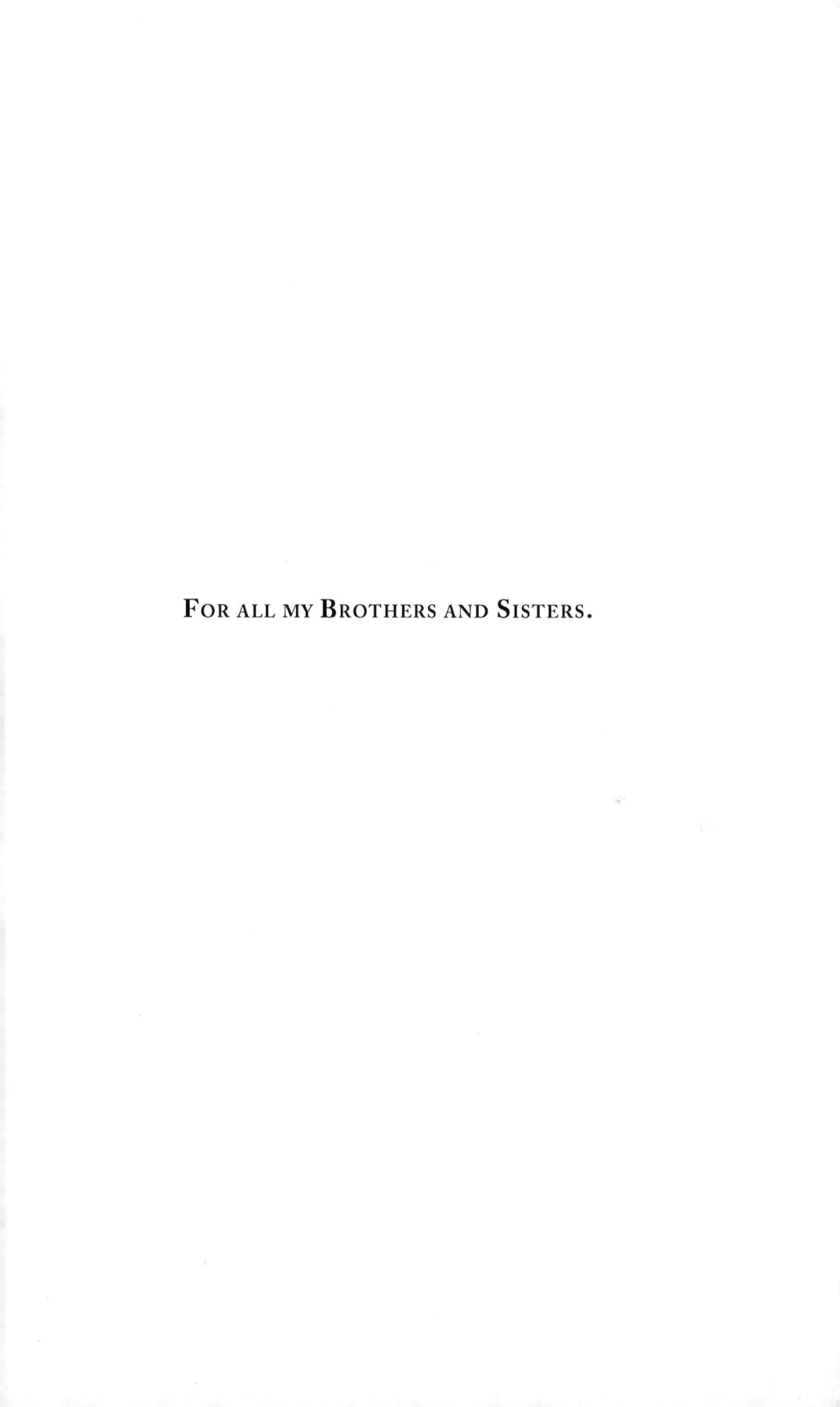

AUTHOR'S NOTE:

History, like memory, defines our identity. And, like memory, in the great course of time, things are lost, suppressed, or erased, leaving gaps in the record of mankind. It is here that God's most precious gift, the imagination, takes over. To know who we are, to understand the great story, sometimes we must invent our history, for while we may lack fact, we can always find truth.

This book is a work of fiction.

IN 357 A.D.

Engulfed in turmoil, the Roman Empire had divided itself in two: the West, overrun by barbarian marauders, and the East, prosperous, encroaching toward the orient, its boarders extending and contracting with battles against Persians. To quell growing civil unrest, Constantine the Great made Christianity the state religion, remaking temples to Jupiter into churches of the Anointed One.

After Constantine's death, his son Constantius took power as Caesar Augustus, high ruler of the Empire, in Byzantium, new capitol of Rome and home of the Senate, then executed all that remained of their family, save his two cousins, Gallus and Julian. Constantius appointed Julian, aged only twenty-three, Caesar of the West, custodian of Rome against the pillaging tribes. An academic at heart, no one in the Empire believed he stood a chance leading the armies of Rome, until one day in Gaul, a great battle altered the course of Julian's career, and changed the lives of two soldiers destined to make history…

Part One:
Death

Chapter I.

He could barely breathe. The August sun burned from its crest in the sky, boiling the slumping marshland below. The thick air, saturated with the odor of unbathed men like onions rotting in the sun, roasting beneath the insulation of black chainmail armor and a ridge helmet, felt like water in the lungs. The stench forced Sergius to pant and choke as he squinted in the sunlight, his head throbbing. He did his best to focus, the cacophony of the battle making his heart pound in his ears. He clutched his spear tight in his hands, crouching down behind the giant wooden disk of his shield. He extended his javelin outward, ready to reenforce the ranks already engaged far ahead of him. The howls of pain made his shoulders tighten as a new smell overlaid that of the sweat and swamp: the metallic smell of fresh blood, spilled into the fields of wheat ahead.

Sergius had fought in battle before, but unlike his comrades, he did not relish the charge of adrenaline that accompanied combat.

He had felt stinging blades slice though his flesh, heard the snap of bones and wails of agony. He had killed men, the light draining from their eyes before he could withdraw his sword from their fresh corpses. So many soldiers felt the same sickening feeling at their first battle, but learned to tolerate, even lust for the killing and destruction of war. Sergius never had; if anything, each cry of death only fueled his anxiety. The more he saw death, the more he feared it.

"The Vexillationes better leave some for the rest of us." Sergius's eyes flickered right to his friend Gaius, a bear of a man, his body as scarred and ravaged as the battlefield ahead. Gaius grinned a mouth of rotten, chipped teeth, his gaze unmoving on the forward ranks, betraying his desire to flaunt his skills of butchery before his comrades.

Sergius let out a sigh. "Are you ashamed of your division?" he asked Gaius, trying without success to mask his fear.

"Not at all," Gaius growled. "We Batavi should be fighting where our Caesar can behold our bravery, not cowering behind him like frightened kittens."

"That Julian is actually here defies all reason," Sergius said. "What experience has he as a general?"

Gaius's tone lowered in offense. "He shows the courage of Alexander just by—"

An equine scream shattered the air, yanking Sergius and Gaius back to attention. In the distance, they could see movement amid the ranks, hissing arrows slicing the air growing ever louder, as did the wails of both man and beast. The acid washed against the walls of Sergius's stomach like the tide across a beach, reshaping the tissue with each ebb and flow.

"Why do the horses scream so near?" Sergius whispered. "The Imperial Calvary should not be so close to the forward ranks!"

"The Alemanni barbarians must be approaching," Gaius uttered with a hint of excitement. "Perhaps we shall greet King Chondomar after all," he sneered. "And what a tribute shall we pay him with our blades!"

The screams grew louder still. Sergius's eyes narrowed, perspiration streaming beneath his helmet. Something had gone wrong; Sergius could feel it in his gut. He unconsciously held his breath, sensing some momentous event careening forward to meet their ranks. Though it seemed hours past, in mere seconds he beheld the anticipated horror, as his fellow soldiers in the forward position collapsed beneath a flood of barbarian troops. For the first time, Sergius had a clear view of the battle ahead: the shining helmets of Rome vastly outnumbered by the greasy heads of the Alemanni.

"The front line is breached!" Gaius cried, a perverse joy buried in his words. The Batavi needed no other command; the unit charged forward, their enormous shields, each painted red and adorned with an inverted black teardrop, plowing before them. Sergius, gasped for air as the unit climbed uphill toward the battle. He could only think of his Emperor Julian, whose life he must preserve at any cost.

Rising in lockstep and crouched together, the Batavi unit looked like a giant red turtle shell as it marched toward Julian's command post. Struggling to keep formation on the downward slope, the Batavi met with the sight of hundreds of Chonmodar's German berserker troops, each armored with a thick wooden shield on his back and a sword in his hand. The barbarians moved with the speed of frenzied insects, their blades stabbing in any possible direction, splintering the Roman formations. The Emperor's Calvary, charging from Julian's outpost ahead, fought back with chaotic fury, their horses crumpling beneath their riders as the barbarian swords pierced the animals' soft bellies, exposed beneath their hanging chainmail armor. Each time a horse dropped, tethering its mounted soldier with it, Sergius could see an enemy soldier hacking through the air at the disabled Roman, the Alemanni's long, blond, greasy hair whipping back and forth with every chop. The sight of such brutality melted Sergius's fear away; now only one thing remained—he had to protect Caesar.

The Batavi formation broke into a mess of flailing weapons against the Alemanni units. Sergius's pace quickened, his eyes fixated on the purple dragon pendant flapping just above Julian's tent, stalks of grain smacking his legs as he ran. With adrenaline burning in his veins, he plowed head on into an unsuspecting Alemanni, knocking the barbarian to the ground with the force of his body behind his shield. Sergius didn't stop, stomping over the toppled body of his adversary and launching his spear through the air like a javelin, its serrated point cutting into the chest of another unsuspecting opponent.

Nothing else mattered now—not his fellow Batavi, nor even his own life. He had one singular focus, his whole existence devoted to protecting Julian. As Sergius drew his sword and engaged the barbarian troops hand to hand, he pushed back toward Caesar's command post, its fluttering pendant high beyond the piles of dead horses and soldiers.

A jagged sword struck at Sergius shield, knocking him off balance, his feet sliding through the bloodied soil, his helmet slumping forward blocking his vision. Sergius struck back in reflex, his Roman blade slicing only air. The Alemanni struck again, this time throwing Sergius stumbling backward.

So fast, Sergius thought. *Have to match their speed.*

Reaching to his chin, Sergius unfastened his helmet, letting it fall to the ground as he charged forward again. The sweat gleamed on his face and in the ebony curls of his hair as his eyes met the gnarly opponent before him. As the barbarian raised his sword again, black and jagged teeth gritted, Sergius swung out his left arm, the thick wood of his shield meeting with the Alemanni blade, pushing backward and colliding with the barbarian's greasy body, tossing him to the ground. Without hesitation, Sergius thrust his sword downward, catching his adversary between the ribs with an audible wet snap. The slain German vomited blood and bile as Sergius withdrew his weapon, once again seeing the face of death in the face fallen before him. He paused only a moment, scanning for Gaius, who had already vanished into the battle. Turning back to his slain opponent, a flicker of guilt rising from his core, Sergius recalled his objective, and forced himself back into the fray.

Sergius stalked toward Julian's post, engaging one Alemanni, then another, then another without hesitation, his fear silencing any other thought. "Bastards," he muttered each time he crossed swords or trampled over the body of a fallen opponent. "Bastard *filth*! Barbarian *scum*!" The swelter and humidity of the day went unnoticed by him now, extinguished the icy chill of hate in his veins. He did not waver, he did not show pity; focused only on his objective: kill anyone who threatened the Emperor.

Sergius pressed onward, dodging the scrambling horses, attacking any Alemanni he could reach. He stopped only feet away from Julian's white linen tent, feeling a tinge of relief at the unassuming sight of the Emperor, his own sword withdrawn, shouting orders at his bodyguards scattered about as his advisors cowered within, peeking outward from the hanging fabric.

It took only a moment for Sergius to spot the enormous advancing barbarian, musculature lean and rippled as a lion's, sword raised, about to leap onto the unsuspecting Emperor.

"Lord Caesar!" Sergius screamed, running as he never had

before, to intercept the assassin. In one swoop, Sergius hurled his shield like a discus toward the advancing German, its spinning edge catching the enemy soldier in the jaw, interrupting his advance.

Julian instinctively backed away, his own sword ready to engage, as Sergius thrust forward toward the dazed Alemanni. Just before his blade could meet with the enemy flesh, the giant chopped through the air with his own sword, blocking Sergius's attack. The Alemanni spat blood, grinning as he engaged his opponent, reveling in the thrill of hand-to-hand battle. He charged again at Sergius who, clasping his sword with both hands, managed to block the attack.

The barbarian's might shocked Sergius as he stood his ground in their duel; he had never confronted a man of such physical power before. Fear welled in Sergius's stomach again. Parry after parry, his muscles ached and began to tire; he wondered how long he could withstand such an attacker, one who moved with such speed and force. Sergius held his sword diagonal to his chest and hurled himself forward onto his opponent, his weight pressing their bodies inches apart, the gleaming edges of their blades threatening to pierce both their flesh.

Sergius inhaled the sour body odor of the Alemanni, feeling the hot blood-tainted breath radiating from his lungs. "For what glory do you fight?" Sergius growled, knowing full well the barbarian couldn't understand his language. "What higher majesty is there than Rome?"

The barbarian thrust back against Sergius, who sprang backward and left, catching the Alemanni's arm with the edge of his blade as their two swords slid down against each other. The man-beast cried out in pain, distracted by his wound, as Sergius slashed out a horizontal lunge, all the weight and power of his body behind the chop. His sword met the barbarian's abdomen, slicing it all the way across, dumping blood and viscera into the field below. The German slumped to his knees with an awful, gurgling wail, dropping his sword, collapsing into the soaking pile of his own flesh.

Sergius gasped for air, exhausted and distracted again by the sight of death. He glanced first to Julian, who gazed in awe at the duelist before him, his mouth agape.

He closed his eyes a moment in relief. He flickered them open again just in time to see another barbarian hurling towards him, sword outstretched as he stabbed Sergius clean into his left shoulder. Howling in pain, Sergius felt his knees give way as the Alemanni brought his sword down again. With the last of his strength, Sergius raised his own sword to block the attack, managing to guard against the lunge, but letting his weapon slip from his hand in a moment of Pyrrhic victory. The barbarian, triumphant, raised his sword again, and then chopped down with incredible power.

In the splintered moment as the sword fell, aiming to split his skull, Sergius closed his eyes, ready to meet oblivion, his only thoughts of his family in far-off Hispania, how his death would disgrace them.

Forgive me, he thought.

His eyes opened again, resolved to meet agonizing death, just as a deafening clang exploded just above his head. Sergius teetered backwards into the grain, catching himself on his right elbow. His left arm incapacitated, he raised his eyes to behold the sight of his rescuer: a great mound of sinew packed beneath shimmering chainmail, polished helmet, and a golden torque about his neck. His shield bore the insignia of a yellow sunburst against background of black, and his sword extended outward catching that of the barbarian with the edge of its blade.

The Roman yanked his sword up, carrying the barbarian's with it as he kicked forward, his sandal meeting the Alemanni's stomach. The German let out a great wheeze, like the cry of an ass, as his lungs deflated and he staggered backward, away from the wounded Sergius. The Roman advanced on the Alemanni, his sword shining like lightning as it chopped through the air, smashing against this barbarian's weapon, disarming him.

The Alemanni dove to the ground, clawing in desperation for the sword. His fingers brushed the edge of the hilt just as the Roman brought his own blade down again with such might that in one swift motion,it smashed into the German shield covering the barbarian's back, splitting through the inches of wood with a deafening crack and continued its thrust, clean into the spine of the Alemanni's body.

The barbarian screamed in agony, his limbs giving way as he collapsed face down in the field like a slaughtered turtle. Putting his foot atop the Alemanni's cracked shield, the Roman freed his sword, and jabbed downward once again into the base of the barbarian soldier's skull. As he withdrew the blade, the Roman spat down onto the corpse of his defeated adversary—one last gesture of disdain.

Sergius heaved, grasping the bleeding wound of his shoulder with his good hand, blood gushing between his swollen fingers, as his Roman savior turned to face him. Sergius gazed up into his countenance, the sun creating the image of a shimmering halo as his golden helmet and torque reflected its rays, silhouetting his face in darkness. The soldier sheathed his sword and reached down, grabbing Sergius by his uninjured forearm, pulling him to his feet. Standing a few inches taller than his rescuer, lightheaded

The Passion of Sergius & Bacchus

from exhaustion and blood loss, Sergius teetered a bit, trying to maintain balance. The Roman reached around Sergius's body with his free arm pulling him close, steadying him until he'd regained his bearings.

Sergius looked down into the face of his savior, beholding the Roman's visage for the first time: simple featured, blond shadow of beard growth dusting his skin, lips cracked and dry, and eyes of pure violet, unlike any Sergius had ever seen. The irises seemed deep and clear as the Mediterranean; amethyst tunnels into a soul of warmth, sadness and pride. Lost in their allure, Sergius forgot the throbbing pain of his wound, and for a moment felt yearning that he never had before, never wanting to leave the sight of so regal a gaze. In all his life, Sergius had never known anything so perfect.

"S-soldier," Sergius stammered, trying to muster words. "I…" his voice trailed off, as the Roman pressed Sergius's body against his own, the chainmail of their armor grinding together. The soldier's arm slid from Sergius's back upward into the soaking curls of his ebony hair. Sergius's balance steadied just as the Roman guided their faces together, their lips meeting in a kiss of electric passion and no battle could ever parallel. The Roman loosed his hold on Sergius body, but Sergius didn't pull away, drinking in the sensuous contact, the earthy taste of the soldier in his mouth, comforting each other amid the stacks of bodies.

As he reveled in the kiss, Sergius body slackened vision blurring as his body went flaccid. The Roman's arm stiffened again, suspending Sergius body above the ground.

"Here!" a voice shouted, capturing the Roman's attention, as the darkness consumed Sergius. The violet eyes darted upward, glittering like two glowing planets in the night heavens.

"Yes, Lord Caesar!" the Roman called back, hoisting Sergius

above the ground, carrying him off. The fallen Sergius heard something strange in the Roman's pronunciation…an inflection he had never heard before. As he lost consciousness, Sergius reflected on the sound of the Roman's voice, on his perfect countenance.

This man is different, he thought. *Eyes like gems, voice so alien… perhaps he is Hercules himself, come to save Rome…*

…come to save me.

Chapter II.

"You ought to have Barbatio flogged to death."

Sergius awoke to an unfamiliar voice, his shoulder throbbing with pain as his vision came back into focus. He shifted, fighting to stay conscious, trying to sit up but unable to muster the strength. He lay under a woolen blanket on a woven mat, a basin of water and towel next to him. He rubbed his eyes, steadying his breathing, his shoulder burning with each inhalation. The thick smell of incense clouded the air, failing to mask the stench of war outside. Still, Sergius found the aroma a comfort.

"I fear that's just what Constantius would have me do," replied another voice, this one more familiar—confident, smooth and with perfect elocution. "Execute one of his favorite commanders; seem to encroach on his authority…"

Sergius blinked, his sight regained, to find himself under a large white linen tent, sparsely decorated with only a few oil lamps, a simple table covered with a platter of fruit, scrolls, a pitcher and set of goblets, four chairs, and, in one corner, a plain soldier's mat and blanket. A bulbous man sat at the table with silver goblet in hand, the other short and lean with his back turned to Sergius, hands clasped together behind him, head bowed in thought.

The man at the table scoffed, sipping from his goblet. "You're probably right," he muttered. "Barbatio deserts, leaving us horribly outnumbered, and he gets protected from penalty by Augustus himself. Instead you suffer the punishment of humiliation before your army."

"My troops suffer the real humiliation," the other man said, voice cool and firm.

"They will remember," said the seated man, words drawn out with dramatic inflection. "Just as you must remember: armies coronate Emperors more than even the Gods," he added, raising his goblet. "Or God, I should say," he grumbled, correcting himself.

"Enough Oribasius!" the standing man snapped, turning to face his companion. "Your words approach sedition, and I have no desire to see you executed." He paused a moment, staring down at the sitting man, as if to emphasize his point. "Besides," he said, nodding in Sergius direction. "We are not alone."

Sergius again tried to sit up, his skin waffled from the texture of the mat. The standing man noticed Sergius's movement, taking a step in his direction. The sitting man turned, and seeing that Sergius's had awoken, went and knelt beside him, taking the towel from the basin, wetting a corner, and dabbing Sergius's brow. As he knelt, Sergius could better see the mustard-colored togadraped over his round body. The man tended to his patient, and after wiping Sergius forehead, pulled back the blanket to examine his wounded shoulder, now wrapped in a bandage of cloth and twine.

"No matter," the mustard-clad man added, checking over Sergius's wound, "he probably doesn't even understand a word."

"What happened?" Sergius groaned, as much an inquiry as a rebuke to his steward's condescension. The man looked up in shock, tossing the towel back into the basin where it landed with a tiny splash.

The deminutive man walked over, fascinated by the wounded soldier before him. As he approached through the dim light, Sergius could finally make out the wine hue of his toga, and the bejeweled torque about his neck.

"You understand the Greek tongue?" the man asked, looking down at Sergius with anticipation.

"I do," Sergius replied, flinching again to clear his vision. As his eyes focused on the face of the standing man, Sergius's pulse leapt with shock. The standing man outstretched his palm in a halting gesture, encouraging Sergius to relax.

"Be still," the other man whispered, keeping a careful eye on Sergius's bandage.

"Lord Caesar," Sergius gasped in horror, trying to push up to his knees that he might properly bow before his Emperor. The pain from his shoulder seared again, and the dizziness returned as Sergius collapsed flat on his back.

"Your wound is deep, soldier," Julian said. "Do not let royal protocol impede your healing." A hint of cynicism echoed in his voice.

"This is my personal physician, Oribasius," Julian continued, folding his arms behind his back, nodding at the mustard-clad man at Sergius's side. "He's the finest in the Empire; follow his instruction and your wounds will heal."

"I've already sutured the tear," Oribasius said, again examining the cloth at Sergius's shoulder. "Quite well, if I may say," he added with satisfaction. "Not one spot of blood through the bandage." Oribasius rummaged through a small pouch on his belt, and produced three tiny brown seeds between his thumb and forefinger and placed them at Sergius's lips. "For the pain," said the doctor, as Sergius choked down the seeds dry. Oribasius patted Sergius's chest with fatherly affection. "It will heal fast."

Sergius shook his head in disbelief; not only had he survived the battle, he now lay in the royal tent at the feet of the Emperor himself, and with the royal doctor tending to his wounds. What kind of Caesar treated so lowly a man with such humanity?

"You protected my life out there today, soldier," Julian declared, voice grave. "I shall see to it the favor is returned." He paused in a moment of reverence. Oribasius looked up at the Emperor, as if waiting for approval. Julian nodded, and the doctor returned to his chair and goblet.

"But tell me," Julian said, taking his own seat. "Who are you, and how is it you know Greek so well? Men from this part of the Empire seldom do."

Sergius writhed again fighting the pain, though this time able to muster enough strength to sit upright. He heaved for breath as sweat condensed on his back.

"Careful or you will tear the stitching!" Oribasius exclaimed with frustration.

"May I please sit?" Sergius asked, rubbing his face, still uncomfortable lying down in front of his Emperor. Julian glanced at Oribasius, who rolled his eyes in annoyance as he returned to Sergius's bedside. The doctor wrapped Sergius's good arm about his neck, helping him to his feet. He guided Sergius, clad only in his loincloth, to one of the open chairs at the table. Sergius heaved as Julian poured water from the pitcher into a goblet and slid it across the table to his ailing soldier.

"Thank you," Sergius sighed, taking a long drink. "Lord Caesar, I am Sergius, son of Maximinus." Oribasius plopped into his chair again, disinterested in Sergius's words, his attention fixated on his patient's dressing, watching for spots of blood.

"You're lucky the barbarian missed the bone," Oribasius grunted. "You might have lost the whole arm."

"Enough," Julian ordered again, bored at Oribasius posturing. He turned back to Sergius. "You were explaining how you know Greek."

"I speak Latin as well, if you prefer sire," Sergius offered.

"No, no," Julian smiled with amusement. "I was raised with the classic tongue in the East; I far prefer it to the language of the West." Sergius bowed his head in acknowledgement. "But if I am not mistaken," Julian deduced, "it is from the far West you originate."

"Yes, my Lord," Sergius answered. "I come from Tarraco, in the province of Hispania Citerior, though my blood traces back within the walls of Rome itself. My grandfather moved to the province as advisor to the Consularius, where he took a wife and estate. My father, Maximinus was raised in Tarraco, though he traveled to Athens to study."

"As did I," Julian injected, putting a hand to his chin, fascinated by Sergius's tale.

Sergius smiled. "Father insisted on my fluency in both the tongues of the Empire and that my brother and I learn the classics, that we should be as educated as he. He forbade us to speak any local dialect, or even to play with other children, lest we forget we were Roman by birth, not conquest. He intended our education to be apparent at all times, that we might someday seek a place in the Senate, or as a Prefect."

"If you are so learned," Oribasius asked, skepticism apparent, "how did you end up a soldier in the swamps of Gaul? How are we to believe you know the classics, let alone have the proficiency enough to read or inscribe them?"

Julian's eyes inched to Oribasius, then back to Sergius. "Yes," Julian purred, "which of the classics is your favorite?"

"Virgil. Orpheus and Eurydice," Sergius replied without hesitation. "That a man would love someone so much as to battle his way past death and the Gods to retrieve her…" Sergius trailed off. "It's a beautiful story."

Oribasius's eyes widened, impressed. Julian smiled. "I much prefer Marcus Aurelius," the Emperor volunteered. "Nothing better expresses the ambition and agony to rule."

"You would know more about that than I, my Lord," Sergius replied with a slight bow. Julian chuckled.

"And so how did a wealthy, tutored man like you end up all the way out here with us? How did your father react to your joining the legions?" Oribasius pressed.

Sergius looked down, took a long sip from his goblet, and then let out a great sigh, wincing at the pain from his shoulder. Julian and Oribasius exchanged glances, intrigued by their guest's hesitation to answer.

"My father, like the rest of my family, is dead. Slaughtered by Germanic marauders, our estate razed, our fortune stolen. I am all that remains of my bloodline. All I have is Rome. I thought it best to memorialize my family by fighting for their country; by defeating the barbarian tribes that destroyed our home." Sergius fell silent in thought. "The animals that took them from me," he whispered finally, hate seething in his voice.

Julian and Oribasius both sat quiet, observing the wounded soldier before them. The doctor glanced at his Emperor, noticing the glimmer of tears welling in the Caesar's eyes.

"Your wound will heal in time," Oribasius croaked, breaking

the silence. "And it is time I took my leave," he said, rising from his seat and patting Sergius on his good shoulder. "And it is time you rested."

"You shall stay here tonight," Julian declared as he stood up. He looked at Oribasius, his glare preemptively silencing any objection from the doctor. Julian turned back to Sergius, still lost in thought. "It will be far easier than trying to move you out to your camp. Besides, you will rest better here."

Oribasius helped Sergius back to his mat, scrutinizing his wound dressing one last time before departing. Julian snuffed out all but one of the oil lamps before lying down on his mat on the opposite side of the tent.

"My Lord," Sergius said as Julian lay down. "You honor me with this hospitality."

"You are a son of Rome," Julian observed, voice clear and forceful as a bell. "You are an asset to your Empire, and a defender of your Caesar. Hospitality is the very least you deserve." Julian shifted, getting comfortable under his blanket.

"Besides," the Emperor added with a hint of tenderness. "We must be delicate for injuries to heal, and you've far deeper wounds than that of your shoulder." He paused a moment, leaving Sergius to wonder how to respond to such frankness from so great a man. As it happened, Julian's next words made it clear Sergius did not have to respond.

"Wounds of the soul…Heaven knows I know something of that."

Chapter III.

He awoke to screaming; screaming pain still emanating from his shoulder despite Oribasius's seeds, the screaming of a mob rising outside the cloth of the tent.

Sergius rolled onto his right side, body wet with sweat and dew from the humidity, the wool of the mat irritating his skin. The single oil lamp still glowed across the makeshift room, but even in the dim light, he could see that Julian's bed lay empty. The cries outside welled again and panic began to rush over his body at the possibility of another Alemanni attack.

Guiding himself to his feet, sheer willpower granting him the strength and quelling the pain of his shoulder, he hobbled for the fabric doorway of the tent writhing ahead of him in the gentle night air.

As Sergius pulled back the curtain, gazing through a crack into the outside, he marveled the sight of the night illuminated by hundreds of tiny torches and campfires freckling the gentle slope below. Moving between the overlapping shadows, thousands of Roman soldiers chanted one word with metronomic rhythm.

"Augustus! Augustus! Augustus!"

Sergius's eyes widened at the notion; the entire assembly of the Roman army in the West now committed an act of rebellion, calling for Julian's ascent to Caesar-Augustus, high ruler of the entire Roman Empire. Burning in the campfires of the hill below smoldered the embers of civil war.

Rapid movement and the sound of horses' hooves distracted Sergius. He spotted Julian mounted on his steed, riding back and forth before the tent, the pendant of his purple dragon in hand, waving with every stride. The sight seemed to frenzy the soldiers even more, as Julian came to a halt just before the entrance to the tent, drawing his sword and holding it aloft to silence the legions before him.

"My fellow Romans," Julian began, "you honor me with cries! But I am only a man, same as you. I am a soldier of the Empire, and like you, I serve my Emperor. Constantius is your Caesar-Augustus, and we must honor him, lest we disrespect all of Rome's majesty." A translator rode alongside the Emperor, repeating his words in Latin for the troops; in Athens, Julian had apparently never learned the Western tongue.

Sergius stumbled backward to one of the chairs, bracing himself against it before falling into the seat in disbelief at Julian's modesty. With half of the Imperial army at his command, and knowing that Constantius's forces were detained in a far-East campaign against the Persians, he actually declined the throne of the whole Empire, even chastising his troops for their support. The title of Caesar-Augustus bestowed godhood on its bearer; Julian would have at his command the new religion of the Galileans as well as the legacy of Jupiter. And yet he refused, calling himself only a man. What kind of Emperor would decline such power that he might wield for the good of the Earth?

"For it is for Constantius we fight," Julian orated, sheathing his sword, "and for the glory of our Empire! Alexander once conquered the world. Julius Caesar took Alexander's Empire and made it Rome's. And so shall we fight, now and until the end of time, these barbarians who would rape her of her glory!" The cheers quieted to stunned silence. "Severus now pursues the Alemanni beasts, and tomorrow, we shall press after them, crushing them beneath our strides, staining their fields with their blood! We will push them until they can retreat no further and then…" Julian paused for dramatic effect, his Athenian oration skills at their penultimate. "Then Chonmodar will bow before the garland of Rome!"

The translator interpreted Julian's words with equal drama as cries of the army shattered the air again as Julian raised his royal banner before his troops. The translator, still at Julian's side, pounded his right fist in the air with the rise of the banner. Sergius listened in amazement, hardly able to process the events of the past day. As he collapsed back into bed, his pain cooling as he reclined, he thought of that purple dragon flying in the wind, and the fortitude that matched its Imperial grandeur, how Julian deserved the Imperial robe and golden garland more than any man he could ever imagine.

As Sergius relaxed into sleep, he recalled another purple: the amethyst eyes of the soldier who had saved his life. His breathing deepening, his eyelids drooping, Sergius resolved to find his hero and show him the same gratitude that Caesar had bestowed on him.

As he lost consciousness, all Sergius could think of were the violet eyes, less ingratiated than awestruck at the soul within, and how, more than anything, he wished to bask in their magical light forever.

Chapter IV.

The next morning, Sergius awoke to an empty tent, with a small loaf of bread, chop of seared beef and goblet of water waiting for him at the table. The pain in his shoulder had muted a great deal, and he found himself able to move about with minimal pain.

At first unsure if he should partake of the meal set before him, he realized that it seemed deliberately placed for him at the same corner where he sat the night before with Julian and Oribasius. *Besides,* he thought, *what Caesar would sustain himself on the modest rations of the infantry?*

As he swallowed down a mouthful of the seasoned meat, he answered his own question: *Lord Julian would. What other commander in the history of Rome would care so much for his troops that he should treat himself as one of them?*

The curtain flung open, and the sight of the doctor Oribasius greeted Sergius. The physician stopped in the doorway, watching

Sergius as he nibbled at the bread, staring down with a look of utter disgust.

"Your Caesar offers you his tent, and you repay him by stealing his breakfast?" Oribasius spat with disdain. Sergius choked on the bread, coughing and spitting, lurching forward against the table as Oribasius broke into a gaudy laugh, walking to Sergius's side and patting him on the back.

"My apologies, son of Maximinus," Oribasius said, his back slapping giving way to a gentle rub. "A good laugh in the morning always leads to good health in the afternoon, especially when one is healing from battle." Sergius glared at his doctor, taking a sip from his goblet. Oribasius plopped down in a chair next to him, the fabric of his toga still rippling from his suppressed giggles.

"Must the laugh come at the patient's expense?" Sergius asked with more than a hint of resentment.

"No, no," Oribasius answered, leaning forward and examining Sergius's shoulder dressing. A tiny rust-colored spot had appeared through the twine and padding during the night, and the doctor poked and pressed about it with his finger. "But it is a fine way to shrug off lingering sleep," he muttered, distracted by the examination. "Are you in much pain this morning?"

Sergius shook his head. "I slept well," he told Oribasius between bites. "And besides, I'm anxious to rejoin my unit, and catch up with Chondomar, show his brutes some retribution."

"High spirits," Oribasius commended. "Always a sign of good health." He nodded down at the remains of Sergius's meal. "Make sure you eat all of the meat. It aids with repair and the blood loss." Sergius obeyed by taking another large bite of the beef. "Though," the doctor added after a moment, "I don't know that our Caesar would have you return to the Batavi."

"Have I displeased him?" Sergius retorted in shock. "My place is with my legion, defending my Emperor!"

"Defending your Emperor, yes," the physician said with fatherly warmth. "But it is Julian alone who shall decide how best you might serve."

Sergius finished the last of his breakfast, washing it down with a final gulp from his cup, watching Oribasius with riveted interest.

"You've proved your loyalty and gained the respect of the philosopher Emperor; not a task easily accomplished," the doctor explained with solemn gravity. A distant look came to Oribasius's eyes. "I have known Julian since he was a boy. In his family…" he trailed off, searching for the delicate words, "…trust is something not easily earned."

Before Sergius could react, the tent curtain flew open again, and in walked the Emperor Julian himself, flanked by a man of tiny stature and rodent-like features: angular cheeks, a pointy nose and huge overbite, dressed in a tunic of white and red peeking out from beneath his chainmail armor, with an ornate torque of gold about his neck. Tucked beneath, Sergius could make out the vague outline of a wooden Chi-Ro, the emblem of Constantine and the new faith. In his arms he carried a small pack of folded cloth. The stranger eyed Sergius with a skeptical glare, but said nothing, standing at Julian's side like an obedient dog.

"Lord Caesar," Sergius blurted, rising to his feet. Julian reacted by hissing and waving his hand about, as if swatting at some annoying insect.

"We've an army to defeat!" Julian declared, "though it's good to see you able to stand again. It means you can ride." Sergius's mind spun, trying to process all that had happened in the past day, as Julian took from his escort the small pack and placed it on the table before him and Oribasius. "May I present Nebridius, of my personal escort *Scholae Palatinae.*" The tiny man bowed slightly to Sergius. "The two of you will get to know each other very well."

"My Lord?" Sergius questioned, his confusion piqued. Julian cracked a smile, exchanging a quick glance with Oribasius. The Emperor looked back at Sergius with a smile, as if concealing some wonderful secret.

"For this I think protocol *is* in order," Julian said to his own amusement. "Sergius, son of Maximinus, legionnaire of the Batavi, defender of Rome, kneel before your Emperor." Sergius complied, dropping to one knee with his head bowed, the formality of his actions somehow putting him at ease before Julian, who placed his hands on Sergius's shoulders, minding the bandage. "For the valor of Aries in defending your Caesar, for your loyalty to Rome and her Empire, for the rare wisdom that glows in your heart as it would in that of Pallas, I hereby promote you to the title of Primercius, in the Imperial bodyguard of the Scholae Palatinae." Sergius eyes leapt up to meet Julian's beaming gaze, as the Emperor helped Sergius back to his feet. Nebridius took the loin cloth from Sergius waist, leaving him naked amoment before unfurling the garment, a flicker of gold spilling from its folds onto the table, revealing a fresh loincloth and red and white tunic, which he placed over Sergius body.

Julian took the piece of gold from the table, which Sergius now recognized as a torque identical to Nebridius's, and fastened it around Sergius's neck. The Emperor looked Sergius in the eye and smiled again, recognizing the soul of a friend.

"You are an asset, Sergius, which I wish to have at my side," Julian uttered in a near-whisper, "an honor to Rome and to your family." A flicker of sadness rippled across Julian's face as he looked up at Sergius, before snapping back to the present.

"Now," Julian said with vigor, "enough of my soldiers kneeling.

It's time I made Chondomar kneel!" He took a step away from Sergius and folded his arms behind his back. "Let us dismantle camp and pursue the barbarian!" He turned to Nebridius. "See to it that our new Primercius is fitted with the proper equipment and given a horse. He shall ride alongside me this day."

"My Lord," Sergius interjected, "I wish to return to my legion of the Batavi." Julian looked at him, eyes wide and nostrils flared.

"You would deny your new promotion?" Julian said, anger concealed beneath his slow enunciation.

"No, Lord Caesar," Sergius explained, "but I've some personal effects to collect. Codices of the classics," he added, trying to prevent any insult to Julian.

"They've likely been filched and used as kindling by now," Julian replied, his demeanor relaxing.

"They belonged to my father, sir," Sergius blurted in desperation. Julian's eyes flashed toward Sergius, before giving a nod of his head.

"Pray they're still intact then. Nebridius," Julian motioned again, "fit and equip him, take him to the Batavi and see to it this camp is dismantled." He traced the outline of the tent in the air with his fingers. "One hour."

Sergius followed Nebridius out into the morning sun, the grass and crushed wheat stalks moist beneath his bare feet, air thick but still cool from the night. As a much taller man, Sergius couldn't tell if his diminutive companion moved at a slower pace on purpose or by nature. Sergius, despite his wound, tried to encourage Nebridius to walk faster, but his fellow Batavi seemed not to notice.

"I'm honored to serve with you," Sergius said, trying to break through Nebridius's icy quiet as they walked toward the armament tent.

"I'm certain you are," Nebridius sighed. "Joining the Scholae Palatinae is no small feat, especially for one to rise in the ranks so quickly." Nebridius looked at Sergius, his overbite pulling back to reveal his uneven teeth.

"The Emperor thinks me worthy of the promotion," Sergius defended, his voice low.

"Obviously," Nebridius shot back. "And what the Emperor thinks is all that matters, yes?"

"Do you not share his opinion?"

"My opinion represents nothing compared to Caesar's. I, as a Roman, understand that."

Sergius stopped in his tracks. Nebridius inched ahead of him before turning back and glaring at him in puzzlement.

"Your opinion is still your own, and I think Lord Julian would agree," Sergius uttered, his inflection slow and deliberate. "Do you think me a fool, disrespectful to him?"

"No," Nebridius replied. "But it is my belief that only Romans should guard the Emperor of Rome."

"Then it is you that questions Caesar's judgment. And it is you who displays his ignorance." Sergius began walking again, passing his escort without even a glance. "I am Roman," he called back.

"Are you not from Hispania?" Nebridius questioned, scuttling to keep up.

"I am," Sergius confirmed.

"Then you are Roman by conquest, not birth," Nebridius contested.

"My family comes from Rome itself. I merely spent my childhood in Hispania, since my family was friend to the Prefect."

Nebridius's demeanor changed in a flash. "Then you serve here by choice?" He asked in disbelief.

"Do you not?"

The Passion of Sergius & Bacchus

"I serve that my family will gain favor with Caesar. We are native Romans, and wish to see the Senate restored to the West." Nebridius sounded apologetic, almost desperate. "I wish to be Prefect one day of an Empire restored to her full glory."

Sergius stopped again, looking his escort in his rodent-eyes. "Then I wish you luck," he said. Nebridius flinched, taking a step back, intimidated by Sergius's candor. "While I wish to hold no political office, I wish to serve Rome in all her glory."

Nebridius cracked a smile. "Then perhaps we want the same thing."

At the armory tent, Nebridius fitted Sergius with a new mail of armor, sword and much-needed Caligula-style boots, their spidery straps wrapping his wet feet. Sergius squatted down, allowing Nebridius to refit his torque over his armor.

"I'll return for my shield and horse shortly," Sergius declared, shifting the weight of his mail over his shoulder wound, fighting the soreness. "I must return to the Batavi."

"Wait," Nebridius called after him. "Your helmet!" Nebridius produced a golden parade headpiece, a helmet adorned with golden features of an artificial face. Sergius halted at the sight of the magnificent craftsmanship a moment, then turned and strode on towards the Batavi camp.

"Keep it. Helmets always pull my hair!" he called back to Nebridius.

Nebridius chortled. "Barbarian curls! Roman indeed!"

It took several minutes for Sergius to make his way through the ravaged field to the already dismantled Batavi camp. His heart pounded as he glanced around, searching for some sign of his belongings. A brief memory flashed through his mind: his father Maximinus reading to him from one of the books as a child in the garden of their estate, gentle breeze flowing in the Hispania sun.

The tale of the birth of Athena--Sergius listened rocking back and forth seated at his father's side, enraputred, his heart racing with every word. The tender memory gave way to the present, and his pulse raced as he began to panic.

"Sergius!" called a bawdy voice, startling him into a tiny jump. Sergius whisked around to see Gaius, arms outstretched, racing towards him with excitement. The great beast of a soldier captured Sergius in bear-like embrace, lifting him from the ground, laughing all the while. Sergius's wound burned with pain, and the pressure of Gaius's grasp squeezed him so tight he could scarcely breathe. Moreover, Sergius could tell Gaius hadn't washed in days; the pungent odor of flith and battle suffocating Sergius's inhalation. "By God, you live!"

Gaius released Sergius, who stumbled across the ground, first gasping for air, then yelping in pain. He grasped his wounded shoulder as tears formed in his eyes.

"You were injured!" Gaius realized, grabbing Sergius with his left hand to steady him, his right gently brushing over Sergius wound. "That's my boy! Taking it from those bastards and giving it right back! Still able to stand!"

"Barely," Sergius grumbled, crumpling into a slouch, glaring up into Gaius's ravaged face.

"Oh, come now man, it *cannot* be that bad!" Gaius retorted, amused by Sergius's pain. "You're a real soldier now, not some dusty scholar in the university!" He took a step backward, suddenly recognizing Sergius's new uniform.

"A Primicerius?" Gaius whispered in awe. "You joined the Palatinae?"

Sergius nodded, a grin of pride across his face. "Lord Caesar thinks highly of me."

"As should we all!" Gaius proclaimed. He raised his arms, head pivoting back and forth to the Batavi troops scattered about the remains of camp. "Brothers!" he shouted. "Caesar has created our Sergius a Primicerius!" Their fellow troops feigned excitement; none of them had much cared for the highly educated Spaniard. His promotion only added to their annoyance.

"You honor your family, and your fellow Batavi!" Gaius intoned, eyes steely. Sergius had never imagined that a man so vulgar as Gaius could show such reverence. For the first time, Sergius felt a true camaraderie, a feeling of belonging he had not felt since abandoning the breezy halls of his family's Hispania estate.

"The Batavi is my family," Sergius replied, solemn and gracious as Gaius. He gazed around at his fellow troops with humility.

"That we are," Gaius said. "Though none of us could replace the family for whom you fight." Sergius bowed his head, pensive, as Gaius pushed his way through the small crowd of troops. In a moment he returned, carrying three worn codices wrapped in a swatch of burlap.

"I kept these aside in hopes that you would survive the battle." Gaius smiled with a sincerity Sergius had never before observed in him. "You the scholar. The philosopher soldier." Gaius nodded. "A man like you deserves a proper funeral. I planned to bury them if we couldn't find you," Gaius confessed, handing the package to Sergius. Sergius unwrapped the burlap with great care, examining the books for signs of damage, and found none. His eyes welled, just enough to glass over but not shed tears, and he appreciated Gaius'ss friendship in a whole new way.

"Thank you," Sergius stammered.

Gaius let out another coarse laugh and squeezed Sergius's good shoulder. "Don't start yourself weeping, man!" he declared. "I'm certain the Caesar has little use for women in the Palatinae!" Sergius nodded, regaining his composure. He smiled, looking around at his assembled Batavi one last time before gazing up into the scarred face of Gaius.

"Thank you, my friend. I shall not forget this kindness." With that, Sergius pivoted on his heel, and set off back towards the Imperial outpost. As he walked, his heart full of pride, he ran his hand across the rough cover of one of the codices, again thinking of his mother and father and their beautiful home, of his childhood innocence, of happy days past that he hadn't appreciated at the time. He'd fought with his father, disrespected his mother. He'd been lazy in his studies much to the annoyance of his tutors. He thought the family estate modest and unremarkable, dreaming of the marble palaces within Rome's gates. And then, he'd lost it all, only to realize just how much he'd had in the first place, replaced by regret and loneliness.

He hadn't appreciated the Batavi either, not until that moment, and realized for the first time that what he sought by joining the army was not just patriotic defense of the Empire, nor revenge against barbarian marauders. He fought for love, to regain the family he'd lost, the joy and hope of years past. He'd realized it at last among his legion, only to lose it again to another higher calling.

Perhaps this is the cycle of my life, he thought, the smashed wheat crunching beneath his boots. *Perhaps to love something, I must lose it.*

Chapter V.

The horse had a coat of light brown, soft like suede, well groomed beneath the sculpted golden plates of Palatinae armor adorning the animal's body. This was not battle armor; merely decorative, the plates covering the length of his face and around the edge of the polished brown leather saddle, reigns intertwined between four horns of the seat. He whinnied and snorted, snout wet and pulsating, blond mane tussling in the morning light.

Sergius never cared much for equestrian sport, short of watching the occasional chariot race, and even then, the race appealed to him more for its social and gambling opportunities. His father had owned a pair of white Andalusians in Sergius's boyhood, and he'd learned to ride then, though years had passed since he'd mounted a horse. His rustiness, coupled with his injury, made for a fiasco when climbing atop his new steed.

The footmen did their best to conceal their laugher at this new bodyguard the Philosopher Emperor had selected. Had

Sergius not proved his mettle in battle the day before, the servants might have questioned Julian's sanity. An accomplished rider by comparison, Julian rode alongside Sergius, basking in the daylight, glancing over every so often to see if Sergius might slide from the saddle to the ground. The new Primicerius held the reigns for dear life it seemed, his back stiff, about to catch himself if he started to fall.

"Lucky for you, Hylas is more experienced at having a rider," Julian joked, referring to Sergius's transport. "He's the brother of my own Demosthenes," he added patting his horse's neck. Demosthenes had the same rich brown coat as Hylas, but a much darker mane. He also seemed more even tempered than his brother, plodding over the flat stone pavement of the road in perfect obedience, without so much as a whinny.

"You honor me again, Lord," Sergius uttered with a hint of disbelief. "You treat me as if you and I were brothers."

Julian laughed. "Well…" his voice trailed off, lost for a moment in another world. He stared out at the road of flat stones and gravel snaking out before them, the army marching with a calamitous smacking as it plodded along the pavement. "I see a bit of my own life reflected in yours."

"How so?" Sergius asked, gripping the horns of his saddle, suddenly even more on edge.

"I had a brother once," Julian began, the glow in his eyes turning to pools of pain. "Gallus. Tyrannical fool that he was."

Sergius let slip a quiet gasp, horrified that the Emperor should compare him to one he so despised.

"Gallus served as Caesar in the East for a time. Having him executed was the greatest thing Constantius ever did," Julian spat.

"I remember," Sergius added. "I joined the army around the

same time. Caesar Augustus moved to fight the Persian front, and his philosopher cousin came to power in the West."

"Gallus's death called me away from Athens to serve as Caesar," Julian confirmed. He lowered his eyes in thought. "Though Gallus may have deserved death, I, like you, would have preferred a scholar's life to that of a Caesar's." He scoffed. "I think Constantius would have it the same way."

"Why should you believe that?" Sergius asked. "He chose you…"

"He chose me because he had left himself no alternative," Julian interjected, voice bitter. "Constantius *slaughtered* my entire family, save my brother and I." He shook his head, disgusted, the pain still ever-present in his heart. "I was only five years old and made an orphan by my own cousin."

"I didn't…I didn't realize," Sergius stuttered.

"Of course not; you're too young," Julian snapped. "*I* am too young to remember."

"I'm nearly twenty-seven, sire."

"And what would a nine year old know of world affairs?" Julian asked slowly. "I'm now in my twenty third year, and I've scarcely a memory of my Mother or Father."

The two rode in silence a moment, Sergius once again awed by his Emperor, Julian lost in bitter memory. For the first time since he'd gazed upon his own smoldering estate, Sergius felt blessed to have known the time he'd had with his family. Each moment with them, even the angry memories of arguments and screaming matches now seemed precious.

Sergius looked off to the side of the road, examining the decimated landscape that stretched on for miles before them, sprinkled with the rotting bodies of Alemanni, cut down by the Romans as they fled Strasburg.

So much death, he thought, staring at the rotting carcasses, scavengers beginning to feast upon the remains. *How can I… Rome…any man survive in this world when death consumes all—man and beast alike? This world is one big executioner's slab, each one of us in line, forced to watch as all those around us die before we too meet Hades's blade.*

"Why were you spared?" Sergius murmured, half to himself, half to his companion. Julian let out a sarcastic chuckle.

"I can't be sure; I've not even met Constantius," Julian explained. "He probably thought Gallus too daft and me too weak to ever pose any threat to him." His eyes narrowed. "He was right on one account." Julian's voice had the timbre of an ominous bell, its bass rumbling the world around it.

"So you see," Julian concluded, his tone more affable, "I know your pain."

They rode in silence for some time after that, sun beating down on their backs as they rode west. Sergius's anguish burned in his stomach, his sweat beginning to soak through his new toga as the sun rose higher in the sky, the air thickening to a soup. He could feel the sweat of Hylas at his thighs, the horse having mellowed to its new owner. Still, all Sergius could think of was Julian—his pain, his responsibility to Rome, and how they all seemed amplified versions of Sergius's own feelings. He understood Julian's affection now, and he reciprocated it with his Emperor.

"You never wear a helmet," Julian observed, breaking the silence.

"No, sire," Sergius admitted. "I find them constricting, tangling with my hair."

"Were your hair not so long, you might not have that problem," Julian laughed. "It's a wonder you've not been mistaken for one of the barbarians."

"I can cut it, sire," Sergius offered.

"No, no," Julian calmed him through a smile. "Keep it as it is. Would that I could keep my hair so long," he said, lowering his voice. "Or even grow a beard." He stroked cleft of his chin with his right hand, suggesting a goat-like spiral like those Sergius had seen in statues of the Greeks. "I'm told, however, that such styles are out of fashion for a Caesar."

"Oh?" Sergius asked, not quite sure what to say.

Julian nodded, looking over at Sergius's uncomfortable expression and smiling. "If you choose not to wear a helmet, I shall not discourage you," he said with familial warmth. "Though keep in mind that blade could have easily pierced your face as it did your shoulder yesterday."

"Yes, sire," Sergius laughed in concession. *He has a point,* Sergius thought. *Had it not been for that other soldier...*

"My Lord," Sergius inquired. "The soldier that rescued me...I wish to find him and show him the same gratitude you've shown me."

"An honorable goal," Julian acknowledged with a nod.

"Know you his name?" Sergius asked, voice shaking with hope. Julian recognized the quiver in his companion's tone, and looked at him, puzzled. His eyes narrowed and blinked, as if trying to detect some ulterior motive in Sergius's desire.

"I do not," Julian admitted.

Sergius's heart sank.

"Though I do recall," Julian added after a moment, "he wore the torque of a Secundarius."

"He's a Scholae Palatine?" Sergius blurted in excitement.

"You didn't notice?" the Emperor chortled, amused and perplexed by Sergius's reaction.

"No my Lord," Sergius admitted. "I remember only the pain of my wound." He paused a moment. "And his eyes," he added. "He had eyes of perfect violet, a kind I've never seen before."

Julian thought a moment. "Interesting details you notice," he observed, ambiguous smirk on his face.

Before Sergius could reply, there came a great clamor: hollering and laugher and screaming of insults. Sergius tried to push himself up on his saddle, but with his left arm still wounded and his balance unsure to begin with, he slid back down onto his seat, craning his neck over the rows of Palatinae on horseback to see the source of the noise.

"Ah," Julian purred with satisfaction. "We've found Barbatio." He steered his horse off the path into the muddy field, with Demosthenes's every step slurping as his hooves landed in the muck. Sergius followed both out of curiosity and bond; after the past two days, he couldn't imagine being away from Julian's side.

Hylas whinnied and lunged about as the horse trotted over the wet earth, though Sergius wondered if his steed's reaction had more to do with the sight before him than the mud. Laying beside the road was the general Barbatio himself, writhing about with hundreds of his own troops cast along the countryside, guarded by an entire battalion, with peppered members of the Scholae Palatinae overseeing their suffering.

Barbatio looked far more like a customary general than Julian: older, tall with brute strength, broad shoulders and dark beady eyes darting about like a frightened rat's. But the sight of a disgraced officer alone did not give Sergius pause. He looked down, horrified, at the general who now lay covered in mud, dressed in a stola, veil on his head, and make-up smeared over his face like that of a whore, as did the hundreds of other troops littering the field. Sergius mouth went slack at the sight of such humiliation, lost in a storm of disgust and pity. Only the sound of Julian's laugh jolted him from his shock.

"And my cousin's general, the mighty Barbatio," Julian proclaimed, as if giving an oration before the Senate. "Defender of the Empire! He who would protect the West from the ineptitude of the Philosopher Caesar!" Julian's voice lowered with contempt. "He who would take the garland for himself, and abandoned his Emperor in time of battle, taking a full *six hundred troops* with him!" Demosthenes bucked and whinnied, mirroring his rider's anger. "Is this how you defend your Empire?" Julian seethed, a bit of spittle flying off his lips.

"Lord Caesar," Barbatio pleaded, his voice quivering like that of a child.

"Do not sully the name Caesar with false humility, for as you do, you disgrace all of Rome! You would see me die and take my crown, just as you would Constantius." Julian's voice grew cold, his eyes winced in disgust. "And so he shall know," he said, his tone low and ominous.

"Captain!" Julian called to one of the nearby guards. The soldier approached, though keeping safe distance from the agitated Demosthenes. "See to it the men remain until at least the Calvary has passed, lest they know what awaits treachery. When the last horse has passed along the road, release the troops and give them back their armor. Tell them they are now under my personal command and will follow me to slay Chondomar or remain with this beast of a traitor." His eyes fixated again on Barbatio, whose body quaked with fear before his Caesar.

"And as for the general," Julian uttered slowly, a hint of sadism buried within his voice. "Send him and his wife back to Constantius, and see to it they share dress all the way into the palace. Let Caesar Augustus see the loyalty of a harlot. Let him see just how weak, dumb, and animal he is, lower than even the soulless deceit of a woman. A man who betrays Rome is no man, but a worthless prostitute begging to be filled."

Barbatio cried out in terror and humiliation, his spirit broken, any sense of pride disintegrated. Sergius had never heard so desperate a wail, not even on the battlefield. He clutched at Hylas's reins, trying to find comfort in his new beast of burden. The horse bucked his head back, as if trying to nuzzle Sergius's arm. Sergius ran his fingers through the soft, wet mane and Hylas let out a great exhale, the two finding solace in one another.

"Lord Caesar, please…" Barbatio pleaded, crawling through the mud to Demosthenes's stomping hooves. "Do not let them steal my manhood! Take my wife! Take my sons! Take anything we own, but please…"

"You have already betrayed your gender," Julian declared, soulless and mechanical. "Did you not want to be made female?"

Barbatio broke into sobs of fear, his body crumpling into the shape of a fetus before the Emperor's horse. Julian grunted with disgust and turned back to the Captain.

"He has made himself a woman in appearance. Do not let your men make him female in the body. He and his wife should be unspoiled when they meet Augustus," Julian ordered. His eyes fixated on the shrinking form of Barbatio. "We are not the Alemanni. Some punishments are too inhuman for Rome. Were they not, I would have him nailed to a cross like the Galilean." Julian turned back to the Captain who pounded his right fist to his heart in salute. Julian nodded in acknowledgment, and lead Demosthenes back onto the highway, paying no further attention to Barbatio or Sergius.

Sergius looked down at the once-great general, now sullied with wet earth and smeared greasepaint. His feeling of pity now overwhelmed that of disgust as he lead Hylas back to the road. Then, struck by a thought, he turned the beast back toward the field and called after the centurion.

"Captain!" Sergius yelled, capturing the soldier's attention. "Know you a Secundarius with purple eyes?" The Captain stared at Sergius in confusion and laughed.

"I do not, sir," the Captain answered. "The eye color of my brother troops is the least of my concern."

"Yes, of course," Sergius replied, a phony smile on his face. He led Hylas back alongside Julian, disappointed at the lack of sign of his savior, his stomach soured by witnessing such grotesque humiliation.

He rode alongside Julian in silence, watching the Emperor's stony face. Only his flaring nostrils betrayed any inner rage; Julian's eyes fixated on the road ahead, expression cool and emotionless.

"I've less use for traitors than I do for women," Julian said at last, breaking the painful silence. "For women cannot help that they are born without soul or strength. Traitors like Barbatio surrender their Roman nature for lust of wealth or power bring shame to the Empire." He paused a moment in reflection, cracking a smile.

"What will my cousin say when he sees that creature before him? Doubtless Barbatio and his wife will be executed, finally sparing them their humiliation. But what of Constantius's own disgrace, for it was he that sent the general to spy on his inept philosopher cousin." Julian laughed at the thought.

"Perhaps he will recall that he alone does not posses the blood of the Empire."

Chapter VI.

The blazing campfires lit up the night sky, their billowing smoke eclipsing any celestial glow as the silhouettes of solders and glimmer of blades danced across the horizon. The Roman legions advanced with little resistance, as the Alemanni ran amuck with terror, their troops falling by the thousands.

Julian had set up his outpost in the ruined city of Concordia, just above the banks of the Rhine. From a crumbling guard tower, he could watch the Roman ranks form a crescent around the barbarians, walling them in from escape, pushing further and further toward the river, until sparkles of water gave him final indication that the Germanic troops had fled into the stream, preferring to drown than face the Roman blade. At long last, he'd trapped Chondomar.

Sergius and Nebridius, hands to their sheathed weapons, kept guard at the mouth of the stone doorway, its door long-ago chopped down during a barbarian sacking. Julian and Oribasius poured over a strategic map by lamplight, looking out through an opening in the collapsed wall toward the battlefield every so often to observe their victory in progress. Oribasius could scarcely contain his glee at his friend's long-awaited victory. Julian, modest as usual, kept his arms folded about his back, his expression stoic, deep in concentration as not to let one moment of arrogance let him slip, allowing the Alemanni to stage an upset in the final moments of the battle.

"It's a matter of time, Julian!" Oribasius reveled. "You'll wear Chonmodar's glittering helmet before dawn!"

"Why would I wear the effete costume of a barbarian?" Julian grunted in monotone. "I've no desire to catch lice." Julian turned out toward the battlefield, the light of the campfires reflected in his eyes. "Chondomar is only the beginning. Look around you." Julian's gaze did not waver, nor did that of his companions, all fixated on their Caesar. "We stand in the carcass of an Empire. This city, like so many others, must be revived for Rome to live on."

"My lord," Nebridius interjected, "is not the maintenance of a city the responsibility of its people? And are those people not the very forces we fight against? Why should a Caesar concern himself with the lives of an enemy, even a conquered one?"

"The loss of this city meant the loss of this region, Nebridius," Julian declared, annoyed. "A conquered people are still an asset, and they must learn that they are now part of Rome, not enemies of it." Sergius watched Julian turned to his other bodyguard, expression stone. "Rome must know that too."

Nebridius swallowed, his giant overbite shifting, nervous sweat forming on his brow. Julian turned back to his view of the battlefield, as Sergius and Oribasius exchanged a glance of discomfort. The room fell silent but for the sound of the battle outside, the Emperor deep in concentration, his companions afraid to speak.

The sound of footsteps coming up the ruined staircase made Nebridius and Sergius jump to attention, each withdrawing his sword, ready to fight. Sergius's wound still hurt when he moved his arm, though thanks to the care of Oribasius, the throbbing pain had reduced to mere soreness, allowing Sergius greater range of movement.

The Palatinae stood down as the weathered face of Serverus, Julian's deputy general, hobbled into the room, a walking stick in his left hand, his right arm wrapped around his back, the hand flapping and shaking like a leaf in the wind. An aged man, the countless battles Severus fought shown in his wrinkled face and receeding hairline, though his muscular frame testified to his still-brute strength. Julian greeted his commander with an embrace, his respect for the man obvious.

"News?" Julian asked, voice awash in anticipation.

"Alemanni can't swim," Severus proclaimed, baritone voice smooth as marble. He limped over to a pile of broken mortar and sat, rolling his walking stick back and forth against his palms, no doubt trying to conceal his shaking hand, Sergius assumed.

"We could see that from here," Oribasius fired back, probing for more detail. Severus looked up at the doctor, a smile appearing amid the wrinkles of his face.

"Victory is immanent," Severus boasted.

"And what of our losses?" Julian inquired with passion.

"Two hundred or so," Severus answered with pride. "Two hundred of three thousand Roman troops, in a battle against forty thousand Germans."

"That's still two hundred too many," Julian observed with reverence. Shaking himself from his brooding he reached out and locked arms at the wrist with Severus, grinning with triumph. "You've done a great service to your Empire, my friend."

"As my Emperor, you should expect nothing less," the old man replied.

"Indeed!" Oribasius ejaculated. "And what a feat for one of so advanced age!" The doctor chuckled at his own joke as Severus rose to his feet and hobbled toward him, eyes like a frenzied bull about to charge. Severus stopped, inches from Oribasius face staring the portly man down. The doctor chuckled again, this time in nervous fear.

The wrinkled skin writhed as Severus ground his teeth together, limping away from Oribasius and toward the door. Severus held a furious gaze as he turned to the Palatinae, cool smile on his face, eyes still burning.

"He thinks me old," Severus uttered low to Sergius and Nebridius. "The physician sees a crutch and assumes its owner lame!" he belted out, insuring both Oribasius and Julian heard, though his gaze never left the two bodyguards. Sergius shifted his feet, unsure of what to expect from the older commander. Severus only smiled.

Then, like lightning, Severus drew up his crutch and hurled it down like a club against Nebridius. The Primicerius had enough time only to draw his sword half way from its sheath before Severus struck against his hand. Nebridius cried out, dropping his sword back into its sheath as he wrenched his hand in pain, just as Severus's cane met with the back of the soldier's knee, knocking him off balance to the floor.

Sergius had not even reacted when Severus's crutch swung at him with the same electric speed. Holding his breath, Sergius managed to pull his sword with his good arm and block the attack, his blade meeting the staff at a perpendicular angle to his body slicing a tiny chip in the wood. Undaunted and unflinching, Severus attacked again, aiming for Sergius's lower extremities. Sword met crutch again, and once more as Severus targeted Sergius head. They held fast against each other, Severus gazing into Sergius's eyes, his head tilting like a curious bird as he stared at Julian's newest bodyguard. Severus withdrew, nodding with approval as Sergius caught his breath.

"Oribasius looks at me and sees a cripple," Severus said with pride. "I look at him and see a blind man." He turned back to the doctor with a defiant smirk, resting against his cane once more. He turned back to Sergius. "I look at you and see the speed of Mercury, which is impressive with that wound." He chuckled to himself and nodded to the doctor. "Especially if this one did the bandaging."

As he passed Oribasius on the way back to his seat, Severus gave the doctor a soft pat on the shoulder, indicating the benign nature of their rivalry, the doctor's eyes following Severus with great interest. The general made no apology to Nebridius, however, who rose again to his tiny height, nursing his sore hand and leg, with a resentful glare. Severus had made apparent his strength, as well as his disregard for perceived ineptitude.

Across the room, Julian seemed bored by the whole exchange, though tolerated Severus's ego. The Emperor glanced over his shoulder, back down at the battlefield for a moment, then started for the door.

"It's time," Julian proclaimed, starting down the stairs without waiting for any of his companions. "Let it be finished."

All four followed Caesar down the staircase and out into the ruins of the city meeting with a score of additional Palatinae. Sergius gazed about, trying to recognize any of their faces in the darkness as they mounted their horses and marched toward the battlefield, but had no success.

On the banks of the Rhine, littered with barbarian corpses in every direction, bodies floating atop the water, flowing downstream with the current, Julian and Chondomar at last met face to face. Brought before the Caesar, the barbarian king, adorned in an intricate golden helmet sculpted to match the face of its bearer, Chondomar knelt bound at hand and foot before Julian. Julian dismounted and with slow relish and sanctimony, removed the helmet from his enemy's head, running a hand over the golden indentations, examining the markings. He then turned back to Chondomar, hunching over for intimacy.

"You fought well for a savage," Julian whispered. A nearby translator reiterated the words in the Alemanni dialect, Chonmodar's eyes darting to him, then back to Julian with understanding. "My cousin shall know that when you meet him."

Climbing back atop Demosthenes, Julian raised the golden helmet for all to see, proclaiming victory with one word all would understand: "Rome!" he cried with a fury erupting from his solar plexus.

The cheers exploded from the legions, and Sergius, for the first time, found himself reveling in the thrill of victorious battle. He looked around at his fellow soldiers, his fellow Scholae Palatinae, and felt a solidarity he never had before. He looked to Julian, who commanded Sergius's respect as no other ever had. He felt proud: proud of his countryman, proud of his Empire, proud of his Caesar.

And yet, in the midst of his joy, Sergius found his thoughts wandering again to those perfect amethyst eyes, and the exhilarating feeling he'd experienced staring into them. He gazed out into the darkness of the battlefield with a yearning that dwarfed his pride.

Battle won or lost, Empire preserved or crumbled, he had to find his savoir before all else.

Part Two:
Amethyst

Chapter VII.

Despite the decisive victory over Chondomar, little changed for the Western army following the battle of Strasburg, and indeed, little changed for Sergius, either. Under the command of Severus, the Roman army slogged on for almost two years back and forth over the Rhine visiting Gaulic villages, demanding tribute from remaining Alemanni warlords, securing the release of imprisoned Romans, and re-annexing territories in the name of the Empire.

Sergius also found that his new promotion and the rush of victory did nothing to pacify his hate for war, or his guilt for killing, which festered within him at every battle. Soldiers still fell by his blade, the life slipping from their bodies, and he felt as though he'd committed some transgression against his race, even for the glory of the Empire. Julian kept Sergius close during these journeys, the latter regaling his Caesar's insatiable appetite for stories of Sergius's boyhood. Having little personal experience with a family, Sergius surmised that Julian took a vicarious solace in Sergius's memories, yearning for a family of his own.

Still his friendship with the Emperor complicated matters. Sergius encountered nothing but distain and envy from his fellow soldiers: the lower legions were always jealous of the elite Scholae Palatinae with their better wages, and even Sergius's fellow bodyguards shunned him as one who had risen too fast within the ranks,with the Emperor preferring his company to other soldiers who he'd fought alongside much longer. To make matters worse, Sergius had also managed to learn some of the Germanic dialects, which made his fellow Palatinae look on him with even more suspicion. Sergius found that his only friend within the Palatinae was Nebridius, a man he thought more annoying than enjoyable, but nevertheless, Sergius appreciated someone with whom he could commiserate.

Sergius's closest companion, however, he never would have expected—Hylas, his blond-maned steed. On his free time from rotation, Sergius often rode into the woods or lay in an open meadow, reading his father's codices, reliving the adventures of Ulysses or the Argonauts. Hylas would keep a quiet vigil at his master's side, often nuzzling him in a sign of affection, which Sergius returned by patting his long equestrian face. Sometimes he'd even murmur the words aloud, as if recounting the story to a child. Hylas always seemed interested, a certain awareness glowing within his mica eyes, never so much as grunting while Sergius read. In those quiet moments, Sergius found a greater peace than he'd felt since leaving Hispania.

Despite the reprieve ganted by his horse, Sergius still brooded over having not located the soldier who'd saved his life those months ago. His searches yielded little hope, as much as from the sheer size of the Palatinae—five units, at five hundred guards each—as from the uncooperative nature of his fellow bodyguards. Though Oribasius had removed the stitches from Sergius's wound after a month, the jagged keloid scar still ached every time Sergius moved his arm. At night, in his barracks, Sergius would rub the tissue, hoping that pain would stop, hoping at the same time that his burning need to find his rescuer would quell. After two years, neither passion had.

Sergius thoughts often drifted, lighting on the visage of his skeleton packed beneath the layers sinew pulling at the bones. After all, was that not the essence of every man: olified dust clad in rotting, delicate flesh, forced to watch the flesh decay until the last breath escaped the ribcage, letting the bones turn to dust, and the soul escape into nothingness.

The swelter of summer turned to the crisp air of autumn, and by November Julian and his army had set up a seasonal base in a modest Roman outpost well protected from any barbarian attack: Paris. The city had once been a center for the conflict between Rome and the Germanic tribes, but thanks to improvements in infrastructure and a towering guard wall around the perimeter, Paris had become one of the most secure bases for governing the region.

Sergius loved Paris, and relished spending time there during the winter months when the cold weather prohibited warfare. With its grand amphitheatre, Forum, quaint shops and grandiose bath house, it reminded him of how he'd always dreamed Rome looked in the glory years. Upon moving into the city, Julian granted Sergius a large insula near the Imperial Palace, complete with running water, latrine and a bondservant. While nowhere near as grandiose as his family's estate, Sergius found the multi-room apartment luxurious, especially compared to the rough mats and crowded tents he'd spent the summers living in.

He'd not expected the servant, either, but Julian had sent him as a personal gift. Called Didymos, he'd come from Constantinople itself, and had served Constantius for a time before his reassignment to Julian. Sergius couldn't decide if the Emperor had given Didymos to Sergius because he also spoke Greek, or because the Julian wanted as little to do with his cousin as possible. Either way, the servant proved competent, keeping the insula clean and cooking savory meals for his master.

Though he loved the city, growing up in the warmth of Hispania had not trained Sergius for the frigid winters of Gaul. The cold weather bothered his health to no end. His head ached, his breathing passages caulked with thick mucus, the post-nasal drip irritating his throat, making his tonsils swell. It hurt to breathe. It hurt to swallow. It hurt to *live*.

One frigid night, on the advice of Oribasius, Sergius set out to the public baths to enjoy a steam, hoping that the warmth might bring him comfort or at leasat unclog his nostrils, granting him a reprieve. Traversing the frosted streets of Paris, dressed in his informal Palatinae uniform—a red and white cape complimenting his tunic, and a thick woolen cloak to shield him from the chilly air—Sergius realized just how lonely his life had become. Joining the army had afforded him a purpose; an opportunity to serve his Empire. His wealth and property were more than satisfactory, and he enjoyed a friendship with the Emperor himself. But despite all these achievements, Sergius couldn't help but feel empty, as if none of them meant anything. His success certainly hadn't filled the loss of his family. He needed someone to take pride in him. His thoughts drifted again to his dead father, and Sergius's stomach burned with regret. He pulled his cloak tight around his body, and hurried to the bath house.

A warm blast of air greeted Sergius as he entered the Parisian baths, delighting him with the sound of echoing laughter and voices. The smooth tiles and mosaics offered him welcome as he paid the balneator his entry fee. The main atrium, its dome arching high above lit by countless oil lamps, casting long shadows, gave the room a sensuality that made the hair on Sergius's frigid arms stand on end. Stone benches lined the chamber, as did posters for plays at the amphitheatre and the gladiatorial games. Stacked along the wall, small tables with merchants sold oils and incense to half-naked patrons. The baths attracted most of its regulars in the afternoon, so most of the peddlers had cleared out by that late hour, though the number that still remained surprised Sergius.

Sergius smiled to himself, glad to connect with people again, even if just through proximity. He entered the dressing room where an attendant helped him out of his clothes and into a towel. Any other day, Sergius would have started with a cool swim in the frigidarium pool, but with his bones already freezing, he headed straight to the sudatorium for a hot steam. Sitting on a bronze bench in the dark and cloudy room, he at last relaxed. His salty perspiration mixed with the flowing vapor, running down his face to his lips. Occupying the bench by himself, he lay down against the warm metal, smiling at the faint scent of cedar in the room, muscles loosening, nasal congestion draining.

As he sat, feeling comfort for the first time in weeks, Sergius's mind wandered back to the days of his youth on the family estate. He thought of his mother and father, wondering what they would say of his adventures in the East, his scars of battle. No doubt his mother would fret over the stab wound; she always rushed to Sergius's side for even the tiniest boyhood scrape. His father, forever a political man, would have choice words to say about their philosopher Caesar and his campaigning to rebuild the Empire. Still, no matter how critical of Julian he may be, Sergius knew his father would take pride in his son's friendship with the Emperor, always hoping to see Sergius one day made prefect.

Finding his eyes heavy and sleep seductive, Sergius thought it best to move on to the caladarium to rinse in the hot water. Besides, far more people congregated and conversed in the caldarium than in the sudatorium, where like him, men tended to sit in quiet relaxation, often dozing in the steam.

The ornate arches of the caladarium and fine tile floor sprawled out in the dim lamplight as Sergius entered the chamber. An attendant welcomed Sergius by rubbing olive oil all over his skin, kneading his muscles in a gentle massage. As he descended the ceramic steps into the pool Sergius noticed the oil of his skin leaving a rainbow sheen atop the water. He smiled; he could see the azure tile beneath the ripples, laid out in the shape of a trident, the sign of Neptune. Other bathers packed the room, swimming about, bobbing up and down on the edges of the pool, discussing everything from politics to chariot racing. Sergius drifted to one side, and swung an arm up over the perimeter, steadying himself, splashing hot water all over his sweaty head, letting it soak his ebony curls.

"Sergius!" called a familiar voice. Sergius's heart leapt as the smile of Gaius greeted him. The two met halfway in the center of the pool, Sergius's overjoyed at the sight of a familiar face.

"My sweet boy!" Gaius bellowed, slapping Sergius on the back. His hand drifted over Sergius's collarbone, his finger running over the tender edge of his scarred wound. "Your scar! You wear it as a badge of honor!"

Sergius looked down at the keloid on his shoulder and chuckled. "I suppose so," he sighed, rubbing over the pink tissue.

"And to think, they said you wouldn't survive five minutes in battle!" Gaius purred. "Now word is you're at Caesar's side day and night."

"The Emperor does enjoy my company," Sergius admitted with a hint of humility. "It's a privilege."

"He would not keep a weak man close to him if he had any sense," Gaius added. "Though I begin to wonder if our Caesar has retreated to his books again."

Sergius looked at him, perplexed. Gaius waved his hand through the air in a gesture of disregard, splashing warm water about the two of them.

"Julian could have been Augustus by now," Gaius contended. "Instead, he lets Constantius issue proclamation after proclamation taking credit for Julian's achievements. *Our* achievements," he spat.

"Julian is a wise man," Sergius argued. "He does what is best for Rome, and, for that matter, what will save him from the fate of the rest of his family."

Gaius cocked his head to one side, realizing Sergius's point.

"A true observation," Gaius confessed. He sighed. "I grow weary of city life. I want to get back, back out to slaughtering barbarians day and night! A man can only feel his mettle in battle!"

Sergius mood soured at the thought. He dunked his head under the water, wiping his jet black curls back over the contours of his skull. His eyes met Gaius's with a gaze of annoyance as he let out a great sigh.

"You'll get your wish soon enough," Sergius moaned.

"Don't be ashamed of your manhood," Gaius said, grabbing Sergius by the nape of his neck. He looked at his timid friend a moment, before a devious grin crossed his scarred face.

"There *are* ways to indulge manhood off the battlefield," Gaius admitted with glee. "Other swords to be drawn. Come!"

Gaius swam back to the staircase and exited the pool, water

running everywhere off his scarred, behemoth form, a thick coat of wet hair on his back clinging to his skin. Sergius followed, suspecting what his friend had in mind. The thought did not bring him comfort.

"I never did congratulate you properly on your promotion," Gaius said as Sergius climbed out of the water. An attendant rushed over with a towel, dabbing the lingering droplets from his bronze skin. Sergius glared at his friend, skeptical.

"My treat," Gaius offered. "And I know just the place."

Chapter VIII.

The giant bronze phallus wrought with green tarnish mounted above the door confirmed Sergius's presumption. An oblong building of unremarkable brick, Sergius wouldn't have noticed it if not for its single adornment, and had he been alone, he would have passed by in disgust. He stopped short, glaring as Gaius plodded up to the weathered door, almost skipping with glee.

"No," Sergius declared, feet planted hard against the frosted pavement. Gaius turned and rolled his eyes. Walking back, he pushed his friend forward toward the brothel. Sergius's heels slid along the street, fighting Gaius's grip.

"You're a man! Act it!" Gaius challenged, halting at the entry, banging on the door.

Sergius relaxed in surrender as the door swung wide, revealing an older, svelte man in a blue toga, graying hair plastered to his head with oil, his upper lip cleft, revealing a mouthful of rotting teeth.

"Gaius!" the man slurred, throwing wide the door, arms outreached in welcome. Gaius entered, dragging Sergius over the threshold into the dark foyer as the svelte man slammed the door, pushing a large deadbolt into place.

"Tigranes!" Gaius greeted back, the two exchanging a quick embrace. "How's business?"

Tigranes waved an enormous hand, fingernails overgrown and yellow. "Always the best," he sputtered. "Always the best!" He eyed Sergius up and down, assessing his newest customer. "Brought a friend?"

"A gift," Gaius explained. "He's joined the Scholae Palatinae."

"Ah, then we are graced by your presence, sir," Tigranes said with a slight bow, putting a hand to his chest. "Welcome. Whatever your pleasure, I'm sure we can accommodate." His slender finger, nails overgrown and tinted, pointed toward a billowing rose curtain, inviting the men to enter.

Sergius coughed at the thick smoke of perfume and incesnse permeating the air. Though the cloud he could see about a dozen women of varying races, builds and sizes, faces smeared with cosmetics, adorned in stained togas of sheer cotton, sitting on benches and blankets around the room, waiting for a customer. Sergius's clenched his jaw as they all began to writhe about like maggots on a corpse, each competing for attention.

"What's your taste tonight, Gaius?" Tigranes asked, taking a step into the room. "German? Greek? Slavic? We even have a virgin!" he boasted, his bony finger pointing out a blond haired girl about ten, hiding herself in a darkened corner. "She's extra, of course," he added with a hiss of air from his cleft palate.

Sergius recognized the look in Gaius's eyes as the same frenzied lust he displayed before battle. He had no chance of dissuading him now, not after his gaze had seized on the prize.

The Passion of Sergius & Bacchus

Gaius watched the girl as she lowered her eyes, hiding from his gaze. He cocked his head back in thought, tongue running between his teeth and lower lip. The girl looked terrified, and Sergius felt a sudden, irrepressible need to protect her.

"What good can she be," Sergius improvised, trying to sound casual, "if she's had no experience?" Gaius flashed him an annoyed glare.

"I can teach her a good deal," he grunted with pride.

"Of course, but…" Sergius's voice trailed off, trying to stall.

"You just want her for yourself," Gaius interrupted. He looked at the girl, then back to Sergius and scoffed. "Well," he said after a moment, "it is you we're celebrating."

"So?" Tigranes interjected, drumming his fingers together. His face oozed lascivious greed, eager to get on with business. His lips curled back in an unsettling rictus, the edges of his cleft palate stretching apart.

"Let him have her," Gaius declared with slow resentment. His eyes lit immediately on another girl, this one dark skinned and a bit older. She matched his gaze with an inviting smile. Gaius reached into a small pouch at his belt and produced a handful of coins which he placed in Tigranes open palms.

"Will that cover the both of us?" Gaius asked.

"Enjoy," Tigranes whispered, pocketing the coins in a pouch of his own.

Sergius watched as Gaius walked over to the chosen girl who took both his hands and pulled him into a darkened hallway at the opposite side of the room. Without thinking, Sergius took a deep breath in disgust, the fumes of incense forcing him to cough again. Beneath the pungent aroma, Sergius could smell the foul stench of sweat and septic filth. He pulled a hand to his mouth, trying to recoil from the air around him.

"So you get the new girl," Tigranes said with enthusiasm. Across the room, the virgin girl's eyes met Sergius's with utter terror.

"No!" Sergius blurted, his stomach churning. Tigranes jumped in shock, taking a step backward, his enormous hands pressing outwards.

"No?" Tigranes asked. "Is she not to your liking?" Sergius could sense the frustration growing beneath Tigranes's voice. Sergius's mind darted, searching for an excuse.

"She's not to my tastes," he said after a moment, watching the child's eyes flicker with hope and relief. Sergius turned to Tigranes, who gazed back at him, perplexed. The whoremonger drummed his fingers again, eyes locked on Sergius, squinting in thought.

"Ah!" Tigranes purred, his long index finger pointed upward. "I understand." He patted his filthy hand on Sergius back, who squirmed against his touch. "Come this way."

Tigranes led Sergius down the long, darkened hall, lined with curtains covering narrow stalls. From within, shadows danced against the fabric accompanied by grunts and moans of carnal action. At the opposite end, the hallway opened into another, much smaller room, less decorated but still unmistakable in nature.

"Here," Tigranes wheezed in presentation, palm outstretched. Six boys crouched together in a corner casting lots for modest coinage snapped to attention before their customer. "Pick one. And don't be embarrassed." His lips curled into a disfigured smirk. "Gaius indulges in the same from time to time."

The six boys stood and lined up shoulder to shoulder, each one familiar with the routine of advertising to customers. Sergius estimated them between the ages of twelve and seventeen, each at varying stages of pubescent development. Unlike the exotic selection of women in the next room, the boys all seemed local:

Germanic or possibly Slavic, with either very fair or dark features. None of them seemed afraid; accustomed to competing for an itinerant job.

"Ah, you like them closer to manhood," Tigranes whispered, jolting Sergius from deep thought. He realized that his blank stare had fallen on one of the older boys with blond tresses and pale blue eyes, a hint of whiskers on the edges of his upper lip. Tigranes motioned, and the boy took a step forward, the others resigning back to their game. The boy looked at Sergius with a grin of seduction—he'd done all this many times before, well enough to know how to attract business.

"Anything you want," Tigranes assured. He turned to the boy and nodded, taking a step back, folding his hands with satisfaction. The boy laid his hand upon Sergius's wounded shoulder, the pressure inflaming his nerves. He fidgeted a bit in the boy's grip, as he lead Sergius back into the hallway and into an empty stall.

A single oil lamp in a brick alcove lit the narrow bunk, no wider than a coffin, the room's sole function apparent from the pillows and blankets lining the floor. Sergius and the boy squeezed in together, the boy closing the curtain behind them.

"So," he asked Sergius, trying to initiate their transaction. "You can inspect first," he said, removing his toga displaying his naked body for Sergius approval. "I've none of the marks of Venus." The boy took the oil lamp in one hand, running it along his naked body. Sergius watched the light fall over the boy's youthful anatomy; a dusting of hair on each pectoral and at his navel, trailing downward to his prize. Most of his baby fat had melted away giving way to the sinewy contours and form of a man, his back lean and firm, legs sculpted and tufted with fuzz.

"Here," the boy said, handing the lamp to Sergius. He bent over, stretching his buttocks open. "No lumps." He stood and took the lamp from Sergius, placing it back in its alcove. "Or you can use my mouth." The boy's jaw hinged wide as he leaned forward to Sergius's face. He snapped his mouth shut with a grin and began to unfasten Sergius tunic.

"That's alright," Sergius blurted, recoiling against the wall. "You…you don't need to…" The boy snickered, and reached for Sergius's clothes again.

"What's your name?" Sergius asked, his voice nervous.

"Justinian," the boy smiled.

"You don't have to do that," Sergius told him, grabbing Justinian by the wrists.

"I want to," he murmured. "Please."

"Will you just sit and talk with me?" Sergius cringed at the sound of his own desperation. Justinian looked at him, quizzical and confused.

"If it pleases you," Justinian shrugged, his blue eyes fluttering. He squatted down against a pillow, crossing his feet and wrapped his arms around his knees, locking them together by gripping his wrists. Sergius crouched down against the wall, trying to leave some space between the two of them, his heart pattering with anxiety. Justinian watched Sergius, waiting for him to initiate their encounter.

"How old are you?" Sergius asked him, voice low.

"I'm not sure, sir," Justinian confessed. "About seventeen I think."

"You're fully grown?" Sergius exclaimed in disbelief.

Justinian nodded. "Tigranes lets me stay because I don't look it. I don't have to scrape off the hair on my body."

"How did you come to this place?" Sergius whispered.

"My mother bore me here. She died when I was small, though Tigranes had cast her out before that. She had a disease that warped her face." Justinian shrugged away the memory, his eyes running over the wooden divider wall of the bunk. "It was good of him to let me stay here and work."

"You like this?" Sergius asked in disgust. Justinian nodded, his whole torso bobbing with his head.

"It's better than living on the street, especially as a child," Justinian reasoned. "Better than living as a slave where I'd have no choice at all. Tigranes takes care of us. He won't let the men beat us or cut us or do any of the awful things to us that the street walkers have to do."

"No child should have to suffer the vices of men," Sergius declared, his voice clear and firm.

"Don't think me worthless," Justinian rebutted, "As a boy it was shameful, true. But I never had interest in the company of women, only men." Sergius reflected a moment.

"Neither have I," Sergius realized with a murmur. "I've never known the touch of a man or a woman." Justinian tried to conceal a snicker beneath his hand, but let a smirk betray his amusement.

"There is no shame in the pleasures of the world," Justinian whispered, a certain seductive huskiness in his voice. He reached over and placed his hand on Sergius thigh, watching his body tense with the contact. "For what you do to me will make you no less of a man."

"And what of you?" Sergius asked. Justinian averted Sergius gaze, a hint of shame in his face.

"I do what is in my nature; what lets me eat. Men cannot marry other man as they once did, for Roman troops are in short supply, and I am ignorant and low born. How else should I survive?"

"Rome is too great to allow her children to suffer at the lusts of wicked men," Sergius growled, shaking his head. Justinian laughed in genuine amusement.

"I can tell you did not grow up poor," Justinian observed. "The world has always been this way, with men of power preying on whatever their desire. Rome is no exception, no matter what Caesar or the Senate or any other power might declare."

"It is wrong," Sergius urged back. Justinian hugged his knees together, thinking a moment.

"For a child," he acquiesced. "As a child men did not desire me for my body, but for my innocence." Justinian's eyes flashed with a moment of pain. "And most of the other boys are forced to betray their nature to survive. But would you condemn my place here as a man, if it is my instinct to desire other men?"

"No," Sergius murmured. "Each man should be true to himself." They sat in silence a moment. "And you may be ignorant," he added, "but you posses wisdom, Justinian."

Justinian leaned forward, reaching out and beginning to unfasten Sergius tunic again. This time, he didn't resist.

"And if it's my nature to desire your body," Justinian whispered, "should I be denied that?"

"No," Sergius whispered back, eyes to the floor, afraid to look Justinian in the face.

"And if you desire mine?" Justinian pulled Sergius to his feet, slipping the folds of his cape and tunic from his body, leaving Sergius in only his loincloth.

"It is my nature too," Sergius sighed, closing his eyes.

Justinian knelt down again, untying the loincloth, leaving Sergius naked in the flickering lamplight. Justinian ran a hand over his olive, Spanish body, feeling the grooves of his muscles, the curls of hair against his skin. Justinian's hand moved lower, meeting with Sergius hardened arousal, both of them silent, quaking with nervousness at what the other might do. Justinian leaned in, his lips meeting Sergius's with a moist, sweet kiss, arousing both of them even further. Their loins brushed against each other with a hint of moisture. Sergius heart pounded, wracked with shame but relishing every moment, as Justinian reached down and started pumping his erection in perfect rhythm.

Sergius's eyes flashed open, and he looked down at the boy before him: a boy whom predators had robbed of his childhood, whom society had robbed of his manhood, his body sewn with the seed of countless men. Sergius took Justinian's hand and knelt to face him, his chestnut eyes meeting the clear blue of Justinian's.

"You are wise," Sergius whispered removing Justinian's hand from his swollen member. "And you are beautiful. And you are true to your nature in which there is no shame. But you are still too innocent, not yet a man." He squeezed Justinian's hand tight in his own. "And though it would please my own, I cannot in good conscience know your flesh."

Justinian's eyes drooped like those of a scolded child, his innocence even more apparent, making Sergius confident in his decision. He kissed Justinian on the forehead and dressed himself as the boy lay naked across the pillows, deep in thought. Not sure what else to say, Sergius lift the curtain to exit the stall.

"You're a good man, Primercius," Justinian said, halting Sergius in his tracks. Sergius looked at him one last time and forced a smile, before ducking through the curtain, down the hall, and out the front door into the streets of Paris without so much as a thought to Tigranes or Gaius.

As he plodded though the frosty streets, breath clouding in the air before him, Sergius felt even more alone than when he'd set out to the baths that night. Heart heavy, wracked with melancholy, he set out to see the only friend he knew would hear his problems.

Chapter IX.

"I'm sorry to wake you," Sergius apologized, "but you tell me: did I do the right thing?" He leaned forward onto the wooden door of the stall, resting his head on his folded arms, watching the silhouette dancing before him in the shadowy torchlight. With slow, heavy footsteps, the dark form stepped toward him as if pondering Sergius's words.

Hylas extended his head into the dim torchlight, his wet nose kissing the side of Sergius face with a gentle nudge. He shook his blond, equine hair back and forth, suggesting a wakening yawn. The horse hung his neck over the edge of the stall gate, against Sergius's arms, his tiny ears twitching atop his head. His eyes sparkled like two onyx stones in the night, watching his master's sullen face.

Sergius reached up and stroked Hylas's long face. "How did all this happen?" Sergius asked, shaking his head, trying to understand. "I almost died in battle. I very well could again, and regardless, nobody lives forever. Am I wasting my life?"

Hylas let out a low grunt, as the sound of footsteps through the Imperial stables made Sergius jolt upright. Another man, built square and firm as a brick, moved through the shadows in full armor. Before Sergius could react, the man called out in a foreign tongue, his voice booming through the stable walls, making the horses whinny and stomp with fear.

Sergius froze in confusion. The man called out again, and this time Sergius recognized the language as one of the Germanic dialects. It took him a moment to process, before he could remember enough to understand.

"*What are you doing here?*" the stable attendant called out, annoyed at so late a visitor.

"*I…visit…horse…*" Sergius struggled. He looked around, searching the air for some unseen cue that would help him recall the vocabulary.

"*Horse?*" the stable man called back, stopping a few feet away, still in shadow.

"Hylas." Sergius pointed to his steed with an uncomfortable chuckle.

"Hylas," the man repeated, stepping into the light. Sergius gasped as he recognized the uniform of a fellow Scholae Palatine, though of a lower rank; a *Secundarius*. He stood shorter than Sergius—but then, most other men did—and wore his full armor, indicating that he was on duty in the stable, guarding the Imperial Calvary. As if the language barrier didn't make it obvious, the Secundarius appeared of local origin: Aryan features, pale skin, with blond locks peeking out from under his helmet. He stared at Sergius, a mix of skepticism and caution.

"*Mine horse,*" Sergius managed, pushing back his cloak to reveal the uniform of a Primicerius, fingering his golden torque.

"Sergius," the Secundarius uttered in amazement through a thick Germanic accent. Sergius stumbled back in surprise, bracing himself against the pen door with his left arm. Hylas perched his head over Sergius's shoulder, watching the scene unfold with great interest. Sergius reached up and patted his long face as a reflex, his subconscious looking for comfort.

"You know me?" Sergius asked in his native Greek, forgetting the language barrier in shock.

"You serve Caesar," the Secundarius replied, forcing the Greek through his natural drawl. Greek had an unnatural sharpness coming from his mouth: "Caesar" sounded harder, more like "Kai-Zair," though the guard managed to get the pronunciation of Sergius's name just right, with perfect elocution.

"Everyone know de great Sergius who save Kai-Zair at Strasbourg," the soldier went on in broken Greek. "Julian love eem."

"Did you fight in that battle?"

The Secundarius nodded. "I come vrom Germania, but I am Roman," he declared, shaking a finger at Sergius with great vehemence. "I not bar-bear-eon." His posture shrank a bit, as if somehow not believing his own words. Sergius, intrigued, stepped toward the stable guard, stroking Hylas's face as he moved away from the pen.

"And you speak Greek?"

"I learn de speech ov my Kai-Zair. I am Roman."

Sergius nodded, his eyes squinting as he examined the curious man before him. Most of the Germanic troops recruited to the Imperial forces retained their native languages or spoke Latin, the tongue of the Western Empire; few had learned Greek, even since the Senate moved from Rome to Constantinople, most of the commanders in the Germanic campaigns had originated from the Latin-speaking West.

"You serve him well," Sergius complimented after a moment. He smiled, then patted Hylas again, intending to leave the soldier to his guard.

"How your scar?"

Sergius froze. He spun around, eyes aflame, breath heaving with shock.

"How did you know about that?" Sergius demanded, striding over to the Secundarius, who cowered backwards, intimidated.

"*I saw you stabbed,*" he said, reverting to his first language. It took a moment for Sergius to process the words. He stared the stable guard, who ducked his face in embarrassment. Sergius didn't waver, watching his fellow Palatinae on edge.

"Here," Sergius ordered, throwing back his cloak again and rolling his sleeve to reveal the pink wound on his shoulder. The German looked up a bit, just enough to gaze at the warped skin. Sergius studied what little of his face he could see, cast in dim light by the torches and hidden beneath his helmet.

The Secundarius took a timid step toward Sergius to closer examine the scar. Sergius watched him very carefully. He reached up and unfastened the soldier's helmet. The German backed away but otherwise did not resist, as Sergius tightened his grip around the chinstrap, not letting him retreat. Sergius undid the fastening, and with both hands slipped the helmet from the soldier's head, unveiling a full head of golden blond hair and soft pale skin. Tucking the helmet under his arm, Sergius put a hand to the soldier's chin, tilting his averted gaze up to meet Sergius's own.

Sergius held his breath, as he gazed into a pair of perfect violet eyes, glimmering in the dim light, awash in fear and embarrassment.

Sergius's whole chest throbbed; he felt his heart might burst forth from within, falling to his savior's feet in homage.

"I am sorry," the stable guard said, pulling back from Sergius's touch.

"You saved me!' Sergius gasped, not understanding the man's humility.

"You devend Kai-Zair. You great man," the soldier murmured, his eyes averting Sergius's again. "Blood Roman. Wealthy. Strong. You…" He paused, struggling for the right word. "Thin-Ker," he managed at last.

"Philosopher," Sergius chuckled, gathering what the German meant. "And I owe you my life." Sergius said, voice quaking with emotion.

The German shook his head, ashamed. Sergius cocked his own head back in confusion.

"I shame you," the Secundarius croaked. "I only vant to show my…admiration." Sergius didn't have to think long to know what the soldier meant. He couldn't believe that something that had meant so much to him, which had haunted him, making his heart weep since that day on the battlefield could cause his savior, a man he so cherished and felt indebted to so much pain. Sergius reached out at stroked the German's cheek again, his gnarled fingers coarse against the soft, pale flesh.

"No," Sergius murmured. His eyes met his savior's, the gems of amethyst as deep and pure and beautiful as he'd remembered. Sergius dropped the helmet, letting it roll across the stable floor. He slid his hand back through the blond locks, pulling him close, their lips meeting in a gentle press at first, crescendoing with intensity into a forceful lock. Their mouths twisted together, gripping at each other as if to draw the life from one another, to merge into one perfect being, each filling the emptiness of the other.

When at last they separated, their eyes remained locked, the only sound the gentle footsteps and breath of the horses, bodies and souls aroused, their hearts pounding like war drums.

"You do not shame me," Sergius whispered, still in awe. "You honor me." The Secundarius didn't back away this time, his gaze never leaving Sergius's own. "What are you called?"

"Bacchus," the guard answered. "I am Bacchus."

Chapter X.

Sergius set off to his duty at the palace under a grey sky, clumps of snow dusting over his shoulders and hood. The cold seeped into the metal of his armor, but he didn't mind. The sight of Paris in winter, the crisp air, the glistening snow all seemed so perfect. He felt as though some great burden had released him, letting him stand tall as he strode through the city.

What a fine life I have, he thought to himself.

Entering the palace, Sergius laughed again as he discarded his cloak to an attendant and proceeded through the Great Hall to Julian's study. Even after more than a month in Paris, Julian had yet to adorn his walls with any of the usual silks and decorations associated with the Empire. Plain walls and common furniture peppered the room which was otherwise barren of the usual mosaics, silk draperies and ornate carvings found in an Imperial palace, making the hall seem even more cavernous. It was nothing like the Imperial Palace of Caesar Sergius had imagined in his youth…more like a town hall where the proletariat might congregate. But even then, public halls usually had some kind of distinction—graffiti if nothing else. Julian's Great Hall had nothing.

Julian's study had only a few more decorations than the great hall: antique furniture from Athens, busts of Aristotle and Marcus Aurelius, and two Persian divans covered in plain wool situated around a flaming cistern. A great window between two columns overlooked the city, though covered in thick curtains for the winter, Julian let it hang open just a crack. A plain table held a silver platter with fruit and a glass pitcher of water, along with a set of goblets.

"You found him."

Sergius froze in his tracks as he entered Julian's study, the Caesar pacing about the room, a stack of letters in his hand. A gentle breeze flowed through the room, as the chill of the outside crept through the curtains and intermixed with the heat of the flaming cistern. Sergius could feel his hair tussle against his forehead as Nebridius, his usual guard partner, looked at him in confusion.

"Lord Caesar…" Sergius mumbled, taken aback.

"Sergius, you may think your feelings concealed," Julian observed as he dropped the letters onto the table. "But in all our time together, I've never seen you smile like this."

Sergius realized Julian was right. In fact, thinking back over his entire life in Hispania or in Gaul, Sergius could not think of a single time that he had found himself smiling for no reason at all but that he was alive, and that living brought him joy.

"You serve me well," Julian complimented, taking a sip from a nearby goblet, "just as your emotions serve you. Congratulate your brother, Nebridius. He has found his savoir!"

"Is it true?" Nebridius asked in quiet dismay. Sergius nodded, beaming from ear to ear.

"You are an observant man, my lord," Sergius complimented, his eyes darting to the tile floor in slight embarrassment.

"Come, what's his name?"

"Bacchus, my lord." Sergius explained how they'd reconnected in the stable, how Bacchus served as a Secundarius, how Sergius recognized him immediately by his unique eye color. Nebridius and Julian listened with great interest, with even the former showing some genuine happiness.

"We shall have a guest tonight," Julian announced, taking a small bell from the table. In a moment a young female servant appeared, bowing to her Emperor and awaiting instructions. "Prepare a feast," Julian ordered.

"A feast on such short notice?" the girl asked in panic. "We've so little time!" Julian laughed at his servant's agitation.

"It shall be for only four," Julian instructed. "Have it prepared by sundown." He waved the servant girl away, and turned to Nebridius.

"Send for the Secundarius guard Bacchus," he told Nebridius. "Make sure he's bathed and rested. Have him here just after sundown." Nebridius stared at the Emperor, awed by such generosity. "Go!" Julian waved, prompting Nebridius to charge out the door, flicking a glare of resentment at Sergius as he departed.

"Lord Caesar, you honor me," Sergius stammered at a loss for any other words. "But I cannot ask…"

"Nonsense," Julian interrupted. "This Bacchus saved the life of one of my best soldiers, and aided in preserving my own. He too, as you so often have observed, deserves gratitude." Julian looked down a moment, his thoughts distant as he chuckled to himself.

"Besides," Julian murmured, "it's not often one of my soldiers is so in love."

Julian's words stunned Sergius. The soldier looked about, again at a loss for any response to his Emperor.

"Don't deny it," Julian smiled. "You love the man whether you realize it or not. Or you will soon enough."

"How do you know this, sire?"

"Read Ovid, my philosopher soldier. You learn to recognize the signs." Julian gazed into the flames of the cistern across the room a moment, his thoughts again distant. "Mutual fulfillment should be the ideal for any couple, regardless of their composition, or so claims Ovid. I have never known this feeling. I hope you are more fortunate."

"Thank you, lord Caesar," Sergius murmured, his heart weeping for his Emperor. Julian cracked a modest smile, sensing his Primercius's compassion.

"I shall look forward to tonight," Julian said, taking the letters back in hand, returning to business.

Chapter XI.

The formal triclinia looked dressed for some state affair, despite the mere four place settings at the great square table; one setting each at two of the four sides, two placed together along another side, and the last left open for service, the one hint that the patrons would dine as equals, not subordinates. A great rack of lamb, its smell of charred meat, garlic and herbs wafting through the air, lay atop a great platter with tender green garnishes. Next to it, a platter of fruit and bowl of leafy salad complimented the roasted meat. A great crackling fire burned in the fireplace beyond the table, the light dancing across wall paintings of Athena, Dionysus and Zeus, the shadowy flicker giving their images an ominous lifelike quality. The couches around the table wore their most regal dressings of bear skin and red velvet pillows, as if expectant of Augustus himself, not mere bodyguards.

Sergius broke a sweat at the sight, as barefoot servants moved about the room, finishing setting the table with bronze cutlery and golden flatware. In all his time at Julian's side, he had never seen the Emperor allow such extravagance. Sergius didn't feel flattered, so much as intimidated by such hospitality.

Much to his relief, Oribasius greeted Sergius with a tall goblet of fine wine and his bawdy laugh. After all the months since Strasburg, Julian still managed to intimidate Sergius—he was Caesar, after all—but Oribasius had a way of putting Sergius at ease, perhaps because of his relaxed demeanor around the Emperor, and perhaps just his friendly persona.

"You finally found him," Oribasius congratulated, slapping Sergius on the back. Sergius took a long drink from his cup, wine burning his lips with its sensuous kiss, his body calming into the gentle tingle of intoxication. Oribasius's hand drifted over to the wound at Sergius's shoulder, the pain having subsided, leaving only the warped scar tissue as a reminder of his injury. "Julian knows how much this means to you," Oribasius said, voice quiet. "That's why he's gone to such great extravagance. The man would never allow this decadence for anyone else. It offends his sensibilities."

"His generosity is not lost on me," Sergius replied, taking another swig from his goblet. "I hope my love of such luxury will not hurt my graces with him."

"No, no" the doctor reassured with a smile. "You saved his life. Bacchus—that is his name, yes?" Sergius nodded.

"Yes," Oribasius continued, "Bacchus. He saved your life; ergo he also indirectly may have saved the Emperor's as well. Julian is a gracious man."

Just then, the sound of sandals against tile captured the attention of the two men. Greeting them, the image of Bacchus, clean shaven, hair meticulously placed, dressed in his formal Palatinae attire complete with shining golden torque, stepped into the room, chistled face aglow in the firelight.

"Bacchus!" Sergius greeted, hardly able to contain his excitement. The two men embraced, and shared a soft kiss without thought at all—a simple reflex at the sight of one another. Oribasius motioned to a servant as he extended his arm to Bacchus.

"At last we find you," Oribasius remarked after introducing himself. Bacchus hung his head low, eyes to the floor in deference to a man of higher social class. Sergius wondered what would happen when the Secundarius actually met the Emperor.

He didn't have much time to dwell on the issue, for just as a servant offered Bacchus a goblet of wine and refilled the glasses of Sergius and Oribasius, the booming voice of Julian himself greeted his party.

"Gentlemen, welcome to my home," the Caesar said, his arms outstretched in a friendly greeting. Dressed in his formal purple Emperor's robes, and despite his average height, the man actually looked to Sergius like the deified Caesars of legend. Bacchus dropped to one knee, head bowed as if for execution at the sight, and Sergius could see his breathing accelerate to a pant, sweat forming on his brow in the firelight. It didn't even occur to Oribasius or Sergius to give more than a respectful nod to Julian, both of them distracted by Bacchus's formal gesture. Julian chuckled, placing a hand on either of the kneeling soldier's shoulders, gave a wry smile to his other two guests.

"Welcome, soldier," Julian intoned with reverence. "Now please, dispense with the formality. I am Caesar, but I am also a man the same as you." He pulled Bacchus by his shoulders to his feet, looked him in the eye, and smiled. "They tell me you are called Bacchus."

"Bacchus, grandson of Iuventinus," the Secundarius introduced himself, his words slow and deliberate to combat his Germanic accent. Sergius could tell Bacchus had practiced his elocution for the party, though he noticed Bacchus's eyes never left the ground, too intimidated by Julian to even gaze on his face.

"Grandson?" Oribasius asked in confusion. Sergius too thought Bacchus's answer odd; he wondered if, in his nervousness, he had forgotten his Greek.

"Grandson of Iuventinus," Bacchus repeated, his eyes flashing across the doctor's face. Julian tilted his head back, intrigued by this new guest.

"Come, let us dine," Julian invited, showing his guests to the table.

Julian reclined onto the couch with his back to the fireplace, Oribasius at his left, and Sergius and Bacchus sharing the place at the Emperor's right. The firelight over the back of Julian lit the Caesar with subtle aura, somehow appropriate, Sergius thought, for a man of such charisma and power.

Sergius thought the food the best he'd had since leaving Hispania; he savored every bite of the roasted meat, the sweetness of the ripened fruit. Sharing the couch with Bacchus, the two aligned themselves one in front of the other, with Sergius at the rear. Every so often Bacchus would recline just a bit, resting up against Sergius's body. He couldn't tell if Bacchus's movements were deliberate, but Sergius savored each touch as much as he savored the meal. As the other men feasted, Julian ate only from the bowl of mixed greens, sprinkling the leaves with a light coat of oil and vinegar. He didn't touch the meat, nor did he drink the wine, content with only vegetables.

"You were explaining your family, Bacchus," Julian said after the men had started well into their dinner. "Where do you come from?"

"From Trier, here in Gaul," Bacchus answered. He stopped eating and sat upright on the couch, eyes again downward, as if receiving orders from a general. Julian snickered and waved his hand at the soldier.

"Bacchus, please, relax and enjoy the meal. I assure you it's the finest in all Paris this night," Julian soothed. Bacchus slouched a bit, relaxing at the Caesar's words. "You originate from Trier. Who was your father?" Bacchus sat quiet a moment, as if unsure how to answer the question.

"I am Grandson of Iuventinus," Bacchus said at last.

"Yes," Oribasius interjected through a mouthful of bread, "but what of your father?" Bacchus's head sank, great shame pouring over his body.

"I am a bastard, sir," Bacchus answered. Across the table, Oribasius let his goblet slip from his fingers to the table with a clang as it spun around on its base, flicking wine about in its gyration. Julian fired off a stern look at his doctor, then turned back to Bacchus with equal gravity.

"Go on," the Caesar ordered, voice cold. Bacchus nodded, taking a deep breath. Sergius could see his leg trembling with fear at having to reveal his story to the Emperor, and reached out to steady it, resting his hand on Bacchus's thigh. Bacchus's hand instinctively flew over and gripped Sergius's own, holding on to it as if for dear life.

"My family has lived in Trier since before the great war with the Alemanni. After Constantine had reclaimed her, Grandfather lived with his wife and sole child, my mother, playing music." Bacchus gripped Sergius hand even tighter, signaling that he had not recounted told the worst. Julian and Oribasius sat riveted at the heavily accented words of the Secundarius, neither of them touching their food as they listened.

"One night, an Alemanni band slipped into the city and broke into the home of my Grandfather. One of the bandits raped my mother. I am the result."

Sergius let out a sigh at the awful revelation of Bacchus's origin. Across the table, Oribasius pursed his lips, trying to hide his disgust: a bastard child in Rome might as well be a slave. Bastard children had no rights under Roman law, and their birth would disgrace their mothers, who no man would ever marry. Julian's brow furled, his eyes intense in the dim light of the flames as he stared at the averted face of Bacchus, whose head hung in shame.

"My Grandfather could not stand the disgrace of his only child, but rather than force my mother to poison her womb, he adopted me, proclaiming me a son of Rome. He taught me Latin, and when I heard of a Caesar of the East, I learned the Greek tongue. I am sorry that I do not speak it better for you."

"You are a son of Rome," Julian interrupted, before Bacchus could reveal any more. "Your valiance and loyalty have earned you that." Julian turned to Sergius, who sat aghast at Bacchus's every word.

"You say you found him in the stables?" Julian asked. Sergius nodded.

"Though I am a Secundarius," Bacchus explained, "some still think me less for my birth."

Julian sat upright, holding his head high, casting a long, towering shadow across the room. He laid both his hands on the table, dark gaze fixated on Bacchus.

"Look at me," Julian commanded, voice still soft, but firm. Sergius could feel Bacchus begin to tremble again as he raised his head to face his Emperor, his gaze still averted in disgrace.

"Look at me!" Julian screamed, lurching to his feet, his voice booming with an unusual rasp, echoing through the dining chamber. Bacchus's eyes met his Caesars, and the two just stared at each other a moment as the soldier trembled.

"You honor Rome," Julian said, his voice a near-whisper. Behind him the coals of the fire crackled and popped, adding some dramatic effect to the Emperor's already powerful tone.

"You Bacchus, Grandson of Iuventinus," Julian continued, "have demonstrated your loyalty, your bravery, your strength. You honor your family, and you are a son of Rome." Sergius could see the sparkle of tears welling in Bacchus amethyst eyes, and sat upright, placing an arm about Bacchus's waist, never letting go of his trembling hand.

"You both are," Julian added, turning to Sergius. "You honor me. You've saved my life, and if all of our army shared in your virtue, the world would unite under the banners of Rome in eternal peace." Julian sat down again but did not recline onto his couch, taking a sip of water from his goblet.

"Sergius," the Emperor asked, "how well do you know the work of Plato?"

"It..." Sergius cleared his throat. "It has been some time my lord."

"Plato observed that at the dawn of time, Zeus tore men in half, mixing and scattering them about the world," Julian explained. "While I have always regarded this sentiment as humorous, I have also come to believe it is true. If a man should find his other half, be it a woman or a man..." He paused a moment, eyes distant. "...he should not let his other half go."

Bacchus's grip on Sergius finally loosened, and the two shifted about, making themselves more comfortable, though they kept their fingers intertwining in a gentle web.

"Julian, really," Oribasius interrupted. "Bastard sons granted full citizenship? Letting your soldiers make one another female?"

He extended a hand to Sergius and Bacchus in a gesture of apology. "With due respect, how are these virtues of Rome?"

Without hesitation, Julian grabbed his golden plate, and in one swift gesture hurled it at Oribasius. The flat underside of the plate struck the doctor in his shoulder with a thundering gong, making him yowl in pain. Julian scowled in disgust.

"You are a skilled doctor, but a foolish man, Oribasius," Caesar declared. "Those elitist and aristocratic prejudices are exactly the root of the decadence that has lead Rome to the brink of dissolution!" His words slowed with emphasis. "And *I* will not have it in my Empire!" He turned back to Sergius and Bacchus, his face red and nostrils flaring with a rage Sergius had never before seen.

"Bacchus, you wish to be treated as a true Roman?"

"Yes, lord Caesar," he answered, his thick accent still distorting "Caesar" into "Kai-Zair."

"And you Sergius, would you not see Rome restored and your family avenged?"

"Yes. my lord," Sergius agreed.

"And Oribasius, have you abandoned the philosophy we have so often shared?" The doctor glanced across the table at Sergius and Bacchus, then met the eyes of his Emperor.

"No, Julian. I still believe."

"Then the three of you will join me," Julian said, voice low with gravity. "Rome will unite the world, and it will be a republic as it was meant to be, where all men are treated as equal under the law." The room fell silent with Julian's proclamation.

"And Sergius and Bacchus," Julian uttered, breaking the quiet, "I will say this: do not give up your manhood to one another for the pleasures of the flesh. Love one another, live as Alexander and his beloved Hephastion, but do not betray your manhood, lest your power as soldiers fade. I have renounced carnal passion for the sake of Rome."

"That he has," Oribasius mumbled. Julian shot him a look of annoyance, but did not address his comment any further.

"I encourage you both to let your sole passion be Rome," Julian said to his bodyguards. "Can you do that for your Emperor? For your state?"

Sergius and Bacchus did not hesitate to answer.

"Yes, lord Caesar."

Both of them had answered on instinct, feeling they had no alternative. Their hands stayed intertwined through Julian's entire tirade, holding on to one another tighter than they had all evening.

Chapter XII.

Nebridius waited outside Julian's study door for his partner, and met Sergius with a look of distaste. Sergius's glad countenance melted to one of question, his brow furling at his rodent-like companion.

"Be prepared," Nebridius warned, his overbite extra pronounced. "They've been shouting nonstop."

"Shouting?" Sergius asked in dismay. In all their time together, Julian seldom raised his voice during a dimplomatic meeting, no matter how heated. "About what?"

"I've no idea," Nebridius said in a hushed voice. "It ought to be interesting to watch, no doubt." His eyes widened at the thought.

"Who is his audience with?" Sergius questioned, still confused and shocked. Nebridius's crooked teeth protruded from his curling lips in a sadistic grin.

"The Prefect," he whispered, voice sanctimonious, beady eyes darting over Sergius's face for a reaction.

The chamber doors flung open for the changing of the guard. Sergius counterpart shot him a look of woe.

Sergius entered to find the cold and rigid room, its inhabitants just as uninviting. The Caesar himself stood hunched over a worktable covered thick with the usual maps and letters, his head sinking in frustration.

Oribasius, seated across the room at one of the divans, sat rubbing his forehead, and acknowledged Sergius and Nebridius's entry with a nod. The doctor's gaze turned back to the Emperor and his guest, a debonair man of some stature, wrapped in the deep folds of a billowing almond-colored toga over a plain white tunic, his face as chiseled as the marble busts across the room. He sat with a casual arrogance across the table from Julian, twiddling a coin between the fingers of his right hand like a child bored by his father's lecture, a shine of defiance in his eyes.

"I'll not see my soldiers who risk their lives at the hands of our enemies die from neglect by their Empire!" Julian yelled, his nostrils flaring, face red and puffy. "They are the soul of Rome! They must be paid." Julian pounded a fist against the table.

"Then as I see it, your only option is to raise the taxes," the bureaucrat rebutted, his speech slow with a hint of delight at Julian's frustration.

"Why not just collect the taxes effectively?" Julian snapped, rising to his full height. "Why not make sure the wealthy pay their full sum? Or would the great Florentius lose some of his popularity with the elite?" Their eyes locked like two dogs', ready to attack. Florentius's lips parted, as if to vent the heat of his anger, his face still cool as stone. Julian smiled, knowing he'd struck a nerve with the Prefect.

"Or…" Julian began, raising a finger to the air. "Why not tax the raving Galileans for once? Their churches generate enough revenue that their clergy can then revel in luxury."

"The Galileans are exempt by order of your uncle, Constantine," Florentius shot back, leaning forward in his chair. "The church answers to only the highest authority; your cousin shares that reverent view. I would think you would as well, considering you are…" He swallowed, raising his eyebrows and reclining again. "Faithful to the true God?" Julian looked down at him, eyes burning with rage, taking a step backward, crossing his arms about his back in his usual manner.

"Of course," Julian said low. He glared down at Florentius, jaw tense, analyzing his opponent. Julian tilted his head back, strolling over to the food table in thought.

"Well, it seems we shall have to take up this matter with Constantius," Julian declared, voice casual. "After all, a Prefect only serves his Emperor."

"Quite right," Florentius replied, standing. "Just as you, Julian, serve your cousin. Constantius has granted me authority on this issue. I know you'll respect that."

"Yes," Julian conceded. "We'll see what he has to say."

"Indeed," Florentius smiled. "I'm sure he'll be happy to know his philosopher cousin is so interested in…higher Imperial policy, especially concerning the true faith."

"As I should," Julian interjected. "I am Caesar; I am of the Imperial bloodline." Florentius gave his host a slimy grimace, and flicked the coin into the air, catching it in the same hand and pocketing it in the folds of his toga.

"Nebridius!" Julian barked. "Show our Prefect to his escort." Nebridius gave a slight bow, opening the door to the study and letting Florentius pass before following him down the hall, shutting the door behind them.

Julian watched the door seal, his face steely and intense. Sergius glanced over at Oribasius, exchanging a quick look, knowing their Emperor was oblivious to their presence, lost in his own rage and thought. The room fell silent, the only sound the crackling logs and coals of the cistern. Sergius studied the details of Julian's posture, noticing a great stiffness in his body, his face turning red again.

Then, with total abandon, Julian spun around, throwing the food and dishes from their table in one great swoop, hurling them across the room, shattering the ceramic pitcher against the tile floor. Oribasius cowered at the flying debris, feet skidding across the couch as he rushed to stand in alarm.

"The damned bureaucrats!" Julian bellowed, arms thrust into the air, fingers twisted like claws. "No wonder the West has crumbled! Its politicians have grown fat and stupid!" Sergius looked to Oribasius for a cue as to how he should react. The doctor looked just as clueless.

"You know who's really behind this? Constantius himself!" Julian spat, an accusing finger pointing toward his physician. "He wants to see me trapped!"

"Lock the door," Oribasius commanded Sergius, who did so without hesitation, sliding an iron deadbolt into place. Nebridius would not be gone long, but hopefully, Sergius figured, would realize the Emperor wanted privacy and wait outside…hopefully out of earshot.

"Damn that man!" Julian ranted. "I try to serve my Empire, to live my life, and he interferes with everything! Does he not know we share the same blood? Is mine so tainted that I am unworthy to bear its responsibility?!"

"Perhaps that's why he had you marry his sister," Oribasius quipped, trying to quell Julian's anger.

"Leave Helena out of this!" Julian snapped back. The Caesar

slouched down in a chair at his worktable, putting his face in his hands, eyes looking through parted fingers at the papers before him. "Constantius wants me to maintain supply with Britain with an unpaid and ill-equipped army. He cares not for his people or his Empire; only to see me fail." Julian reclined in the chair, looking up at the plain ceiling. He plunged into thought again, wracking his brain for a course of action.

"I recommend," Oribasius began, placing a hand on Julian's shoulder, "that you relinquish the matter for the moment, and turn to other affairs." Julian grunted in reply. He glanced at his physician with a soft blink, recognizing Oribasius's concern, and thanking him with a slight smile. The Emperor's gaze then lit on Sergius, still standing guard by the door, not wanting to further agitate Julian.

"And what say you, my philosopher guard?" Julian asked Sergius, sitting upright again, resting an arm on the table. Sergius froze, put on the spot and terrified of saying something that would further enflame Julian's temper.

"I would say, sir," Sergius answered, voice aquiver, "that Augustus enjoys his popularity, and would not see it threatened."

"That much is obvious," Julian prodded. "Offer a greater wisdom. I know you possess it." Sergius mouth hung open as he searched for words, for some tidbit that could aid his Emperor.

"The only way to defeat a man so powerful as Florentius," Sergius observed, "is to gain favor with Constantius."

"Yes, and how would I gain favor with him who would see me fail?"

"Through one who can influence him." Sergius looked up at Oribasius. "And if I might remind you, my lord, your wife is Constantius's sister, and though she be a woman, if ever one of her gender held influence..." Sergius paused a moment, the thought of

Bacchus flashing into his mind, coaxing a smile to his face. Julian smiled back, cunning and calculated, following Sergius thinking.

"That woman is a nuisance and has bore me no sons," Julian observed. "Her mind is simple and ignorant, her tastes decadent and extravagant." The Emperor smirked. "She is very much her brother's sister. But she does have her attributes."

Chapter XIII.

Sergius had never seen anyone so thin, even among the starving, diseased beggars of the Parisian streets. Helena, the Empress of the West, looked like a canvas stretched over sharpened bones, each protruding through the thin layer, threatening to tear it with every step. That she could support the rattling golden jewelry about her ears, neck and wrists only furthered the wonder as she strode into Julian's study, the sheer fabric of her stola protected beneath a long cloak of white wolf skin, the portrait of Roman aristocracy.

Nebridius bolted the study door as he escorted the Empress into the room, her dark eyes filled with a childlike insecurity as she bowed to her husband, a man she barely knew. Julian looked on her with an annoyed condescension, his disgust for her luxurious taste as apparent as his distain for her ignorant gender.

"Can you believe this?" Nebridius whispered to Sergius, a hint of excitement in his voice. True, few outside the royal family ever witnessed an interaction of this sort; Sergius again felt as intimidated as he did honored to be granted such insight.

"My Lord," Helena cooed, an echo of yearning buried in her voice. Julian's posture did not change, treating his wife with the same business-like formality as he had Florentius.

"Helena," Julian greeted back, motioning for her to sit. Helena looked around, noticing the carnage of Julian's earlier tantrum, even more intimidated by her husband. "Sit, please," Julian ordered, impatience obvious. Helena looked around not sure what to do, as Oribasius rushed forward to pull a chair out from the table for her to sit. Julian rolled his eyes, disgusted that the woman had not even the sense to seat herself.

"Helena, a critical argument between myself and Florentius has arisen, and I'm afraid we've no choice but for your brother to arbitrate," Julian began, his arms folded about his back, pacing back and forth as if giving a lecture. Helena watched him with a dumbfounded gawking, her head bobbing back and forth in confusion with Julian's every step. Julian paused and stared at his wife's blank expression, cocking his head back with a groan.

"We need you to appeal to Constantius," Oribasius explained, as if translating Julian's words. "Julian must be allowed to control the tax laws if he is to regain control of the Western territories."

"My Lord, I know nothing of taxes or war," Helena said in a girlish chime. Her eyes dropped to the floor, ashamed. "Just as my Lord knows nothing of my womanly affections."

Julian looked uncomfortable, as his eyes rolled back, his tongue running over his back molars creating a protrusion in his cheek in annoyance. Sergius thought it looked as though the Emperor had to choke back the urge to scream at his wife, frustrated that she would equate the good of the Empire with something so insignificant as their marital consummation. Julian let out a deep breath.

"We need you to send a letter to your brother, Helena," Julian instructed, leaning over the table, his words slow and deliberate as if to keep his temper in check, and to let his wife's slow brain process his direction. "We need you to tell Constantius that I alone must control the taxation of the West if our army is to be prepared to retake Britain and rebuild Gaul."

A flicker of understanding flashed in Helena's eyes. "But why would Florentius oppose you in this?" she asked.

"Because he's a spoiled, greedy fool," Julian told her, his eyes burning with ferocity. "Think of it as your duty to the Empire, and to your husband. Constantius will give your words consideration."

"But why me?"

"Because you are his sister, and he cares for you," Julian said, voice suddenly gentle. "One of the few he loves," he added, muttering under his breath.

"You say it is my duty?" Helena asked, erecting her skeletal posture.

"It is, my lady," Julian agreed, he too rising to his full stature. Helena sat quiet a moment, staring blankly at the table before her. Her eyes darted up to meet her husband's, a sudden fire of thought glowing in their dark irises.

"And what of your duties as a husband?" Helena questioned, her voice awash with a newfound confidence. Sergius had to crack a smile; the cunning of the Imperial Dynasty ran through even the blood of its women.

"What of them?" Julian moaned.

"Are not your obligations to your Empress as great as those to your Empire? Is it not your duty to sire an heir?" Helena ran a bony hand across her abdomen, as if to cover a gaping wound. Julian slouched at the question, glaring across the room at Sergius.

Sergius heart pounded, realizing that Julian had included Helena in the matter at his suggestion. If she didn't respond to Julian's orders, or worse, if she told Constantius of Julian's plotting against Florentius, Julian would not be the only one to meet with the executioner's blade.

"Guards," Julian called out, motioning them toward the burning cistern. "Doctor," he added as he passed Oribasius, stomping across the room, leaving Helena confused in her seat.

"Your counsel brought us to this juncture," Julian observed to Sergius as the four men gathered around the fire pit. "Perhaps you've another suggestion as to how to this woman's involvement might benefit us? Or you, gentlemen?"

Sergius and Nebridius looked at one another, then to Oribasius, who shared their nervous apprehension.

"An heir would insure your legacy, my lord," Nebridius said, his voice quivering.

"True," Julian snapped back. "And threaten Constantius, which would in turn threaten me."

"I'm not sure she's even able to conceive," Oribasius added in Nebridius's defense. "Not that your highness as put forth much effort." Julian glared at the physician, his anger mounting by the second.

"Carnal passions are a mere distraction from the true problems of life," Julian spat. "I've less interest in them than in her fashions." Julian nodded his head back towards Helena, who turned in her chair, watching the men with obvious anxiety. The Emperor's gaze lit on Sergius, bright and passionate.

"And what say you now, my philosopher?" Julian inquired of Sergius, ready to unleash his anger on the Primicerius. Sergius thought a moment, straining his wits to find some answer that might suit his Emperor.

"Medea helped Jason steal the Golden Fleece, did she not?' Sergius asked, recalling his classic training. Julian's head shifted, his eyes narrowing on his bodyguard.

"She did," the Emperor answered, intrigued.

"And what compelled her to do so, to betray her father in the process?"

"The frailty of womanhood," Julian growled.

"Perhaps," Sergius agreed, not wanting to contradict his Caesar. "But what did Jason offer her in return?" Julian's eyes lit up, a sly grimace coming across his face. "That which she wanted most," Sergius added with a slight nod toward the Empress.

"Marriage," Julian added.

"Not just marriage. She betrayed her own blood for love," Sergius went on. "And Jason succeeded. Are we not to learn something from these classics?"

Julian nodded, slow and pensive, a great look of satisfaction coming over his face as he stared at Sergius.

"What desperate acts will men commit for love?" Julian purred, glancing back at Helena. He turned back to Sergius, reaching out and laying a hand on the bodyguard's wounded shoulder. "You are as wise as I thought, Sergius."

"But how will this help in the matter of Florentius?" Nebridius asked, lost in the exchange.

"It means anyone can be bargained with, if there is something he wants," Julian explained, turning back to his wife. "And I will do what I must," he added with a whisper. The Emperor's gaze lit on his physician. "She will not conceive," he ordered. Oribasius gave an uncomfortable nod as Julian strode across the room to his wife, taking her emaciated hand in his own, a charming smile on his face.

"That man is not a bureaucrat," Oribasius muttered to the guards as he watched Julian stroke Helena's arm. Julian spoke in an intimate, inaudible whisper across the room, Helena smiling at his words. The doctor and bodyguards watched as Julian uttered something to his wife, who let out a gleeful laugh, taking his other hand in her own.

"He is a pragmatist," Oribasius concluded, watching the scene before them. "A true politician."

Sergius nodded in agreement. "And that is why he shall win."

Chapter XIV.

The bitter chill of the air had subsided, and though still cold, the embryonic spring of 360 had started the icicles dripping, melted the powdery snow into viscous slush and filled the woods outside of Paris with gentle snaps and crunches as the load of the precipitation grew more weighty on the trees. The sun had begun to peek through the overcast skies, every so often reflecting off the shimmering frosted landscape with a blinding glare. Very soon, Sergius knew, the boots of Julian's army would tread down the muddy and puddled roads, marching off to battle once more, leaving behind the quaint comforts of Paris.

Very soon, but not yet.

Still wrapped in their winter cloaks, wringing their bare hands for warmth, Sergius and Bacchus hiked through a modest wood just outside Paris, a quiver and arrows slung over Bacchus's back, an overstuffed leather purse crossing from Sergius's good shoulder to the opposite side of his waist. Neither spoke, their movements careful and deliberate, as Bacchus scanned through the trees.

Bacchus halted, raising his left hand against Sergius's chest, stopping him in his tracks. Sergius's eyes darted around at the cause of their stop, but saw nothing. He turned to Bacchus, perplexed, who gently raised his hand about Sergius's neck, adjustiniang the direction of his head to face a clump of trees and snowy brush. Bacchus extended his arm, pointing straight at the brush. Sergius squinted, looking for their prize.

At last he saw it—a young stag grazing through the trees, oblivious to the two soldiers watching its movements. Without a sound, Bacchus handed the bow to Sergius and pulled an arrow from the quiver. Standing behind his companion, Bacchus helped him load the arrow and raise the bow, their arms covering one another, aiming with great care. Bacchus took a step back, letting Sergius complete the aim on his own.

Holding his breath, Sergius let his fingers wrap tight around the bowstring, the taught fibers forming stinging grooves against his frigid fingertips. The jagged arrowhead fixed on its target, Sergius released. The arrow sliced through the air with a loud whirring, heading straight for the unsuspecting stag, landing erect in the mud just short of the animal's sinewy body. Terrified, the stag rushed further into the wood, leaving its would-be hunters groaning in frustration.

Sergius slouched forward, half laughing, half grunting, tapping the bow against his head in frustration. Bacchus shook his head and rolled his eyes, stepping forward and patting Sergius on the back in comfort.

"You are no Calvary," Bacchus laughed. "You are lucky you never must hunt."

"Agreed," Sergius said, handing the bow to Bacchus. "I've no feel for it at all." He thought a moment, imagining the dead stag, the arrow protruding from a growing patch of blood, its lifeless eyes petrified in one final look of pain and fear. "I've no desire to kill," he added at last, eyes distant. Bacchus gave him a soft kiss on the cheek, Sergius's stubble tickling his lips.

"No shame," Bacchus comforted, stroking Sergius's cloaked back. Sergius let out a sigh.

"Shall we rest a bit?" he asked. The two found a patch of ground close to an evergreen tree free of snow, the earth soggy from the thaw. There, Sergius laid out the contents of his purse: a loaf of bread, a few strips of dried meat, a bottle of wine and two shiny red apples, courtesy of Julian.

The two Palatinae squatted over the wet ground, sharing their lunch in silence, Sergius still pensive over his failed hunting attempt.

"You hurt?" Bacchus asked, breaking the quiet. Sergius's gaze met his violet eyes, and found himself comforted.

"I'm alright," he answered with a smile. "I've seen so much death in my life. I have to wonder if there is nothing more than pain and decay in this world…if all I am capable of…all Rome truly stands for…is destruction."

"Rome is what Caesar makes it," Bacchus replied after a pensive moment. "If he reunites the world, the killing will stop."

"No it won't," Sergius rebutted, a hint of bitterness in his voice. "The wars may end but the killing will never stop. The Imperial family will tumble over themselves to grasp the laurels of power with daggers bared." Sergius drew his cloak in around him, fighting a sudden chill. He reached down and took a long swig of wine from the jug and offered it to Bacchus, who followed in kind.

"And what of our deaths?" Sergius continued. "Is that what

awaits all of us? The rot and worms? Incineration in the fire of Tartaurus?"

"The dead feel no pain," Bacchus interjected, not quite knowing what else to say.

"But the living do," Sergius observed. "And we go on alone, waiting for our own dissolution into oblivion. I watched my whole family die. Will I have to watch my Emperor? Will I have to watch you?"

Bacchus clenched his jaw in thought. He let out a sigh, and then without a word, dug deep into the folds of his cloak, and produced a weathered lyre, which he positioned against his left arm.

"Where did you get that?" Sergius asked in total surprise.

"My grandfather." Bacchus wrapped his cloak under him as he sat down onto the wet ground. He lurched his right arm forth from within the sheets of fabric, twiddled his fingers, and began to stroke at the melodic strings of his instrument.

"You had that hidden with you this whole time?" Sergius asked, a smile coming across his face.

"I wanted…" Bacchus paused, searching for the word. "…to surprise."

Sergius rested his arms against his knees and leaned forward as Bacchus began to play a soft refrain, his technique perfect, years of training at his grandfather's side evident with every note. Sergius's heart welled with joy and sadness, as he contemplated the death of his own family, and the magnificent man now playing before him. Bacchus played with effortless precision, every note in tune, the sound glowing through the snowy forest. As he plucked the strain, Bacchus seemed distant, adrift in his own melody, and doubtless, pondering the man who taught it to him.

The Passion of Sergius & Bacchus

Sergius exhaled and realized he had a great smile across his face, lost in Bacchus and his music. For all the morose conversation, for all the discomfort of the wet, cold air, his soul felt light and carefree. He had the feeling again of unadulterated happiness, just sitting close to Bacchus, listening to the vibrations of his antique lyre.

Bacchus looked up from his instrument and suddenly stopped playing as he gazed upon Sergius's grimace.

"Why do you smile?" Bacchus asked, a chortle in his question. The violet of his eyes sparkled with the sunlight reflecting from the snow. Sergius shrugged.

"You play very well," he complimented, grin persisting on his face. Bacchus let out a modest laugh, his look darting to the ground in humility. A great smile of his own lit on his face, his lips curling over his teeth. Sergius had never actually seen Bacchus laugh or smile before, at least not with such broad feeling. For the first time he noticed that one of Bacchus's molars was missing, leaving a vacant socket just under the line of his cheekbone. The flaw didn't bother Sergius; somehow, in only made Bacchus's handsome looks more interesting.

"You flatter," Bacchus said, his sparkling eyes meeting Sergius again.

"I do not!" Sergius protested. "You honor your family with your skill." Bacchus laughed again, his cheeks flushing with blood. "What is it?" Sergius asked, watching Bacchus's every movement. Bacchus shook his head, denying anything special about his music.

"You embarrass me," Bacchus confessed, cringing a bit in self-consciousness.

"I don't mean to," Sergius soothed, forcing his smile into a mere grin. Bacchus relaxed a bit, tucking the lyre away, too nervous to keep playing.

"Your tooth," Sergius asked, pointing to his own corresponding molar, "how did you…?"

"Battle," Bacchus revealed, matter of fact.

Sergius reached out and stroked Bacchus cheek, caressing the skin over the gap beneath. Their eyes locked, deep brown chestnut aligning with shimmering ametyst, the two of them lost in one another's gaze. He longed to plant his lips upon Bacchus's own with the same abandon they had known on that battlefield in the face of death, apathetic and oblivious to the world around them. Sergius yearned for his own body to press up against that of his companion, their skin rippling into gooseflesh, every nerve activated with warm friction, reveling in contact.

"You are very brave," Sergius whispered, the callus of his thumb lingering in its stroke of Bacchus's face. Bacchus's breathing hastened as he leaned forward, his lips meeting Sergius's in an electric, passionate kiss, as powerful and intense as their first on the battlefield so long ago. Sergius gripped Bacchus face tighter, reveling in the feeling, channeling the fervent power with each passing moment, their mouths widening, tongues exploring. He felt as if their souls tried to flee their bodies and merge into one perfect, transcendent being, luminous and trumpeting as the dawn, hovering high above the snowy trees, locked together for all time.

Sergius lost track of time as he and Bacchus expressed their physical passion; hours could have passed without him noticing. When their lips did finally part, Sergius found his hand interlocked with Bacchus's, their fingers intertwining in a gentle web.

"Let's go home," Sergius murmured his eyes still locked into Bacchus's sparkling own. The two cleaned up the remnants of their picnic, and then without thinking, joined hands again as they trudged through the slush and mud. As they approached the edge of the forest, a foul stench stopped Sergius in his tracks, his eyes darting about for the source.

It didn't take long before he found the origin of the smell: a stillborn fawn, its skin still pink and fetal, lay rotting on the ground. An opossum tore chunks of the carcass's flesh away, its body decaying into the liquefied dirt. Around it, an oily, reddish sheen of blood mixed with the wet earth, forming an eerie aura around the remains. The scavenger looked up at the two soldiers and scampered off into the woods, a mouthful of the tender meat still hanging out of its mouth.

Sergius gagged and spun his face away in horror. Bacchus gripped his hand tighter in an instinctive gesture of comfort, before averting his own gaze, his face twisted in disgust.

As the two made their way out of the wood and through the empty fields leading back to Paris, Sergius couldn't shake the nauseous feeling at what he had seen. Death invaded everywhere, everything, destructive and indiscriminate, waiting to tear, rape and decay everything that ever lived, just at it had his family. Just as it had to Julian's family, or Bacchus's or any of the dozens of men he had killed on the field of battle. How had men survived so long? Was killing the weapon Rome must employ to save the world? Was there no mercy from oblivion?

Bacchus squeezed his hand, jolting Sergius from his morbid questions. Sergius squeezed back in thanks, his anxiety slightly alleviated.

It was the first time he ever felt comfort in the face of death.

Chapter XV.

The Parisian tavern resembled some cross between the fine wine shops of Roman ownership and the Germanic halls of the north: soldiers dressed in tunics and togas congregating around mosaics and triclinas amid a crackling fire in a stone hearth, high wooden ceilings and handled steins in place of ceramic goblets. Winter and supply problems had made wine a precious commodity—Sergius had to use his best connections to secure a bottle for his picnic with Bacchus—and the gentle sting of grapes had been replaced almost entirely by a hearty local brew called mead.

Sergius hated mead, as did most men who came from the Mediterranean climate, and the very odor of it made him cringe as he and Bacchus entered the crowded tavern to warm themselves after their jaunt back from the forest.

"Sergius!" a voice bellowed as he and Bacchus stepped over the threshold. The hulking form of Gaius rose from a triclina deep in the tavern walls, his arms outstretched to meet his old friend.

"The philosopher soldier!" Gaius said, squeezing Sergius tight. The two parted and Gaius's attention flashed to Bacchus, his face stone and unwavering as he watched Sergius's former Batavi cohort with suspicion.

"Hoo arr yew?" Bacchus hissed, his thick accent reappearing with his aggression. Gaius narrowed his eyes with a quizzical look at the Secundarius.

"This is Gaius, a friend of mine from my time with the Batavi," Sergius explained. Bacchus relaxed at the words, but his eyes never left Gaius face. Gaius extended his arm in greeting to Bacchus, and the two shook in introduction.

"Gaius, this is Bacchus," Sergius added, puzzled but amused by Bacchus territorial posturing. "He's the one who saved my life at Strasburg." Gaius's face lit up in recognition.

"God save you, my boy!" he said, pumping Bacchus's arm even harder. "You've done your Empire a great service. Sergius is a fine soldier."

"Yes," Bacchus agreed, his Germanic accent evaporating with his aggression. The cool look in his countenance softened, and Sergius smiled in relaxation.

"Come, join me!" Gaius invited. The three reclined into Gaius's triclina, as a young maid with braided hair served three steins of mead. Gaius and Bacchus both grinned as they sipped theirs. Sergius just stared at his, as the foam atop the liquid fizzled.

"Not taken to the local specialty?" Gaius asked with a laugh. "All those years drinking wine and reading books softened you! With that fair skin and ebony curls…if I hadn't seen you in battle, I'd think you a woman!" Gaius glanced back and forth between Bacchus and Sergius, waiting for some kind of reaction.

Sergius watched as Bacchus concealed a smile beneath the rim of his mug. His gaze moved back to Gaius, and he could see in his friend's eyes an implication, a suggestive look that implied the Batavi knew the nature of their relationship.

"He's no woman," Bacchus interjected, before Sergius had time to rebut Gaius insult.

"Nor is Bacchus," Sergius added with a cool smile. "But if you think us lovers…you are correct."

Gaius snorted a laugh, examining the seriousness of his companions' faces.

"Isn't he a bit old?" Gaius asked Sergius, ignoring Bacchus's presence. "I mean, the beauty of young boys is impossible to resist—I enjoy it myself. But he's fully grown!"

"And I wouldn't change that," Sergius replied, matter-of-fact. "I like him more for it." From his peripheral vision, Sergius could see Bacchus's head subtly hang, as if trying to conceal some shame. With a slight shift of his weight, Sergius edged his body over, grazing it against that of his lover, catching the Secondarius' attention. He gazed into Bacchus's face, the two sharing a moment of transcendent affection.

"Psh!" Gaius retorted. "I think the stab of the blade that day gave you a taste for unusual penetration."

"There are other things men can do," Sergius reminded. "Or are you so inexperienced with the flesh that you don't know?" Gaius dropped his stein to the table, the mead swishing out onto the wooden surface, cracking a smile as it did.

"Heart of a lion," he muttered, regarding Sergius. "That's what makes you a great soldier. That's what makes you a great friend." Gaius glanced over at Bacchus. "And great at other things, apparently." Sergius and Bacchus laughed, the latter reaching over and resting his hand on that of the former. "So tell me," Gaius said, reclining in his couch. "What has hardened Caesar's heart against his own troops?" Gaius's words shocked Sergius, who, heart pounding, rose to Julian's defense.

"How can you speak such words!" Sergius exclaimed, his dark eyes wide and dilated. "You once proclaimed him Augustus! Is he not the same man who triumphed at Strasberg?"

"He was a different man then. He had the fire of Julius Caesar himself," Gaius spat with disdain. "Our brother soldiers starve in Britain! They freeze in Gaul and Germania!" Gaius reached into the folds of his robe and produced a crumpled pamphlet, a caricature of Julian with a goat beard and horns on the cover. Sergius took it and peeled the pages open, scanning the contents.

"And this latest insult," Gaius continued. "Our Caesar has announced today that several legions will now be transferred to the Persian fronts in the East.

"What?" Sergius gasped.

"It's too soon," Bacchus ejaculated. "The ground is still frozen. No army could make the trip."

"And he sends us anyway," Gaius snarled.

"These orders," Sergius injected, raising a hand as he read over the pamphlet, "they come from Constantius."

"And our philosopher Emperor follows them!" Gaius exploded. "He's a fool! Had he any strength at all, he would have cowed Constantius as he did Chondomar, and taken the golden laurels of Augustus for himself by now!"

"Your words," a gravely voice boomed, "approach sedition." The three companions looked up to see the frightening countenance of Severus, his face covered in blisters, tremor in his hands now a wild shake, hobbling against his cane over to the table. Dressed in his formal armor, the man looked rabid and old, eyes burning with madness. "Have you a problem with the divine orders of your Augustus?"

"His orders come not from the One God," Gaius snapped back. "He is not ordained by the false gods like Nero, nor does he claim to be the Anointed One as Caligula might."

"And yet you serve under the Chi-Ro," Severus hissed back, leaning into their triclina. "Our lord Constantine was given the Chi-Ro by the Lord himself. It is under that sign you fight. It is for your holy Empire!"

"The One God may be all powerful," Gaius said, rising to his feet, "but Constantius is not the One God. Let Julian challenge him! Let him protect his soldiers as he would protect Rome!" He stared into the crazed eyes of his superior officer, showing no flicker of doubt. Sergius could not believe what he was seeing.

"Traitor," Severus whispered. "I'll see you executed." Gaius didn't blink.

"Coward," he said, the pitch of his voice rising with condescension.

Severus gnashed his teeth, and with his characteristic speed, brought his walking stick down across the cheek of the unarmed Gaius. Gaius spun around, crying out in agony as he slumped down over the table dumping the steins of mead all over Sergius and Bacchus. Gaius lunged backward, plowing into Severus, the two of them stumbling backward as patrons jumped out of the way of the fight. The whole room stopped but for the two men wrestling in battle; the room knew by the colors of their tunics that both were high-ranking men.

The two men fell to the ground, Severus attempting to pull his walking stick up around Gaius's throat. As he chocked for breath, Gaius reached down and drew Severus's sword from his belt, managing to slit the general's wrist as he did so. Severus screamed in pain as blood splattered across the tile floor and Gaius scrambled to his feet. Plunging down, Gaius shoved the blade towards Severus's abdomen. Still, the old man, even in his sickened condition, still had enough speed to deflect the stab with his staff.

Severus leapt to his feet as if unwounded, even as the blood gushed from his arm, pooling onto the floor and charged at Gaius, staff meeting against sword as the two pushed back at each other in unwavering stalemate. The blood poured faster from Severus's wound with the pressure against his body, and the old man began to flinch as if dazed.

Sergius looked on at the two men as they circled each other, the sword cleaving into the thick wood of the walking stick, when Severus finally wavered. Slipping in the warm gelatin of his own blood, the general staggered backward, off guard. Gaius seized his moment to slam his blade down against the weakened staff, snapping it into two jagged pieces and sparking against Severus's formal armor. With the general stunned, Gaius rammed the blade between the plates of Severus's armor, stabbing deep into his side with a wet slice. As Gaius withdrew the blade, more blood gushed. The patrons scampered away, widening the circle around the growing puddle. Sensing his last moment at hand, Severus gripped his jagged staff with all his might, and thrust it straight into Gaius's larynx.

The two men fell together into the splatter, Severus clutching his right side, Gaius sputtering and clawing at his neck, the great piece of wood stuck through his windpipe. The barkeep rushed to the fallen Severus, crying out for help. As several patrons rushed out the door in search of a doctor, Sergius and Bacchus knelt before the dying Gaius trying to elevate his head, as their friend managed to grasp some ornament about his neck under the folds of his tunic.

"Gaius," Sergius said, feeling powerless, tears welling in his eyes. "Why you fool?!" Gaius snapped the necklace from around his neck, just as his body went limp. His balled fist fell to the floor sliding into the warm blood, the contents of his hand dropping out and forming a tiny ripple in the plasma.

Sergius felt Bacchus arm on his shoulder in comfort as the pain and shock overwhelmed him. The two looked down at the tiny charm Gaius had dropped them, almost as if he'd wanted to share one final thought with his friends.

A tiny wooden fish, its mouth hanging from a line of broken thread lay motionless in the sea of blood before them.

Chapter XVI.

Sergius lay on his left side atop the simple wooden skeleton of his bed, his shadowy bedroom lit by a single oil lamp atop a modest end table. Adorned by the creamy ceramic of the lamp, along with two alabaster amphorae of scented oil, the table added a hint of class to the modest room. In his left hand Sergius clutched Gaius's wooden fish charm, in the other, the hand of Bacchus, who sat at his side in a leather folding chair. He had cried for hours; Gaius, brash though he could be, had been Sergius friend—in fact, his only friend in his first years with the Batavi. They'd fought along side each other, and in Gaius Sergius had found a surrogate brother, a bit of comfort from the great waves of fear and guilt that would drown him at every battle. And just like the men who scarred Gaius's face all in all those battles spread over all the years, Gaius now lay dead, every bit of his spirit lost for all time.

Sergius grasped harder at Bacchus's hand, who matched the pressure in kind. He said nothing, just letting his companion's sorrow pour out with his tears, hoping that soon the reservoirs of both might evaporate.

A modest knock at the bedroom door, and Bacchus turned to see Didymos enter with a goblet of warm broth as an offer to his master. Bacchus waved him away, knowing that even the strongest wine would not bring Sergius peace this night. Nothing could.

"Here," Bacchus whispered, lifting Sergius's limp body into his arms. "You should sleep." Sitting Sergius upright, Bacchus began to undo the knots and belts of his robes, stripping the blood stained clothing from his body, piling it on the floor. Frigid air made visible Sergius hot breath, as Bacchus removed layer after layer of fabric stripping his host down to his loincloth, and resting him back in bed under a deerskin blanket. Stroking Sergius's hand, he took the small charm of the fish, then gathered the fabric in his arms and slipped out of the room. Didymos met him in the tiny hall separating the great room from the bedroom.

"Here," Bacchus said, handing the fabric to the servant. "Good luck getting the blood out."

"I will sir, Didymos whispered with a slight bow. Bacchus fingered the tiny fish in his hand, debating what to do with it.

"Take this too. It belonged to Gaius so I know Sergius will want to keep it. Clean it up and repair it too." Didymos looked at the necklace with astonishment.

"Gaius was Galilean?" Didymos gasped. Bacchus shrugged.

"Just clean it up, and leave your master to sleep. I'll make sure he has all he needs tonight." Didymos nodded and scurried off towards the kitchen, staring down at the small charm in his hand.

Bacchus re-entered the bedroom to find his whimpering brother balled like a fetus under his blankets. Bacchus crouched down and brushed the ebony curls from Sergius olive skinned forehead, placing a tiny kiss on it, intimating his impending departure.

"Stay with me," Sergius pleaded, grasping Bacchus hand again. "Lay here." They looked in each other's eyes, pools of watery chestnut meeting amethyst, looking deep within the irises into each other's souls. Bacchus stroked the bristly hairs of Sergius's arm, hesitating a moment.

"I don't care," Sergius whispered, his gaze unwavering. "Stay with me this night if no other."

Bacchus rose to his feet and started to remove his own bloodstained clothing, looking down at Sergius with a passionate gaze. The light blond hair on his chest, muscled as if cut by a sculptor, ran down the length of his body creeping into his own loincloth. He leaned forward to slide into bed, when Sergius grasped both his arms in a gesture of pause. Dropping the tiny blood-splattered necklace to the floor, Sergius reached down and removed his own loincloth, revealing his naked form to Bacchus. He could feel the heat radiating from his Germanic body, smell the day of hunting on his skin; it only made Sergius yearn even more for his touch.

Sergius reached down and undid Bacchus loincloth, his genitals slipping from within the folds. Bacchus made no attempt to stop him. The two men stood there, both naked in body and soul, inches apart, neither sure what the other would do next. Bacchus reached out with his right hand, and pulled Sergius close in a dizzying kiss. Their bodies pressed against each other, the heat of each merging together into a column of burning passion. Sergius could feel both of them hardening below the waist, their hearts pounding in their chests. He wrapped his arms around Bacchus, as if trying to suck the life force from him, let their souls join just as they had on the battlefield those years before. The two men slid into bed together, their hands moving faster and faster over the tender flesh of each other's bodies.

Bacchus pulled back a moment, his eyes meeting Sergius's again. He stared into the sparkling chestnut rounds, running his callous fingers over the stubble of Sergius's beard, before reaching for one of the amphorae.

"What?" Sergius asked, voice hushed.

Bacchus's eyes never left Sergius's face as he lifted the top from the amphora with a glassy *clink*. The milky white of the bottle shown like a moonbeam in the dim lamplight as Bacchus tipped it, spilling jasmine-scented oil into his free hand, letting it flow down over his palm and pour between his fingers. Placing the amphora aside, his eyes never leaving Sergius's face, Bacchus shifted his legs apart, and, tilting his pelvis upward. He reached down below his perineum, massaging the oil against his bottom, a quivering sigh escaping his lips as he rubbed. Sergius hand shot out and gripped Bacchus's wrist, but the Secondarius resisted.

"I would make myself female for you," he whispered in the flickering lamplight. He reached forward, stroking Sergius's loins with the excess oil on his hand. "I want to."

"But you could never be a woman to me." Sergius replied. "Nothing you do with your body could change that. Your soul is that of a man; there is no question. It's what made me love you."

"As is yours," Bacchus said. "Which is why I love you."

Bacchus raised his head up and laid a soft peck on Sergius's lips, just as he laid a hand at on Sergius's waist, edging him forward until their oiled bodies met. Sergius gasped as he felt his body enter Bacchus's own, his jaw going slack at the sensation as Bacchus winced at the sensation. Resting a moment, feeling each other from within, Sergius could feel Bacchus's pulse race along with his own. His whole body tingled with discovery, his heart throbbing with a fiery joy he'd never known before, as if his spirit screamed with relief at finally being made whole.

The two kissed again in searing passion, both their hearts aching with pain and joy and sadness and comfort. The night melted around them into a shapeless meld of color as they writhed under the blanket, their sweat and fluids soaking one another. Neither had experienced anything like it before, but as the cool night air kissed their moist bodies, they knew nothing on Earth could ever keep them from doing it again. They had discovered their nature: two men, powerful on the battlefield, loyal to their country, desperately in love with one another.

Chapter XVII.

"The old man had lost his mind! OW!" screamed Julian, who lay with his head above a warm pool of water. The Imperial bathing chamber, like the dining room, reminded Sergius of the fabled luxuries of Rome and Greece of old: opulent curtains draped from the ceiling, servants running around attending to the temperature of the water, and Julian's personal barber crouched over the Emperor's head with a pair of oversized tweezers, grooming kit at his side. Julian recoiled with each tweeze, as the barber sifted through his curls plucking out gray hairs.

"He had lost his mind, and he's part of the reason our troops drag through the mud of winter into battle," Julian went on, resuming his thought. "It was that damned shaking disease, a result of his incessant fornicating." The barber plucked out another hair and Julian let out a grunt before slapping his hands away, sitting upright in the steaming pool. "This is why I prefer celibacy."

Sergius and Bacchus, both dressed in formal armor, stood

watching as Julian continued his rant, his voice echoing against the ceramic tile walls. Both felt on edge: as witnesses to Severus death, they could be considered accessories to murder. Yet Julian didn't seem too concerned with the death of his top commander. In fact, he actually seemed relieved.

"My Lord," Sergius asked, slight hesitation in his voice. "What shall become of our troops on the front lines?"

"Constantius will send us a new general, and I hesitate to think who." Julian tilted his head back again as the barber dug through his tool kit, producing a very sharp silver knife and a tiny hand-sized mirror. Kneeling and moving with slow, deliberate action, he began to run the razor blade over the side of Julian's face, shaving off the bristles of his beard up one cheek, then down the other, hands quaking with nervousness. "You said he mentioned the Chi-Ro?"

"Yes, lord," Sergius acknowledged. "Fighting for the One God."

"The Chi-Ro," Bacchus asked. "Is that not the symbol of..?"

"My uncle, yes," Julian cut in. He snatched the glass from the barber, who yelped in nervous shock. The frightened servent collapsed onto his haunches, dropping the knife and holding his head in panic. Hovering the mirror over the steaming water, Julian let it fog, then drew a character in the condensation:

The Passion of Sergius & Bacchus

"He always said it was the sign the One God, sent him to convert to the faith of the Galileans," Julian explained as he slid the mirror over to Sergius and Bacchus. "I've tried to remove it as much as possible, but apparently my uncle lives on." He gave a sarcastic grunt. "The Galileans promise to live forever. Constantine *is* doing just that."

The barber waved the knife over Julian's face, trying to reposition himself, to pick up where his work had left off. The Emperor waved him away in annoyance.

"Leave it," he said, running the hand over the stubble on his chin. "I like it." Without a word the barber gathered up the rest of his tools into his work case, shuffled across the room, and snatched the tiny mirror from Bacchus hands. With a snobbish glare, he disappeared into the halls of the palace.

"Strange that Severus should mention a Galilean symbol in his last hours. He never was a man of much faith," Julian reflected, reclining again into the pool for a few moments relaxation. "The Gods know what replacement I'll receive." Sergius and Bacchus glanced at each other with intrigue.

Julian sat upright and clapped. A servant appeared with his plain cotton robe, wrapping the Caesar in it as he stepped out of his bath.

"My philosopher soldier," Julian asked, "what do you suggest? Constantius would see me executed, this I know, and I have yet to receive an answer to Helena's letter about Florentius. Severus's death only compounds matters. My cousin's sword is drawn."

"In that case, lord Emperor," Sergius answered, "I would see to it I was surrounded by friends." Julian thought on this a moment and nodded. His eyes met Sergius's and he nodded again.

"A wise answer, Sergius," Julian declared. "Perhaps it is time I surveyed my own arms." He paused and thought a moment. "I already know the symbol which I shall carry into Byzantium."

Chapter XIX.

"I didn't realize he was a Brother, master," Didymos said, holding out Gaius's repaired fish necklace by the chord.

"A Brother?" Sergius asked, confusion in his voice.

"It's what we call one another. We Galileans are only Brothers and Sisters. We are all one family in the Anointed One." Didymos handed the necklace to Sergius, then tipped his head as he scurried to the fireplace to tend to the coals.

"I didn't realize you were also Galilean," Sergius said, reclining into his lectus, turning the wooden fish in his fingers. Didymos had managed to get most of the blood off the wood, but a few dark spots remained along the aquatic form. Sergius thought it appropriate—it was said that the leader of the Galileans died under the reign of Emperor Tiberius long ago. How fitting that Gaius would stain his emblem with his dying blood for the same reason.

"I am a Brother, master" Didymos acknowledged without looking up as he stoked the fire.

"Why?" Sergius blurted. "Is it not said that your Anointed One rose from the grave, and that he will restore the Jewish Kingdom?"

"He will erect a new Heavenly Kingdom," Didymos corrected, failing to conceal his annoyance. "And he is risen."

"Then where is he? Where is his Kingdom?"

"Not here." Didymos rose from the fire pit. "And I might remind my master that the Emperor himself practices the Galilean faith."

"He bows to the Chi-Ro, not a fish," Sergius contended. "And besides, he's not here to hear me." He gazed at his servant, dark eyes of stone, ordering him without words to remember his position. Didymos bowed and tried to leave the room.

"And why did you take up the faith?" Sergius queried. The servant shrugged.

"I want to believe that we can live forever. That God loves all of us equally. That the dead are not lost…that we will be reunited in a Heavenly Kingdom." Didymos looked at his master, face grave, eyes sad but bright in the glow of the fire. "Gaius believed. Perhaps it's worth thinking about."

"And what's the difference," Sergius inquired with genuine interest, "between the fish and the Chi-Ro?"

"That question would be better answered by my deaconess. She too, comes from the East. You both speak the Greek tongue. You should meet her. You and Bacchus both."

Didymos left the room, leaving Sergius to stare at the charm in his hand. He gazed into the flames of the fireplace, deep in thought.

Sergius flipped the fish once more in his fingers, then wrapped the twine around his neck and tucked the charm into the folds of his tunic. He ran a hand over the fabric, feeling the smooth wood against his skin. As he watched the fire burn, he had the most invigorating feeling that something immense crept toward the present, something that would reshape both he and Bacchus's lives.

Something wondrous.

Chapter XX.

The nondescript house could have sheltered any common family in Paris; it had not even one distinguishing mark about it—a perfect match with the rest of the Roman-Parisian architecture. Didymos trudged up through the puddles in the street lit by moonlight. Sergius and Bacchus followed the servant locked hand in hand in their formal armor and heavy winter cloaks, their faces hidden by raised hoods. Pausing at the door, Didymos knocked three times. A tiny shaft of light appeared in the midst of the heavy wood, and Sergius noticed for the first time a tiny notch which the inhabitants must have used as a peephole. Sergius knew something mysterious and secretive must transpire within those walls, and his heart fluttered as he wondered what awaited him.

The great wooden door swung open, revealing another man in the plain tunic of a peasant, a bushy auburn beard covering his face. He eyed Sergius and Bacchus up and down a moment, then stood aside to let the three enter the house.

Once indoors, the three guests joined their host inside a cramped foyer, the far wall covered by a curtain sewn together of fabric scraps. The host closed and bolted the door behind them, and Sergius and Bacchus pulled back their hoods.

"*You bring Scholae Palatinae?!*" the host hissed at Didymos in the Germanic tongue. Didymos struggled a moment, trying to remember the proper words.

"*They are…master…*" Didymos searched his memory, eyes closed and hands pounding at the air in concentration.

"*Didymos is my companion's servant,*" Bacchus injected, much to Didymos' relief. "*He brings us here to learn more of the Galilean faith…the faith of the fish, not the Chi-Ro.*"

The host looked at Bacchus, stunned. Sergius couldn't decide if Bacchus command of the German language had taken him so aback, or if his candid explanation of their visit had shocked him so. After regarding the three guests a moment, the host pulled back the curtain, allowing the three travelers to enter an even greater room, this one decorated with strange symbols which Sergius had never seen before.

A windowless chamber lit only by oil lamps and candles, a single table served as the only furniture adorning the scant room. The table stood at the far end, covered with more lamps and a thick folio lying open atop it. On the wall, a great wooden cross with the vague carving of a man hung over it, giving the whole room a creepy, sanctimonious feeling.

Didymos walked toward the altar and sat a few feet away, as if routine. Sergius and Bacchus followed and did the same, still unsure what to expect in this strange place as the host disappeared through another door next to the altar.

"Didymos, what is this?" Sergius asked, on edge from the proceedings.

"This is the true faith, Sergius." In his years working for the Primercius, Didymos had never once called Sergius by name. The directness of his comment took Sergius aback, making offensive tension bubble in his stomach.

"Do not scold him, Palatinae," came a cool, feminine voice, as if detecting Sergius's thoughts. "In this place there is no slave, and there is only one master." Sergius and Bacchus looked up to behold a towering woman—almost as tall as Sergius—with a high, shining forehead, buttery brown skin, and long, silken ebony hair stride into the room. Dressed in a plain tunic, she somehow had a regal and powerful air about her. In her arms she carried a basin of water, and over one arm, she had draped a plain towel. Sergius figured she couldn't be much older than he by her youthful energy, though premature graying at the roots of her hair suggested a worldliness to her sprit.

The woman sat with her back to the altar, the glow of the lamps and candles casting a warm aura around her, as if the light came from her skin. She smiled, and placed the wash basin between her and her three guests.

"I am Macrina," she introduced in perfect Greek, brushing back her shining hair over her shoulder. "Welcome to our church." Sergius and Bacchus looked at each other, then back at this unconventional woman before them.

"Thank you for receiving us," Sergius said, not quite sure what to say to such a strange host. His eyes darted about the plaintive surroundings. "Your church is a most unusual one."

"It is a true church," Macrina snapped, curt in her tone. "Not some redecorated temple to Jupiter." She shifted her body against the stone floor. "This is a church like that of the first apostles, like that the Master himself would have preached in."

"The Master?" Bacchus asked in genuine perplexity.

"Yeshu," Macrina answered, matter-of-fact. "Our Lord and Savior."

"We accept Yeshu as our one true Lord and Master, who will grant us eternal life in exchange for faith in his teaching," Didymos explained.

"You refer to the crucified Jew, yes?" Sergius muttered, his voice hoarse with discomfort.

"Crucified by Pontius Pilate, buried, and risen again by God himself." Macrina nodded with reverence. She reached out to Sergius's foot, motioning to him to give it to her. Rocking back on his elbows, Sergius extended his leg toward Macrina, who undid his sandal and rested his foot in the water basin, massaging the dirt from it with her bare hands.

"The Master asked that we do this," she explained, "that we always show hospitality, lest we commit the sin of Sodom."

"I know not of that legend," Sergius confessed.

"It is an old Jewish tale," Didymos injected as Macrina went about washing Sergius's feet. "One night angels came to the city of Sodom and were granted lodging by the man Lot. The other citizens however rebelled against Lot's generosity, wishing to rob and rape the angels. It so offended God that he destroyed the city."

Sergius recoiled at the strange tale, his foot splashing about in the basin. Macrina raised her eyes to him, cold, judging his reaction, searching for its root. She patted his foot dry, then motioned for Bacchus to surrender his feet.

The group sat quiet at Sergius and Bacchus contemplated the story, and Didymos and Macrina waited for some response. Bacchus reached out as Macrina scrubbed at his toes and stroked

Sergius's hand. Macrina's eyes darted between the two soldiers, an ambiguous look on her face.

"Is it not said," Sergius uttered, breaking the awkward silence, "that the Galilean God is one of mercy and forgiveness? How should a god of mercy murder entire cities?"

"They had sinned!" Didymos shot back. "Sin is an affront to God! Why should he keep them alive?"

"Brother Didymos," Macrina cut in, voice stern, forcing him silent. "You forget Yeshu's commandment: 'Let he who is without sin…'"

"'Cast the first stone,'" Sergius finished. "I have heard this saying. But how do you reconcile the teachings of Yeshu with the action of an angry god?"

"The sayings and stories of Yeshu come before all else. He is the begotten son of our Lord God. The Divine incarnate," Macrina declared, drying Bacchus's feet.

"You still have not answered my question," Sergius pressed. Macrina gave an evasive grin.

"Tell me Primercius, why do you know so much of our faith?" Macrina asked. "Have you practiced it?"

"No, madam," Sergius offered. "But I have studied the world. The Galilean faith is not unknown to me."

"And what do you believe?"

Sergius paused at the question, not quite sure how to answer Macrina.

"I put my faith," he said at last, "if that is what you mean, in the wisdom of the ages. I follow no deity." Macrina nodded and turned to Bacchus.

"And you, Bacchus? Where is your faith?" she inquired. Bacchus too fell silent, thinking.

"I put my faith in Rome," he declared, eyes to the ground. Macrina regarded them both, her face steel and cold.

"I see. My brother Basil," she began, "has too studied the classics, even at the side of Caesar Julian himself. Your friend Gaius too believed in Rome. Both men put their faith in Yeshu, for believing in one does not negate the other. And for that belief, they shall both live forever."

"Gaius rots in the grave!" Sergius spat with rage. "His belief did not save him from Severus's blade!"

"He believed in the sacrifice of Yeshu," Macrina said, her tone maternal. "When the end of time comes, he too will rise as Yeshu did. He will be part of the new Kingdom."

"Oh, so he must wait?" Sergius retorted in sarcasm. "And where will this new Kingdom exist?"

"Not here."

"No, of course not," Sergius replied, his anger rising. "And why should I choose to believe in this new Kingdom?" Macrina finally smiled a genuine smile, her teeth showing between her parted lips.

"Because," Macrina cooed, "in this new Kingdom, there will not be male nor female, free nor slave, neither rich nor poor. And there will be only Yeshu and his Father, our Lord God, ruling over all mankind. And we shall live forever."

"I've heard all this before," Sergius grunted. "This is the same faith of the Chi-Ro. The faith that Constantine…"

"It is *not!*" Macrina yelled, breaking her cool exterior. The Emperor has introduced a new god, yes, and he would call it the god of Yeshu, but it is not. It is the god of the Imperial throne. The faith we practice here is the original faith of Yeshu, not the faith of Constantine. He has bastardized and corrupted the Lord's teachings!"

Sergius glanced over at Bacchus enough to see him cringe at

Macrina's words. He took Bacchus by the hand and climbed to his feet.

"We are finished here," Sergius declared, pulling Bacchus up along side him. "Didymos, you may practice your faith as you like, but you are never to mention the name of Yeshu in my home, is that clear?" The servant looked at his master, horrified, then looked to Macrina for help. The deaconess said nothing.

"Yes, my lord," Didymos said, hanging his head low.

"These are the teachings of hypocrites and words of sedition. I'll not tolerate them," Sergius finished. Turning for the door, he led Bacchus along with him when Macrina spoke.

"If I offended you," she whispered, just loud enough to capture the two soldiers' attention. "I apologize. But I will not apologize for my belief."

"I do not ask you to."

"Then know that our door is always open, and there is always a place at our table, Sergius and Bacchus. You both are welcome here whenever you please, should you choose to believe." She climbed to her feet, head held high and statuesque.

"You speak ill of my birth," Bacchus fired off, his accent beginning to erupt. "Vy should Ay sty here?"

"There are no high or low births here, Bacchus" Macrina apologized. "Only brothers and sisters in one family, the family of Yeshu. Our Lord's parents were not married either; his social class will not preclude him from ruling the greatest Kingdom of all. And you are both invited."

Sergius and Bacchus took one look at each other and walked out into the night, not even bothering to shut the door behind them.

Chapter XXI.

Didymos brushed at the tiles of the insula floor beside a bucket of murky water, trying to find some hint of progress in returning them to their true color of white. Thus far, he had found none, as Sergius sat patiently next to the warmth of the hearth reading the tale of Oedipus by the firelight.

"That's enough," Sergius declared after what seemed like hours of irritating grinding. Didymos sighed and made a slight bow as placed his brush back in the bucket of water, rising to his feet. "And Didymos," Sergius added, "have breakfast for two ready tomorrow morning. Bacchus will stay here tonight." Though his master made no point of the sleeping arrangements, Didymos knew this also meant he had to make Sergius's bed up for two as well, and so he exited to the room to go about preparation.

Animosity burned in Sergius's heart against his servant. Until meeting Macrina, he'd had no objection to the Galilean faith, simply lumping it all together with the myriad of religions he'd studied as a boy. Something about this one though, or at least Marcina's cult of it, intrigued him as much as it offended him. The idea that people could live forever simply by *believing* in those absurd stories of resurrection. How could anyone believe something so impossible?

Sergius didn't have much more time to brood before Bacchus arrived looking splendid in his formal armor. Sergius rose to meet him with a kiss, dropping his cherished codex to the ground before either of them spoke. Their lips tangled and tongues explored in ecstasy, and Sergius could smell the jasmine oil Bacchus had scented his body with. Their mouths parted, but Sergius let his embrace around Bacchus linger, and the Secundarius didn't seem to mind.

"Hi," Sergius whispered with a huge grin on his face. Bacchus said nothing, just squeezing Sergius tighter in his mighty arms. When they released each other, Sergius just stared into Bacchus's amethyst eyes, reveling in their beauty, enjoying the swell of pride that the soldier before him—*his* soldier—could look so splendid.

"You look handsome," Bacchus said at last, much to Sergius surprise. He'd not expected that kind of compliment; indeed, he could not recall a time when anyone had given him one. He kissed Bacchus again, quick and simple in a gesture of thanks.

"*You* look handsome," Sergius repeated to Bacchus, as if his beauty paled in comparison to his fellow Palatinae. Their fingers intertwined, overjoyed at reuniting after even the shortest parting from one another.

Bacchus averted his eyes suddenly, gazing down at the fresh-cleaned tile. Sergius recognized the look at once.

"What troubles you?" Sergius whispered. Bacchus shook his head.

"I lav you, and vould gif all ov my body and soul to you,"

Bacchus creaked through his re-emerging accent. "But Ay feer I shame Kai-Zair by making myzelf female."

"You shame no one," Sergius decried, "and you are no woman. You are a man, valiant and strong, and Caesar takes pride in you." Bacchus soft eyes raised to meet Sergius's and the two shared a soft kiss of comfort, even Sergius could tell Bacchus still struggled inside.

"Caesar will take pride in both of you," Didymos added as he re-entered the room. He walked over and picked up the Oedipus codex from the floor with great care, brushing dust from its pages. "It is telling that he would invite the two of you to a formal dinner with heads of state. You must be important counsel."

"It is Sergius," Bacchus declared, squeezing his hand. "Caesar cherishes his wisdom as much as I do."

"You both flatter me," Sergius demurred, smiling wide, eyes to the tile floor in embarassment. He looked back up at Bacchus, whose violet eyes shined with pride and smiled a toothy grin. Bacchus did the same, smirking so wide that the socket of his missing tooth showed. Sergius didn't even notice.

Finding his annoyance with Didymos quelled, Sergius thanked his servant for all his help as he and Bacchus set out into the chilly night for the palace. The two walked in silence, just happy to be together, the sound of the evening traffic of horses and carts the only noise between them. Halfway to the palace, Bacchus broke their silence.

"Have you been thinking about the Galileans?" Bacchus asked.

"I have," Sergius admitted with a nod. "Macrina intrigues me as much as she infuriated me. What are your thoughts?" Bacchus swallowed, trying to phrase together his words.

"I do not think she meant offense," he declared. "She is… passionate. She believes what she says."

"I agree. But why should someone believe something so absurd?" As they both reflected on the question, Bacchus took Sergius by the hand and raised it to his lips, laying a soft peck across the back of his palm. The two walked hand in hand the rest of the way to the palace.

As they approached, another noise permeated the air—the sound of a metronomic grunting, like a chorus of wild apes. The two soldiers slowed their pace in hesitation and exchanged looks of puzzlement. They walked slow, and as they beheld the great Imperial palace lit up by torchlight, casting long, eerie shadows over itself against the night sky. Then the lovers saw the mob, fists pounding the air, screaming at the palace walls, their military garb unmistakable even in the darkness of the night.

Fear stabbed into Sergius's gut at the horrible vision, especially as he recognized the crumpled pamphlets littering the ground—the same propaganda that Severus had waved around in the tavern. The same that incited the fight that ended with both he and Gaius's death. Was this a seditious mob of troops, come to murder the Emperor they'd once proclaimed Augustus? Had the unrest grown that bad?

Fortunately, Sergius and Bacchus blended with the rest of the mob as they weaved through it towards the main palace gate. As they approached, Sergius could make out Nebridius and a dozen other soldiers standing guard at the door, deflecting the occasional hurled stone or rotten vegetable with their Palatinae shields.

"Sergius!" he called out in desperation. "Please say you've come to relieve me!"

"I'm here to see Caesar," Sergius confessed, a hint of sympathy in his voice, grasping Bacchus hand even tighter.

"Watch for flying stones when you enter," Nebridius warned as he moved his tiny frame to shield Sergius and Bacchus. He hurried them towards the gate, where another sentry scrambled to open it for the guests.

"What's all this about then?" Sergius yelled over the noise of the mob.

"Inaction," Nebridius replied. "Julian is up meeting with senior commanders now, trying to calm all this down. They trusted Severus, and now that he's gone, the troops want more direct involvement from Caesar to fight the supply shortages and outrageous strategies of Constantius."

Nebridius pushed Sergius and Bacchus into the entry hall, dodging a flying stone as they entered. Bacchus hurried to check over he and Sergius armor, to make sure it had not been blemished by the debris.

"Enjoy dinner," Nebridius hissed with sarcasm. He raised his shield and charged back outside as the palace gate slammed behind him.

Sergius and Bacchus looked at each other, winded by the strange encounter outside. Not quite sure what to say, Bacchus reached out and placed his hand on Sergius scarred shoulder. The Primicerius looked at him and smiled.

The two ventured into the shadowy palace towards the formal dining chamber, a separate dining area used only for functions of state. Decorated more in the local style, it featured an elongated table and chairs allowing for individual seating, and a great chandelier of candles hanging from the rafters high above. A single mosaic of Jupiter along the back wall served as the only indication of the Roman presence.

Sergius and Bacchus entered to find Oribasius, goblet in hand, speaking with a man neither had ever seen before—dark skinned, dressed in tight fitting robes more akin to the dress of the Persians rather than the Romans. On his head he wore a circular hat of exotic colored fabric, his long, dark hair twisted up beneath it.

"Boys!" Oribasius called with his usual flare, apparently unaffected by the riots which they could still hear outside. "Meet Euhemerus, our new friend from Libya."

"Soldiers," Euhemerus greeted with a slight bow. Sergius and Bacchus returned the gesture.

"Sergius and Bacchus are favored amongst all the Scholae Palatinae," Oribasius added. Euhemerus raised his brow, eyeing the two infamous bodyguards. It dawned on Sergius that their initiation to this formal dinner might have greater meaning than he or Bacchus anticipated.

"Where is Caesar?" Bacchus asked. He eyed the great table which had five place settings. Servants rushed in and out of the room preparing it, arranging each setting as well as a centerpiece platter of fruit.

"Still with the generals," Oribasius answered. "Trying to grant any request in his power to quell the unrest."

"He will be along soon," came a modest, feminine voice. The four turned to see Helena stride into the room looking like Venus herself. Clad in a red stola, hair piled atop her head with golden and ivory combs, a necklace of finger-like golden rods about her skeletal neck, she looked vibrant with life. It seemed to Sergius that the Empress showed a newfound confidence in her posture—this was not the submissive girl he had seen weeks ago, but a woman aware of her own stature.

"Please, everyone, take your seats," Helena urged. "We can begin the first course without him.

"No need," Julian declared, entering the room in a lavender tunic. He looked exhausted, eyes sunken and black, the lines about his forehead pronounced and leathery. Without any more greeting, he took his seat at the head of the table and flicked his hand into the air, motioning the other guests to sit.

Sergius and Bacchus sat next to each other at Julian's right, while Helena, Oribasius and Euhemerus sat at his left, his wife looking regal with a warm smile on her face. Her eyes never left the face of her husband, though Sergius knew the Empress would be the last thing on Julian's mind given the present climate.

Dinner consisted of wild boar, greens with olives shipped all the way from Rome itself, and a centerpiece of assorted fruit. Sergius noted that Julian again shied away from the meat, consuming only the fruit and vegetables. Moreover, no wine was served, and Sergius could see the displeasure in Oribasius face as he washed down his dinner with a goblet of plain water. During the meal, Sergius also noted the doctor drop a pinch of some unidentified powder into Helena's cup. He recalled the discussion Julian had with his counsel when he decided to employ Helena's assistance in appealing to Constantius. Sergius assumed Oribasius had just followed his order to make sure Helena would not conceive.

The party ate in silence, the echo of the mob outside providing an eerie background noise that made their stomachs churn. Sergius himself lost his appetite by the time the servants sliced the wild boar. Not wanting to insult his host, he forced it down anyway.

"Servants, leave us," Julian ordered as the group finished their meal. The servants complied, scuttling out of the room like frightened bugs, scurrying in every direction for the doors. When the room had emptied, Julian himself checked every door, locking in from the inside before he returned to the head of the table, remaining standing. Sergius knew Caesar was about to reveal their purpose in this bizarre dinner.

"My friends," Julian began, taking a swig of water from his goblet. "My wife," he acknowledged with a slight nod. "I've called you here tonight because you, above all others, I trust in my court." Bacchus reached under the table and took Sergius hand. Sergius looked at his companion with a glance of pride before turning back to the Emperor.

"With Helena's help I have appealed to Constantius regarding the issue of Florentius and taxation, as well as our campaigns in Gaul and in Britain and the breaks in our supply chain. Our Augustus has not responded to my requests, nor has he addressed my accusations that Florentius has embezzled much-needed tax funds to his own purse. Instead, he chooses to ignore me. He ignores the situation of his troops here in the West. And thus, he ignores his duties as Emperor."

Sergius tightened his hand around Bacchus's in anticipation. He had long expected Julian to defy Constantius, but just how far he would defy him remained in question.

"Therefore," Julian continued, "I cannot in good conscience stand for this treatment any longer. It is said he makes fun of my appearance, that he calls me a coward, that he has never taken me seriously as his Caesar of the West. Indeed, his perceived image of me as a fool might be what has kept me from execution all these years. But the time has come to remind Constantius that I too have royal blood in my veins. Caesar Augustus must mind his troops, he must believe in the true ways of Rome. This Galilean religion has separated us from our roots, and though I have practiced it since childhood, my heart and soul have always been faithful to Rome, and to her deities. It is Jupiter, not some dead criminal that personifies the best of our Empire. It is the audacity of Mars, the affection of Venus, the courage of Mercury that defines Rome, and without our gods to guide us, our Empire will meet with destruction and death."

Sergius could not believe the words Julian spoke. The Caesar was not only pledging his faith in the old gods, he was actually talking about re-converting the Empire from the Galilean faith. Moreover, his hot criticisms of Constantius were more than just complaints…they approached treason. Sergius held his breath, anticipating Julian's next words.

"I have spoken to my commanders, and they are with me. I have enlisted Euhemerus, whose troops in Libya can be called in to open a second front in the event of full-scale civil war. Constantius can no longer be allowed to destroy the Empire of our fathers, even if it means I must destroy the capitol to find him. Constantinople will be called Byzantium once more, and the wretched legacy of my uncle and cousin will be undone." Without looking, he reached out and took Helena's hand. The Empress beamed at her husband.

Julian sighed for dramatic effect. "At dawn you may no longer call me Caesar, for a new day will begin for all of Rome."

Sergius eyes widened. He held his breath in anticipation.

"At dawn the restoration of the glory of Rome begins. The reign of Constantius is over.

You may call me Caesar Augustus."

Chapter XXII.

"I've known you your whole life, Julian," Oribasius cowed, leaning against a pillar in the shadowy room. "And I have known you to be both audacious and bold. But you are sparking a civil war…"

"The war began the day Constantine and Constantius murdered my family," Julian said, his voice ringing like an ominous bell. "It ends at dawn. And should my cousin object, I shall meet him in battle."

Sergius adjusted his armor over his chest, tense and uncomfortable since Julian's announcement at dinner. The heavy red meat of the roast boar rested in his stomach like a brick, and moreover, without the presence of Bacchus, he felt alone and vulnerable. The darkness of the room didn't settle him either; after dinner, Julian demanded Sergius and Oribasius join him in his study where he barred the servants from the room and declared that the torches and cistern remain unlit. The resulting atmosphere made for a black and cold chamber as melancholy as the thoughts of its Caesar.

As for Julian himself, he stared out through a heavy curtain over the crowd of chanting soldiers below. The generals had returned and joined the mob, trying their best to placate their rage.

"I informed the generals that Constantius demands the division of our legions," Julian explained, distant as he stared out over the Parisian landscape. "He would send half of our forces to Britain, and then another third to the East to aid him in the Persian campaign. It would reduce our forces to battle the remaining bands of Alemanni to the point of futility. Chondomar may rot in a Roman cell, but a new king, Vadomar, tries to reunite the clans in opposition to our advances. Without our full army, we cannot hold our reclaimed territories. Constantius wants to see me fail. I'll not give him the satisfaction."

Oribasius and Sergius watched Julian with pregnant silence, waiting for him to explain the rest of his plans. The doctor scowled, knowing full well that Julian kept them in suspense on purpose.

"So what will you do?" Oribasius asked.

"Keep my forces united, and stay true to my original objective: preserving the Western territories." Even in the darkness Sergius could make out the puzzlement on Oribasius face. He shared it.

"Civil war would only destroy both regions of the Empire. Declaring myself Augustus holds claim to my sovereignty and allows me to continue my campaign. I shall starve off any armed conflict as long as possible, and I suspect with the Persian campaign going as poorly as it is, my cousin will do the same."

"It's an awful risk," Oribasius observed.

"A necessary one," the Emperor responded. "There is more." Julian walked toward Sergius and motioned for the doctor to join them. Oribasius tripped through the darkness, grunting as he stubbed his toe on a table, and limped the rest of the way to his companions. Julian let out a great sigh, as if a tremendous weight fell on his shoulders.

"Sir…" Sergius began, trepidacious.

"Helena is with child," Julian blurted. Sergius grunted in shock and turned to Oribasius. He knew the doctor was actively trying to prevent the Empress from conceiving, and feared for Julian's wrath.

"How can you know?" the doctor asked with incredulity. "I've been feeding her contraceptives. There is no way to know without an examination…"

"I'm an educated man, Oribasius. I know the symptoms. Her bleeding has stopped. She suffers cramps of the abdomen. Her appetite is monstrous for a woman of her size. She believes she is carrying my child."

"And…" Oribasius cleared his throat. "You believe this?"

"I need you to find out for sure, for if she is, it will only heighten our danger. Constantius has no heir. Any offspring of my own would only threaten his power even more." In the dim light, Sergius recognized a nod from the doctor.

"I shall go at once," Oribasius said with a tiny bow.

"Good," Julian agreed. "And have them prepare. I'm crowned at dawn."

"We lack the royal laurels," Oribasius reminded Julian. "Perhaps we could use some of Helena's jewels."

"Keep my wife's feminine trinkets away from me! I'm no Empress! I'm Caesar Augustus. Find another way!"

Oribasius exited the room, and as light flooded in from the unbolted door, Sergius recognized a look of fear on his face that he'd never seen before. Helena's pregnancy changed everything in the contest between Julian and Constantius, including the Caesar's demeanor. Sergius had never seen him so angry among his trusted friends. Sergius moved to leave too, to run back to Bacchus and tell him all the exciting news.

"Primercius," Julian said, "wait a moment. Close the door." Sergius obeyed, replacing the deadbolt as Julian threw open the curtains, dowsing the room with cold morning air. Over the Parisian rooftops, the sky lightened from the black of night to the early blue-purple of morning. Even with so little light, Sergius recognized the total exhaustion in his Emperor's face.

"Sergius," Julian began, "I want you to know something. I want you to know because you are a loyal, dependable soldier and I trust you. I consider you among my closest advisors, and more importantly, I consider you a friend, a luxury most Emperors cannot afford."

"My lord," Sergius uttered, flattered.

"I've known for some time of your carnal relationship with Bacchus. I find it unusual that two grown men should seek the flesh of one another over that of women or even youth. Many in my court disapprove." He paused a moment. "Do you love him?"

"Yes, my lord," Sergius answered without hesitation. "More than anything." Julian nodded, a gravitas in his gesture.

"Then stay with him. I have not desired love, nor wished to know the flesh of another. That I've devoted my life to the preservation of Rome is a tribute to my deceased family. But..." Julian paused. "Helena has ignighted my emotions like I never thought possible. I find myself thinking of her when I should think of my Empire." Sergius eyes widened at the Caesar's admission. Julian slouched over to the triclina, lounging down in it, his face a twisted portrait of agony.

"Constantius denied me that chance to know my mother and father, and now…" Sergius watched as tears formed in the corners of Julian's eyes. The Emperor bowed his head, wringing his hands back and forth.

"Lord Caesar," Sergius cooed with tenderness, kneeling at the Emperor's side. "You needn't say more."

"I do!" Julian snapped. "Do not waste your time with him! Glean every moment with Bacchus and forget what judgment anyone else might pass, that it's disgusting or shameful or anything else! Being together brings you joy in a way you could never have any other. Stay with him. Let nothing ever separate you."

"Yes, my lord," Sergius accepted after a shocked pause. He reached out and laid his hand on Julian's own, and the Caesar did not recoil. The two sat there, silent, neither needing more words. Sergius watched in compassionate awe as the tears of the most powerful man in the world fell to the cold tile floor in the early morning light. Sergius never wanted to leave his friend, only wishing that Bacchus were there to hold him.

Chapter XXIII.

The golden light of daybreak cast long, glowing beams through the corridors of the Parisian Imperial Palace as servants rushed about their morning duties, and Sergius followed Julian through the halls about to commit what he knew as an act of treason. Caesar looked exhausted: dark circles around his eyes, jowls deep set in his face, crow's feet cracking the smooth contours around his eyes, stubble dusting his cheeks in a goat-like beard. For a man of his mid-twenties, Julian looked at least ten years older. Yet his fatigue showed not in his resolve, as plodded on with deep resolve, his slight figure clothed in his purple robes.

Nebridius and Oribasius followed the Emperor as well, along with Euhemerus, his flowing Libyan dress rippling against the friction of the air at their brisk pace. No one spoke, each man aware that their very participation in the morning's assembly would be cause for execution. As the group headed to the upper levels of the palace, Nebridius exchanged a nod with Sergius and disappeared into a separate hallway, determination in his walk. The rest of the group headed to the top level of the palace, making their way to the westernmost balcony overlooking the city.

As they approached the open curtains, the cold of the morning kissing their skin, Sergius could hear the rhythmic chanting of the army down below. He wondered if, after the dinner, Bacchus had gone out to join them. He wished his companion were with them now, to share in such a momentous occasion.

The rhythm of the crowd turned to outright cheering as Julian took to the balcony, the sunrise lighting the palace with a halo, as if the light of the world emanated from its grand architecture. Julian let out a deep breath, which coalesced into white fog as he raised his fists over the screaming army below. Their cheers immediately amplified at the sight of their Caesar in his full glory, and even the modest Julian cracked a smile at feeling his own popularity. He opened his palms, waving them downward, calming the crowd before him. When their cheers had finally settled to a dull rumble, the Emperor spoke.

"My fellow Romans," Julian began, "I have heard your cries, and the divine hath sent me a vision!" Caesar's eyes darted about, exchanging knowing looks with his companions that the divine force he referred to was not the Galilean, but the majestic Jupiter. "I have seen two trees, one tall, one a mere sapling. As I approached, I could see the tall tree stood curving toward the ground, cut down by some unseen woodsman, while the sapling hung suspended above the Earth."

Sergius and Oribasius traded a perplexed look, both wondering what odd metaphor Julian fed to the masses, and more important, how their uneducated minds would digest it.

"As I stared at the two trees, the tall one dying, the sapling so fragile and unprotected, a voice said to me 'Alas for the tall tree, for not even its offspring will be preserved. But take courage, for while the small tree roots still in the soil, so shall it be uninjured and established more securely than before.'"

As Julian spoke, Nebridius crept up to the balcony, something massive in his arms wrapped in a blanket. Sergius looked at his fellow Palatinae and flinched with confusion.

"My fellow Romans, I know what this vision portends," Julian went on. "Citizens, you stand with your armies. Soldiers, you stand with your generals, and generals, you stand with your Emperor!" Julian raised his hands to the heavens, screaming out with full dramatic flare. "Hear me Constantius, for your reign is dying. From this day forward, the sapling outgrows the falling tree, for I am your Caesar Augustus!"

The crowd erupted in a deafening cry the likes of which Sergius had not heard since the Battle at Strasburg. The citizens of Paris, awakened by the early commotion leapt up and down with excitement. The soldiers raised their shields, the round insignias of their divisions pounding toward the sky with chants of "Augustus! Augustus!" Julian spread wide his arms, as if to embrace the populace below, a smile of genuine satisfaction glowing on his face. He turned around to face his companions, his teeth still shining in the morning light.

"Nebridius," the new Augustus said, waving the Primercius toward him. Nebridius's tiny rodent body crept towards Julian with slight hesitation, unwrapping the contents of the blanket in his arms. Under the folds, the golden bridal of a Julian's horse Demosthenes glimmered in the morning light. Nebridius held it out towards the Emperor, timid.

"That's the best you could do?!" Julian bellowed. "The armor for my *horse?!*" Julian dropped his arms to his sides, slack jawed with shock.

"You declined all of your wife's jewels!" Nebridius reminded the Caesar. "Finding golden laurels at short notice is not an easy task!"

"And so my options are decline my new title, be crowned a beast or a woman?" Julian asked, his voice flat. "Can we do no better?" Sergius stared down at the bridal, realizing just how pathetic Julian would look before his army wearing a horse's armor. It would not be the best start to his new administration.

"Here," Sergius injected. Thinking fast, he undid his golden torque about his neck and held it out to Julian. The Emperor glanced down at it a moment, then met Sergius's eyes with a grin.

"You do the honors, philosopher," Julian purred with a smile. The Caesar turned back towards the crowd and held out his arms again, as Sergius with great sanctimony, raised the torque above his head, before placing it atop Julian's locks with gentle care. The crowd below screamed even louder as Julian teetered to balance the loose torque atop his head, and for the first time in recent memory, Sergius watched as the new Augustus laughed without hesitation.

After minutes of reveling in the cheers of his subjects, Julian decided to take an inaugural march through the city. The entire Scholae Palatine assembled by division, each soldier in formal armor, following as the new Augustus rode Demosthenes through the Parisian streets. Sergius followed in formation atop Hylas, still without his torque which Julian used for his crown. All along their way, citizens rushed out to join in the cheering from their homes, from the baths, from their shops. As they rode by the brothel, Sergius nodded to Tigranes and Justinian, both of whom had joined in the revelry. Justinian met Sergius's gaze and held it as long as he could, until the procession was long out of sight.

Sergius felt a swell of pity in his gut, that he could do nothing to rescue Justinian from his circumstances. He wondered how many countless other children, both male and female, had to suffer sexual humiliation from infancy in order to survive, how many of them died from starvation or disease, or how many just went plain mad from misery.

Such tortures are not fitting of Rome, he thought, *not fitting of Julian's new rule.*

As the soldiers marched on, these thoughts weighed on Sergius's mind. He wondered if, in Julian's new order, there was something he, Sergius, could do to prevent children suffering.

The shadows along the cobblestone pavement lengthened as the sun set from afternoon to evening, just as the procession entered the southwestern corner of the city, near Florentius's palace. By that time, the thought of any objection against Julian's new title had purged itself from Sergius's mind—the city had received the new Augustus so well that he'd begun to think the army could ride all the way to Constantinople with only cheers and accolades to guide their way. And there, in the shadow of Florentius's palace, Sergius heard the first cries of dissent.

They began in low, almost indiscernible from the rest of the crowd's cheering, so muted in fact, that Sergius questioned if he actually heard them at all. The first crack of a stone against his armor confirmed what he thought he'd heard: the crowd accused Julian of treason.

No doubt composed of Florentius's confidants and Constantius's loyalists, another stone hurled toward Sergius, bigger this time, enough to knock him off balance. Hylas whinnied and stopped in his tracks, rearing up on his hind legs and bucking as Sergius held on to his reigns for dear life. When the horse had settled, Sergius hurried to dismount and inspect his equine companion for any injury. Finding none, and with stones still flying, Sergius drew his sword and raced toward to head of the procession to find Julian and Demosthenes encircled by bodyguards, fighting off an angry mob. Sergius raised his shield, and plowed into the frenzy.

Though he kept his blade handy, Sergius relied on his shield to break up the crowd, slamming it into the bodies of the protesters, knocking them to the ground amid shouts of "Traitors!" and "Constantius is the true Augustus!" Sergius paid their words no mind, focusing on his sole purpose; the same it had been since Strasburg: protect Caesar. Yet Julian, perhaps emboldened by his new title, would not stand for any protest.

"Storm the palace!" he commanded, raising his own sword to the heavens. "Bring me Florentius alive!" Before he'd even finished his orders, soldiers and looters alike charged for the palace gates. Sergius followed, taking one last look up at Julian, inspecting the Emperor, making sure of his safety. Julian caught the glance of Sergius and pointed his sword downward into the face of the Primercius.

"Alive, Sergius!" Julian ordered again. "See to it!" With a nod, Sergius charged for the palace walls. Inside, he found the ornate decorations of gold and silver already torn from the walls, bodies of fallen soldiers loyal to Florentius, and general chaos of frightened servants, panicking guards and thieves using the commotion as a cover for looting.

Sergius ran through the confusion into the maze of dining rooms, studies, parlors servants' quarters and baths, searching for some sign of Florentius. The palace itself resembled Julian's but on a smaller scale, and much more extravagantly decorated by its occupant, though the silken curtains and golden plates were quickly vanishing. Several of the servants had stopped to fight off the looters; Sergius couldn't afford to pay them any mind. If Florentius escaped and made it back to Constantinople, Constantius would no doubt withdraw troops from the Eastern front and bring the battle to the West and decimate all the cities and forts Julian had spent years rebuilding. All of Rome would be at stake.

Racing to the second floor of the palace, Sergius encountered even more of the same chaos. Out of the corner of his eye, he spotted an old servant woman staring at him, terrified. Sergius's glare lit on her as she took of into a limping run towards a door at the end of the hall. He had no problem overtaking her as she tried and failed to open the bolted door.

"What's inside?" Sergius barked, grabbing the old woman by her tunic. The crone screeched in terror and panic, crying and howling in hysterics. "Is he in there?" Sergius repeated, shaking the woman in frustration.

"The...bedchamber..." the old woman managed to cry between pants. Sergius released her with a look of disgust, turning to the locked door, unable to open it himself. The woman took off running again, this time headed to the ground floor of the palace, no doubt trying to escape Sergius's wrath. Sergius had no intention of harming her, of course, but given the choice between inflicting harm and brutal intimidation, he chose the latter.

As he struggled against the door, another cry, this one bloodcurdling, captured his attention. In a dusty corner near a bend in the hall, Sergius beheld a young girl, no more than twelve years old, her clothes torn and scattered about as three men in plain dress forced themselves on her, two holding her to the ground, another pumping back and forth atop her. At once, Sergius forgot his main objective and charged down the hall, this time, ready to use his sword.

He never had a chance.

Out of nowhere, another bodyguard, a Secundarius, leapt atop the perpetrators, and in one swift move, grabbed the rapist by his throat and jabbed his sword into his abdomen. The violator's mouth sprayed blood out into the face of the Secundarius, who dropped him into a bloody heap like a butchered animal. The two other men rushed to their feet, ready to attack, just as the soldier lashed out with the disc of his shield, catching one square in the jaw. The man hobbled around in a daze before collapsing to the floor, just as the Palatinae engaged the final molester with Herculean strength, slashing him across the stomach, digging his shield against his face and, with one arm, lifting the attacker by his tunic, its seams tearing with a large shredding noise as he hurled the man into the air and down the hallway.

Sergius dove out of the way as the bloodied rapist skidded across the tile, his head bouncing against the floor as he landed, leaving a crimson stain across the ground. Regaining his bearings, Sergius looked up to see the Secundarius comforting the girl, covering her with her torn clothing. Stunned by the whole scene, Sergius ran to his side, grabbing the soldier by his left arm, and spinning him around.

The moment their eyes met, chestnut and amethyst, they didn't need words; both knew the other had not sustained any injury. Unable to help themselves, Sergius tore Bacchus's helmet from about his head as their mouths met in a ferocious kiss, Sergius's stubble grinding against Bacchus's smooth skin, lubricated by the splatters of blood on his face.

"Come on," Sergius declared, pulling Bacchus down the hall. They returned to the bedchamber door, Sergius again struggling to get it open. Without a word, Bacchus pushed him out of the way, and with one swift kick sent the wood splintering to the ground. He and Bacchus rushed into the room, only to behold a deserted chamber, save one cowering old man now covered in dust and debris. The old woman rushed past the two soldiers into the cloud of sawdust hurling herself atop the old man, the sound of her sobs howling over the noise of the battle.

Sergius's heart sank and his stomach knotted; the old woman must have just been looking for her husband. He and Bacchus looked at each other just long enough to share a moment of fright as the voice of Julian rang over the commotion of the palace.

"Escaped?!" the Emperor bellowed, marching down the hall, flanked on either side by two other Palatinae. Julian stepped forward into the room, scoffing in disgust at the old servant couple, inspecting the carnage a moment before turning to Sergius.

"You manage to find Bacchus but not the man you were sent for?"

"He's not here, my lord," Sergius acquiesced. "He must have gotten word and escaped before the procession even neared the palace."

Julian nodded, taking the torque from off his head and handing it to Sergius with a dismissive posture. Sergius sheathed his blade and took the torque in one hand, and reached out to Bacchus with the other. Bacchus pulled Sergius close, and wrapped a protective arm around his lower back. Julian studied the two of them, along with the stoic faces of his other bodyguards.

"Put on your torque, Primercius," Julian ordered with muted fury, turning and striding back down the hall, the other bodyguards chasing after him.

Without thinking, Sergius reached up and touched the scar tissue of his shoulder. Though Florentius's flight put Julian's rule in question, one thing was certain: a great battle lay ahead.

Chapter XXIV.

They had three amazing weeks together, caught up in the jubilation of their friend's ascent to High Emperor. Bacchus had transferred his few belongings to Sergius's insula, and the once-quiet apartment now turned to a bastion of laughter and conversation. Stories of childhood in Hispania and Gaul, of relatives past and hopes for the future accompanied every meal. The crackle of the evening fire now joined with the melody of Bacchus's lyre, or punctuated the speech of Sergius, as he read aloud the stories of old. Sergius would recline in the triclina with Bacchus kneeling on the floor, his head resting on Sergius olive-skinned legs, listening with absolute intent. Sergius found Bacchus drawn to the tales of Homer, of Paris and Helen and the Great War of Troy that followed, and of Odysseus and his beloved Penelope, and their undying love for one another. Sergius loved the way his eyes would glisten in the firelight, always riveted by the epochs of love and needed no further assurance of Bacchus's own feelings.

The spring brought with it nature's cycle of rebirth, and Sergius and Bacchus alike found their bodies throbbing with heat. Almost every moment they spent together, the two found a way to touch, the softest caress walking the Parisian streets to passionate lovemaking by lamplight, each physical contact intimating their affection for one another. In the dead of night, as the air turned warm and humid again, the two men would slide into bed together, their naked bodies adhered together until morning when Didymos would serve them both a modest breakfast before their duties as soldiers beckoned. Some days they neglected the food altogether, choosing instead to make love again, or to lay in each other's embrace a little bit longer. Others, Bacchus would sulk, again preoccupied with the compromise of his gender to which Sergius would offer comfort, reminding him of his valiant courage, and that their love transcended Earthly bodies. They found it harder and harder to arrive to their posts on time, reveling in every second together, not wanting to spend a single unnecessary moment apart. Despite this, both men found a way to avoid tardiness, their loyalty to Rome still the upmost priority.

Still, even in the days and nights of bliss, fear haunted Sergius. The blossoming spring meant that soon the armies would assemble and march again, and with Florentius still unaccounted for, their pace would be exhausting as they made for Constantinople. Worse, attacks by the re-emboldened Alemanni marauders disrupted supply chains to Paris and its outlying regions. The city had foodstuffs in reserve, so the pains of shortages had yet to creep within the walls of the metropolis. On the trail of war, however, the armies would fight the pains of hunger as hard as they would fight the barbarians as they slogged on across Gaul, and worse, marching into war meant separation from Bacchus.

Nightmares of Bacchus's death already plagued Sergius's

nights. He could see the fields, muddied with blood and manure, trampled by the feet of soldiers, decimated with piles of slaughtered bodies of Roman and barbarian alike. Sergius would run across the hellish landscape, his heart pounding, stomach churning with acid. Inhaling the stench of decay and death, he would look for his beloved. Atop the highest mound of bodies Sergius would find the remains of Bacchus, his bowels spilled, skin rent, amethyst eyes crushed into jelly like squished eggs. Sergius would try to pull at the cadaver, only to sink deep into the mountain of bodies, as if the hands of corpses pulled him further and further in. Bacchus would fall atop him forcing him down, suffocating him in death.

Sergius would awake drenched in sweat soaking through the bed linens, his whole body atremble as he gasped at the night air. Sometimes he would cry out like a child, overcome with fright, waking Bacchus with the spasms of his limbs. Those nights Bacchus would simply cup himself around Sergius, squeezing his body tight against his own, and lay a gentle kiss on Sergius's maimed shoulder. Without fail, Sergius would nestle himself against Bacchus, his gasps relaxing and heartbeat slowing, as his senses returned to the present, to the arms of the man he loved. Still, he pondered night and day the thought of separating from Bacchus, and the very real possibility that one or both of them could die in battle, far away from one another. No amount of kisses could stop that reality.

Death loomed ever-present.

After a night of the most horrific waking dreams, Sergius found himself on a morning walk through the streets of Paris. Bacchus had already departed for guard duty, and Sergius needed a way to kill the hours before Julian required him at the palace. Sergius took some comfort in the walk; he loved to imagine that Paris was Rome itself in the glory days of the republic, merchants and their carts clamoring over the stone streets, the public negotiating for goods in loud and vigorous voice. The crowd, the noise, made the whole city feel alive, the rows of shops and merchants the contours of a sensuous body, the noise the sound of her breathing, this woman of knowledge and peace, presiding over the good of the world with her mothering. Sergius paused in his steps, and island in the flow of the city commerce. *One day, I shall stand in Rome like this,* he thought. *One day, Julian will restore her to the glory of the world.*

Sergius took a deep breath, and looking around recognized the plain house of Macrina and her Galilean fellowship. Sergius pondered the coincidence: *of all the twists and turns of the streets of this city, strange that I should end up here.* He reached up and fingered the wooden fish, still memorializing Gaius beneath the folds of his tunic. *How could so brave a man believe in this faith?*

Sergius meandered towards the door gazing at the heavy wood a moment, and not quite sure what else to do, banged his fist against it. A few moments later, the tiny slit opened, revealing a pair of dark feminine eyes in the shadowy foyer beyond. The eyelet slid closed with grinding clack, and the door swung open, revealing Macrina inside. Without a word, she stepped aside in a gesture of invitation to Sergius.

"I prayed you'd return," Macrina said, her voice cool and husky as she and Sergius entered the sanctuary. Sans doors or windows, the room looked much as it did the night he and Bacchus had first ventured to the secretive church. With the changing seasons, dampness had crept into the hallowed room, and the rank smell of mildew made Sergius recoil.

"It is one of our principles," Macrina explained, "that everyone deserves forgiveness." She slunk over to the altar, lit by ceramic oil lamps, dim around the oversized folio, and knelt before it, motioning for Sergius to do the same. "I hope that you can forgive me for offending you."

"I am not the one you should ask," Sergius countered, kneeling beside his hostess. "It is Bacchus's birth you insulted; comparing it to something you hate so." Macrina nodded.

"Then I hope he one day forgives me too."

Sergius watched the angles of Macrina's face as they curved up into her long flowing hair. Her form reminded him of the Egyptian glyphs he had seen during his studies; images of women with slender necks and long headdresses crowning their cosmetic-painted faces. Macrina wore no such vanities, her dress plain and modest, though her skin still glowed without the aid of make-up. Somehow, in her modest lifestyle, she still managed to project beauty.

"Why did you return, Primercius?" Macrina asked, her voice quiet. Sergius thought a moment.

"I'm not sure," he confessed. "I just found myself here on a walk through the city."

"Then perhaps it is the Master that led you here," Macrina suggested with a grin.

"You believe his ghost controls our actions?"

"Not his ghost," the deaconess corrected. "His spirit. He is risen."

"Ah," Sergius nodded, rolling his eyes. "You believe he conquered death." As he spoke, the words gave him sudden pause. "And how is this different from Osiris, or Dionysus or Mithras? Surely you must know their legends as well…"

"Osiris and Dionysus never existed," Macrina said, her voice flat. "Yeshu lived. He was a man…"

"Just a man, like Mithras," Sergius argued, "but without the prestige of being a soldier or an aristocrat. Yeshu was a poor, illiterate peasant. Why should any God raise him from the dead? Why not David himself, the great king of Israel, or Constantine, he who converted Rome to the Galilean faith?"

"Constantine did not convert to the true faith, I've told you!" Macrina contended. "He called a political counsel under the pretense of determining the true faith, but used it only as a means to strengthen his power!"

"Even so, even if Constantine never truly believed, why should you? Why should I? Why would the lowest criminal of the greatest empire the world has ever known be anointed as king of the Jews—not just, but over all humanity—and risen from the dead?"

"Because if the lowest criminal of Rome can achieve salvation, anyone can," Macrina answered, matter of fact. "That is what we Galileans believe."

Sergius watched her exotic face a moment, studying it for any flicker of doubt or fear. He found none. Macrina proved herself greater than her sex, as a wise, intelligent and articulate sage. Yet she claimed to believe something so absurd…she put her faith in something that made no sense, no matter how egalitarian. How could this be?

"Why," Sergius asked, shaking his head. "Why do you believe?"

"You approach the question as if it were one of reason, Sergius," Macrina whispered, an ambiguous smile on her face. "It was never a question of reason, but one of faith. I believe because I *choose* to."

Sergius watched her a moment, flabbergasted, searching for some response. The longer the silence between the two of them, the more Macrina's eyes seemed to shimmer in the dim lamplight.

"And so your God has no place for reason?" Sergius said at last. Macrina giggled.

"Quite the contrary. Reason and knowledge are two of our

tenants, though some would have it otherwise. But at the core, our belief is one of faith." The deaconess motioned toward the altar. "Look."

Sergius followed as Macrina presented an oversized folio containing a Greek manuscript, open to a page with four parallel columns running down it. Glancing over the page, Sergius found himself even more confused: each column seemed to tell the same story, at times even with identical wording.

"This is one of the few gifts of Constantine to the faith," she explained, running her hand along the page. "This is a collection of our Holy Scriptures—the writings of the earliest evangelists and tales of the life of Yeshu. My parents, being highly thought of as missionaries, were given a copy that they might spread the good news."

"These passages," Sergius noted, "they're almost identical."

"Not quite," Macrina contended. "It is said that there was once only one collection of the words and tales of Yeshu, but that book is now lost to us. These four are based on that collection, each one of them containing variations on Yeshu's teachings. Only through reason, by reading the four together and noting the similarities and differences, can one understand the true mystery." Sergius smiled.

"It is a strange religion you follow."

"Would you learn more, philosopher guard?" Macrina asked, raising the pitch of her voice. "I ask not that you choose to believe as I do, but merely that you learn more about Yeshu and his teachings." She paused a moment, wetting her lips, as if to approach her next words with caution. "We believe the world can be united in peace, much as you do, but that peace cannot come from Rome or from death. Only from the heart."

Sergius thought a moment. The story of this odd religion did intrigue him, most of all the idea that all, men and women, rich and poor alike, could live forever in a Kingdom of bliss. The thought of living forever with Bacchus appealed to him most of all.

"It is worth considering," Sergius decided. "I will consult with Bacchus." He glanced down at the weathered pages of the folio, scanning the words. His eyes set on one passage in the third column:

I have come to set the world ablaze. How I wish that it were already kindled! But I have a baptism to undergo, and how distressed I am until it is accomplished! Do you suppose that I came to grant peace on earth? I tell you, no, but rather division.

The saying echoed in Sergius mind, as he thought again of his nightmares, of the fields of the dead, of Bacchus's decaying body. He reached down and touched the writing, squinting in thought. "Your Yeshu speaks of destruction and division coming to all. Are you certain of your interpretation of peace?"

"To dwell in the Heavenly Kingdom is to divorce the Earthly one," Macrina answered, her dark eyes darting to the floor. They rose again slowly to meet Sergius's face. "You must leave behind all Earthly desire to join the family of Yeshu."

"Does that mean leaving Bacchus?" Sergius asked, his anger seething forth from his cool exterior. Macrina laughed, her eyes meeting his own.

"Of course not, if you love him," she contended through her ambiguous smile. "Loving another is the first step to entering the Kingdom." She raised her eyebrows. "But you will have to learn temperance and self denial. I can promise you the two of you will live together forever with Yeshu, but only if you can deny the sins of the flesh."

Chapter XXV.

That night, with Bacchus's sticky body pressed against his own, Sergius stared up at the plain ceiling of the bedroom, his thoughts dwelling on the words of Macrina. Was it logical to believe that love, not conquest could unite the world? How was that possible with such a diversity of people? Should the pagans be converted? Or the Jews? Or the Persians, or the Egyptians….how could the death of one peasant be the answer to all the problems of the world? And how could celibacy be the path to immortality?

Sergius shifted beneath the woolen blanket, his skin peeling away from Bacchus as he rolled over onto his right side. Bacchus jolted from sleep, his eyes opening into tiny slits, observing his partner, recognizing the restlessness within him.

"What is it?" Bacchus whispered, running the back of his index finger down Sergius spine. Sergius writhed ad the ticklish feeling, rolling over to face Bacchus.

"I saw Macrina again today," he confessed. "And she had some interesting things to say." Bacchus face hardened at the mention of Macrina's name. Sergius frowned and squinted, as if to admit guilt to his beloved. Sergius told him of their conversation, of Macrina's apology, of the belief that only love could bring about peace and utopia, of the Galilean tenant of asceticism. Bacchus listened with scrutiny, his eyes locked with the dilatation of Sergius's own.

"Do you believe her?" Bacchus asked after Sergius had recounted the whole tale. The Primercius shrugged.

"I'm not sure. I think she believes in what she says. And her philosophy of love does make a certain sense. After all, if I could love the world as I love you, I would never want to raise my sword again."

"As it is," Bacchus observed, "you never want to raise your sword against another." Sergius smiled, pulling Bacchus close, the coarse hair of his chest pressing against the smooth flesh of Bacchus's own.

"True. Perhaps this is why I suddenly find myself drawn to such an absurd faith." Sergius thought a moment. "Is it absurd not to wish to kill others, even in the name of Rome and peace?" Bacchus rolled over onto his stomach, the contours of his vertebrae gleaming like tiny hilltops in the dim light. He propped himself up onto his elbows, resting his stubbly chin against the pillow. Sergius could feel the heat radiating from his naked body in the sensuous chill of the night air.

"No," he said after thinking a moment. "It is not in your nature to kill. It is your nature to love, Sergius. That is why you prefer the halls of study over the battlefield. Within yourself, you have always believed the world's problems could be fixed through study and knowledge, not with killing. That is why you are the philosopher." He leaned over, kissing Sergius's scarred shoulder.

The Passion of Sergius & Bacchus

"That is why I love you." Sergius smiled and kissed Bacchus on the mouth.

"Then perhaps we should go. Are you willing to forgive Macrina's rudeness?"

"If you do, I can," Bacchus answered, nuzzling his face against Sergius's shoulder. Sergius wrapped his arm around Bacchus and pulled him close again. "You are the wise man," Bacchus murmured, shutting his eyes again for sleep. "I believe in you. I trust your choice."

"Even if it means we can never be like this again?" Sergius pressed his naked front against Bacchus's side, the Secondarius turning to face him as they exchanged a passionate kiss, their bodies hardening with passion.

"I told you, I would make myself female for you," Bacchus cooed. He bowed his head a moment, wrestling with some internal conflict. With a sigh, his face tightened with resolve as he raised his eyes to meet Sergius's. "I would do anything," he uttered with assurance.

"Even be damned?" Sergius asked, his voice taking on a sudden gravity. "That would mean we could never be together, consigned to oblivion beyond this world."

"Only if you believe her," Bacchus observed. Sergius eyes scanned Bacchus face, its gorgeous Arian features, the perfection of his golden tresses, still sparkling in the darkness. What god could create a man so beautiful, a man so dear and still deny any form of physical affection? Why?

"I think I do," Sergius hesitated, "though I don't pretend to fully understand all her doctrines. Still, if love is the ultimate belief, then surely there is some answer for us." Bacchus leaned in and kissed his forehead, then stared back into his eyes, a mischievous smirk on his face and gleam in his eyes.

"Well if we must give each other up each other's bodies to convert," Bacchus said, rolling over, pulling Sergius on top of him. "Then we should use our time together." Sergius could feel Bacchus's plumb pressed against him, the soft flesh hardening with every second, its speed matching that of Sergius's own. They kissed again between chuckles of bliss and made love until dawn, when they fell asleep in each other's arms.

Chapter XXVI.

Didymos had packed up much of the insula, leaving travel packs for both his masters. The rooms had fallen silent again, no sounds of music or myth or mirth to enliven the empty halls. The next morning would see the armies march from Paris, lead by Julian in a campaign against Vadomar and eventually against Constantius himself in a war that could slog on for years without end, dividing the empire and claiming innumerable lives along with it. That night, as Oribasius and Julian prayed to Mars for courage and strength, Sergius and Bacchus found themselves again in the house of Macrina, though this time not alone.

A fellowship of about twenty people, all of them peasants seated on the hard floor and dressed in tired wool populated the rest of the room, the smell of their unbathed bodies making Sergius frown. In his time spent in the Imperial Palace, even under Julian's frugal and simplistic tastes, the Primercius had grown used to the scent of oils and incense.

What torture of poor hygiene awaits me on the battlefield, he thought.

Macrina began the service by washing the feet of each congregant, an act that shocked Sergius, even as he had come to expect such modesty from their deaconess. As she washed, the room buzzed with fellowship as the parishioners chatted and with the familiarity of a family meeting for an evening dinner. Yet not one person, save Didymos spoke to the two Palatinae. Indeed it seemed as if most of the crowed avoided the two soldiers dressed in formal armor on purpose, occasionally firing off suspicious looks at the two men seated at the back. When, at last, Macrina arrived with her bowl and towel and began to rinse Bacchus's feet, Sergius made no effort to hide his disgust.

"You say we are all one family in Yeshu, but none of our brothers and sisters greet us," he said, voice gruff. Macrina didn't look up from her bowl, only scrubbing harder at the dust of Bacchus's feet.

"They greet you with skepticism for your friendship with Julian," Macrina declared, her voice taking on the familiar coolness. She ran a towel over the top of Bacchus's foot, the blond hairs rippling like gold across his pale skin. She scooted over and undid the straps of Sergius's Caligula, running water over his bare foot, beginning the washing process. "All know of the Philosopher Guard."

"You said all were welcome," the Primercius countered.

"And so all are," replied the deaconess. "Still, you are both still strangers, unbaptized and unfamiliar with the ways of the church. That will change tonight."

"We are to be baptized?" Bacchus asked, his surprise obvious.

"If you are to join the church," Macrina declared, matter of fact. She fired off a cold look at Bacchus, impatient with his question. "You will see."

The Passion of Sergius & Bacchus

When she'd finished cleaning Sergius feet, Macrina walked to the front of the room and placed the basin atop the altar. The crowd before her fell silent in attention. Oil lamps atop the plain table silhouetted her with an eerie glow, creating a corona around her shadowy form. Shafts of light seemed to come from within her, dancing across the room with even the slightest of her gestures. Sergius wondered if she didn't plan her stance on purpose, to suggest an inner divine light to her congregation.

"Brothers and Sisters," she began, "welcome to tonight's fellowship. We gather here tonight, as always, that we might honor the Anointed One, and pray for his return, and for the coming of the new Kingdom. And tonight, we welcome two new seekers of the teachings of Yeshu." She motioned towards Sergius and Bacchus, as the crowd turned their scrutinizing eyes toward the two soldiers. Bacchus scooted closer to Sergius and clutched his arm, suddenly self conscious before the crowd.

"I have heard your whispers," Macrina went on, "and you forget Yeshu's commandment that all should be greeted with love, that you must love your neighbors as you would love yourself, and do not bear ill-will toward them for their station in life, for as the teacher Paul reminds us, each part of a body has it's own function, yet it is still part of the same body. We are one body in Yeshu, my Brothers and Sisters, and we serve one another as we serve the Anointed One."

Sergius felt a churning in his stomach, an odd kind of nervousness that he'd not felt except in those first days with Julian. Something about Macrina's voice made the words resonate with a certain power; he raised his head and furled his brow, intent on hearing the message of this odd religion.

"Sergius and Bacchus," Macrina called, shocking them both to full attention. "We invite you to our table, but ask that you keep what you hear and witness a secret. Here, we will speak of a learning God, one who hides things from the wise and reveals them to the simple, to those who have faith."

"They serve the Emperor!" yelled a voice in the crowd. "They'll have us all flogged to death!"

"Judge them not Brother," Macrina commanded. "I would not allow them here tonight if I thought it unsafe. Sergius?" The beams of her corona seemed to penetrate Sergius soul as she reached out toward him.

"Yes, deaconess?" Sergius answered back, humbled by her defense.

"I know it is the soul of a friend that brought you here tonight, our departed brother Gaius. I hope that, for his memory if nothing else, you keep what you see and hear tonight a secret, even from your Emperor, for while his power is great, there is the Highest Power of all, and it is his commandments we discuss tonight. Have we your word?"

"Yes," Sergius and Bacchus said in unison, Bacchus tilting his head with a slight bow. He reached out and took Sergius hand in his own, preparing to enter this new world with his own greatest love.

"Good. Then there is one thing more you should know. In Yeshu we become one body within his spirit, through the rite of baptism. Since you have not received this rite, your flesh and blood has not inherited a place God's Kingdom. When you receive the spirit of Yeshu, he will transform your souls that you might live forever as we do, that instead of meeting death, you will be transformed into bodies of Heavenly flesh in the splendor of God." Macrina held out her hands at her sides, like a mother waiting to embrace her child. She wore the same ambiguous smile across her face, reveling in her own mysterious words and, Sergius thought, actually believed every bit of them. This woman was no charlatan, no cynic preacher hoping only for her own fortune and glory. Macrina believed with all her heart in her own teachings, those of the crucified Jew and the converted tax collector, for while they seemed absurd, she still managed to find an ultimate truth within them.

Macrina went on, describing the coming of the Kingdom, of the day of Yeshu's triumphant return when the dead would rise from the grave in Heavenly flesh. She spoke of charity, of living a modest life and spreading the good news that God loved all people, and that all could partake in the Heavenly Kingdom if they chose to believe. As she closed her homily, Macrina raised her voice as if to emphasize a special point to the crowd. Even in the dim lamplight, Sergius could see her dark eyes locked on him and Bacchus as they crouched in the back of the room.

"Remember always," the deaconess commanded, "that to prepare for the Kingdom is to divorce one's self from all desires of this world. Eat not meat, drink not wine, know not the flesh of another, for this will keep your souls pure as it would keep your bodies pure."

Sergius released Bacchus's hand in shock. Bacchus turned to the Primercius to find some immediate comfort or wisdom. But Sergius could offer none as he sat flabbergasted by Macrina's teaching. *Why should love of the body pollute the soul?* he wondered. *Why is physical affection unholy?*

The service concluded with an odd ritual in which Sergius and Bacchus did not take part. Each parishioner, before departing, met Macrina at the altar, taking a scrap from a loaf of bread and a spoonful of dark, crimson wine taken from a wooden chalice. In a faith full of absurdities, this struck Sergius as most odd, since the deaconess herself had just spoken against consumption of wine.

When the rest of the congregation had vacated the dark room, leaving it rank, damp and echoing as it had when Sergius and Bacchus first entered it, the two soldiers approached Macrina as she cleared the bread and wine from the altar.

"You must have innumerable questions," she said without looking up, voice tired. "I cannot answer them all for you; I can only promise that should you join us, you will understand."

"And why…" Sergius began, annoyance evident in his tone.

"Why would you join now?" Macrina interrupted. "I don't expect you to. But you are a thinker, Sergius. I expect you to ponder what you've heard tonight. You too Bacchus, though you deny yourself credit. Then you will decide." She gathered the bread and chalice into her arms. "Wait here," she added in a curt tone before disappearing behind a curtain into the next room. Sergius and Bacchus looked at each other, both overwhelmed at the evening's proceedings.

"What do you think?" Bacchus asked, his eyes sparkling like those of an inquisitive child. Sergius took a deep breath and exhaled. He shook his head, not quite sure what to say next, just as Macrina re-entered the room, her arms loaded with two woolen blankets.

"These are for you," she offered, holding out the blankets folded in her arms. Sergius and Bacchus each took one, puzzled. "You march out soon. Take them with you as a sign of my friendship and affection."

"Thank you," Bacchus said with a bow, embracing the blanket. Sergius looked his over, still suspicious of Macrina's intent.

"A blanket will not help me convert," Sergius declared, voice firm and cool. "You cannot buy my faith."

"I would not try to," Macrina said, matching his cool tone. "So I have something else for you." She reached into the folds of her robe and produced a small codex. "This belonged to my brother

Basil. He gave it to me when he went off to Athens." With a sigh, she offered it out to Sergius, who took it in his hand with a gentle grip. "It is a collection of our Holy Scriptures. I pray you read it and understand the great mystery."

Sergius parted his lips as if to say something, but no words came to his mouth. He turned the codex over in his hand, amazed by Macrina's generosity.

"I can't," he said at last, offering the codex back to Macrina. "It's too precious. It should stay in your family."

"We are all family in the Anointed One," Macrina reminded him. "And besides, the love of family is not embodied by physical objects, but by the spirit that possesses them." She put a hand to his scarred shoulder. "Take it Sergius. Read the stories of Yeshu. Learn his teachings."

"I may never see you again, Macrina," he reminded her.

"You will," she replied with a beaming smile. "I have faith."

"Be that as it may," Sergius declared, unrebuffed by her dismissal. "A question lingers, which I must pose to you." Macrina smiled, but the wrinkling crevices around her eyes betrayed the weight in her heart.

"You wonder why you must forsake each other's bodies," the Deaconess observed without prompting. "But you miss the greater issue. You must love Yeshu with all your heart and obey his commandments. It is he, not I, that would forbid your carnal lusts. You must give up Earthly temptations to enter the Kingdom." Sergius opened his mouth to reply—

"There is one thing I would not," Bacchus interrupted, words throbbing with a confidence Sergius had never before encountered. Their eyes fell to the Secondarius, the room tense with anticipation.

"No one, no Emperor, no King, no God could ever take from me my love for Sergius," Bacchus affirmed. "I love him more than anything—more than my Emperor, more than my mother or my grandfather, more than my own life."

"So you would defy the Lord?" Macrina interrogated as her body froze but for her eyes, her gaze crawling over Bacchus.

"Yes," Bacchus said without hesitation. "For a God of Love would never ask me to forsake his greatest gift to me!" Macrina's eyes narrowed as she took a step toward Bacchus. "Without my love for Sergius, I could not believe," Bacchus whispered, his voice wavering. "For every time I look upon him, I feel comforted. I feel strong. I feel *my life*. And ay zee on-lee zee face uf Yeshu…" Bacchus reverted to his natural accent, his words quaking with emotion. "Zee face of Got." He clenched his teeth and swallowed. "I did not know love until I found Sergius," he continued, careful with his pronunciation. "I love Sergius more than my own soul, for my life is empty without him."

The room fell silent, all overcome by Bacchus's words. Sergius never dreamed his beloved capable of such power with words—and not even in his native language! As he stared at Bacchus, so confident and unyielding in the face of spiritual inquisition, Sergius failed to notice the warm tears flowing down his own cheeks, twinkling as they washed over his stubble, refracting the dim light. His jaw went slack, mouth open in awe.

Macrina bowed her head in thought. A moment of absolute quiet passed, until Sergius reached a shaking hand up and laid it on Bacchus's forearm. The Secondarius uttered not a sound, only leaning his body against Sergius's chest, eyes averted.

"You know the question we must face," Sergius muttered, at last breaking the quiet.

Macrina's face twisted into a sneer of utter frustration. She grunted and began to pace the length of the room like a caged lioness, her hands contorting into claws, the tendons of her fingers bugging out beneath her dark skin.

"We have known each other's flesh," Sergius confessed, unrepentant.

"That much is obvious," Macrina scoffed in disgust. "I can smell the oil on you! You defile your bodies…"

"We do not!" Sergius yelled. "There is no shame in knowing the man I love!"

"You must prepare, for the Kingdom is at hand!" Macrina screamed back. "Keep your body and soul pure! Renounce the carnal temptations of this world!"

"Yeshu did not command that!" Sergius cried back in frustration. "Paul did, and he never even met the Lord on Earth!"

"Yeshu appeared to Paul in vision giving him authority!" Macrina froze in her tracks, left index finger extended toward Sergius's face like a spear. "It is from Paul's letters that we gain the most spiritual guidance! They are older than even the Gospels!"

"Which one?" the Primercius seethed. He stepped toward Macrina, chestnut eyes wide with fury, leaning past her finger to face her eye-to-eye, their faces only inches apart. The deaconess did not flinch, nor did she back away. "Do not think me some ignorant lamb. I have studied the scripture you cite and taken it to heart, have you?"

"Paul's letters are the oldest writings of our faith," Macrina admitted, voice suddenly hoarse. "All the more reason why his teachings hold authority. All the more reason to seek celibacy." Sergius stood upright, his head raised and defiant, still holding Macrina's gaze. Neither of them blinked.

"When Bacchus and I love each other with our bodies, it is not to serve our flesh, but our hearts…to unite our souls as deeply as we might," Sergius contended. "And you Macrina," he continued, rising to his feet. "Have you never known the touch of a man?"

"No," Macrina replied in defiance.

"You never loved a man?" he questioned.

Macrina let out a subtle gasp, blinking away from Sergius's gaze. The stone mask of her face vanished again, replaced by a scowl of turmoil. Sergius knew that for all her resilience, he'd finally reached a vulnerable part of her spirit.

"I was betrothed once, in my youth," Macrina admitted, wariness pouring forth in her words. "He died, and I decided to devote my life to serving Yeshu."

"And had he lived?" Sergius interrogated.

"I don't know," Macrina confessed, pacing the room again, averting her eyes from any of her companions.

"If you had married, would you have known his body?" Sergius cooed, his voice tender.

"Paul allows fornication if a man and woman are married," Macrina chimed. "But only as a last resort, for those who cannot tolerate celibacy," she reminded him as she continued to pace. "That is what a husband and wife do!"

"Then it is natural for Sergius and I," Bacchus reasoned. "It is in our nature to love each other, part of our essence that the Lord created in us, part of the gift of love he has granted unto us by finding one another."

"If the God of Yeshu has made it so," Sergius soothed, "if his greatest gift and his first commandment is to love, if he would allow a man and woman to marry so as to consecrate their union that they may not commit sins of the flesh, why should it be any different for Bacchus and I?" Macrina stopped in her tracks.

"No man should make himself a bride!" Macrina crowed. "That is in the law of your Empire! Even now the bishops—John in Constantinople, Augustine of Hippo—preach against of what you speak!"

"An Empire you call corrupt, and bishops appointed by a murderous charlatan who, by your own admission, seeks to control the faith! Those very men would call you heretics and see you killed!" Sergius bellowed.

"And they may yet," Macrina ceded in a murmur.

"Well if you want to worship like them," Sergius went on, trying to compose himself. "Then go to the converted temples of Jupiter and Athena that Constantine called churches and surrender to their teachings. But if you believe otherwise, if you still have the ability to think and reason and interpret Scripture as you would, than you owe us an answer. Why should it be any different for us in the eyes of God than it is for you?"

"I'll not argue this any further," Macrina declared, spreading her arms wide as if to raze the air. "If you choose to enter the faith you must abide by the commandments of Yeshu and undergo baptism. The choice is yours." She strode through the open room to the front door and threw it open, frosty air pouring into the warm house.

"And if we do not?" Sergius pressed. "If we never see you again?"

"Then may the Lord have mercy on you both," Macrina spat, eyes averted in disgust.

Moments later, Sergius and Bacchus walked back through the streets of Paris in silence, blankets tucked under their arms, thoughts of the evening heavy on their minds. The bitter undercurrent of cold had subsided at last giving way to dewy night air of spring. The stone streets glimmered with the moisture, glowing in the light of the moon.

"So," Bacchus broke the silence, "will you undergo baptism?" He watched Sergius face for some indication of his thoughts.

"I cannot say," Sergius admitted. "Will you?"

"I will believe as you do, as I always have," Bacchus declared. Sergius looked at him, his face twisted with concern.

"You must decide for yourself," Sergius urged. "Do not believe or submit to the irrational commands of the faith simply because I do."

"But it is you I love most," Bacchus said, his voice meek and yearning.

"And so you would put your faith in the teachings of a dead Jew?"

"My faith would be where it is always," Bacchus rebutted. "My faith would be in you."

Chapter XXVII.

The fields of Gaul rolled out like emerald carpet, the trees budding and grass glimmering with fresh chlorophyll under a morning mist. The metallic stripe of the Roman army on the march stretched for miles in either direction, the clanking of their armor and horses breaking the natural serenity of the countryside. The sun glowed overhead, but did not yet burn at infernal temperatures; rather, it warmed the country just enough to melt the lingering snow into soggy ground and mud puddles about the road. Birds chirped over the cacophony of the march, and Paris had long since shrunk beyond the horizon line.

Had he still resided in Paris, Sergius would have thought it a perfect day to hike through the woods with Bacchus, listen to him play the lyre, enjoy some wine and relish each other's embrace under the shade of a towering oak. However, this day, he bobbed back and forth like a bladder on a stick, his body limp with defeat, his mind melancholy with depression. He rode in silence alongside Julian, who didn't need to ask the reason for his most beloved soldier's mood. Rather, the Emperor rode on with his eyes set on some invisible prize off in the distance, not needing to ask his most trusted soldier the reason for his distant, sour mood.

Sergius and Bacchus had bid farewell in the early hours of morning, just before the dawn lit the streets of Paris with orange light, casting long, waking shadows over the tile rooftops. After a night of weeping and passionate lovemaking, Sergius walked Bacchus downstairs to the entrance to the insula, taking one final moment with his savior, his lover, his joy before bidding them farewell.

"I wish I could be with you always," Sergius mustered, fighting back his cries of sadness. "I never want to be without you."

Bacchus took Sergius in his arms and held him tight, rocking softly back and forth. Sergius stared over his shoulder into the glowing morning, wondering what would become of either of them. Sergius had met with a blade once before; he'd survived because of Bacchus. Without him there, could Sergius have survived the attack? Could Bacchus, for all his brute strength and prowess in battle, manage to survive another war? How many men could he fight off at once before falling? Two? Three? Ten? Would some miraculous savior be there to rescue Bacchus just as he had saved Sergius? Was it possible for both of them to survive this war alive, let alone unmamed?

When at last their bodies parted, their eyes locked again, both searching for the right words, both of them with too much to say. Bacchus looked down at the ground, his body heaving with stifled sobs, fists balled, head cocked to one side like a beaten animal. His lower lip furled, jaw tensed and his body began to shake.

"Rrememberr I luv youuu," Bacchus said at last, his accent emerging with full thickness.

Sergius let his tears flow; he knew he couldn't stop them if he tried. He took a step toward Bacchus and gripped his right arm, steadying his balance, pulling him close. Sergius reached up and laid his palm across Bacchus's breast, feeling the pounding of the heart within.

"Remember," Sergius urged, "I think of you every morning when I wake, every night as I sleep. And if I cannot find you on the battlefield, my heart will find you in my dreams. You mean more to me than any Empire or religion, you are the reason I fight. Promise me you'll stay alive." Bacchus nodded, his own tears flowing now, as he reached up and laid his own hand over Sergius's. "I found you once. I will find you again."

Their lips met just for a moment, before their two bodies met in another long embrace. When at last they parted, Sergius watched as Bacchus walked off into the dawn before disappearing into the early morning traffic of carts and horses preparing for the business day ahead.

Sergius looked out over the marching infantry again, knowing that somewhere his beloved Secondarius strode onward in the name of Rome and her Emperor, ready to defend both with his life. Sergius felt such pride in him and tremendous honor that out of all the men and women in the world, Bacchus would fall in love with him.

"You're thinking of him, aren't you?" Julian said, his tone rhetorical. Sergius looked up at the Caesar and nodded, needing to say no more. "I understand," Julian assured him. "I find myself thinking of Helena, and what our future may hold." He chortled. "Not something I ever imagined I would do. Nor do I believe you ever thought you would opine for another Palatinae."

"No, lord Caesar," Sergius admitted. He ran his fingers through Hylas's soft, blond mane, taking some comfort from the spirit of his steed. "And yet," he added, "it's more wonderful than I ever imagined. And more terrifying."

"Then fight for him," Julian roused. "Fight for him as you would for your family honor."

"I will, sire," Sergius agreed, but with no vigor. Julian watched his Primercius, and realizing him inconsolable, quickly changed the subject.

"Consolidation and infrastructure, those are they key to holding Gaul," Julian declared. "I fully intend to inspect every Roman fortress from here to Vienne and squash the barbarian scum at every given opportunity." Julian raised his head and narrowed his eyes, staring of into the distance as if looking into the future at some great treasure. "We'll see the supply chain restored from Rome to Britain, and once again, the West will thrive." Julian looked at him with a confident smile, his head raised and shoulders thrown back like a bird displaying its full plumage.

Sergius feigned excitement a moment, but right away slouched back into his posture of malaise, mad at himself for not sharing the joy of Julian's vision. A reunited, flourishing Rome was what they both wanted; after all it was part of what made them bond those years ago after Strasburg. Nevertheless Sergius could find only sorrow in his spirit, his separation from Bacchus now coloring every moment of his life. Rome, Yeshu, wars, nothing mattered now; he could think of only his beloved.

"Does it hurt again?" Julian asked, again capturing Sergius's attention. Sergius looked up in confusion, only to realize that he now clutched at his wounded shoulder, rubbing back and forth over it as if the blade had just pierced his flesh.

"I guess it does," Sergius realized, looking down at his

shoulder. He withdrew his hand and stared at the palm as if it had a mind of its own, wondering how he could have clutched at his own shoulder without realizing it. Indeed, the wound did feel tender again; Sergius wondered if the riding may have somehow triggered sensitivity in the nerves.

"I'll have Oribasius examine it tonight," Julian declared, his eyes filled with puzzlement and concern. "Strange that it should bother you after all this time."

"You know the nature of old wounds," Sergius muttered. "Even the slightest disturbance of the scar tissue and the pain can return." Julian nodded in agreement. They rode in silence for a few minutes, the clatter of the horse hooves the only sound as both men got lost in their own thoughts.

"You miss him that much?" Julian wondered with a slight hint of awe. Sergius eyes welled and he gritted his incisors, fighting the emotions back down his throat.

"More than I've ever missed anything."

PART III: BROTHERS

Chapter XXVIII.

Every morning Sergius thought the tears had stopped, but every night they would return. Sometimes they'd come in shuddering howls, other times in warm, delicate droplets running down the contours of his face trailing salt behind them. Either way, he would bury his face under the blanket Macrina had gifted him like a child frightened of the dark, praying for his nightmare to end. Night after night, it never would. What little sleep did visit him would overflow with visions of Bacchus dead, maimed, or scarred beyond all recognition. Worse, insecurities plagued his thoughts. What if Bacchus was hurt and couldn't remember him? What if he somehow lost his manhood in battle? What if he'd somehow fallen out of love with Sergius?

Worst of all: What if Sergius had fallen out of love with Bacchus?

Ravaged by worry, Sergius found that the lush spring of Gaul had a dullness about it—the normally vibrant colors of trees and grass and the sky above all seemed muted, as if all the life had gone out of them, just as all the joy had drained from Sergius's heart. Sergius wondered if the whole of the world might end, broken like his spirit. And the sun would rise and set, indifferent to his plight, almost mocking his anguish, as if the cosmos tried to say: *you don't matter, Sergius.*

He wanted to tear his skin off, to release the pressure of the suffocating emotions stockpiled in his chest. How he longed to let it pour upon the Earth like bubbling pitch; viscous, fuming, nauseating. He wanted the whole world to stop and acknowledge his anguish, to take some pity on him. Let the wars end. Let he and Bacchus live their lives in a peaceful Rome. He knew peace, if ever it would exist, would come only when Constantius and Julian declared it, and even then, what of the Alemanni, or the Persians, or some other tribe? How could the killing ever end?

"Do you miss your wife?" Sergius blurted one night. He and Nebridius stood guard outside Julian's tent, the Caesar somnambulated within the rippling sheets of linen. Nebridius turned his rodent face to Sergius with a look of total puzzlement and surprise. For as long as they had worked together, Nebridius and Sergius had remained on only the most cordial of terms, neither prying into the personal details of the other's life. Yes, Nebridius knew about Sergius relationship with Bacchus, and Sergius knew that Nebridius had a wife and children tucked away in Rome that he had not seen in years. However, despite these particulars of one another's lives, the two men could hardly claim to know one another. Until this moment, neither had shown any interest in changing the situation.

Nebridius drummed his fingers against the hilt of his sword, then relaxed a bit as he regarded Sergius. His beady eyes narrowed, searching his fellow Primercius's face for some hint of teasing, some ulterior motive. As he did so, he reached into the folds of his tunic, and pulled out his necklace to reveal the Jovian emblem having replaced the Chi-Ro, its curved legs reminiscent of the lightning of the god it symbolized.

♃

"I apologize," Sergius demurred. "The absence of Bacchus weighs on my mind."

"No need," Nebridius deflected. "I think of my family often, though you are the first to ask me about them." He paused a moment, grinding his crooked rat-teeth together in thought. "I wish more of our soldiers did ask me. I wish Caesar asked me. I want to talk about my daughters, even if they are just females. I miss them so." Sergius nodded in understanding.

"How old are they, your daughters?" Sergius asked, still timid.

"Now," Nebridius said thinking, "they would be seven and four. I wonder if either has any recollection of me."

"You've not seen them in three years," Sergius realized with dismay.

"No. My greater duties are to Rome," Nebridius sighed.

"You are a loyal soldier," Sergius admitted with a nod, half a realization, half a cynical observation. Sergius smiled as best he could, then turned his eyes back out over the field of glowing campfires surrounding Julian's tent. They stood quiet a moment, Sergius scanning the field, hoping against hope that he might spot Bacchus among the army.

"You've been studying the Galilean faith, haven't you?"

Nebridius asked, jarring Sergius from his thoughts. Sergius moved his lips in silent speech, struggling for the right words to, what he realized, could be a dangerous question.

"I studied the faith at University," Sergius said, making a true statement but a deceptive one on purpose.

"Ah," Nebridius responded, almost tripping on Sergius's response. "Of course. The Philosopher Soldier."

"Yes," Sergius stammered. "An odd religion. Strange how their holy scriptures contradict one another at times, and at others, tell an identical story using the identical words."

"I'd never noticed," Nebridius confessed, his voice cool, his eyes scrutinizing.

"Really?" Sergius asked in genuine disbelief. "They also contradict the letters of the teacher Paul."

"I never noticed," Nebridius repeated.

"Yes," Sergius replied, suppressing his impulse to discuss the matter in further detail. He swallowed and stretched his shoulders back, trying to force himself to relax and ignore Nebridius's scrutiny. The fellow guard continued to stare at Sergius, his lips pursed and wriggling about as if gnawing on a piece of fat. He exhaled, batted his eyes, and cracked a smile, looking out over the killing fields.

"I wonder," Nebridius mused, "how Julian will take to Galileans within his army." Sergius's eyes darted to meet Nebridius's, twinkling in the light of the surrounding campfires with a mischievous glow. "Undoubtedly the day is coming when he will seek them out for heresy against the gods of Rome, just as they once were under Nero."

"Julian is a tolerant and peaceful man," Sergius debated. "These battles are fought out of necessity, not lust for war. He would never repeat the genocide inflicted on the Jews or the Galileans as in the old days." Nebridius smirked.

"Of course not," he said through his rat-smile, oozing sarcasm. "True Romans have nothing to fear. And though it's taken me years to declare, you are a true Roman, Sergius, as is your beloved Bacchus. I've fought in many battles, and rarely have I seen the kind of devotion or valor the two of you demonstrate." He took a deep breath and gave a slight nod of his head. "I was wrong about you both. I hope you accept my apologies, as a brother soldier, and a fellow citizen of Rome." Nebridius extended his right arm to Sergius who met it with his own, the two men clasping at each other's wrists.

Silence fell again between the two. Sergius exhaled, running his hand up over his own tunic, feeling the tiny wooden frame of the fish hung around his neck. He squeezed it between his thumb and forefinger, looking out over the fields again.

The two guards said nothing the rest of their shift, though it lasted hours into the night. Worry plagued Sergius, preventing even the lightest of conversation with Nebridius. When their watch had ended, Sergius set out across the battlefield, hoping that he might spot Bacchus among the troops. Still, his quandary of the Galilean faith distracted him from even his search for his beloved as he walked among the muddy fields.

Sergius stopped before a great bonfire of slaughtered barbarian corpses billowing with black smoke and a stench so overpowering it threatened to suffocate him where he stood. Yet Sergius remained, staring into the flames, watching the bodies cremate into dust before his eyes. Would Bacchus suffer this fate? Would he? The thought of all the lives now reduced to ash before him coupled with the foul odor of burning flesh nauseated him, and Sergius sank to his knees before the fire. The heat radiated against his face, forming droplets of sweat within his ebony curls. His skin reddened as they ran down his the curves of his forehead.

There had to be more, more to believe in than just the dust. What he and Bacchus shared transcended all things. Their love would outlast any battle. If Julian died at the hands of Constantius, if Rome itself crumbled, Sergius would still have Bacchus. No edict of the Galileans or the Pagans would separate them. Their love would live forever.

And in that moment, staring into the flames of death, Sergius realized what it meant to possess life eternal. He knew what Yeshu had tried to explain with his parables, what those convoluted and confusing scriptures tried to preach, what Macrina's strange rituals of humble foot washing and sharing of meals tried to symbolize—love was the one true God which would outlast all history, which would encompass all people, which create a new world of magic and wonder, of peace and creation greater than the body, or the Empire, or the whole of the universe; a Kingdom of souls united, together beyond time. His love for Bacchus proved that. It made him believe in absurdity without doubt. He and Bacchus would live forever because they loved each other.

He would find Bacchus again, and this time, he would see to it they would never part. He would find Macrina's odd cult and confess that he had chosen to join, finally understanding the great mystery she could never explain. He would believe, and no edict, no Caesar, nothing could deter him from his faith.

In that moment, Sergius became a Galilean.

Chapter XXIX.

Sergius had the most unusual feeling of relaxation. As he sat under a tree reading from his Galilean codex, Hylas at his side, the horse every so often giving an affectionate nuzzle, waiting for the remaining battalions to dismantle camp and return to marching, he found himself less anxious than he had been in months. True, the thought of Bacchus's safety still occupied every moment of the day, lingering like some feral beast ready to pounce at any moment in the back of his mind. His gushing tears had not yet stopped their flow every night, but Sergius had a newfound trust that helped qualm his fear. He had no assurance that he neither he nor Bacchus would survive this war unharmed. Nevertheless, some inner light comforted him like a mother embracing her infant. Hope blossomed in him with every passage he read, not because of the content, but because of his own burgeoning faith; his choice to believe that he and Bacchus would both survive.

"How dare you rest when the Emperor demands your presence!" came a booming voice. Sergius's heart leapt as if he'd just heard a crack of thunder, dropping the codex to the ground and scrambling to his feet, only to meet with the bawdy laughter of Oribasius, his face red with amusement.

"Sorry my philosopher soldier!" Oribasius said between chortles. "I couldn't resist the temptation of giving you a start! The rush is good for your health!"

"As if the thrill of battle weren't enough," Sergius groaned. Oribasius raised his eyebrows, considering Sergius point and patted himself on his bulbous stomach. The Primercius reached down and collected the codex, then swung an arm up over Hylas's back, leaning against the steed and making no effort to hide his annoyance with the doctor.

"Our new Caesar Augustus would speak with you though," Oribasius said. "There is much on his mind."

"He seeks my counsel?" Sergius asked, running his fingers through Hylas's mane. The horse whinnied and brushed his wet nose against Sergius back, as if to offer his rider counsel of his own.

"More than that," Oribasius explained. "I've come here to speak with you first."

"Without the Emperor's knowledge?" Sergius inquired, cocking his head back with incredulity.

"Well..." the doctor hesitated. "Yes. You see, I've grown worried about Julian's state of mind. The possibility of civil war, coupled with his continuing campaign against Vadomar, and his rebuilding of the Empire, *and* the..." He paused. "The health of the Empress...all these matters weigh heavily on his mind. He grows restless and temperamental. I worry for his mind."

"So you come to warn me of this?" Sergius's eyes narrowed, still trying to understand the doctor's point.

"Not exactly. You see Sergius, Gaul is without a Prefect…"

"I'm aware," Sergius crecendoed with anticipation.

"And the Emperor must know that whomever he chooses to replace Florentius must be loyal to him and to Rome, especially with Constantius's deputes still hiding in the shadows." Their eyes met, as it dawned on Sergius what Oribasius hinted at.

"He wants me as Prefect?" Sergius gasped, eyes wide, his head hunching down to look Oribasius straight in the face.

"He trusts you above all others," Oribasius said, as if Sergius should already know. "You are loyal and well studied, more qualified than even Florentius was."

Sergius slumped back against Hylas, the horse shifting against the weight of his owner, hooves clopping against the dewy grass. The soldier stared at the physician, holding his mouth slightly agape unable to find words to express his shock.

"Come," Oribasius insisted. "Caesar Augustus awaits."

Julian looked transformed when Oribasius and Sergius entered his tent. The Emperor's eyes looked sunken from stress, his beard now grown out into an odd curly twist at his chin, resembling the whiskers of a goat. Sergius thought the facial hair made him look ridiculous, like some antique Grecian philosopher parading about Athens hundreds of years prior. *There again,* Sergius thought, *that is probably exactly what Julian wants.*

The Emperor greeted Sergius with open arms and genuine cheer, hugging him tight as he might a brother. The interior of the Imperial tent, as usual, stood free of accent but for Julian's massive work table, which, of late, had accumulated even greater piles of letters, maps and other important papers. Their dishevelment suggested that Julian never stopped pouring over them, attempting to develop a ruling strategy without rest. Careful not to disturb the table, Nebridius and another Palatinae dressed as a Primercius drew two chairs from the table and set them up facing one another in the middle of the tent.

"My philosopher soldier," Julian greeted, motioning for Sergius to sit. Sergius obliged, as the Emperor took a seat across from him. Nebridius and the other soldier slipped back outside the tent, the former giving a knowing nod to Sergius as he vanished. Sergius's heartbeat pounded in his ears, his palms beginning to sweat. He hadn't felt so nervous around Julian in years.

"We've an urgent matter at hand, and I need your help," Julian started in as Oribasius walked over and stood at his side. "Florentius has fled to Byzantium, and I've not the troops to spare to pursue him, nor have I the resources to hold Gaul without a trusted Prefect in place. I received a letter from my cousin this morning chastising my insurrection." He scoffed, glancing back at Oribasius. "It seems Constantius thinks me ungrateful for all he has given me, for raising me up as his only family, for making me Caesar," he said, his tone mocking. "My father's murderer reproaches me for being an orphan!"

Sergius clasped at his knees, still on edge. He didn't want the job of Prefect—the responsibilities would be great, not to mention, if Julian's coup failed to secure the laurels in Constantinople, it would mean death for all those who assisted him, including Sergius.

"If you ask me who might take over as Prefect, I have but one suggestion," Sergius blurted, interrupting Julian's fuming.

"What? Who?" the Emperor questioned, taken aback by Sergius directness. The soldier lowered his eyes.

"I know that you would consider me for this position, and while I am flattered and will do what my Emperor commands, you should know that it is not a role I desire, nor think myself suited for."

The Passion of Sergius & Bacchus

"Sergius," Julian whispered, gentle but perplexed, "why do you resist?" The Caesar rose and walked over to Sergius, laying a hand on his scarred shoulder, kneeling down next to him. "I need you. You are wise and loyal. This is our chance to restore Rome as you and I would have it—glorious and flourishing with educated minds and our national traditions. This is your chance to get away from the death of the battlefield which sickens you so!"

Sergius didn't dare confess his fear that Julian's insurrection might fail, and that Constantius would have all of Julian's deputes executed. He did, however, have a matter just as pressing on his mind.

"And what of Bacchus?" Sergius pleaded. "Would he return to Paris with me?" Julian swallowed, pursing his lips.

"I cannot spare any troops at this moment, Sergius, especially one with the might of Bacchus. He could return to you when Byzantium is secured, I promise you. And the sooner we have the West consolidated under our control, the sooner the East will fall to us as well." Julian squeezed the scar tissue of Sergius's wound, causing it to ache once more. Sergius tried to shift without seeming to recoil from his friend; the last thing he needed was to trigger Julian's volcanic temper in the midst of such a delicate conversation.

"Lord Caesar," Sergius muttered, "I would rather face death if it meant being closer to Bacchus. He met the Emperor's gaze, watching his eyes narrow in thought. Sergius stared back unflinching, firm in his conviction that he should stay on the battlefield, his most dreaded of environments.

"You love him so?" Julian asked, half in disbelief.

"I do," Sergius admitted, shaking his head. Julian took a deep breath and rose again, placing both hands behind his back.

He paced the length of the tent, eyes burning in thought and frustration.

"And if not you, than who?" Julian bellowed. Oribasius looked at Sergius as though he had lost his mind. *Perhaps I have,* Sergius wondered.

"Nebridius," Sergius answered as a reflex. "Send Nebridius. Let him live with his wife and children."

"Nebridius!?" Julian repeated in a near-shout of disbelief. So loud boomed his voice, that Nebridius himself rushed into the tent in a panic at the call of his name.

"My lord," Nebridius said, his voice quivering. Julian stopped his pacing and stared at the other Primercius now in his midst, studying his rat-face a moment. The Emperor looked momentarily at Oribasius, then turned to Sergius before facing Nebridius again.

"Sergius, leave us," Julian ordered, his eyes never leaving Nebridius's confused face. Sergius looked at Oribasius, searching his countenance for some signal of comfort but meeting only with an expression of stone. With a slight bow, Sergius exited the tent into the baking sunlight.

The sun above poured heat down on Sergius, soaking his ebony locks within moments of his stepping outside. He and the other Primercius didn't speak, both of them squinting in the light over the camp before them. The green hills of Gaul rolled out before them, carved by the Rhine with elegant majesty. Sergius wished again that Bacchus stood at his side; Bacchus who so loved the beauty of nature. Seeing his beloved happy brought the kind of joy to Sergius heart that he so desperately needed at that moment. How he opined for winter, when the army would set up a long-term encampment, when battles with the marauders would cease, and he and Bacchus could lie in each other's arms again.

Minutes later—hours even? Sergius wasn't sure—a messenger

dressed in military garb rushed up to the tent. Sergius and the other Primercius both reached for their swords on instinct, but the heaving breaths of the boy, who could not have been more than ten or twelve years of age, let both soldiers know he stood little threat to the Emperor inside.

"A message…for lord Caesar Augustus…" the messenger gasped, holding out a scroll sealed in wax. That the boy referred to Julian as Caesar Augustus indicated the friendly or at least benign origin of the letter. Sergius grabbed it without hesitating, noticing the indentation of the Imperial seal of a ram's head in the wax, and burst back into the tent.

Inside, he found Nebridius displaying his crooked, oversized teeth in a broad smile, his tiny frame almost quivering with excitement. Julian, by contrast, looked graver, and Sergius knew that the Emperor had offered Nebridius the job of Prefect, and that his fellow Palatinae had accepted.

"Lord Caesar, I apologize for the interruption," Sergius declared with an obligatory bow. "This letter has just arrived for you, and it bears your seal."

"Mine?" Julian asked in confusion, taking the letter and examining the wax. He broke open the seal and unscrolled the letter, the color draining from his face as he read. His knees loosened and he began to lose his balance, prompting Oribasius and Nebridius to rush forward to support him.

"My lord, what is it?" Oribasius asked with urgency.

"Get to Paris, Oribasius," Julian ordered, his voice shaking with emotion. Oribasius looked at the Caesar as though he'd gone mad.

"Impossible," the physician stammered, as he and Nebridius gently sat Julian in one of the chairs.

"Go now," Julian said, his voice with the pitch of a low bell.

"But Lord Caesar," Oribasius sputtered. "It would take weeks, even with the fastest horse and the best of riders to return to Paris in such a short time! I possess neither attribute!"

"You must go," Julian said, gripping Oribasius arm with the force of a vice. The soldiers and the doctor exchanged glances of confusion, none of them knowing what to say or do. Indeed, in all his time serving as a Primercius, Sergius had never seen the Emperor react in such a way. Sergius held out his hands, as if ready to offers some bit of counsel or service, but found himself at a loss for either. Fortunate for all of them, Julian spoke, sharing his horror with his companions.

"Helena bleeds."

Chapter XXX.

Hours of pleading would not wrest Julian from his solecism that somehow Oribasius could ride back to Paris and Helena's aid. Sergius had never seen the Emperor in such a state; it seemed counter to his entire nature. Usually so articulate, he stammered his words. Usually so collected, he paced the tent like a caged wild beast, throwing papers about, alternating between cool denial and furious shouting. Sergius just watched in silence, knowing that no words he could speak could console his friend.

Only when the second messenger arrived a few hours after the first did Julian at last face the truth: Helena was dead, her life drained away by hemorrhaging, their child and heir dead before birth, a relic of Julian's dream of restoring Rome and redeeming his family line. Like his wife and child, his hope lay cold and lifeless.

Night had fallen, and the glowing oil lamps cast long shadows through Julian's tent and across the face of the mourning Caesar. The dancing darkness over his countenance made him look like a cadaver—sunken cheeks and hollow eyes, flesh grey and sagging off his skull. Sergius watched him with the care of a father, waiting for some emotional outburst, for some opportunity to rush to his side in comfort. Yet Julian sat still as the marble statues of Rome, staring down at the table between them. Servants had cleared the papers away, replacing the day's work with a loaf of bread and two bowls of leafy greens. A pitcher of water provided drink for the meal which sat untouched by either diner. Sergius didn't dare eat in front of the self-starving Emperor, nor did he have any hunger to do so. Like Julian, his appetite had vanished with the news of the Empress's death. The Caesar and his Primercius sat quiet, Sergius eyes never leaving Julian's face, Julian's staring into the void.

"A chariot," Julian said after a long while. "Had I a chariot, I could have sent Oribasius back…" His voice trailed off as his lower lip furled and his head pivoted side to side in gentle motion. He stood up and started to pace the room again, fire in his eyes, the restless beast returning. "I must always have a chariot with me," he affirmed. "From this day forward."

"My lord…" Sergius began.

"By the gods, call me Julian, Sergius," the Emperor declared. "I call you by your name, it hardly seems fair."

"You are Emperor, sire," Sergius observed. "It goes against royal protocol."

"Forget the protocol!" Julian blurted in annoyance. "I am only a man, same as you, just with a different title. You're my brother. We're alone. Call me Julian."

"Julian," Sergius edged from his lips. "Even the fastest chariot in the world could not have journeyed to Paris in time." The blaze quashed in Julian's eyes, leaving only morose darkness again.

"I know," Julian admitted. He put out his hands, fingers twisted like avian claws, as if to grasp some invisible weight in the air before him. Grunting, he clenched his teeth in frustration, trying with all his might to maintain his composure. "I'm a fool," he growled. "Helena was a worthless, stupid woman, sister of a man who is now trying to kill me! Who killed all my family! I married her because I had to!"

"Sire…"

"Don't call me that, Sergius!" Julian grasped his head with both hands in frustration, crumpling over, falling down into a squatting position, teetering on his toes, about to crash to the ground. "Why? Why must I care about the death of a woman I did not love? I did not even mourn for my family this way!"

Sergius closed his eyes, taking a deep breath. He ran his hand across the coarse wood of the table, searching for some word of consolation. He opened his eyes again and flicked at the edge of his plate. He knew full well why Julian mourned. Surely, in some way, he had come to care about her even if he could not admit it to himself—she loved him, a feeling to which Julian was not accustomed. Moreover, in the recent months, with her own lobbying of Constantius, she had become an invaluable political asset. Still, as Sergius watched Julian's throbbing red face, he knew the greatest cause of Julian's sorrow.

"She carried a son, didn't she?" Sergius asked, his voice delicate. A wince of agony crossed Julian's face as he nodded in confirmation.

"My son," the Caesar gasped. "My son." At once his eyes welled as he pulled his arms up over the back of his neck. Sergius watched as Julian rocked back and forth, withered and hunchbacked like an emaciated Atlas, muttering and babbling like an infant, "My son, my son, my son…" He heaved a great breath in and held it, afraid of the cry that might slip out if he released it. Sergius felt powerless to help his friend. Unsure what else to do, he crept toward Julian with his arm outreached.

"Don't touch me!" Julian screamed, his vocal chords shredding in his throat. Sergius recoiled as he watched the Caesar run his clawed hands through the curly locks of his hair, pulling so hard that it straightened, puckering the scalp beneath. He gritted his teeth and cocked his head back, exhaling at last. He then collapsed forward toward the Earth, catching himself just short of the surface, the veins and tendons in his hands and arms bulging with tension. He shuddered and panted as Sergius watched. Minutes passed, and the Primercius did nothing afraid that even a slight movement might disrupt Julian's emotional stasis, sending him into a violent fit.

"It doesn't matter anyway," Julian growled, his eyes locked on the dirt in below him. He raked the earth with his hands, back and forth, over and over until his nails had blackened with soil. He raised his face to meet Sergius's gaze, and wiped the fledgling tears from his eyes with the back of his wrists. "Doesn't matter," he echoed.

"Julian," Sergius pleaded.

"No," the Emperor affirmed, pointing his index and middle finger out at his bodyguard. "No mourning. I've more important concerns. I've cities to build, armies to defeat." The light flickered from his eyes a moment, pupils dilating, his mind distant. "We crush the barbarians, then we set out for Vienne. We'll form a base there to prepare to fight my cousin." He nodded, immersed in his own thoughts. "That must be my objective above all. I must not waiver, I must not hesitate. I will kill Constantius for what he's done, and to protect my Empire."

"Yes, my lord," Sergius uttered, not sure what else to say. The

Emperor's eyes met his again and after a long, silent look, Julian placed both arms behind his back and furled his brow.

"Dismissed," Julian declared with unusual formality. Sergius nodded and turned toward the curtained doorway. He'd already pulled the fabric back for his exit when Julian stopped him.

"Sergius?" the Caesar asked. Sergius turned to find the Emperor looking distant again, as they held a long, silent pause before Julian spoke again.

"What you feel for Bacchus," he began, "the longing, the loneliness, the fear that you might lose him to death, or even that he may one day leave you..." Sergius back tensed at the thought. "Is it worth…is it worth the moments of pleasure?"

"Yes," Sergius replied, half puzzled without hesitation. He studied Julian a moment, his clothes and hair disheveled, eyes swollen and dark. The exhaustion lines cracked his young face, his curly beard as disheveled as a slaughtered goat's. Their eyes locked, and it seemed as though Julian had discovered some part of his friend that he could not recognize, some alien quality he did not understand. The Emperor squinted at Sergius, then waved him away, hanging his head in thought once more.

Sergius exited the tent into the warm air of the night, the dewy grass wetting his boots as he walked. Something had changed in Julian that night. The Emperor had, for all his life's hardships, always had more love in his heart than he realized—for Rome, for his family, even for Helena. And now only one remained, and a fickle object it was. Rome could never return Julian's love the way Helena could, and its affections could change without reason or warning. Such a lover would almost ensure heartbreak, and Sergius wondered just how much more Julian could withstand.

Chapter XXXI.

A full six months passed before, despite his declared paganism, Julian allowed Helena a traditional Galilean funeral, sending her body from Paris to Rome where a priest would oversee the Eucharist and her daytime burial. The Caesar, of course, would have preferred a sensible Roman funeral, cremating her remains and keeping her ashes in a decorated urn or spreading them out at night over an Elysian field. Moreover, a pagan funeral would send a message to the rest of the Empire about the return of the old religion, setting an example for the lower classes to follow. Still, out of honor and respect for the mother of his dead child he chose to exalt her according to her own beliefs, no matter how absurd he found them. He would send a message of tolerance to the Empire: under this new Caesar Augustus Rome would be true to herself again, but would also allow the other faiths to co-exist. To Sergius though, it indicated a truth to which his Caesar would never admit: Julian had loved his wife.

Julian never shed another tear—at least not that Sergius witnessed—beyond that first night of agony, nor did he mention Helena's name again after making the funeral arrangements. In the months between her death and burial he acted as though he'd forgotten the whole of her existence, though his mood suggested otherwise. To Sergius, the Emperor seemed slower, unfocused. He slept longer hours in the morning and became irritated over the most trivial of matters, barking at servants over the quality of his dinner or a half empty pitcher of water. Even among his trusted friends he seemed rigid and formal, hiding behind the very royal protocols he once despised. For most of his life, Julian managed to quell the anger and resentment of the loss of his family and treatment by his uncle and cousin, keeping it at bay, preventing it from corrupting his soul. But with the loss of Helena, a woman he would never even claim to love, bitterness had crept into his spirit.

Sergius could relate to Caesar's anguish. In six months, he had no sign of Bacchus condition or whereabouts, despite the best of his searches. Granted, Sergius faced huge obstacles in his quest: Julian demanded much of his time, less as a bodyguard than as an advisor after leaving Paris. The Emperor consulted his Primercius on everything from building aqueducts to rationing food for the troops, keeping him close all the while, much to the jealousy of his fellow Scholae Palatinae. Even more frustrating, Sergius struggled with the language barrier—the majority of the units still comprised of Germanic men undergoing Romanization, most of whom still spoke their native dialects. While Sergius had managed to learn some rudimentary phrases in his time with the Batavi, most of them he'd forgotten since Julian, his advisors, and Bacchus all insisted on speaking Greek. Sergius found himself feeling like the dejected outsider again, enduring the whispers and stares of guards and servants around Julian's camp. How he missed Bacchus, and the simple feeling of the two of them lying together in a triclina or in bed, the soft touch of their togetherness as they stared out into space expressing feelings more than words ever could.

Sergius found some hope as Julian entered Vienne and the various units took up residence in the city's barracks—with the army consolidated in one location, he had far less ground to cover in his search. Still, Julian demanded most of his time and Sergius began to wonder if the Emperor even *wanted* Sergius to find Bacchus at all.

"You'd do well not to think of him," Julian declared one night, prompted by Sergius own distant thoughts. Sergius, Oribasius and the Caesar along with an armed escort made their way through the quiet streets of the modest city—though it sported a theatre and a small palace, it came nowhere near the grandiosity of Paris, a gentle snowfall sparkling in the moonlight, the low echo of the January wind whistling between the tiny buildings.

"I can't help it, Lord Caesar," Sergius pleaded. "My heart breaks every moment for him."

"Which is why you would do well to forget him," Julian contended, firing of a chilly look at his Primercius. "Love and carnality only distract us from our real functions and goals in this world. They only make us vulnerable." Sergius didn't dare argue. He knew doing so would only enrage the Emperor, who, he realized, could make his search for Bacchus almost impossible if he chose.

"I understand," Sergius managed though his tightened jaw as he drew his cloak about him, shielding himself from the cold. He wrapped his arms up around his broad chest in a self-embrace and squeezed, pretending for a moment that it was Bacchus who held him in comfort.

The group left tiny footprints in the dusting of snow as they climbed the stairs to the church of Vienne, an already-ancient temple of classic Roman columns on three faces and a solid inner chamber on the fourth elevated from the ground on a platform only five or six feet high. Inside, lit cisterns cast bright patches of light and shadow across the towering spires and standing crowd, as a Galilean service celebrating the arrival of Magi to the child Yeshu was well underway.

"Why exactly are we here?" a bored Oribasius grunted as the group reached the top of the platform. He ran his hands across his arms with great vigor, trying to keep warm, impatient with his Emperor. "Has our Caesar decided to convert?"

Julian glared daggers at his physician, his brow wrinkling, his curly beard sparkling with tiny water droplets of melted snow. Oribasius took a step backward in deference, bowing his head in reflex. Julian sighed, shaking his head in annoyance.

"To survey this temple," Julian explained. "It once housed statues of the first Augustus and his wife Livia. It was a monument to heroes of Rome and to our heritage. Now, the Galilean fools desecrate it with their rituals. You see there?" Julian pointed toward the far back wall of the church, which housed an inner sanctum where the priest presided over an altar, leading the crowd in prayers. "That room is sacred. It should house the gods of Rome, not memorialize some criminal!" The Emperor shook his head in disapproval. He took a step toward the threshold of the inner building, stopping just outside the columns, unwilling to enter during such sacrilegious proceedings. Sergius stepped up alongside him, letting the currents of heat from the inside warm him. He watched Julian's repulsed face for some sign of purpose, some reason why he should want to witness a service that he knew he would find objectionable. Julian just stared into the church, the light from inside reflected in his eyes like flames, no doubt matching the burning anger in his soul.

"My lord…" Sergius nudged, hoping to illicit some explanation from Julian.

"Disgusting," Julian spat, rage seething in every syllable. "Hypocrites. They would call Augustus and Livia false gods, their deification by vote in the Senate the work of heretics. Do they not understand the Galilean was deified in the same way at Nicaea? And Augustus was a hero, bringing order to the Empire after twenty years of civil war! The Galilean sought to incite rebellion, and they worship him for this?!" The statement gave Sergius pause—he had never considered the divisions within his new faith, nor just how much it emulated the religion of Rome. But it was not the deification of Yeshu that had drawn Sergius to the faith; rather his teachings of love and forgiveness. Did Caesar not understand that it was Yeshu's message that attracted the crowds to his altar? In Rome anyone could become a god with the right clout, but not everyone could purport to teach like one…

"My lord," Sergius stammered, "do not the Galileans believe in peace…"

"Peace!?" Julian blurted. He rotated his head to face Sergius, inching it around with a deliberate and dramatic effect. "Do you not recall how my family died? Do you not know of the slaughter of their own bishops—*their own bishops*—after the council of Nicaea? Of those who dissented with its creed?" His face flushed red, and his nostrils flared, his fury oozing through his cool exterior. "You may empathize with their commandments, Sergius, but their actions do not match their words. That is why they threaten not just Rome but the whole of the world. This religion must be quashed!"

Julian spun around on his heel, his boot squeaking in the snow against the marble of the church platform and plodded down the stairs back into the street. Oribasius and the guards hurried to follow him.

"We will reconsecrate this temple as soon as I reach Byzantium!" The Emperor exhaled a deep breath, misting in the cold night air before him.

Sergius lingered a moment, staring in at the congregation, realizing the gravity of his situation. He would have to keep his newfound faith a secret, even from his most trusted friends. Though he planned religious tolerance during his rule as the Empire transitioned back to its pagan roots, Julian's hatred of the Galileans was unyielding. The most Sergius could hope for would be to convince the Emperor that he could not hold culpable an entire religion for the actions of a few power-hungry hypocrites or crazed fanatics.

"And now they celebrate Magi bowing to a peasant child?" Julian glowered. "Idiots."

Help me Lord, Sergius prayed to himself as he chased Julian down the stairs. *Help me spread your words. Help Julian understand.* He pulled his cloak in tight again as the burning chill of the wind flooded over him away from the radiating warmth of the church. *I have faith in you.*

And please, Lord. Help me find Bacchus.

Chapter XXXII.

Sergius prayers had still gone unanswered. One night, several weeks later he carried a bundle of firewood through the streets of Vienne. The snow had continued to fall almost nonstop since the visit to the temple with Caesar until a mild thaw abated the cold, melting the piles of snow in the streets to slush, browned with a mixture of dirt, sewage and filth. The odor of ash from the hundreds of stove fires from around the city clouded the air dusted the snow with blackness. The frigid wetness made for an even more uncomfortable walk than if Sergius had ventured out in a blizzard as the cloudy moisture seeped through the spidery straps of his Caligulas and poured over his bare feet. He frowned, jutting his legs about like a newborn deer trying to find its footing as he attempted to find the driest spots on the street to no avail. Would that he had Didymos to run such errands for him, but Julian had only just sent for the palace servants—Sergius loyal butler included—after spending several weeks in the city, feeling assured that the route by which they would journey was well protected from raids by marauders. In the meantime, the Primercius would have to suffer household chores himself in addition to attending to Julian's needs.

Forced to tend to his own meals and household duties, Sergius had limited time to search for his beloved Bacchus. Trips to the army barracks yielded little hope, as had visits to the army stables. Sergius figured if he could find his savior there once, he might find him there again. Yet there he found only the welcome of Hylas, whose onyx eyes somehow managed to quell Sergius's loneliness and longing. His steed could offer little more than a nuzzle or whinny, but the simple love of horse for his master seemed the only thing that could make Sergius smile in those barren days of winter.

Sergius's Vienne home occupied the top floor of a tiny apartment building not far from the palace, putting him at close range should Julian desire his sudden counsel. To reach his front door, Sergius had to enter a tiny alcove and ascend a narrow staircase to his doorstep. As he trudged up the stairs to his insula, wet feet squeaking against leather with every motion, arms loaded with kindling, he noticed the lumpy shadow perched atop the staircase. His climb slowed and heart raced as adrenaline pumped into his system, readying him for a fight with some thief or assassin come to murder the Emperor's advisor. He dropped the firewood, letting the logs clink and roll down the stairs as he reached for his sword. The shadow lengthened as the stranger rose to his feet. Sergius clawed at his waist, only to realize that he had left his sword inside, not believing that he would need the blade for a simple off-duty trip to the market. In a panic, he grabbed at one of the sticks at his feet, raising it up in his right hand like a club, ready to bash at the shadow, when he heard the familiar voice.

"Sergius?"

Sergius blood ran cold as he dropped the firewood to the floor with the rest of the scattered kindling. He held his breath, stumbling up the stairs, thrusting himself against the blackness of the stranger. He felt the curves of his body beneath cold metal armor, the visitor's woolen cloak scratching against Sergius's skin. The Primercius pulled his body in close, recognizing at once the scent of a man who had sweat in battle, marched over hundreds of humid marshlands, snowy fields, fought to defend his Empire masked by the thick aroma of jasmine—the smell of courage and patriotism, of a hero: the unmistakable bouquet of the man he loved.

"Thank you, God!" Sergius blurted, his voice shattering with emotion. He buried his face against the man's shoulder. "Bacchus!" he cried. "Bacchus!"

Bacchus held Sergius tight, feeling his beloved wobble under the support of liquid knees. He tried to steady him, but even with all his might Bacchus stumbled against Sergius's weight, sending the two of them tripping backwards and slamming against the wall. Sergius reached his hand up beneath the woolen hood, running his palm across Bacchus face before pulling back the fabric and staring into the faint outline of his beloved's countenance. Even in the dim light of the hallway, Bacchus's eyes sparkled. Their lips met with electric force the likes of which they had not known since that first day in Strasburg, when Sergius had also fallen limp in Bacchus arms, and the Secundarius had offered him comfort.

"Inside," Bacchus whispered with a wide grin. Sergius reveled in the sight of Bacchus's smile, complete with the socket of his missing tooth. It seemed to him like a unique flaw in some carbuncle gem, less an imperfection than a unique signature, as if the Creator had deemed it not just beautiful, but special. Sergius pawed at his waist for the bronze key to the insula door. He managed to regain his composure long enough to find it and fit it to the tarnished lock, fitting it through a keyhole, turning it, and haplessly feeling around for the prongs of the key to meet with the slots of the bolt. Bacchus steadied Sergius's hand, as the key fit into place and slid the lock open with a metallic pop.

The door opened, and Sergius wrapped his arm around Bacchus's neck again, pulling him into a kiss, walking backwards into the darkened room. As he did, he felt a burlap parcel brush against his left ankle, giving him pause a moment, looking down into the blackness for what it might be.

"Careful," Bacchus urged, reaching down for the sack, sliding it into the room as he shut and locked the door behind them. With privacy assured at last, the two soldiers began to undo each other's cloaks, letting them fall to the floor in great heaps before unfastening their armor, tossing it without care into the darkened chamber. Sergius pulled one leg up to try and undo his sandals, hopping about in the blackness, struggling for balance. Bacchus laughed and eased the foot back to the floor where he undid the straps to both of Sergius's shoes, kissing each ankle as he did so, letting out a tiny chuckle of adoration. In turn, Sergius did the same, and slipped Bacchus out of his uniform, smiling for the first time in months as he did so. When the two men wore nothing more than their loin cloths, Sergius lead Bacchus through the darkness into the bedroom. The cold air of the night erected the hair of their arms into bumpy gooseflesh. They reached the bed, and Sergius yanked at Bacchus's loincloth, tossing it to the floor, leaving the man naked in the night. Sergius kissed Bacchus neck, drinking in the luscious smell of jasmine, closing his eyes and running his own stubbly face over Bacchus's pale skin.

"You stopped at the baths, didn't you?" Sergius mused as Bacchus unfastened his loin cloth, freeing his hardening pomp from its swaddling. Bacchus laughed.

"I had to be clean for you," Bacchus demurred. "Months on the battlefield do not make a man smell sweet." Sergius appreciated the hygiene, but no amount of oil and perfume could erase the odors of a soldier, and Sergius reveled in those of Bacchus: they served as reminders, trophies of Bacchus's survival and bravery— the very qualities he respected most in his beloved. The two men fell into bed, one atop the other, their gnarled hands moving over the tender flesh of one another's bodies. Sergius closed his eyes and inhaled, savoring every sensation of Bacchus: the subtle taste of salt and oil on his skin, the smooth of his chest, the sound of his breathing, and the sinewy form of his body in the near-pitch blackness. Sergius own muscles seemed to melt with every touch as he writhed against the blankets, wanting to pour his whole existence into an inseparable mixture with Bacchus's own, never parting, united forever in all things. God had answered his prayers, and though carnal lust may have been poor thanks for such a blessing, even the thought of eternal damnation seemed a modest price for the opportunity to merge body and soul with Bacchus.

After they finished their lovemaking, the two cupped themselves together under the warmth of Macrina's blanket, silent, their faces pressed against each other, eyes shining in the darkness. Sergius ran his hand over the smooth crevice of Bacchus's lower back, closing his eyes and reveling in the feeling, as he prayed a silent thanksgiving to the God of Yeshu for Bacchus's safety.

"Oh!" Bacchus grunted, hopping out of bed and stumbling into the next room. "I forgot!" Sergius hunched upright against the mattress, trying to follow the silhouette of Bacchus as he stumbled around blindly in the next room. Without the warmth of Bacchus's body, he shivered against the frigid night air, and whished that he'd had time to start a fire before meeting Bacchus again, or at least get the firewood stored inside the insula. No doubt thieves had pilfered it from the stairwell as the two had enjoyed their reunion.

Dim light shown from the living room just as Bacchus re-entered the bedroom carrying the burlap package under his right arm, a lit wick in his left hand. He set the parcel a moment on the edge of the bed as he lit the oil lamps about the room, bathing the room in a butterscotch glow. Sergius bunched the covers against his chest, watching the perfect sculpture of Bacchus's naked body move about the room. It was in the dim light that Sergius first noticed the weathering to Bacchus's once-perfect face. He, like Julian, looked older now, his face chapped and dry, cheeks red with burst capillaries—the face of a soldier who had braved the marshy summers of the country as well as the bitter wind of winter. Had he only lusted for Bacchus, Sergius might have found the sight repulsive and mourned the loss of youthful beauty. But there, as he watched Bacchus with squinting eyes in the low light, he felt a spring of pride well in his chest: Bacchus was a survivor, and a testament to the strength and bravery of Rome.

"I bring you a gift," Bacchus said, a faint echo of his Germanic accent in his voice as he unwrapped the parcel. From inside, he produced smaller bags of dried apples, figs, cranberries and a jug of wine. Draped within a softer cotton cloth lay Bacchus's lyre. He smiled wide at Sergius, proud of his romantic endeavor as he too shivered a bit in the cold, pouring the wine into a pair of goblets before hopping back into bed with Sergius. Sergius leaned up and gave Bacchus a soft kiss before sipping from the cup, letting the gentle acid of the vintage tingle at his lips.

"So," Sergius began after a moment.

"Wait," Bacchus said. He reached over and grabbed a fig, dangling above Sergius mouth, who reached up like a hungry fish and chomped the fruit down with one bite. The two giggled at their infantile behavior, reveling in it all the while.

"So," Sergius continued, still chewing the seedy pulp of the fig. "Tell me of the war." Bacchus took a long swig from his goblet and shook his head left to right. His face seemed to darken as he thought.

"It was war," he observed, taking another sip. "You have fought in many battles; you know it well." He fell quiet, lost in distant memory. "I killed sixty-five men," he admitted. "Maybe more. I remember the face of each one." Sergius reached out with a tender grasp at Bacchus's arm, his own eyes unwavering from the ravaged face of his beloved. The two sat quiet as Sergius stroked at Bacchus wrist.

"Do you feel guilt?" Sergius asked after a moment. Bacchus flinched, his lips wringing as he thought.

"I feel sad," he declared. "I am proud to defend Rome, but I am not proud to kill." Sergius nodded in understanding. Another silence fell between the two men.

"I have come to believe," Sergius began, "that Rome cannot save the world by war, that peace will not come from killing."

"You read the words of Yeshu, from Macrina," Bacchus presumed. Sergius nodded in admission.

"Yeshu teaches that only love will bring peace—love for each other, love for the One God. And I have begun to believe in him." They locked eyes, deep brown meeting amethyst, Bacchus trying to understand Sergius. After a moment, the Secundarius nodded.

"I trust in you," Bacchus said at last. "If you believe in Yeshu, then so shall I. But what of Macrina's words, that we should not love one another's bodies?"

"I think she bases that on the words of the teacher Paul," Sergius explained. "Paul never knew Yeshu, but was one of his earliest followers. He popularized Yeshu's teachings by proclaiming that all people, not just the Jews, could enter the Kingdom. He also taught that to ready ourselves for the Kingdom, we must forsake Earthly pleasures, for they so easily lead to Earthly problems."

"But what would that gain?" Bacchus wondered. Sergius shrugged.

"A focus on a Kingdom not of this world. Freedom from distraction."

"Paul sounds like Julian," Bacchus observed. Sergius chuckled and sipped his wine.

"Caesar would not enjoy that comparison. Nor would Paul, I think," Sergius grinned. "What I find odd is that Macrina would take Paul's words as if they were those of Yeshu. Yeshu never spoke of celibacy as a need to enter the Kingdom." Silence fell between the two again as they contemplated. When Bacchus finally spoke, he squeezed Sergius hand to wrest him from his deep thoughts.

"What do you think we should do?"

Sergius looked at the blanket which covered and warmed him and Bacchus, certainly as much as the heat of their bodies warmed one another. He thought of Macrina and her small congregation, and how it differed from the massive assembly at the church of Vienne.

"I think we should be baptized as Galileans," Sergius asserted, watching Bacchus for his reaction. "But we cannot do it openly, not in the church here. The Emperor's hostility toward the faith would put us in danger. Besides, Macrina's mass seemed very different than the one performed by the priest here."

The Passion of Sergius & Bacchus

"So what then?" Bacchus asked, puzzled. Sergius shook his head, as if looking for options and finding none.

"We must find Macrina and ask for her help. When Didymos arrives, he will know how to find her." Sergius yawned and reached over Bacchus to place his goblet on the floor. The wine had flowed into his brain, and the cold of night had made him tired. He kissed Bacchus on the shoulder and reclined into the bed. Taking his cue, Bacchus did the same, pulling Sergius arm over and wrapping it around his own waist. They lay there a few minutes in the dim glow of the lamps, squeezing their bodies together for warmth as much as for affection.

"What made you believe?" Bacchus asked, voice creaking and quiet, just as Sergius drifted on the boarder of sleep. The Primercius's eyes shot open and he sighed, contemplating Bacchus's question.

"My love for you," Sergius answered without hesitation. "That I could find one so beautiful, one I loved so in this world of death and war…that could only be the work of the God of Yeshu—the God of love and peace. I need no greater proof than that."

Bacchus pulled Sergius's hand to his mouth and kissed it, long and soft, before returning it to his abdomen and pulling Sergius in close. Sergius drifted into sleep soon thereafter, and for the first time since leaving Paris, he slumbered without weeping.

Chapter XXXIII.

The thunderous banging woke them from their blissful slumber, rhythmic, unceasing, insistent. Sergius winced at the morning light pouring in from a tiny window just above his bed, picking the crust from the corners of his eyes, trying to discern the source of the pounding. He sat upright, looking down at Bacchus who grunted and cowered, pulling the blankets up over his chapped face, leaving only locks of his blond hair visible. Sergius noticed for the fist time that Bacchus's hair too had darkened, now almost auburn in color, though still speckled with the golden threads that Sergius loved so. Sergius ran a hand over Bacchus's head as he leapt from the bed to the cold tile of the floor. The frigid surface stung at Sergius's feet, making him hop and dance around as he searched the littered clothing about the insula for his loin cloth. Unable to find it, and with the banging at the door incessant, Sergius grabbed Bacchus's undergarment and wrapped it about himself, making his way though the apartment to the door. Before he could even call out to the visitor, a familiar voice snapped him to attention.

"Sergius!" screamed the voice of Julian. Sergius snapped open the bronze lock without hesitating and threw open the door, revealing the sight of his Emperor. Julian charged past his host and into the insula, trailed by Oribasius and two guards. Awestruck, Sergius stumbled back, allowing his guests into the room without comment. Caesar paused a moment, scanning the room as one of the guards slammed the door shut. His gaze then fixed on Sergius, eyeing up him and down, frowning with slight disgust at the slight of his scantily-clad Primercius.

"Lord Caesar," Sergius stammered, not quite sure what to say to such an invasion of his home. Julian ignored him, stepping around the scattered clothes toward the bedroom.

"Good morning, Sergius," Oribasius chimed with a cheery smile, patting Sergius about his keloid shoulder. The doctor followed his Emperor towards the bedroom, and in turn so did Sergius, glancing back at the guards who stationed themselves, expressionless, at the front door.

"Lord Caesar," Sergius began again, entering the bedroom, "you grace me with your visit. What…" The sight before him in the room gave him pause, even as Oribasius grunted and shook his head: Julian knelt at the side of the bed, shoving handfuls of dried fruit into his mouth. Sergius's jaw went slack at the image, as he mouthed without speaking, at a loss for words.

"He thinks Constantius is trying to poison him," Oribasius explained with dry boredom. Julian rose to his feet, chewing at a dried apple, glaring at his physician. "I tell him to make the servants taste his food for him, but that doesn't seem to reassure him."

"How can I trust the servants if they were assigned to me by

Constantius?" Julian contended, gnawing at his apple. The sound of Julian's voice made Bacchus peek his head out from under the covers, squinting in the light for a moment before rocketing out of bed to his feet.

"My Lord!" Bacchus exclaimed as the cold air and floor burned his naked skin, forcing him into a shiver. Julian regarded the nude Secundarius with ambivalence, as Bacchus yanked a blanket from the bed and wrapped it about his waist.

"Glad to see you two found each other again," Julian said, swallowing the apple.

"Caesar, to what do I owe this visit?" Sergius asked, moving alongside Bacchus and helping him to tie the blanket at his hip.

"Forgive the interruption of your fornication," Julian said, making no effort to hide his annoyance. "But a problem has arisen."

"Lord Caesar," Sergius demurred, "should you need my counsel you need only send for me."

"I didn't want to wait," Julian declared, placing his arms behind his back. "Besides, I needed time out of the palace. I find my residence here so constrictive."

"And he was hungry," Oribasius added with a smirk. Julian glared daggers at his doctor, whose expression evaporated. Neither Sergius nor Bacchus made a sound.

"The Alemanni have been committing raids along the Rhine," the Emperor explained. "This would not be surprising but for the season; battle in winter is just as unkind to the barbarians as it is to our own legions."

"Can the local forces not withstand the attacks?" Sergius wondered.

"It's more complicated than that," Oribasius injected, voice grave. Julian sighed.

"We've intercepted a messenger on his way to Byzantium,"

Julian revealed. "He had letters from the barbarian king Vadomar, sent to Constantius. It appears the two are in league." Bacchus gasped. Sergius took a timid step towards his Emperor.

"You mean Constantius is encouraging these raids?" Sergius inquired with disbelief.

"Vadomar refers to me," Julian chimed, words slow and simmering with resentment, "as a rebel Caesar. Not Caesar Augustus. Not one with a right to the golden laurels. A rebel. They are trying to trap me."

Sergius blinked his eyes, trying to process such devastating news. Fighting barbarian tribes was one thing, but the idea that Constantinople would encourage such attacks—even aid in them—meant almost certain defeat for Julian and his armies.

"Then we must move to stop Vadomar," Sergius contended. "If we lose the territories you've fought so hard to rebuild over the past years, you'll look weak, and the Empire will never stand behind you."

"I've considered this already," Julian blurted, raising his voice. "I've also sent word to Euhemerus in Libya for help, though I fear he will be of little assistance should our messenger even reach him."

"So what advice do you seek, my Emperor?" Sergius asked, shaking his head in disbelief at such revelations. Julian sighed, his eyes falling on the food again. He reached down and took a fig, bit into it, and chewed it in silence, leaving his host pregnant with suspense.

"My focus must remain Constantius, and taking Byzantium," Julian said, gnawing on the seedy pulp of the fig.

"Then you must negate Vadomar's influence," Sergius observed.

"That is obvious," Julian snarled. "But how?"

Sergius wracked his mind for some idea. The very idea of

war seemed more repulsive to him now than ever, especially with Bacchus's return. That any man or woman could risk losing their beloved on a field of snow and mud over a quarrel between cousins seemed absurd, even if one of those cousins was Julian, and even if Julian deserved the throne more than Constantius. And what of the Alemanni? Did they not have lovers, spouses, children that would suffer the loss of a soldier just following the orders of his king?

Sergius found his thoughts drawn to Yeshu, who would have opposed the whole political mess, advocating peace and love above all else. Still, even Yeshu warned, as Mark's Gospel recorded, that war was sometimes immanent before the coming of the Heavenly Kingdom. If Julian could provide a path to that Kingdom…if Rome could transform itself from a warrior's Empire to a Kingdom of love and peace…

"Is it not said," Sergius remarked, "that the Galilean was betrayed by one of his own followers?"

"The Galilean!?" Julian exclaimed in puzzlement.

"Yes," Sergius continued, "at a supper with his followers. One of his chosen turned him over to Rome in exchange for silver." Julian regarded Sergius a long moment with great scrutiny. Sergius wondered if his analogy had perhaps raised the Emperor's suspicions.

"You make a wise observation," Julian said after what seemed like forever. "If a man will surrender his messiah for wealth, what barbarian would not surrender his king, eh?" Julian exited the bedroom toward the insula door, and Oribasius dutifully followed, with Sergius and Bacchus darting after him. "And a supper sounds like just the opportunity for an arrest." He scoffed. "It was for that seditious Jew."

Julian motioned to the guards who opened the door, flooding

the room with frigid morning air. Bacchus clung to Sergius for warmth, the heat of their bodies merging at the touch of their skin. Sergius closed his eyes a moment, enjoying the feeling of Bacchus against him, and the comfort it offered from Julian's intimidating presence.

"I'll see you at the palace, Sergius," Julian declared, pausing in the doorway. "And Bacchus, welcome home. Was it you that provided those tender morsels?"

"Yes, Lord Caesar," Bacchus confessed.

"Must have cost you a good deal given the season," Julian observed.

"Yes, Caesar," Bacchus repeated. Julian cracked a smile that Sergius took for a friendly gesture. Sergius just wished the Emperor would close the door and leave them alone.

"I'll see to it you receive payment for them then," Julian decreed. "And I'll make sure the two of you have food provided to you. You've something to celebrate."

With that, the Emperor and his doctor left the insula and closed the door, shutting out the wind if still leaving the room freezing. Though Sergius found his gesture of payment for the food he'd taken a humble one, something about Julian's demeanor left him feeling uneasy, as if the Caesar held a deeper resentment he tried to mask; an anger that had little to do with Vadomar or Constantius. Sergius grasped Bacchus hand and squeezed it tight.

Chapter XXXIV.

The tiny palace rooms in Vienne only added to the tense and cunning air which surrounded Julian in the weeks following Bacchus's return to Germania. The trapping of Vadomar became the top priority for the Caesar, who took every precaution that no one outside his inner circle would know of the plot. Curtains were drawn, doors bolted, guards dismissed and servants chased away as Julian reduced his advisory staff to only Oribasius and Sergius when discussing the matter, usually by torchlight and with hushed voices in some tiny, plain room away from the Emperor's main study. Julian's newborn paranoia amazed Sergius. Granted, as a rebel Caesar Augustus Julian had more to fear than ever before, more so than even during the purge of his family. He'd committed treason, and if he could not wrest the laurels from Constantius while maintaining order in the West, only one fate could await him, along with those who had pledged their loyalty to him.

The specter of Julian's failure weighed on Sergius without

reprieve, for if the Emperor did not succeed, it would mean Sergius's own execution. Though his newfound belief in the One God and the teachings of Yeshu brought him some comfort, his own overpowering fear of death still haunted him—even if he had found a way to face death, he had not found a way to escape it. Moreover, those destined to enter the Kingdom had to undergo baptism, a rite which Sergius had yet to experience.

The thought of dying without his ceremonial spiritual rebirth didn't frighten Sergius so much as he expected. Somehow, believing in a God who loved an Emperor as much as a slave, remembering the sacrifice of the Anointed One and knowing the love of Bacchus—absolute, unwavering and without question—brought him a comfort he never before felt, greater than even the most joyous and gleeful childhood memory of laying in the arms of his parents watching chariot races. With Bacchus's love, Sergius discovered a fresh reservoir of courage and faith—anything seemed possible.

That optimistic sentiment proved comforting as he poured over a crude sketch of the Alemanni territory alongside Julian, Oribasius and Bacchus, the four men sequestered in a tiny storage room of the fortress. Chalk marks, some distinct, others smeared, dusted over the inky scrawling of trees and roads, indicating the most up-to-date division between Roman and Alemanni land. Beneath it lay a more elaborate map of the entire Empire, the city of Rome occupying its center marked by an icon of a wolf in a red circle like the heart of the Earth, its sprawling highways snaking all over like arteries sustaining civilization.

"Here," Bacchus said, pointing to a tiny blank spot on the map outlined by trees and traced by a thin blue line representing a shallow creek, his eyes burning with concentration in the lamplight. "In this spot the trees have receded, leaving the forest bald. It is close to Alemanni territory, so Vadomar will not suspect an ambush." He tapped his rough finger, as callous from battle as from years of lyre plucking, at the tiny space.

"We bribe one of his guards to convince him to settle there for reconnaissance," Oribasius added, following Bacchus's line of thinking. The doctor buroughed his hand into a burlap sack of some unidentified seeds, tossing handfuls of them into his mouth, his molars grinding them with a low *crunch*, underpinning the tense dialogue of the room.

"And then send word that he's stationed there. And when he does," Bacchus continued, "we capture him."

Julian stepped forward, gaze staring down at the map, eyes fixed and unblinking as he considered the plan of his Secondarius. His lips twitched with subtle tension as he clenched his incisors beneath them, deep in thought.

"Those trees will not provide us much cover," the Caesar noted in a pensive monotone without looking up. "And we will need full-force ambush to insure our victory. I cannot afford anything less."

"Darkness will help hide our numbers," Sergius injected. Oribasius glanced at him, cheeks puffed out as he chewed. Bacchus looked up with an affectionate glimmer in his amethyst gaze, cracking a smile at his beloved. Julian ignored the exchange, still concentrated on the plans before him.

"True, Sergius," Julian acknowledged. "But even in the shadows Vadomar could spot our soldiers."

"Then let us break into smaller groups," Bacchus volunteered.

"Yes!" Sergius exclaimed, taking a step towards Bacchus and resting a hand on his shoulder. "Groups of five men, lightly armed—only bows and swords—for greater speed and mobility spread out through the surrounding area." He returned Bacchus's look of pride, feeling the Secondarius' hand brush against his thigh. "And no helmets," he quipped, eliciting smiles from the other men, save Julian.

"And we position them here, here and here," the Emperor noted, tapping out three different areas surrounding the clearing. He took a step back, as if trying to absorb a great image before him, eyes still fixed on the map, oblivious to the quiet affections of Sergius and Bacchus, or Oribasius's noisy munching. Julian reached up and tugged at the whiskers of his caprinian beard, twisting the curly hairs into a tight peak, eyes widening. "May the gods help us; it's our best chance," he decided at last.

"Then when do we begin?" Sergius asked with anxious enthusiasm.

"Tonight," the Caesar declared, turning toward his soldiers. "We shall send our agent to infiltrate their ranks—someone I can trust implicitly, someone who's Germanic heritage is not in question. Someone who knows the area." Sergius felt the tides of acid rise in his stomach, his grip on Bacchus's soldier tightening as the rhythm of Oribasius chewing slowed to a pause. The Primercius held his breath, sweat beading amid his ebony curls, his heartbeat a rapid drum in his chest. Julian glanced at Sergius, then to Bacchus.

"I need you to do this, my Secondarius," the Emperor ordered, compassion buried in his tone. "You and Sergius are among the few I can still trust, and while I know the two of you would rather stay behind, drinking wine, playing your lyre and knowing each other's flesh, I must ask this of you, for the sake of Rome."

Sergius's twisted, his breathing shallow in a near-pant, vision fixed on Bacchus's face, purple eyes aglow, shadows from the lamplight dancing at upward angles across his rugged face. Sergius knew Bacchus would never reject an Imperial order, but even if he could, the Primercius recognized the undaunted power in Bacchus's countenance: he would serve Rome no matter what the cost.

"By your command, lord Caesar," Bacchus accepted with a slight nod. He swallowed, betraying a hint of his own fear as Sergius moved his hand from Bacchus's shoulder to meet his clammy palm. The two soldiers' fingers interlocked in a vice grip, silently expressing their love, but still accepting their duty.

Julian looked grim as he placed his hands behind his the small of his back.

"May Aires protect you," he sighed. Sergius watched the Emperor, sensing his empathy, understanding his decision none the less. Julian's sincere words rang hallow in Sergius ears, feeling less a comfort than a tin platitude.

Lord of the Anointed One, Sergius prayed to himself, *watch over my valorous Bacchus on this mission of patriotism. Forgive us our sins. Protect us all.*

Chapter XXXV.

They said nothing as Sergius fastened Bacchus's cloak over his shoulders. The Secondarius postured at attention, watching Sergius's face. The Primercius's gaze eluded Bacchus's, with Sergius vision casting over the Alemanni-style woolen tunic and worn leather pants that Bacchus now donned. Sergius couldn't bear to look at Bacchus on the eve of this mission. It seemed every time the two found each other fate yanked them apart again, each separation a sadistic arrow of Cupid driven into their chests. The Lord had brought them together; why would he tear them apart at every opportunity?

"Do you have all your supplies?" Sergius asked, still avoiding Bacchus's stare. Sergius moved about the darkened living room, the crackling fire the only source of light. The flames cast morose shadows over the tile floor, as Sergius looked for any discarded or forgotten accessory to Bacchus's mission.

"I've my pouch," Bacchus noted, running a hand over the

cinched leather bag tied to his left hip, then letting it drift to the rough hilt of a sheathed blade at his right. "Sword. Cloak. Quiver."

"Bow!" Sergius declared, raising a finger and looking around the room. He spied the weapon tucked away against the wall, shrouded by the darkness of the room.

"Bow," Bacchus repeated, taking the unstrung limb and tucking it in his quiver. He sighed, his lips pulling into a half-smile as he locked eyes with Sergius at last.

Sergius felt his stomach knot and his cheeks tense as unbearable anxiety flushed though his body. He ran his hands over his tunic, as if trying to grab at some unseen crutch and finding none just clawed at his own body. He panted, unable to hold Bacchus's gaze for more than a moment, ducking his head in embarrassment away from his beloved.

Bacchus stepped forward and wrapped his thick arms around the shaking figure of Sergius, pulling him in tight, his hand gently manipulating the Spaniard's head to rest on his shoulder.

"I'm sorry," Sergius whispered, choking on his words. He returned Bacchus's embrace, running his hands over the muscular contours of his back, trying to find the most comforting place— the *safest* place—to grip onto him. Bacchus just held on to Sergius unwavering, trying to keep him clam and steady as possible.

"Do not apologize," Bacchus answered, voice soft and tender. "Do not shed tears. This duty…" He paused, loosening his grip on Sergius, leaning back that their eyes might connect, beholding each other's naked soul. "This duty is a gift from Caesar. It is an honor that he trusts me with this task. It is an honor that I serve Rome."

"I do not fear for Julian, or for Rome," Sergius decreed. "I fear losing you."

"Do not be afraid," Bacchus soothed. "You are also a gift, my greatest gift, from the Anointed One, from the God of love. I cannot believe he would take you from me."

"It is not my life at stake here," Sergius snapped back, "but yours." He placed his palm on Bacchus cheek, running his thumb over the blond stubble. "I believe the Anointed One brought us together too. But he also took my whole family from me. Why should you be any different?"

"That was not the God of Love," Bacchus responded, a newfound gravity in his voice. "Those were barbarian filth. That is why I must go tonight—to see to it that no other families must suffer as yours did." He tiled his forehead against Sergius chest. "Or mine." Sergius exhaled, surrendering to Bacchus's wisdom, shutting his eyes in acceptance.

"You truly believe the God of Yeshu has brought us together?" Sergius questioned, raising his eyes and toward the darkened ceiling, the timbre of his words ringing like the basso chime of a great bell.

"I could not believe otherwise. Only a God of love could create someone as perfect as you."

The two men locked mouths in a fiery kiss, their nostrils fairing as they gasped for air. Neither wanted to pull away; their life forces charging one another with hope and faith. An unparalleled feeling consumed them: that in everything, everywhere, God existed, and that the almighty didn't watch over them, but lived *within* them, awakened and empowered by their love.

Sergius saw Bacchus to the edge of Vienne, standing in the street and watching his beloved's form until it disappeared into the night. He stood there for some time after, just staring at the blackness, hoping that somehow the smooth darkness might ripple and shift to reveal Bacchus. How he wished for one last embrace, a final kiss, another chance to speak of love and devotion. But the Secondarius did not appear, and Sergius at last surrendered to reality: Bacchus had gone, and he was alone again. Bowing his head, weight of the universe sinking in upon him, Sergius paced back into the streets of the city, wandering without aim, lost in his own anxiety. As he walked, the sickly feeling in his stomach only worsened, his face beginning to sweat and twisted hands clawing over his body with nervous fervor.

What would Macrina tell me in this moment, Sergius pondered. *What comfort would she offer?* Sergius stared up to the heavens, the light of the stars eclipsed by dense black clouds hanging low from the sky, threatening to crush the world below. He thought again of Holy Baptism, and the frightening notion that he or Bacchus might die before undergoing the rite, leaving the uninitiated condemned to oblivion for all time. Sergius paused in his tracks, dwelling on the thought.

Indeed, what God of love would damn a man so virtuous as Bacchus? True, Bacchus had killed, but only in the name of his country. He and Sergius had fornicated, but for the sake of love, not lust. But most important of all, Bacchus *believed* in the teachings of the Anointed One, holding them in his heart and mind with true and unwavering faith. Could the God of love and forgiveness abandon a man of pure faith and devotion, simply because he had not undergone a sanctimonious and theatrical ceremony on Earth?

Sergius's eyes narrowed, running the tip of his tongue over the edge of his incisors as he reflected. He recalled the teachings of Yeshu from his days as a scholar, as well as those of the teacher Paul who courted Gentiles to the Galilean cause. Paul had noted that keeping the Jewish traditions of Kosher and circumcision mattered not in the eyes of God, for a man's worth came not from his lifestyle, but from his soul.

The Passion of Sergius & Bacchus

No, Sergius decided. *Mystic rites and ceremonies are there for men, as a sign of devotion to which they might bear witness as a demonstration of one's faith to those who cannot see what God already does; they matter not in the Kingdom. I love Bacchus, and I place my faith in Yeshu's wisdom. That is what matters.*

Sergius felt his shoulders drop as his head tilted up, his back erecting to an upright and relaxed posture. The burning tide in his abdomen had receded, and though his fear persisted, some flicker of hope lit the darkness of his soul. He inhaled a deep breath of cool air, the odors of midnight fires flavoring the air and shocking him back to the present. He looked around at the sleepy, empty streets before him. Bacchus might have gone, and Sergius, for the moment, might walk alone, but loneliness did not sting him any longer.

Yeshu was with him. He believed.

Sergius began his walk again, this time with renewed energy and purpose—he had a destination. He would go to the palace, to Caesar, to put his nervous hands to use. They had to prepare for battle.

Chapter XXXVI.

Two days after Bacchus's departure, Julian received word that Vadomar was on the move, and the barracked army of Vienne sprang to attention. They kept a rapid pace even without the aid of their horses, moving under the camouflage of night. The battalions dissolved into groups of no more than ten men, each armed with only a bow, arrows and a sword, forsaking the great wooden shields that designated their units. Julian ordered the entire city scoured for spare fabric as well, that as many of his soldiers as possible might don a cloak over his armor, preventing any possibility that the Alemanni might catch a metallic glimmer of reflected starlight in the darkness.

Sergius, of course, never left his Caesar's side, helping to prepare in any way he could—organizing troops into their new guerilla units, distributing supplies, and doing anything he could to keep from worrying about Bacchus. As the army departed the city under cover of night, scurrying like rats out of the city gate to keep their operation clandestine, Sergius felt a wave of relief calm his burning gut. Though the march of battle had always made him sweat with fright, Sergius felt calmed at the thought that his suffering away from Bacchus might subside, even if it meant his own end.

Before uniting with Julian to set off for battle, Sergius resolved to make one final stop, to make use of a final opportunity to thank and love a loyal friend.

The nighttime stables still sounded with clicks and whinnies of its inhabitants as Sergius roused his beloved steed from sleep with the sound of gentle kisses. Hylas stirred, his onyx eyes fluttering open and walked to the edge of his stall to greet his master, shaking his blond mane as if to preen and look presentable to Sergius. He extended his long equine face out over the his stall door with a low grunt and a sigh, his wet nostrils contracting with his breath which lingered in a cloud of white moisture in the cold, nocturnal air.

"Hylas," Sergius whispered, stroking the soft fur of the horse's face. Sergius leaned forward and laid a soft kiss on Hylas's snout, and the beast again shook his mane and lunged out with his neck, softly nuzzling him to return the affection.

Strange, Sergius thought, *that I should find so much love in a stable.* The Primercius chuckled at the thought, but he could not deny the fact. Those early months as Julian's advisor, Sergius doubted the loyalty and trust of everyone and everything around him, but for Hylas's own; indeed, those peaceful afternoons reading Plato and Sophocles in hushed voice to his horse stood out as the only moments of levity in the beginning of his tenure as Julian's personal bodyguard. Moreover, without the bond Sergius shared with Hylas, he might never have found Bacchus toiling away as a stable keeper. Sergius grinned to himself at the realization that so much of the love in his life should be born in a stable. And still, in a way it all seemed appropriate. After all, did the God of Love not send his son Yeshu to be born in a stable?

Hylas brushed his wet, equine snout against Sergius's chest again, his wise mahogany eyes blinking with intuitive empathy. Sergius realized Hylas said goodbye with his affection, wishing him safety, hoping that the two would ride together once again. Sergius embraced his horse, patting his long neck and stroking his blond mane, letting a sigh of resolve escape his throat.

The time had come.

The muted lumens of hidden campfires flickered across the rushing creek, their light peering through the bunched trees where Julian, Sergius and their dispersed troops crouched against the marshy soil. Sergius squinted and strained his vision in hopes of beholding a glimpse of Bacchus among the Alemanni soldiers—some confirmation that his beloved still lived.

"Quit looking for him," Oribasius wheezed beneath his burlap cloak. In the dim light, the doctor's massive silhouette made him look more like a bear fattened for hibernation than a man prepared for battle. Sergius frowned, annoyed as much by Oribasius's harassment as by his own transparency of emotion.

"I look to see if he's completed his task," Sergius growled, making no effort to conceal his anxious resentment.

"Both of you be silent," the Emperor ordered, his own gaze fixated on the Alemanni camp across the stream. "We've one chance here; if we fail, it could mean losing the whole Empire to Constantius. We must succeed."

Just then, a scurrying noise through the brush caused all three men to reach for their blades.

"My lord," said a foot soldier, pulling back his ragged cape to reveal the shimmer of his Roman armor. Sergius and his Caesar stood down their arms. Oribasius did the same, grunting in annoyance as he did so. "All units are in position."

"And Vadomar is among their ranks?" Julian questioned.

"Our spy has confirmed it. The king dines here."

Sergius heartbeat leapt to a frenzied throb—Bacchus lived, at least for the moment. Should the Alemanni realize the traitor in their midst, they would make Bacchus their first target.

"Then our moment has come," Julian declared, rising to his feet. "Aries and Zeus be with us." The soldier bowed in acknowledgement and crept off into the dark, the foliage rustling under his feet. Sergius and Oribasius rose with their Emperor, adJustiniang their armor for comfort, preparing for battle. "You both serve Rome well," Julian said, his voice grave and sanctimonious. "And you are my friends. May the gods protect us all this night."

Julian turned and fixated on the tiny lights of the campfires in the clearing across the stream again, his posture leaning forward in readiness. Sergius breathed deep, closing his eyes a moment, meditating, preparing himself for dreaded combat.

"*Lord of Yeshu,*" Sergius prayed to himself, "*protect us this night. Be with my Bacchus, and help me guard my Emperor that Rome might find peace in this world, that the death and killing might end.*"

A thundering blast from a horn, unmistakable as it echoed through the forest jolted Sergius to attention, blood pumping with a nervous adrenal rush. All around him, he could hear the sound of mud globing, of cracking twigs and plants crushed beneath the pounding boots of the Roman Army. The low rumble of war cries rose up from the marsh, as Julian drew his sword and held hit high and resolute.

"Now!" he commanded, charging forth toward the water, Oribasius following not far behind.

"God help me," Sergius muttered aloud, drawing his own

sword as he broke into a run, fighting his way through the brush and into the battle ahead.

Chapter XXXVII.

The frigid water of the creek washed up over Sergius legs and soaked through his loin cloth, freezing his male extremities as he struggled with the quiver slung over his back and pumped his legs in a frenzy, his feet struggling to find tracking in the muck below. All around him, he could see the glimmer of drawn swords in the night shining over the water and glinting in action in the clearing ahead. Through the battle cries, the shriek of arrows piercing the air began to sputter, as did the wails of pain and woe on the shore. The Romans had succeeded in the surprise element of their attack; whether or not the Empire would triumph in the battle remained an open question.

Just ahead of him, Sergius could see Julian struggle to keep his own head above water, his sword dipping below the surface as he fought for buoyancy. Sergius fought through the current to Caesar's side, and wrapping his weaponed arm around Julian's waist. He pulled the shorter man up above the face of the creek, steadying him. The Emperor panted and grunted, catching his breath, glancing at Sergius with a grateful smile.

"Philosopher. Bodyguard. Buoy. You've many uses, Sergius," the Emperor chuckled between gasps. Sergius felt his balance solidify as they reached the shallow water of the creek bed and lowered Julian to his own stance. The two men staggered up through the mud to the dry land, their wet legs pimpled with gooseflesh in the freezing night air. Sergius's jaw locked and his teeth chattered as he watched Julian for direction. The Emperor stood like a mighty pillar in the night, cheering his men into battle, waving them on as they reached the shore. Julian's gaze shot around to Sergius, the Caesar's eyes desperate with confusion.

"Oribasius," Julian uttered, his eyes scanning the soldiers as they came ashore, looking for some trace of his physician. Sergius lips parted as he searched for some pearl of comfort, when suddenly, like the great Scylla rising from the seas above Odysseus's ship. The sopping wet form of the doctor lurched forth from the water, tripped onto the shore and collapsed in a great mound in the mud. Sergius and Julian rushed to his side, helping the massive doctor to sit upright and catch his breath.

"Lord Caesar," Oribasius choked. "Julian. You'd better defeat these bastards, or else you'll need to find a new doctor!"

Julian scoffed as he pulled at Oribasius's arm, helping the aging medic to his feet.

"Catch your breath, old man," Julian commanded. "The rest of us will fight for Rome whilst you wallow in the mud!" With that, Julian motioned to Sergius, and the two men darted off toward the fighting. As they approached, the chaos and bloodshed gave Sergius pause.

Alemanni tents burned. Arrows sliced the air. Blades flickered reflected light amid the twisting bodies, as the corpses piled with increasing numbers around the clearing. The blood of barbarian and Roman alike mixed in the mud, indistinguishable in death.

Though he stayed close to his Emperor as his duty would dictate, Sergius attention fell to only one objective: locating Bacchus. In the strobe of the firelight, even with the blazes rising as the campsite burned, Sergius could not tell Alemanni from Roman, their dress too similar to differentiate one from another. His ears pounded with his rushing heartbeat, paralyzed with horror and disgust at the seething orgy of death surrounding him. His stomach burned and his breathing accelerated to a rapid pant, hoping against hope that Bacchus still lived, that the God of Yeshu had protected him from the pain and suffering he'd helped to incite.

"Lord, please..."

No sooner had the words meditated within Sergius's panicked mind when his dark eyes lit on a mighty figure, his face and body obscured by a rough cloak, launching a steady torrent of arrows into the twisting mass of soldiers, each one landing square in the chest of its target.

Sergius took off running across the field, dodging arrows, climbing and wrestling his way through the mass of soldiers, making his way to the archer.

"Sergius!" Julian yelled after him, but even the call of his Caesar could not deter him, Julian's words dissolving and lost in the cacophony of battle surrounding them. Sergius clawed and kicked through the battle, forging a path to this frantic soldier, even as the arrows poured down like hail.

"Bacchus?" Sergius cried with hopeful anguish, only a few feet away from the archer. "Bacchus!?" The head of the cloaked figure turned and spotted Sergius in the churning fight, the object of its gaze unmistakable. Hope quaked in Sergius's chest, even as the soldier reached back and drew another arrow from his quiver. Sergius froze, eyes wide in panic as the archer, without any hint of hesitation, loaded the arrow onto his bow, raised it, and aimed it directly at Sergius.

Paralyzed with terror, Sergius couldn't even think, his mind reduced only to the animal response of pure emotion, eyes wide, holding his breath with anticipation.

The warrior released his arrow, sending it whirring straight for Sergius at blurring speed, its head cutting through the smoky air with a crecendoing charge. Sergius felt his body go numb as the arrow torpedoed toward him, passing only inches from his face as it roared past his head and lit with a *chock* between at a target behind him. Sergius spun around to behold an Alemanni soldier, the arrow dug square in his temple, slouch to the ground as the life evaporated from his body.

Sergius turned again in time to see the archer pull back his cloak, a pair of amethyst eyes glowing in the firelight—magnificent, perfect, unmistakable.

Sergius rushed toward Bacchus, sword still in hand, as a barbarian soldier leapt for the Secondarius, his own blade drawn, ready to strike. With a lightning reflex, Bacchus took a step back, reaching for another arrow, only to claw an empty quiver. His violet eyes widened, helpless, as the Alemanni poised to stab right at his neck. In a flash Sergius darted forth, his own sword raised in both hands. With a flicker of steel, Sergius parried the attacker's lunge, catching his sword with his own, thrusting the soldier backward and away from Bacchus.

The Alemanni raised his sword again, and brought it down with all of his strength against the chest of his new target, only to have Sergius block the attack once more. The barbarian stabbed again at Sergius's neck, and again at his loins and once more at his chest until, with one mighty gesture, Sergius batted his sword against that of his attacker, sending the barbarian's weapon hurling off into the night just as Sergius plunged his sword through the thin leather armor of the Alemanni.

It took less than a moment for Sergius to realize what he'd done. His face contorted with horror as the soldier went limp, falling to the muddy ground, Sergius's sword buried at a right angle to his abdomen. Sergius slouched to his knees, conflicted, disgusted, guilty as Bacchus rushed to his side. The Primercius knelt forward, placing a quivering hand across the dying man's chest, Sergius's own chestnut eyes meeting the clear blue of his victim's. Blood rushed forth from the wound, soaking the Alemanni's body, gushing over Sergius's quaking fingers.

Sergius toiled for words, unsure what to say or do, when the Alemanni made a sudden grab at Sergius's wrist, grasping it with unyielding pressure. With slow precision, the dying man raised Sergius's stained hand, the blood oozing from his fingers like dripping honey, and positioned it against the handle of his embedded sword. He held Sergius limp palm there, his grip tight as a vice, waiting for Sergius to finish what he'd begun.

Neither man spoke as Sergius gazed into woeful face of his victim, recognizing their desperate plea. Hand still blood soaked and quivering, Sergius grasped at the hilt of his sword, feeling the Alemanni's grip begin to loosen. Tears welled in the sparkling eyes of both men as the soldier's hand tightened again, begging Sergius for merciful peace that life no longer could afford him. Holding his breath, Sergius plunged all of his weight down against his sword, driving it all the way through the Alemanni's body and into the soft Earth below.

The soldier vomited blood and his body convulsed, contorted with incredible tension for a split second, then went limp, releasing

Sergius from his grasp as the light drained from his blue eyes forever.

Sergius had killed men in battle before, driven by his own terror of death and his patriotism for Rome. But this night, as he knelt there in the bloody soil, a great wave of pity and sorrow engulfed his heart. Something had changed within his soul, some beam of empathy, glowing with absolute purity and filling him with some charge of transcendent power. War…death…Emperors…barbarians…all of the constructs of his life seemed so feeble, so insignificant. But what had changed?

Sergius found his answer as a gentle hand fell upon his keloid-scarred shoulder, , a callous thumb brushing over the rough burlap of his cloak. He looked up into the face of Bacchus—golden locks feathered over his head, blond stubble dusting over his face, and the two perfect glowing gems of his irises. In that moment, Sergius knew that Bacchus held the same divine lumen within him, that what they felt for one another had taught them to love and forgive all mankind—rich and poor, German and Roman, royal and slave, man and woman—not despite their distinctions, but because Sergius and Bacchus knew the truth that Yeshu had espoused: there was no difference.

War would stop, though not from conquest. Death would end, though not from passivity. Peace and Life Everlasting would only come from love.

A cry from across the battlefield jarred both men from their meditation. They turned and spotted the bear-like form of Oribasius struggling against two Alemanni soldiers, trying in vain to protect a diminutive figure hidden beneath a rent cloak. A quick exchange of gazes, and Sergius knew what to do. Tearing his quiver from across his body, he tossed it up straight into the air. As it hovered, Bacchus snatched forth two arrows with one fell swoop. The quiver landed back in Sergius hands, as Bacchus tossed one arrow straight up where it peaked for a moment several feet above his head—just long enough for him to load the other arrow into his bow in a fury of movement and fire it off. The arrow had not yet reached its target when Bacchus caught the other arrow, and with the fluid movement loaded and launched it as well. The two arrows skewered across the field toward Julian and Oribasius and their attackers, each projectile striking an Alemanni in the shoulder. Oribasius's jaw went slack and Julian threw back his cloak, exposing his goat-like face beaming with amazement as the two Alemanni dropped their swords and coddled their wounds, screaming in pain.

Neither men's watch leaving their Caesar, Bacchus reached down and locked arms with Sergius, helping his beloved to his feet. Across the battlefield, Oribasius fended off the two weakened soldiers with ease, as Julian cocked his head back, eyes radiating pride and awe.

"The speed of Hermes, Bacchus!" Julian howled in triumph. "Now let us end this struggle!"

A slight bow to the Emperor and Bacchus turned to Sergius.

"Vadomar!" Sergius uttered with resolve. Bacchus nodded, gazing off across the field, stars in his eyes. He let out a pained cough of exhaustion.

"I know where he is."

Chapter XXXVIII.

The once-muted fires of the Alemanni camp had swelled to mighty blazes, consuming much of their shelter and supplies, even threatening to spread to the trees of the nearby forest. A few of the Germanic soldiers had withdrawn from the raging battle, trying to fight the fires with buckets of icy water from the nearby creek, but as the Roman troops flowed forth from their hidden pockets surrounding the area, the Alemanni forces became even more disorganized and chaotic as their invaders began to overtake them.

Julian, flanked by Sergius, Bacchus and Oribasius along with several other Palatinae, stalked through the camp on a predetermined course. They paused only to cast their disguise cloaks into one of the fires, letting their Imperial armor glow in the flickering light—all but Bacchus, who, though still donned in his Alemanni disguise, let his drawn Roman sword quash any illusion about which army he might have sided with.

"This way Kai-Zair," Bacchus said, his natural accent leaking out as he led Julian's force to the edge of the clearing still unsullied by the spilled blood of the battle. Julian followed his Secondarius with unblinking eyes, despite the smoke and cacophony of the surrounding destruction. Though sealed lips, Sergius could observe the Emperor gnashing his teeth with anxiety, using all his willpower to conceal his nervousness from his army. The very fate of his life—of all their lives—might have hinged on what they discovered next.

Bacchus stopped before what seemed an insignificant supply tent, its minuscule size barely enough to conceal the sacks and baskets of food within. Julian observed the tent with disdain as he motioned to Sergius and the other soldiers to search it.

"Try not to ruin their stores," Julian ordered. "We will have use of their plunder in our own march to Byzantium." The troops obeyed, unloading the supplies with care, placing them along side the tent against the tree line in hopes they might remain protected from the chaos permeating the camp. Sergius looked to Bacchus in confusion as a soldier removed a final sack of grain from the tent, leaving it empty with no sign of the Alemanni king. Bacchus held his breath under the skeptical gaze of Caesar, who stood waiting for an explanation, his impatience growing. Bacchus gestured with his sword to a small patch of burlap in the center of the tent, and Julian nodded with understanding.

"He hides like a vole," Julian uttered in disgust. He motioned to Bacchus, who pulled back the sack cloth to reveal three long, flat planks of wood covering a carved out space in the ground. As he did so, the other soldiers made no delay in tearing out the boards, unveiling a group of cloistered Alemanni screaming and cowering below.

"Bring them," Julian commanded, spinning around on his heel, making for the center of the battlefield. "Oribasius, sound the horn." The doctor bowed and rushed off towards the creek bank, as Sergius rushed to escort the Emperor should he encounter any resisting Alemanni as he walked to end the battle.

"Eno smiles on us this night," Julian whispered to Sergius as they waded into the chaos. Dead Alemanni bodies carpeted the clearing, covering the ground from the woods to the water; great bunches of arrows standing erect in the corpses like overgrown weeds, the sway of a gentle night breeze adding to the effect. From the creek bed, the Roman horn sounded again bringing the remaining fighting troops to attention, as they shifted from hand-to-hand combat to imprisoning the Alemanni in tiny clusters spread across the clearing. An eerie silence fell over the battlefield; the only sounds the crackling flames and the whimper of men weeping for their fallen brothers. A few stray Roman soldiers, taking direction from Oribasius, began to fight the fires of the engulfed tents, pillaging what supplies they could, gathering them at the water's edge.

Julian positioned himself with his back to the creek, looking on the clearing as if it were a great proscenium, the flames and trees a backdrop of some Greek epic. He twisted the spiral of his beard in thought as Bacchus and the other Palatinae arrived with their prize: six Alemanni solders, disarmed with their hands bound around their backs, one with a grain sack covering his head. Bacchus escorted the captive himself, thrusting the bound and blinded soldier to his knees before Julian, then taking his place beside Sergius, running his hand down the Spaniard's back with discreet affection.

"Bacchus," Julian asked, "can you translate?" Bacchus nodded, and took a step forward, ready to repeat Julian's oratory.

"Alemanni tribesmen," Julian's boomed, his voice taking on a lower resonance with more gravitas. Bacchus mimicked Julian—

grave tone included—calling out in the local dialect. "Your swords break under the boot of almighty Rome! Behold your camp in ruin!" He spread his arms wide, embracing the wreckage around him. "Behold, your king fallen before Caesar Augustus!"

Julian stepped forward and snatched the sack from the kneeling Alemanni's head, tossing it away, revealing his prize. Sergius gasped at the sight: Vadomar, king of the Alemanni—a boy aged no more than thirteen years. Nary a whisker on his face, the king had cheeks pocked with carbuncles, light brown hair greasy and messed, his svelte build in oversized Alemanni dress making him appear even more childlike. Most pronounced of all, Vadomar's transparent fear raged before his captor: that of a boy thrust into the role of a man, caught in a struggle between two Emperors, alone and broken before his own people. The sight even gave Julian pause, who fell silent as he looked upon the boy. His own eyes suddenly distant, the sight of Vadomar recalled some haunting memory from the Caesar's past.

Julian drew his sword, holding it high above his head that all those present could witness him wielding a deadly weapon before the fallen chief. He stood that way a moment gazing down at Vadomar who closed his eyes and quaked with fear. Sergius could see pity swell in Julian's eyes, conflicted about what sentence should befall this rival.

"My lord," Sergius whispered, edging to Julian's side. "He's only a child."

"He is an ally of Constantius, and my would-be murderer," Julian hissed back. "What would you have me do?"

"Forgive him," Sergius answered without hesitation. "Show him mercy. The kind of mercy Constantine would not bestow upon your family. The kind denied to my own by the marauders who pillaged our estate. This conflict is greater than him…"

"You would dare compare my execution of this war criminal to cold-blooded murder that Constantine inflicted on my parents?" Julian seethed, nostrils flaring with growing rage.

"My lord, killing only begets killing," Sergius declared, unwilling to back down even in the face of his Emperor's wrath. "Kill Vadomar and another chief will take his place, and the Alemanni will fight you to their last man. Gift on him life and win their allegiance. And win his gratitude." Vadomar looked up from his cowering kneel, unable to understand or speak the Greek tongue of Julian and Sergius, but his eyes begging for mercy in universal yearning. Julian looked down at Vadomar, then back at Sergius, lowering his sword in consideration.

"Peace will only come from love and forgiveness," Sergius pressed further, sensing Julian's resolve wavering. "Spare him."

"Though he would have killed me, given the chance?" the Emperor contended.

"Peace and prosperity come only from love and forgiveness, Julian. War ends when you want it to."

The eyes of Caesar and his Primercius met each other, shimmering in the dim light from the flames. Julian's face became a mask of stone as he regarded Sergius a moment, then looked down on Vadomar again, raising his sword in the air once more.

"Exile then!" Julian proclaimed, sheathing his sword at his waist. Bacchus repeated the Emperor's words to cheers from the captive Alemanni as Vadomar looked up to Caesar, gasping for breath in disbelief. Julian cocked his head back with an arrogant grimace. "I think we'll send you to Hispania Citerior," Julian mused. "Perhaps there you will learn the same wisdom as my Philosopher guard." The Emperor looked at Sergius with a soft expression of concession. "Is that agreeable to you, Primercius?"

"Thank you, Lord Caesar," Sergius uttered with a bow. Julian nodded, placing his arms behind his back. He motioned to two guards to take Vadomar away and prepare him for captivity, his eyes never leaving Sergius's own. He stood quiet a moment and glanced over at Bacchus, then faced Sergius again.

"I know not if love has made you soft, my friend," Julian said. "But it certainly has made you bold."

"It illuminates me, lord Caesar. Love and forgiveness from Rome will heal the world."

"That remains to be seen," Julian contended, words slow and punctuated. "You almost sound like one of those Galilean hypocrites."

"There is no hypocrisy here this night," Sergius assured, his eyes drifting to Bacchus with warm affection.

"That remains to be seen," Julian reminded.

Just then, there came a great splashing noise from the creek which drew the attention of all those around. Distant yelling only added to the confusing spectacle as a group of soldiers gave way to a scroll-carrying man, his clothes soaked from his ford, teeth chattering amid cloudy breath. Sergius recognized him right away as one of the palace messengers.

The messenger fell to one knee before Julian, raising the scroll to his Emperor. Sergius marveled that although he could see water droplets fall from the messenger's hand, somehow he had managed to keep the scroll completely dry and sealed in his crossing.

Julian took the scroll and cracked the wax, unrolling it with an annoyed frown. A moment later, his expression melted into total incredulity, lips parting in awe, his balance teetering as he tried to digest this message.

"My lord?" Sergius asked, reaching out to steady Julian. The Emperor waved off the help of his Philosopher guard, eyes never leaving the page in his hand.

"Zeus favors us with great triumph this night," Julian mused, voice light and quaking. "We triumph, Sergius."

"Lord Caesar?" Sergius asked again, his confusion only mounting. Julian shook his head in disbelief.

"He's dead, Sergius. The gods have united Rome once more."

Sergius took a step forward, stretching out his arms, palms open at Julian's sides, making no effort to touch his Emperor, but holding him in an imaginary embrace.

"Constantius?" Sergius questioned, voice rising with anticipation. Julian's stone face broke into a wide, toothy smile, a great cackle erupting from his throat.

"My bastard cousin is dead!" Julian proclaimed, gripping Sergius at the wrists. "I am the undisputed Caesar Augustus. Rome is ours!" Julian spun around to face the bewildered crowd of soldiers around him, drawing his sword once more and stabbing it up to the heavens. "I am Caesar Augustus!" he shouted. "We march to Byzantium! The Empire is ours!"

Bacchus stumbled over his words, trying to translate to the crowd amid his own excitement. All the troops, Roman and Alemanni alike, exploded with cheers and raised swords, fists pounding at the air in victory. Their frenzy surmounted even that of the armies at Strasburg, even that of Julian's coronation in Paris. Sergius rushed to Bacchus, the two uniting in a furious kiss, their shadows merging in the firelight, their shared joy palpable to all those who witnessed it.

Julian rushed to his impassioned bodyguards and tore them apart, embracing each with his Imperial arms.

"Byzantium, Sergius!" Julian cried. "Byzantium! Now we will return Rome to her glory! You will finally see the majesty of the capital! The Senate! Our dreams realized!"

"Hail to you, Caesar Augustus!" Sergius said, words bursting with joy.

"And both of you at my side!" Julian declared. "You shall have everything you desire, my wisest and bravest of soldiers!" He sighed with satisfaction. "Our dreams are realized, my Palatinae! Peace again! The old gods will return! Our destiny awaits!"

Even as Bacchus squeezed Sergius's hand, smiling so wide the gap left from his missing tooth became visible again, as he reveled in joy he'd not felt since finding Bacchus that night in the stables. Yet, some tinge of fear flickered in the pit of Sergius's gut. Byzantium and triumph lay ahead indeed, but as he prayed to the God of Yeshu, fingers interlocked with Bacchus's, watching his Caesar Augustus laugh with joy, Sergius couldn't help but feel that the future still lay in ominous shadow.

Part IV: PASSION

Chapter XXXIX.

They slogged on for months through freezing rain as it turned to swelter, back to freezing rain again and then into snow over swampland, sprawling fields, jagged mountain peaks. They stopped countless times to resupply, regroup, and declare Julian's sovereignty before the crumbled roads of the West gave way to the smooth flagstone highways of Anatolia. By the end of their trek, though the year had bore on into December, the warm air of the sea kept Sergius's awful sinuses at bay, and made the thousands of troops now following the new Caesar Augustus effervescent with morale. A joyous optimism drew smiles on the faces of infantry and cavalry alike fostered by the incredible feeling that, by some divine act, the great wars against the tribes of Gaul and Germania had finally been won. Treasure and commerce would soon heal and revitalize the land from Rome to Britain birthed by a great peace brought on by a wise and just Emperor. By the final days of their journey, though protocol among the divisions kept him from seeing Bacchus much, Sergius welled with excitement as Julian and his armies came face to face with the sea, turning East for their final entrance into Constantinople.

The sight of the Sea of Marmara brought Sergius vivid sense-memories of his childhood on the Mediterranean, of the vibrant color of the indigenous flowers and foliage and the bronze light of evening as the Sun descended below the horizon. He understood right away the nickname of the landscape: the Golden Horn A peninsula dividing the Mediterranean and its tributaries from the Black sea, it bridged the gap between trade routes of West and East, a land of melding culture and business rife with wealth, all lit from above by the magnificent Oceanic Sun.

As they neared their destination, the armies encountered more and more fellow travelers, merchants and villages, all sustained in the corona of the new Roman capitol. All welcomed Julian with cheers and fanfare as well as reverential gratitude for his troops. The Empire, it seemed, welcomed its new Caesar Augustus with open arms.

Nonetheless, no amount of flourish could prepare Sergius for the first sight of his new home. He knew the history well from his childhood studies: the city had started as a modest fishing village with an enviable location along trade routes, not to mention a unique and enviable strategic position against both land and sea attacks. With the tribal raids in the West growing ever more violent, and with the city of Rome in disarray, Constantine opted to convert the provincial town into the seat of his Empire. Seeking to recreate the glories of Rome, Constantine rebuilt Byzantium as a majestic fortress surrounded by walls of white marble, outfitted with the most advanced and meticulously planned infrastructure of roads, sewers and aqueducts found anywhere in the world and adorned with magnificent art and architecture pillaged from

The Passion of Sergius & Bacchus

Rome and Athens. With the Senate transplanted from Rome, full governance emanated from Constantine's new capitol—"Nova Roma," he'd called it. The Hellenistic populace, ever-grateful for the Emperor's investment and the deluge of commerce and growth it wrought christened it with a name of homage: Constantinople.

Sergius thought the amplitude of the midday sun must have affected his vision, but as his rubbed his eyes and pushed back the pearls of sweat from his forehead into his ebony curls, the sight of Constantinople did not forfeit its grandeur. The whole of the metropolis seemed to glow from within, spiking minarets and bulbous domes climbing into the sky as luminous as the sun itself, enwrapped in a perimeter of opulent white. He would have shielded his eyes at a sight less beguiling, but couldn't bring himself to look away from the marvel of the city, each detail of its construction becoming more recognizable with every one of Hylas's forward strides.

"By the heavens," Sergius muttered in disbelief. Julian, riding proud next to his Primercius atop Demosthenes, chuckled through a toothy grin.

"Just as you dreamed, my philosopher?" Julian asked with transparent glee.

"No, Caesar," Sergius murmured back. "No *man* could dream of such a glorious place. It's as if Heaven descended onto the Earth and left its most majestic structures behind."

"My Kingdom," Julian said with a sly arrogance, palm outstretched in a dismissive shrug.

"It looks worthy," Sergius marveled, unable to take his eyes off the city. In the distance he could see an enormous archway breaching the perfect shimmer of the white marble, the opening itself aglow with golden adornment. Julian laughed again.

"You've not even seen the palace yet," Caesar purred, only piquing Sergius's anticipation even more.

High atop the marble walls, mighty trumpets blasted, announcing the arrival of Caesar Augustus to his new home as the procession passed through the Golden Gate. Sergius almost fell off of Hylas, causing the horse to whinny and fidget to steady its rider as he observed the ornate reliefs carved in the gold and marble of the doors: detailed sculptures of Heracles and Theseus, of the Emperors of old and their conquering armies, all crowned by a golden inscription:

Theodosius adorned these places after the downfall of the tyrant. He brought a golden age who built the gate from gold.

Hylas jostled Sergius back to attention, the soldier turning back at the long parade of ranks following the Emperor, trying to catch one last glimpse of the artistry of the Gate. How he longed to examine the details up close! How wonderful, perhaps, to hire a city guide who could provide a precise history of the construction and annotated explanation of each relief! What a wonderful outing with Bacchus it would make!

Sergius pondered touring the city with his beloved, the two sharing in the triumph of their Emperor and reveling in the opulence of their new home. If Paris had fostered shy romance between the two, Constantinople would ignite passionate love, unyielding to the pressures of any social convention or religious doctrine. Nothing could sway him from making love to Bacchus at first opportunity, then exploring the city hand in hand, drinking the local wine, feasting on the native cuisine.

Sergius closed his eyes a moment, praying thanks to the God of Yeshu for this blessing—for peace, love and comfort. Though Macrina's words still wrestled in his heart, and though the regret of not undergoing baptism weighed on his shoulders, he felt the presence of the Lord with him, nestled within every throb of love he felt for Bacchus and gratitude to his Caesar Augustus.

The soft caress of a lotus petal brushing against his cheek woke Sergius from his daydream. As they rode down the Mese, the primary thoroughfare of the city, it seemed every citizen had come out to the streets hurling flowers and waving palm branches to welcome Julian home. Sergius waved and nodded to a few as he passed by, feeling a bit embarrassed at such ovation.

"Marvelous," Sergius blurted out to no one in particular.

"Marvelous?" Julian taunted. "As I say, wait until you see the palace!"

"I can't begin to imagine," Sergius replied, eyes now lit on a bronze-domed church atop a hill in the distance. Julian laughed.

"And of course…" The Emperor trailed off, tantalizing Sergius even more.

"What?" Sergius begged, sensing something even more wondrous buried in Julian's pause. Caesar laughed and turned again to his Primercius.

"I have something special for you," the Emperor teased. "Something for you and your beloved Bacchus."

"Julian!" Sergius exclaimed. In an instant he'd gritted his teeth chastising himself, calling the Emperor by name in public. Julian only smiled; the rest of the procession seemed oblivious, distracted by the cheering crowd.

"Later," Caesar declared. "For now, thank your public."

They rode on along the Mese, Sergius marveling at the city all the way. He'd never seen a city so clean and elegant, somehow encapsulating the best of the Empire and its history, still glittering with polish and newness. Rome *lived*.

Still, for all the sights of majestic churches, thriving shops, aqueducts and military installations, the first sight of the palace made Sergius gasp with awe. The procession had rode past the first two fortress walls before it even dawned on him—the Imperial Palace, Julian's new home, took up nearly a fifth of the entire city! Within the palace walls stood military barracks to house hundreds of Scholae Palatinae, a full harbor, an enormous basilica called the Hagia Sophia constructed in a mix of Hellenistic and Oriental styles. A handful of mini-palaces welcomed visiting aristocrats and a full-sized Hippodrome, a stadium constructed for every variety of sporting and gladiatorial events provided a meeting place for Emperor and beggar alike. Then there was the Emperor's residence, if a building of such size and splendor could even hold the title. Julian would live with the Senate chamber, three sets of Triklinos for his royal guard, elaborate baths, no doubt offering every amenity imaginable, and of course, Julian's own private rooms. Sergius could not even begin to imagine what brilliant mosaics and tapestries adorned those walls.

"Your uncle Constantine may have committed many terrible deeds," Sergius mused as he dismounted Hylas as the procession arrived at the Emperor's residence. "But the man had excellent style."

"My uncle was a fiend and charlatan," Julian bristled. "This decadence is a disgrace!" Sergius watched as Julian dismounted and adjusted his armor and stroked at his beard, twisting it into a perfect peak; preening before entering his new home and greeting his new staff. Sergius thought it bizarre that a man so disgusted with the vanity of his predecessors should fuss over his own looks before entering an over-indulgent palace. "He and Constantius sat on a throne of gold cushioned by silken pillows while our soldiers in the West starved!" Sergius ducked his eyes down in deference to his Emperor.

"Still," Julian muttered, climbing the steps to the Palace gates—two enormous doors of solid bronze, flanked on either side by a dozen Eastern Palatinae, their armor identical to that of the Western soldiers, albeit buffed and polished, shimmering in the daylight. "Even I must confess, it is welcoming." He cracked a smile, waving Sergius to a halt.

"I have to tour my new home," Julian said. He glanced up at the enormity of the Palace building. "And that shall take a good deal of time. I'll need your counsel again soon, Sergius. Go find your beloved. Use this opportunity to see your own new residence."

Chapter XL.

The two Palatine tried to conceal their resentment and show respect, but their sour faces betrayed their inner feelings to Sergius. For his part, Sergius could not blame them; to have to escort a soldier of the same rank—a Western one at that—to some new residence which most obviously was not part of the army triklinos cast a pall of humility over their pride. Sergius tried to show as much gratitude as he could, making polite conversation as they marched through the crowded streets of the city just south of the Palace and Hippodrome. There, in a quiet district of recently constructed estates built into the skirt of the city's so-called Second Hill, they found Bacchus sitting outside on the grassy lawn of a Byzantine residence.

The lovers made no secret of their affection, rushing into each other's embrace, sharing a long and sustained kiss between giggles of delight. Sergius couldn't stifle his own giddy laughter at seeing

Bacchus again, and for the first time relishing their triumphant arrival into Constantinople.

"Seer-ge-us," Bacchus uttered, forgetting his affected diction. "I never dreamed…"

"I know," Sergius whispered, bestowing one more kiss upon Bacchus's lips. "It's magnificent."

"Sergius, son of Maximinus," one of the escorting soldiers declared, capturing Sergius and Bacchus's attention, but not wresting either from their tight embrace. The soldier stepped forward as Sergius regarded his dark complexion—brown skin and eyes, angular nose and square jaw peeking out from under his sparkling helmet. "I am Minos, son of Anthemius; this is Tarasis," he motioned to the other shorter, barrel-chested guard, "son of Sebastian. We are Primercius of the Eastern Scholae Palatinae. Our lord Caesar Augustus has ordered us to bring you here, your new home."

Sergius and Bacchus released each other, both looking around in confusion. Only when Sergius beheld the estate house's luxury did turn back to his escorts.

"You mean…*this?*" Sergius waved to the manor.

"Indeed," said Minos, his resentment festering again. "This house, until recently belonged to one of Constantius's finance ministers. For whatever reason…" Minos paused, smacking his lips. "For whatever reason, our new Emperor sees fit that you and your companion, Bacchus, should have it." The Eastern guard reached into a leather purse, rifling around until he produced a bronze key and presented it to Sergius. Sergius gazed at the key in amazement, unable to comprehend the gift Julian had just bestowed upon him.

"What have we done to deserve this?" Sergius blathered. "We are mere soldiers, like you!"

"We do hold the same rank," Tarasis observed, his low and glottal. Minos turned to his fellow escort with an icy glare, eliciting Tarasis to grunt and duck his head, folding his arms across his chest.

"Lord Caesar holds you in the highest regard," Minos spat, his voice projected at Tarasis. He sighed and turned back to Sergius and Bacchus. "And for reasons known only to him, Caesar has gifted it to you." Minos took a step back, regarding the new residents with puzzlement. "I surely hope you have saved his life."

"He has!" Bacchus injected with pride. Minos's dark eyes shifted to Bacchus, his lips tightening over his incisors with disgust.

"I certainly hope so," Minos purred. "I would hate to think one of Constantinople's finest estates should house a pair of fornicating barbarians."

"Ve arrr Ro-Manz!" Bacchus growled, his passion igniting his native accent again. Minos's scowl turned to a bemused grimace as Bacchus realized the irony of his speech. "We are Romans," Bacchus repeated, his Germanic intonation vanishing into perfect Greek elocution. "Same as you."

"Of course," Minos conceded.

"Do you think us otherwise?" Sergius interrogated without a hint of fear. Minos and Tarasis exchanged a quizzical look.

"What matters is what Caesar thinks," Tarasis declared.

"Julian is our Emperor, chosen by God." Minos closed his eyes and swallowed. "Chosen by the gods," he corrected. "Who are we to question the wisdom of Caesar Augustus?"

"Who indeed," Sergius said, his voice flat. He clutched the key hard in his hand, both the ringed and the forked end sticking out at either end of his fist. He took a deep breath. "Thank you,

Minos and Tarasis. I look forward to knowing you both," Sergius offered with genuine gratitude.

"An honor, fellow Primercius," Minos replied, his tone far less sincere. "We bid you good evening." Both escorts gave a slight bow, then swept around and stalked off back up the hill toward the Palace. Sergius and Bacchus watched in silence as the two disappeared into the city.

"Julian flatters me," Sergius grumbled. "Though I fear to the point of embarrassment."

"They envy you," Bacchus offered, placing his hand atop Sergius's scarred shoulder. Sergius let out a deep exhalation and smiled at Bacchus.

"Of course they envy me," Sergius said with false modesty. "I have you."

"I wondered when you would arrive!" called a familiar voice. The lovers spun around to behold Didymos clad in an elegant green tunic and new sandals, his beard shorn and hair trimmed. Sergius smiled with delight; had he not employed Didymos as a house servant for years, the Primercius might have mistaken him for some traveling merchant lost in the house.

"Brother!" Sergius greeted him with glee, the two soldiers rushing forward to embrace their long-estranged friend. "How is it you've come here before us?"

"A blessing from the lord," Didymos replied, voice quaking with humility. "Our new Caesar Augustus thought it fitting I arrive with your belongings to prepare your new home." He sighed. "I must thank you both, for I never thought I would live to see my beloved Constantinople again. I've already reunited with old friends and family. It's like a dream."

"I know what you mean," Bacchus interjected. He shifted his posture over, giving Sergius a gentle brush with his body, enough to capture his lover's attention who returned the affection with a glowing smile.

"Come then," Didymos urged. "You must see your new dwelling!"

Sergius and Bacchus followed their servant into the house of stucco walls and autumn-colored tile shingles, joining hands as they crossed the threshold.

"Tell me, though," Sergius asked, "how long have you been here?"

"Three weeks, brother," said Didymos. "I received orders in Vienne to make haste here along with several of Caesar's palace servants that we might prepare your way."

"But how could you arrive here first?" Bacchus pressed.

"I needed no special urging for speed; I couldn't wait to return home," the servant answered. "Besides, I had no need to stop to supply an army or mint coins along my way." Sergius's eyes widened at the thought; the arduous slog to Constantinople had taken far longer because of the numerous stops Julian had to make to solidify his rule.

"Have you seen the new coins?" Didymos queried with jest. "The likeness to Caesar is remarkable, right down to that ridiculous goat beard he wears!"

"Not yet," Sergius replied. "We…" His voice trailed off at the first sight of the interior of the new estate: a large sitting room laden with cream-colored tile, walls adorned with white curtains covering arched windows, silk cushions stacked in a half-circle around an enormous fireplace. A doorway on the far wall lead back into a kitchen, and a staircase along the wall paved the way up to a second floor.

"These are my quarters," Didymos said with pride.

"What?!" Bacchus exclaimed.

"In Constantinople," Didymos explained, "the masters live upstairs. Come." The servant directed his masters to the staircase with an outstretched arm and a playful bow, as Sergius and Bacchus rushed up the stairs like mesmerized children beholding their first toys.

The second floor of the manor yielded even more amazement for the soldiers. There, they gazed upon a wide-open great room adorned with ornate mosaics of ivy covering the floors, elegant furniture of Eastern style—legged tables erect high off the floor, raised couches and chairs covered in cushions of green and golden silk, their arms rising in swollen, carved spirals and an ornate fireplace crested with an intricate tapestry depicting the tale of Zeus and Ganymede. Light poured in through the arched windows accented with red curtains drawn back against the wall. A dining table of some exotic wood stood next to a doorway flanked with auburn shutters thrown open to reveal a balcony with a magnificent view of the Sea of Marmara below. Sergius and Bacchus rushed out to the balcony, the gentle sea breeze kissing their faces with a delicate caress.

Sergius felt his knees go weak at the sight as he steadied himself against the stone guardrail of the balcony. He'd not beheld a place so beautiful since—

Tears welled in his eyes, as for the first time in—how long? Twenty? Twenty five—years he felt the same comfort of his estate in Hispania. He could almost hear the sound of his mother's laughter under the sound of the far off surf, see the prideful face of his father as he read the classics to the child Sergius, nestled snug on his father's knee staring at the faded words on warn parchment.

Joyous laughter sputtered out from Sergius's gut amid the heaves of sorrow, tears flowing down over his rounded cheeks.

The Passion of Sergius & Bacchus

Julian planned this, he thought. *Caesar knew exactly what he was doing.*

A gentle hand stroked Sergius's back as Bacchus pressed his face against Sergius's arm, needing no further explanation for his beloved's passionate sobs.

"Caesar is generous," Bacchus murmured. "The God of Yeshu blesses us."

"Yes," Sergius managed to whisper, his emotions too aroused to say any more. "Yes."

"Outside in the rear of the house is a small garden," Didymos gently interrupted, "with a trellis of grapevines, already rife with fruit. There's also a bedchamber prepared for two stocked with exotic perfumes and spices in bottles of colored Persian glass." He paused and cleared his throat. "As well as a large amphora of body oil."

Sergius and Bacchus both chuckled in slight embarrassment before their bondservant. Sergius wiped the tears from his face and gazed into Bacchus's amethyst eyes—how they sparkled in the coastal light of day! He took Bacchus by the hand and squeezed it tight.

"I think we'd better see this bedchamber," Sergius declared with a self-conscious giggle, leading Bacchus back inside the house.

"One last thing," Didymos begged, following his masters inside. He motioned to the dining table, a small parcel wrapped atop it. "The Emperor ordered me to present you with this, along with the manor, as small tokens of his friendship and gratitude toward the two of you." He prodded the cloth wrapping the parcel, finally managing to loose it. "I can't imagine what happened on the path of battle that the two of you should gain such high favor," he added, looking up at his masters.

"Much to tell," Sergius replied, eager to see this final gift that he and Bacchus might enjoy their new bedchamber.

Didymos removed the cloth from the parcel, revealing an ornate golden box, its faces paned with intricate glass etchings of roses. Through the clouded glass, Sergius could make out the form of a yellowed cylinder inside.

"I'm told Caesar sent for a Venetian merchant for this box. It must have come at a heavy price." He looked up to Sergius and Bacchus as he hinged back the lid with great care, unveiling a crumbling papyrus codex, bound with a plum silk ribbon.

"This, I'm told, is the real treasure," Didymos presented, hands hovering over the codex as if afraid to touch it. Sergius took a step forward, intrigued, taking the box in his hands, examining its contents. Bacchus moved in close to his beloved, studying the box and codex with awe.

"This codex tells the story of Orpheus and Eurydice," Didymos explained. "It's said to date from the time of the Punic Wars with Carthage, written in Athens."

"Unparalleled," Sergius uttered in amazement.

"Rumor has it Caesar Augustus scoured the whole of the Empire looking for an ancient copy," Didymos said, making his way to the staircase. "What favor you must hold with him!"

"We are undeserving of such luxury," Sergius declared, closing the box.

"One final revelation," Didymos added as he made his way down the stairs. "Macrina is here in Constantinople. And she wants to see you right away."

Chapter XLI.

The splendor of the bedchamber matched that of the reset of the manor. A table with a looking glass stocked with amphorae of delicate gilded glass, painted with images of flowers and vines and a magnificent bed framed in carved cherry wood with an overstuffed mattress adorned in red linen bedclothes decorated the room. Sergius and Bacchus almost felt guilty about sullying the room with their oily fornicating for hours on end. Almost.

Afterword, the couple dined on a sumptuous meal of crusted sea bass, fresh bread and a bottle of wine. Didymos had outdone himself—Sergius could not remember the last time he'd tasted fish so well prepared or, for that matter, the last time he'd even *had* fish. Still, he could see that his bondservant had found new command of his culinary talents, no doubt from the satisfaction of returning to Constantinople. It seemed the blessings of Julian's reign filtered down to even the lowest classes.

With bellies full, though not as weighty as the usual brick-in-the-gut after dining on red meat which had sustained the Palatinae for the past four years on the battlefield, Sergius and Bacchus set out to find Macrina, lead by Didymos. The night air had grown cold with wind blowing in from the sea and though not anywhere as frigid as even the warmest days of the Paris in winter, the night air had enough to make the soldiers don cloaks. They walked through the quaint and clean grid of city streets, following Didymos to a tiny insula near the sparkling fountain of the city's Great Nymphaeum. The couple paused to admire the grotto, an arched rotunda filled with plants and potted trees where citizens of all classes banded together, some just to fill pitchers with water, others to sit and socialize amid the evening torchlight. Sergius longed to mingle among the citizenry, to know his neighbors and experience a feeling of civic community he'd never known, even as a boy. But, Macrina had called, and with issues of the spirit weighing heavy on his mind since their last meeting, he and Bacchus forsook the Nymphaeum and ducked into a narrow alleyway and climbed a darkened staircase to the insula door.

Sergius knew they'd found the right place—the heavy door had a crude drawing of a fish scratched into the wood. Sergius knocked, and true to form, the door opened a crack, revealing a suspicious eye to examine its callers.

"Good evening," Didymos greeted. "We come to see Macrina. I am the Brother Didymos, and these are the soldiers Sergius and Bacchus."

"We've no need for soldiers here!" a rusty voice creaked back as the crack in the doorway began to close.

"It's alright," called a familiar voice as the door swung wide to behold the statuesque form of Macrina dressed in a toga of undyed muslin. The grey in her hair had inched longer, shimmering ebony replaced by galvanized silver twisted and braided into a bun-shape atop her head. Her skin, however, still glowed, as did her dark eyes with passion and vitality. No doubt years of travel had changed her, much as Sergius had observed his own metamorphosis of aging.

Accompanying Macrina, a tiny, frail woman dressed in a faded green tunic, white hair wiry and thinned, face lined and grey but for a few crimson patches of burst capillaries in her cheeks frowned at the two warriors, grunting with disapproval as they entered the shadowy insula. Sergius's attention fixated on the old woman's mouth, on the creases and wrinkles around her lips hinting at once robust beauty deflated by age. The twist of her disapproving scowl also suggested a deep bitterness, not just toward Roman Soldiers, but to the whole of humanity issuing silent disgust at the world around her.

"They'll have you burned, Macrina!" the old woman crowed, voice creaking. "Just as Nero burned our brethren to light the city streets!"

"You forget the Lord's teachings of hospitality and love, Phoebe," Macrina declared, raising her voice. Sergius had never heard anger spout from Macrina's words before, though he could tell from the deaconess's icy glare and tense posture, this old woman grated fast on her nerves. "We are to welcome *all* our neighbors."

"Only those who believe!" Phoebe croaked.

"They do believe!" Macrina rebutted. She walked to a window sealed by planked shutters, opening it a crack and inviting the cool night air into the room. The lamplight flickered at the current, shadows dancing with their unsteady glimmer of the sparse room, devoid of chairs or other adornments, save a thick table pushed against one wall, carved with ornate precision. Somehow a table so elegant seemed out of place in the modest surroundings.

Macrina leaned against the wall next to the open window, rubbing her high forehead with her hand, releasing a sigh. Her eyes lit up and locked with Sergius's. "You do believe, don't you? Is that not why you have come?"

Sergius and Bacchus looked at one another, exchanging a silent agreement between them. Sergius took a deep breath, held it, and met the gaze of Macrina once more.

"We do," Sergius affirmed, releasing his inhalation. "We wish to be baptized as Galileans."

The stone mask of Macrina's countenance melted into a full smile of warmth and triumph. She clasped her hands together with joy, then stretched out her arms and rushed across the room to Sergius, capturing him in a tight embrace.

"I'm so happy for you, my soldiers!" Macrina said, releasing Sergius and throwing herself into Bacchus's arms. "You will be cherished in God's Kingdom!"

"Hrmph!" Phoebe grunted, shuffling over to a table pressed against the far wall, steadying her balance at the edge. "Roman soldiers!"

Macrina spun around, her cool demeanor restored.

"If a wealthy fabric merchant can enter the Kingdom, than so can two soldiers," she answered, wresting herself from Bacchus, taking a step towards the tiny woman.

"I gave up much of my Earthly wealth to the faith!" Phoebe countered. "I host meetings in my home outside the reach of the Emperor and his converted temples! The Chi-Ro is not the sign of Yeshu, but the mark of Rome conquering the faith! Executing our brethren who will not submit to their canon of Scripture, their creed and edicts concocted by bishops appointed by a murderous, pagan Emperor! I'd give up anything in the name of Yeshu!"

"And so would Sergius and Bacchus," Macrina spat back. "A heart of stone is not a virtue espoused by the Lord! Leave us in peace!"

"I invited you here for a purpose tonight," Macrina said at last. She exhaled, wincing with her escaping breath. Her eyes glittered, dark and ominous.

"There is something you must know."

Macrina braced herself against the window sill, head bowed in thought. The others watched in silence as she reached up and undid her braids, letting her long, ebony hair—twinkles of grey scattered among the locks—fall down her back, loose and free catching against the rough weave of her muslin garb.

Without a sound, Macrina swept back across the room and collapsed to her knees before Sergius and Bacchus, placing a hand on each of their arms. She gazed with sparkling eyes at Didymos a moment, then let her head fall in thought again, breathing a deep sigh.

"My whole family has devoted itself to the spread of the Gospel," Macrina began, "to the glory of Yeshu and his message." She sighed again. "I had another brother called Naucratis, older—born between Basil and me." She raised her eyes to Sergius. "You remind me so much of him—the beauty of your youth, your talent with words, the fire in your soul. He chose to devote his life to Yeshu by caring for the elderly and sick, forsaking the temptations of the city and living a solitary life in the wilderness. He forbade any of his family to accompany him in his life as a recluse, save one: a servant named Chrysapius."

"Why would your brother allow such a thing?" Sergius questioned, intrigued. "Did he not possess your gift of stubbornness?" Sergius cracked a smile as he felt Bacchus squeeze his hand.

"Naucratis shared a great affection with Chrysapius," Macrina confessed. "They spent every moment together—meals, worship, study." She smiled, her eyes distant. "And sport! Oh how they loved athletics! Hunting! Fishing!" She laughed out her words. "They would fish every day, bringing home a fresh catch for the servants to cook for us, and with enough bounty to have a surplus to feed the starving beggars too! He found no greater joy than to fish, and always with Chrysapius at his side!"

"And yet he chose a life of solitude?" Didymos injected. "Why should he abandon such blessings? How could he serve Yeshu better in alone?"

"The life of the city proved distracting," Macrina reminisced. "Our neighbors spoke of he and Chrysapius very highly at first, but then…" She paused, running her lower incisors over her upper jaw, creating an overbite at the remembrance. She winced. "They neighbors began to speak of them too much."

Sergius could see a thought dawning on Didymos, his eyes widening at Macrina's tale. Bacchus let out a low sigh—a stifled laugh, Sergius could tell. His beloved could read the foreshadowing of Macrina's story.

"And so they left, consigned to the wilderness," Sergius added, pressing Macrina to continue. "But why together?"

"Naucratis and Chrysapius both sought to serve the God of Yeshu, to profess his message. But even they…" Macrina's voice cracked with emotion, her lips trembling, eyes flooding, shimmering in the lamplight. She nibbled at the edge of her thumb, trying to pacify her emotion with a nervous distraction, but to no avail. Sergius could see the agony building inside of her, blistering against her cool, constructed façade, threatening to envelop her in a massive explosion of sorrow and guilt. She fought back, trying to steady herself, before a primal wail finally escaped her lips. She pressed a hand over her mouth as the tears poured down her face, her mind distant and fixated on her lost brother.

"They couldn't forsake their greatest blessing," Macrina cried.

"Naucratis...he could resist any temptation, quell any desire for sinful pleasure! But he couldn't leave Chrysapius...he couldn't! They..." Her voice faltered.

"They loved each other too much," Sergius whispered, unphased by the words which frightened Macrina so.

"Great affection," Macrina reiterated, still unable to acquiesce to Sergius's observation.

"And what became of your brother?" Sergius questioned, his voice taking on a cool tone, still confrontational despite Macrina's agitation.

"We don't know," Macrina croaked through her tears. "He set out with Chrysapius one day to tend to the elderly men in his care. He hadn't been sick...his body showed no wound, but he fell on the trail clutching his chest. He died in Chrysapius's embrace." She took a deep breath, wiping the tears from her cheeks. "Some old men from their service route came and fetched townspeople to come to his aid." She stopped suddenly, her eyes again betraying her overwhelming fear.

"Why not Chrysapius?" Bacchus asked, suspicion ringing in his words. Macrina closed her eyes and gulped.

"Because he wouldn't leave Naucratis, even in death." Macrina opened her wary eyes again. "And because when the old men returned with the other villagers, Chrysapius was dead too. He cut his own throat."

Didymos grunted in shock. Bacchus clutched even harder at Sergius's hand, pulling him closer, reaching his free arm around the front of Sergius's waist. The Primercius's eyes never left Macrina, even as she tried to hide her agonized face beneath her hands.

"That was when I began to travel, to spread the Gospel," Macrina explained. "To fulfill my brother's work. And my family... none of us ever could discuss what happened. It pained our poor mother so. Basil, our brother, refuses to speak of Naucratis at all. He's afraid. He fears having to admit…"

"*You* fear that Naucratis and Chrysapius might have been…" Sergius paused, careful with his words. "That your brother and his servant might have been of the same nature as Bacchus and I."

"You don't know that!" Macrina blurted. "Naucratis had great temperance. He and Chrysapius loved each other, I am certain! But it does not mean their love was carnal!"

"Regardless…if it was," Sergius declared, "would it change his service to Yeshu? Would his love for Chrysapius be any less a blessing to him?"

"No," Macrina admitted.

"Either way then," Sergius soothed, "should not the God of Yeshu bless their union, that they might be together in this life, as well as the next?"

"You are," Macrina said, shaking her head and laughing through her tears, "silver tongued." She smiled, the warmest expression Sergius had ever seen cross her face. "So much like him." She rose to her feet, releasing a deep breath, smearing the last of her tears from her face. She fell into stoic quiet a moment, deep in thought, before the smile returned, along with the tears. "Our Lord is just." She smiled another quaking grin. "My Sergius. My Bacchus. Love is always a blessing and, for your love, and for that of Naucratis and Chrysapius, and all others of your nature… for respect to our Lord Yeshu, your love should be recognized and you two be joined that you might sin no more or less than any other lovers so blessed." She clasped her hands before her, raising her head in an officious posture. "All are welcome at Yeshu's table. You will be baptized, should you still desire it so, and, if your love is true, if you would forsake all others, than we, your Brethren, would give praise for what the Lord has given you, that you two be bonded in death as in life. As it would be in the Kingdom. As it will be for all time—life everlasting."

Chapter XLII.

Despite all their exhaustion, Sergius and Bacchus agreed to undergo baptism that very night, resolved that their souls could not wait. Macrina prepared the room with aid from Didymos and Phoebe, who produced bread and wine for a Eucharist, a pitcher of water and a great wooden bucket for anointing and set them atop the table. Also decorated with candles, crowns of grapevine and the copy of Constantine's Bible, it became a makeshift altar. Sergius and Bacchus both used the preparation time to pray on their own and reflect on the symbolism of the rite in which they would partake.

Sergius knew the history, at least in the broadest strokes. The Jews used to undergo a purification ritual by immersion in running water, just as the Gospels recorded Yeshu underwent before his ministry. Mikvah, as they called it, symbolized rebirth without sin, and converts to the faith always had to undergo the rite before joining in temple practice. The Galilean sacrament retained the same ideas of purification and rebirth, though it symbolized acceptance of Yeshu and his message as much as for forgiveness of sins. Sergius wondered if, when the water poured over his head, he might feel some magical presence of God enter his body, if his fears of death and loss might fade, his anger at the world quelled once and for all.

As the cool water moistened his ebony curls, weighting them in to sopping clumps messed against his forehead, Sergius felt no special change within him, nor did he witness visions of doves or fire enveloping his soul. Stripped to his loin cloth and kneeling in the bucket as Macrina poured, he felt only the water, nothing more.

"In the name of Yeshu, I baptize you," Macrina declared in her most sanctimonious tone. "Rise Brother, and sin no more."

Sergius climbed to his feet, the water streaming in tiny droplets over his muscled chest and rolling off his ankles. Macrina kissed him on both cheeks and directed him out of the bucket to Didymos, who greeted him with a warm smile and soft towel to dry himself.

"Peace be with you, Brother Sergius," Didymos said to his master with all the sincerity and affection of a genuine kinsman.

"Thank you, Didymos," Sergius whispered, blotting the towel over his chest. His attention leapt to Bacchus, also clad only in his loincloth as Macrina and Phoebe helped him into the bucket.

"We ought to be doing this down at the shore!" Phoebe complained. "That's the way it was done in the first days!"

"Given our new Brothers' position," Macrina observed in cool monotone, "baptizing them before the whole of the city and under Caesar's gaze might prove…compromising." She fired off an annoyed glare at the old woman. "Yeshu would understand."

Sergius watched as Bacchus knelt before the deaconess and she tipped the pitcher over his head. As the water dispersed over the sinew of Bacchus's muscled body, it's flow twinkling in the dim lamplight, Sergius could see a brief flicker of violet as Bacchus looked up to him. The Primercius sighed with satisfaction as Bacchus rose, accepted Macrina's kisses and dried himself, taking his place beside Sergius, grinning with an enlivened spirit.

With their new Brethren anointed, Phoebe and Didymos dragged the wooden bucket to a corner of the room as Macrina stepped towards the altar. She flipped through the pages of the great folio, searching for a particular passage, index finger scanning over the lettering on each page. Finding her desired Scripture, she paused a moment, letting a pregnant silence fall over the room. Raising her posture to her full height, she hesitated a moment, then turned back to her congregants.

"Brothers Sergius and Bacchus, come forward," Macrina said, palms open, arms outstretched. The two men did as she asked, just as Didymos rushed forward and gently collected the towels from his masters. The soldiers stood there, quiet with anticipation, and Sergius could feel the acid burn in his stomach again, not unlike all those moments of terror he'd lived on the battlefield. Yet this felt different, for while death symbolized the end of all things, this moment which he'd so yearned for over the course of four years –the moment when he and Bacchus could surrender all fear of abandonment or loneliness, when he could feel protected, needed and *balanced*—somehow radiated with a fierce vibration of energy. He pondered this strange agitation, at a loss to describe the emotion when a sudden realization clued him to understanding.

Sergius had started to smile, broad and wide, without even knowing it.

His heart gushed and his stomach fluttered as it dawned on him: *this is not death*, he thought. *This is joy; primal excitement!* He pursed his lips and closed his eyes. *This is life.*

Macrina took the right hands of both men and placed it atop the parchment of the Scripture.

"Face each other," she requested. Her voice took on a more officious and ceremonial character. "Where there is love, hatred does not rule, demons have no power, there is not sin. For it is said 'these three things endure—faith, hope, and the greatest of all, love.'" She handed each man a candle, then held up a lamp, nodding for each to light his own. As he lit his, Sergius felt the callous finger of Bacchus brush over his own as it lay atop the Bible. He looked up and smiled into Bacchus amethyst irises which seemed to have taken on their own incandescence. Sergius couldn't help but smile again.

"May the Lord be with you," Macrina continued.

"And with you," the four patrons replied.

"To my mind, no one has ever done this before," the deaconess mumbled. "But, it is also said 'there is nothing new under the sun.' Let us hope I satisfy the Lord!"

"Love always does," Phoebe declared with reflective wisdom, much to the shock of the others. Sergius watched the old woman's face for any sign of bitterness or disapproval, but in the glow of the Holy candlelight, he could find none. Her wrinkled lips twisted into an approving grin which, to Sergius, echoed that of his own mother. It gave him comfort.

Macrina raised her palms to the sky, cocking her head back and gazing toward the heavens as she began:

"God, who made man in your image and likeness, in this Holy place we beseech you now, that these servants, Sergius and Bacchus, become partners not bound together by blood, but worthy of unity of the Holy Spirit and in the mode of faith. Grant them to love each other and to remain unhated and without scandal all the days of

their lives. Because it is you, oh Lord, who does bless and sanctify those who trust in you in everlasting glory."

Macrina paused again to revisit the altar, this time taking the crowns of woven grapevine, their still-green leaves and fledgling, curled stems accenting the design like gems. She stretched up her toes, and placed each crown atop the heads of Sergius and Bacchus. She regarded them a moment, the clasped her hands before her and continued.

"It is through love that we glorify God, the father of our Lord Yeshu, the Anointed, who has called us together from different places to come and see the treasury of love, which all his apostles have desired and embraced as an unfading crown, and brought to God as a worthy gift. Oh Lord, who did grant to us all those things necessary for salvation and did bid us to love one another and forgive each other our failings, bless and consecrate these, thy servants who love each other with a love of the spirit and who have come here to be blessed and consecrated. Grant to them unashamed fidelity and sincere love, bestow upon them joy in thy power that they be joined together in spirit more than flesh. Forasmuch as it is you, oh Lord, who does bless and sanctify all things and yours is thy glory!"

Macrina leaned forward and snuffed out both candles, taking them from the couple and laying them aside on the altar. She took their hands from atop the Bible, guiding them to clasp together as she placed her own across their intertwining fingers. With a deep breath, she closed the book of Scripture and lifted it to Sergius's lips, then to Bacchus's, letting them both kiss the holy tome. She placed it too, back on the altar, before kissing each man on the cheek.

"Sergius and Bacchus, on this night you are made Brothers, and you are united as one by the Holy Spirit in the eyes of God and in the eyes of all your Brothers and Sisters in Yeshu." Turning again to the table, she fed each man a small crust of bread, and held the cup to their lips, letting them both sip from the chalice. "Kiss each other now, and go from this place, united forever in this world, and in the life everlasting."

The Brothers happily complied, grabbing each other and locking mouths with the same intensity as when they'd kissed on the battlefield years before. The kiss morphed into an embrace, Bacchus's heart throbbing with strength enough that Sergius could feel it through his chest, as if it were his own. He nuzzled his face down against Bacchus's shoulder, pressing his nose against Bacchus's skin, drinking in the fragrant smell of myrrh and manhood of his Brother.

"I love you," Sergius murmured, brushing his stubble against Bacchus's soft flesh. "You exalt me. My equal."

"Always," Bacchus whispered back. "Now and always."

The streets of Constantinople had quieted as the allure of nightlife gave way to the tired hours of morning, and Sergius and Bacchus found the streets deserted as they walked hand in hand back to their new estate, crowns of grapevine still atop their heads. Sergius realized he should have felt tired—between the long march into the city, the arrival at their new home, their great debates with Macrina and the ceremonies that followed, he'd exhausted more energy than in any battle—yet he felt more energized than he could ever recall.

As the road dipped down toward the sea and curved around to parallel the shore, leading up to the house, Bacchus paused, his grip on Sergius's hand anchoring the Primercius and retracting him from his blissful thoughts.

"Look," Bacchus urged, pointing out over the water. The blackness of night had begun to creep further west, replaced by a layer of lightened sky. They stood and watched for a few minutes as the violet stratum ascended higher, elevated by a layer of blood horizon as the glowing ember of the sun dawned over the city.

"A new day," Bacchus said, leaning over and kissing Sergius on the shoulder. "A new life."

"I don't think I lived until that day at Strasburg when I first saw you," Sergius chimed. He tore his gaze from the rising sun to face Bacchus. "That kiss as I lay wounded…you breathed life into me, just as God breathed into Adam. I thought death would swallow me, but you…you gave me life for the first time."

"No," Bacchus objected. "Today…" He raised their intertwining hands to his lips, bestowing a soft kiss on Sergius's. "This is life."

They kissed again, their silhouettes merging against the backlight of the rising sun, the white of their Palatinae tunics reflecting the light like an aura around them. They drank the breath from one another, oblivious to the shimmering golden domes of their adopted city and the encroaching crimson as it rose in the heavens dissolving the dark of the sky in its wake.

Chapter XLIII.

He could have spent weeks in bed with Bacchus, not speaking, not making love, but just laying there in united bliss beneath the elegant sheets, their Brother-making crowns hung on a corner of the headboard. But, as he had so many times before, Sergius found himself wrested from domestic bliss by the demands of his Emperor. Only a day after their ceremony, Julian had sent word for Sergius to meet him alone at the city's Great Harbor. The port lay along the Strait of Bosporus, a small inlet connecting the Sea of Marmara in the south with the Black Sea in the north just beyond the walls of the Great Palace. Sergius obeyed without question, and though Bacchus clamped his body in a great bear-hug, muttering objections in a half-asleep whine, the Primercius dressed himself in his formal uniform and placed his golden torque about his neck, adJustiniang himself in the looking glass as he dressed.

Though Julian had observed Sergius in the roughest of appearance, and though Sergius knew the Caesar Augustus would pay little attention to Sergius's grooming, the cosmopolitan air and majesty of Constantinople inspired Sergius to a new level of vanity. Centering his torque on his neck, Sergius's gaze drifted to the reflection of Bacchus, now clutching a pillow between his arms in place of his united. The fair skin of his bare chest and blond locks glittered like the gilded minarets and domes of the city in the morning light. Sergius looked on his beloved with tender adoration, amused and soothed by the sight of the Secondarius asleep in the bed, his muscled chest expanding and rising with each slumbered breath.

The unsupressable smile had returned to Sergius face.

Laying a soft kiss on the bare skin of Bacchus's neck, Sergius set out from the manor heading uphill into the core of the city and toward the Great Harbor. The streets already bustled with shoppers and merchants, soldiers and Senators all going about their day with a heady enthusiasm, all somehow aware that they lived in the most important city in the world. His golden torque and red and white tunic elicited many a nod and bow from passers-by, and Sergius, still wearing his broad smile, reveled with each acknowledgment. He'd waited all his life to walk the streets of the capital, and though Constantinople was not Rome proper, *Nova Roma*, as Constantine had intended to name the city upon relocation of the Senate, satisfied his wildest fantasies.

The Great Harbor on the Bosphorus only added to Sergius's excitement. The sight of dozens of vessels, from tiny fishing boats to massive naval ships crowding together in the crescent of the harbor, their masts jutting upward like the erect quills of a porcupine, sails rippling in the wind made him sigh with amazement. He stood in the midst of the cascade of carts, merchants, sailors, soldiers, barrels and nets, all making their way up and down the slope of the harbor, creaking over the weathered planks of the docks. Sergius hardly reacted when a nondescript man in a brown toga and cloak, face hidden under a hood, came and stood alongside him.

"My Philosopher," said a familiar voice. Sergius twisted around to meet with the shadowed face of Julian, a smirk like a naughty child plastered across his face.

"My lord!" Sergius cried, jumping to attention.

"Shush, calm yourself!" Julian ordered, raised palm dismissing Sergius's formality. "Don't attract attention."

"Lord Caesar…er, Julian," Sergius corrected himself. "You should not travel without Palatinae to guard you!" Julian grunted.

"I find the Palace stifling," the Emperor spat. "Hundreds of servants and bodyguards following me, fussing, *annoying* me! Not to mention that they all served my cousin or my uncle, or both. How am I to trust any of them?"

"All the more reason to travel with Palatinae," Sergius urged. "Pick men you trust, from the West!"

"Thank you for that elementary observation, Sergius," Julian droned. "Don't worry, I'll have a full escort soon enough. I merely wanted to escape the palace undetected. I come here on official business."

"Should you not wear the robes of Caesar Augustus then? Or at least the laurels?"

"You know my distaste for decadent frills of royalty," Julian reminded Sergius. "Besides, I'd have an army of lecherous Palace staff chasing me down, and while I have called you here on official business, I do not wish to distract from the real spectacle. Besides, I think it best that the citizens of our capital see their Augustus not as a god, but as a common man who stands for the interests of all of the Empire."

"And exactly what business are we here to conduct?" Sergius

questioned. He studied the Emperor's face as Julian looked out over the crowded harbor, watching for something particular.

"Closure," Julian chimed. He took a step forward and threw back his hood, letting his mahogany tresses rustle free in the sea breeze. "And here comes the Serb now."

Sergius followed the Caesar's line of sight to a stout, round soldier dressed in full regalia, hobbling his way up the slope from the docks. The shining plates and ornate designs of his armor and fluffed plumage of his helmet proclaimed his rank as a general, and judging by his slight limp, Sergius thought, an experienced one at that.

"General Jovian!" the Emperor greeted, waving and extending an open palm to the approaching soldier.

"Lord Caesar?" the general retorted in disbelief. The man stopped in his tracks, examining Julian with befuddled skepticism.

"I am he," Julian remarked, walking to meet Jovian, his arm still extended.

"I should have known by the beard!" Jovian exclaimed to himself, dropping to one knee and tearing his helmet from off his head, revealing a mess of stringy, greased dark hair like a sparrow's nest woven around a shining bald spot covering the back of his scalp.

"Enough, enough!" Julian grumbled, prompting Jovian to his feet, shaken at this unusual breach of Imperial protocol. He hesitated a moment and grasped Julian's outstretched arm at the wrist, a perceived meeting of equals rather than one rank deferring to a superior. "I welcome you back to Byzantium. A pleasure to meet you face to face at last! May I present Sergius, son of Maximinus and Batavi centurion, my personal advisor in all matters."

"A Primercius?" Jovian uttered in disbelief, looking over Sergius head-to-toe. Not knowing what else to do, Sergius extended his own hand to the general who looked at him in puzzlement.

"My Philosopher Soldier," Julian explained, annoyance in his voice. "He is my most trusted counsel."

Sensing his Caesar's frustration, Jovian shook hands with Sergius, forcing a polite smile to his face. It seemed obvious that the general had never experienced such an informal meeting with an Emperor, or, for that matter, one who valued friendship and intelligence above social status.

"Is the procession assembled and ready to march?" Julian inquired, returning to business.

"Yes, Lord Caesar," Jovian answered. "My soldiers bring the coffin as we speak."

"Good, good," the Emperor purred. "Then let the cortege begin."

Sergius, still confused by the exact nature of the business his Emperor had requested his presence to conduct, looked up to see the answer wheeling toward him. Draped in mauve fabric and adorned with vibrant flowers came a cart pulled by three soldiers on either side, its oblong cargo hidden beneath the decorations, but its contents obvious to Sergius eyes. Cased in a box of plain wood, lay the remains of Constantius, transported all the way from the Persian front for burial. Before he'd even had time to marvel at the sight before him, Julian called him back to attention.

"Gentlemen," Caesar declared. "Let us be done with this." The Emperor spun around, leading the funeral march back up into the city. As he and Jovian rushed along to keep up with Julian, Sergius could hear him utter: "at long last."

The procession took the city off guard, as the bustling citizenry fell silent. Julian led the remnant of Constantius's Eastern army, the late Augustus's body in tow, uphill through the heart of

Constantinople. Julian guided the procession ally the way to the Church of the Holy Apostles, a basilica encased in walls of bronze and capped in a golden dome that glowed as the Sun itself in the warm winter light. Julian seemed oblivious to the reverential crowds, his eyes fixated on the looming building of the church, distant in thought. With Constantius encased in a marble sarcophagus, Julian would not only have buried his most formidable enemy, but his greatest obstacle toward his desired reforms and the restoration of Paganism to the Empire.

Still, as the procession entered the cruciform walls of the Church of the Holy Apostles, Sergius marveled again at his Emperor's humility. He'd arranged a full Galilean burial for his predecessor, a man for whom he'd seethed with contempt; a man who, Sergius imagined, would not have extended the same respect to Julian were he in the coffin. Sergius glanced over at his Caesar as they walked, again marveled by his dignity.

Constantine had commissioned the Church of the Holy Apostles as a consecration of his new capitol. Designed in the shape of a cross, and adorned in etched marble, brass and gold inside and out, exterior dome constructed to withstand the torture of the elements and the interior to glorify Yeshu as God, the late emperor meant to rival St. Peter's Basilica in Rome, further intimating to the world that the majesty of Rome lived on in his new city.

The funeral ceremony within the church further dumbfounded Sergius, as a stoic Julian stared at the coffin of Constantius with icy fixation. Jovian seemed more impressed by the ornate, shimmering porticoes running the perimeter of the sanctuary up to the altar where an elderly bishop dressed in immaculate robes of white and black presided over the funeral rite, his shuffling figure accented by clouds of flowing incense hanging in censors around the coffin.

The Passion of Sergius & Bacchus

"The Galileans believe a man can live forever," Julian remarked, "which is utter folly. However, a man's ideals may grant him philosophical immortality. I am about to seal Constantius in a marble box. I must bury his principles to decay along with him."

"And yet you treat his funeral with such splendor and reverence?" Sergius pressed.

"He was Emperor of Rome," Julian observed, casting a sideways glance at the Primercius. "And since Rome is sacred, he must be treated with dignity and respect, no matter what my personal grudges against him. Besides, to take vengeance on a dead man displays pettiness of mind and spirit." The devilish smile came across his face again, turning to Sergius with relish. "Make no mistake, my Philosopher; just as Constantius rots, so will his legacy, and intend for this to mark my final visit to a house of Galilean worship. And just as I turn my back to Constantius and his faith, so will all of Rome. I shall see to that."

Chapter XLVI.

The arching hall smelled of dank mildew even in the gentle winter months along the Bosporus. Sergius plodded along behind Julian flanked by Oribasius, Bacchus and Jovian, the creaking leather of their Caligula's echoing against the red brick and mortar of the passage. Two hapless servants, each dressed in a crimson tunic with golden trim along the hems chased after them like skittish puppies, afraid to leave their master's side. Far ahead, Sergius could see an overturned half-moon of white light, the only luminescence to guide the party down the long corridor toward their destination. They moved in silence but for the sound of their sandals, beholden to the proletariat roar emanating from beyond the light.

Bacchus reached over and tapped his callous fingertips against Sergius palm, and the Primercius intertwined his beloved's digits with his own, smiling as he did. A feigned cough from Jovian tore the Brothers' attention from one another to the commander who greeted the lovers' affection with a cool gaze of disapproval. Sergius locked eyes with Jovian, defiant and unapologetic with his stare as they continued down the shadowy pathway. *And why should I care?* Sergius wondered to himself. *I've the blessing of my Emperor and my God; I take pride in the man to whom I'm joined. What more approval need I seek?*

Sergius doted on this thought as the group emerged from the tunnel, squinting in the afternoon light, the temperate breeze ruffling their tunics. As Sergius vision returned, he gasped in marvel at the most awe-inspiring sight he'd ever beheld: the Hippodrome of Constantinople. Sergius had, of course, enjoyed equestrian sport as a boy, but even in his wildest hyperbolic visions could the arena's he'd visited inspire him to imagine the splendor of the stadium before him. The sheer length alone outstretched half a dozen city blocks, even the size of the Imperial Palace itself! A great median—itself home to a magnificent collection of bronze statues plundered from the temples and shrines of the Empire—divided the elliptical racetrack down the center of a dusty plain, the earth ground to a fine powder beneath the relentless wheels of dueling chariots. Presiding from the center of the median, a three headed snake coiled into a pillar of bronze and encased in a golden tripod, regarded the spectacle in ominous silence. Rising up from the track, tiers of seats stacked atop more tiers formed a great bowl climbing toward the heavens, inviting tens of thousands of spectators to watch the events. Sergius knew as he awed at the sight that this circus had to be the greatest of its kind, the most incredible the world had ever known.

"Magnificent, is it not?" Julian chortled, jolting Sergius from his marveling. Only then did the Primercius notice his immediate surroundings—the Imperial Loge, a seating box for Caesar and his court adorned with bronze trim and flagged by purple masts bearing the emblem of golden laurels. Julian stepped to the edge of the terrace, looking out at the arena sprawled out before him. With a slight cock of the head, he raised his right hand to the crowd, inviting thundering cheers from his subjects below.

"They greet me as if I were Zeus himself," Julian spouted, raising his voice to be heard above the crowd. "No doubt Constantine planned that when he built this place." The Caesar took his seat on a throne of ivory, motioning for his courtiers to do the same at various folding chairs adorned with gold and mauve fabric about the box. Bacchus tugged at Sergius's arm with giddy excitement, taking a seat alongside Julian. As Sergius joined his beloved beside the Emperor, he caught another disapproving glare from Jovian as he plopped himself down in his own chair. Sergius grinned with defiance, prompting the general to avert his gaze in annoyance. Jovian shifted in his seat, careful to avoid eye contact with Sergius as he craned his neck to get a better view of the track below. With a grunt, Jovian rose again and snatched up his chair, thrusting it down alongside Oribasius at the opposite side of the loge from Sergius and Bacchus. The two servants stood with their arms folded behind their backs on either side of the tunnel entrance at full attention, ready to tend to any request from their host. Sergius eyed them both with pitied amazement—he'd never seen valets so nervous. He could only imagine the abuse they must have suffered under Constantius to condition them into militant submission.

"I've five pieces of gold bet on Green today," Oribasius declared, livening the mood. "I pray my horses do not disappoint!"

"Gambling again, old man?" Julian uttered. "Don't think that because I'm Augustus I shall finance your debts!" The Emperor leaned back in his chair, palms gliding over the ivory arms as his doctor grunted in embarrassment. "That kind of spoiled and unjust favor is something I would expect of the profligate Galileans." Julian turned his head to face north across the stadium at another elevated box at the head of the racetrack, this one adorned with bronze and gold and crowned by a team of four glittering bronze horses, marking the accommodations for rich aristocrats.

As Sergius examined the aristocrat loge from afar, a blasting horn trumpeted the start of another race, as four chariots, two decorated in green, two in blue, each pulled by four horses rocketed onto the track, spouting brown plumes of billowing dust behind them. A great swell of tension erupted from the stadium as nervous gamblers sprung to their feet, with other specators doing the same to maintain a view of the race. Sergius and Bacchus both leaned forward with anticipation as Oribasius leapt from his seat to the guard rail of the terrace, right fist clenched and punching at the air in anxious beguilement. Down below the chariots weaved back and forth overtaking each other, the dust thickening in their wake, obscuring the view as the racers neared the far end of the arena, the crowd screaming louder and louder as they turned around the median.

Bacchus jumped to his feet in anticipation, inspired by the crowd's excitement, and Jovian and Sergius did the same in reaction. The chariots drew close again, the curdling sinews of the horses flashing in the sunlight and detailed enough to see even from the distant Imperial loge. A blue chariot pulled up alongside a green, both competing for the win, the two drivers whipping their teams in frenzy. The blue inched ahead of the green, mere feet from the white chalk line bisecting the course denoting the finish. Just before he crossed, the green chariot lurched sideways colliding with the blue, launching the blue driver into the air as his chariot twisted and splintered, his horses yanked to the ground, collapsing into crumpled masses of flailing hooves. The green chariot crossed the finish line as the masses let out a deafening scream, Oribasius's own cry chief among them, just in time for the blue driver to land face down in the dust, leaving skid marks as he slid through the dirt. The two other drivers yanked at their reigns, diverting their chariots around the wreck, fighting to keep their balance as they did so, making for the finish line in a final act to claim some kind of victory.

But the crowd was oblivious, the triumphant green charioteer taking a victory lap at a leisurely jaunt around the track, arm raised to the screaming crowd, basking in his win. The excitement of the crowd spread right up into the Imperial loge, where Oribasius lead Jovian, Bacchus and Sergius in applauding the victor.

"Five gold pieces!" Oribasius proclaimed. "Five gold pieces!"

"I hope the blue isn't too hurt," Bacchus muttered to Sergius. The two soldiers turned to look back down at the track, as a handful of attendants rushed out to the fallen chariot—three to unteather the horses, two helping the disgraced driver to his feet.

"Oribasius should offer his services, methinks," Sergius quipped to Bacchus's delight. The physician still relished the victory, oblivious to Sergius's joke. The Primercius glanced over at Julian, hoping to have elicited some levity from the Emperor, but the Augustus sat back in his chair, fist to cheek, slouched over one of the ivory arms in thought.

"Are you alright, my lord?" Sergius asked, taking his seat next to Julian. The Caesar shifted in his throne, jarred from his brooding, glancing at Sergius as he straightened his posture. Sergius studied the Emperor's face a moment, noticing for the first time the set lines over his face, which had seeped even deeper into his skin since leaving Germania, his once ebony hair and beard now freckled with threads of silver-gray.

"Just ruminating, my Philosopher," Julian said. He sighed.

"Not sleeping again?!" Oribasius bellowed in amazement. "The most luxurious palace in all the world, your power unrivaled, and you still can't rest?"

"Concern for my Empire distracts me," Julian grunted back. "And I do not find the wretched decadence of this palace relaxing."

"And it shows in your face!" Oribasius scoffed.

Julian glared at his physician, eyes ignited with fury, at once more present than he had during the excitement of the race. Oribasius shrank back as Julian stood, purple robes rippling in the gentle breeze, his diminutive height eclipsed by his powerful charisma.

"Do you imply that I look *old*?" Julian pressed, further intimidating his doctor. Before Oribasius could answer, Julian silenced him, raising his left middle and index finger to the physician. "What say you, Bacchus?" the Emperor asked, his words slow and deliberate. Taken aback, Bacchus flinched in the sunlight, his lips moving, failing to produce any sound as he searched for tactful words.

"Well, lord Caesar," Bacchus replied at last, enunciating each word with care. "You've lived thirty years. The marks of wisdom and experience are bound to appear on the body."

"Your beloved is a poet, Sergius!" Julian laughed. He turned to one of the servants. "Fetch me a barber!" he ordered, sending the footman rushing off through the palace tunnel with a bow. "I'll not have the spider's silk creeping into my hair before I establish my administration!" His expression turned grave as he clasped his hands behind his back, eyes squinting with cunning.

"I shall weed the gray from my head to preserve my youth," Caesar declared. "An Emperor must be groomed as a testament to the sophistication of his people. And just as I would groom myself, so shall I groom Rome." He nodded to the aristocrat loge across the stadium. "Constantius may be dead, but many of his allies remain. I shall weed the old from Byzantium!" The four Imperial guests watched their Caesar with great anticipation.

"I mean to establish a tribunal," Julian explained, "to identify and reprimand those who stood behind my predecessor. Jovian, I beseech you with this task."

"Yes, lord Caesar," the commander accepted with a nod.

"Law is reason exempt from desire," Julian went on. "He who governs must observe the laws; he must recognize the nature of justice, not override it for his personal vendettas. Therefore, Sergius, you will be my eyes at this tribunal. Together, the two of you will see to it my rivals are dispensed, along with justice, regardless of evidence."

"Of course, lord Caesar," Sergius replied, "but is it not hypocrisy to insure conviction of your enemies without damning proof?"

Jovian gasped at Sergius's directness. Unlike Oribasius and Bacchus, the Eastern commander had yet to realize the Primercius's full importance to the Emperor. Jovian's incredulity only increased at Julian's reaction: a chuckle and warm smile.

"It is not hypocrisy, my Philosopher," Julian contended. "It is politics."

Before Sergius could respond, the footman returned, heaving for breath, accompanied by a flamingo of a man, his toga of green silk and gold thread, gilded belt of ornate, etched plates, each finger bearing a ring of gold, and a case of fine leather in his hand.

"Lord Augustus," the gaudy man chimed; almost seeming to sing his words. He took a slight bow and placed his case on the ground, opened it, and produced a pair of tweezers in one hand, and a pair of shears in the other, both instruments made of shimmering brass.

"I sent for a barber, not a rationalis!" Julian hissed, disgusted the decadent beautician before him.

"I am one of the palace barbers, my lord," the barber explained, oblivious to Julian's revulsion. "Now, if I may ask that you sit, I can pluck the gray right off your head!" He leaned forward with the tweezers, ready to pick. Julian caught him by the wrist, clenching it with a vice grip.

"Tell me," Julian ordered, seething anger bubbling under his words. "What are your wages, that a barber could afford to dress as an aristocrat?"

"I am paid twice the salary of a Scholae Palatinae," the barber said, words quaking with a sudden nervousness. "I also receive an ample amount of food for myself and my servants, along with fodder for all my cattle."

"A palace servant with a staff and livestock of his own?!" Julian exclaimed in utter disbelief. "You are not a barber, you are a leech! Go home and pluck the gray from your cattle and the servants from your home, and find somewhere else to plunder the Empire's wealth!"

"My lord, I…" the barber pleaded, his body trembling with fear.

"Go!" Julian ordered, motioning to the two footmen to escort the former servant from the loge. They complied, dragging the hysterical barber screaming from the Hippodrome.

"Disgusting!" Julian raged, his own bellow eclipsing the screaming pleas echoing from the tunnel. "This is Constantine's legacy! A peasant criminal for a god, and all the treasure and worship for himself! Begin the tribunals at once!" he raged, nostrils flaring as he thrust himself back down onto his throne.

Sergius took a step back from his erupting Caesar, brushing against Bacchus as he did, grasping for his beloved's hand out of instinct. Even in the bleakest of nights of the Western campaign, facing barbarian raids and civil wars, Sergius had never seen the Emperor so infuriated. Julian rubbed his temples, his face a contorted mask of frustration. Sergius squeezed Bacchus's hand, a feeling of tarring dread welling in his stomach at the sight of the Philosopher Emperor, once so controlled and hopeful, as he slumped into his throne, a neurotic and vengeful monarch.

Chapter XLV.

Sergius could not decide if he held an enviable position, or an unfortunate one. Julian poured forth his wrath onto the armies of servants at the Imperial Palace without yield. All at once, a thousand barbers, cooks, and butlers found themselves unemployed and homeless, their florid belongings reclaimed to the Imperial treasury as the Caesar reduced his staff to but a handful of aids. Julian resolved himself to proclaiming a new image of modesty and determined to smash the image of a decadent court, replacing it with one of a People's Emperor, a man who cast his gaze to his Empire, not to the heavens. Though Sergius, like most of Constantinople, thought Julian's downsizing of the palace admirable, the sight of discharged, moaning servants brought the Primercius no pleasure. Still, even faced with the option of a sight as obnoxious as former courtiers crying like spoiled children, Sergius wondered if it might be preferable to the equally pathetic commission to which Julian had assigned him.

Just across the Bosporus sat the mining town of Chalcedon,

the site of marble quarries dedicated to feeding the city's ever-growing thirst for monuments. The citizens of Constantinople held open distain for the people of Chalcedon, in general of lower class. Their city lay in constant disorder and ruin after years of invasion by Persians, Barbarians and any other would-be conqueror of Constantinople. Constantinople itself had never fallen, with the Romans' always eventual reclamation of Chalcedon, never bothering to rebuild it. Julian had selected the city as the site for his tribunals against Constantius's remaining allies, at safe distance from any sympathy the trials might invite from the citizens of Constantinople. It also removed—in public perception, anyway—from direct interference from Julian himself, further reinforcing Caesar's new model of Emperor as common man.

Even so, as Sergius kept vigil in the corner of the dilapidated great room of a crumbling manor, selected by Julian as a makeshift courthouse for dolling out punishment to those who would undermine his authority, or to whom the Caesar held personal animosity. Observers from both Constantinople and Chalcedon crowded into the house to gawk with sick fascination as a judiciary comprised of five men, handpicked by Julian, presided over the trials. Though the general did not head the committee, to Sergius's eye the real authority lay with Jovian who, despite the appearance of a balanced jury made up of unified former rivals, saw to it that Julian's will befell each of the accused, regardless of concrete evidence. In the first weeks of the trial, one-by-one each of Constantius's former advisors found their way into the court and by turns, to execution of varying brutality. None of this came as a great surprise to Sergius as he had watched the new Caesar Augustus grow weary and bitter over the past year. But nothingcould have prepared Sergius for the day Florentius found his way into the courtroom…

Though the other accused, regardless of their crimes, had all been treated with dignity before their trials, Florentius came to the court bloodied and beaten, his face greased with cosmetics, his blood soaking through a torn and worn out stola.

"The treacherous bitch at last!" Jovian proclaimed as the crumpled and shivering Florentius fell to his knees before the court. Jovian rose to his feet, circling round the plain table of court officiators, grandstanding without a hint of self-consciousness to the crowd.

"Name! Rank!" Jovian demanded, clasping his hands around his back, strutting toward his cowering defendant.

"I am Florentius, Imperial Prefect of Illyricum in Gaul under our Lord Emperor Constantius," the beaten accused sputtered. "I am a loyal Roman!"

"Loyal?" Jovian interrogated. "How can one such as you be loyal to Caesar? Did you not seek to murder our Lord Julian? Did you not side with Constantius in his attempts to treacherously execute our innocent Emperor?" Florentius's body quaked with panic, as the humiliated governor searched for some way to defend himself.

"Under Emperor Constantius," Florentius explained, "I served as an agent of Rome, loyal always to the golden laurels of Caesar Augustus! I thought only of the welfare of the Empire!"

"Lies!" Jovian spat. "Did you not also serve as an executioner to our Lord Julian's brother, Gallus?" The General paced a circle around the kneeling Prefect like a lion to its prey.

"I followed the orders of Caesar Augustus!" Florentius whimpered, voice quaking.

"And did you not falsely attest to treacherous actions on the part of Gallus? Did you not provide evidence for Gallus's execution?"

"I did," the Prefect mumbled, "always what Caesar Augustus

asked of me." His desperate eyes fluttered to meet the gaze of Jovian. "I'm a loyal Roman!" he pleaded.

"And still you would bear false witness against the Imperial bloodline…"

"I served my Caesar Augustus!" Florentius screamed back, a sparkling wad of spittle ejecting forth from between his lips. "Was he too not of royal blood? He, the cousin of Gallus, the cousin of our Caesar Augustus Julian!"

"Julian," Jovian growled, his prey finally ensnared in his trap. The general leaned down and grasped Florentius's stained cheeks, further smearing the makeup over his rough face. "And did you not try to murder our Emperor Julian while he was Caesar of the West? Did you not flee your estate in fear?"

The room fell silent but for the flutter of nesting birds in the rafters above, all eyes fixed on the unfolding trial. Sergius could feel his heart pounding into his throat, a sudden wave of sympathy for Florentius washing over him. From across the room, he could see the sparkling tears welling in Florentius's eyes—his spirit broken, the dark specter of inevitable death staring him in the face.

"You did," Jovian breathed, his quiet words audible over the silence of the room. "You plotted the death of an Emperor, and for this, there is no greater disgrace." Jovian took a step back from his prisoner, flinging his arms wide in a great, dramatic gesture. "This man plotted to kill our Emperor! He is a traitor to the crown, and a traitor to all Rome!" he bellowed. "This is his crime!"

Jovian stepped back to the table where the four other judges watched in silence. Exchanging a look with each, the general gave a slight nod, snatched up a quill, and scrawled his signature across a sheet of parchment. Scrolling it up, he held it above his head for all the room to see.

"Florentius, son of Apomodius, you stand convicted this day of false testimony against Gallus, Consul of Rome and of plotting to murder our Caesar Augustus, Julian. These are not crimes against men but against all Rome!" Jovian boomed. "You are henceforth to be taken from this place to the city of Constantinople where you are to be flogged as punishment…" He paused, crumpling the scroll in his fist, stepping toward Florentius with perfect theatricality. "And from there," he continued, his voice low and grave, "you are to be taken to the Imperial Hippodrome, where, before all eyes, you shall be burned alive!"

Florentius cried out in primal horror, crumpling to the ground as his twisted hands clawed down at the tile like some frightened beast trying to escape. He kicked and grasped at the floor, skidding about as two guards lurched him from the ground, dragging him through the crowd and outside the manor.

"Justice be pleased," Jovian uttered, passing the crumpled scroll off to another officer, taking his seat at the judicial table. "Bring in the next accused!"

But the words of the general melted into indiscernible noise as Sergius followed the agonized howls of Florentius echoing back through the courtroom. He panted for breath, eyes unflinching as all the muscles of his body tensed at once, a great chilling shock running through his system. Without a second thought, he raced out of the manor and into the slummed boulevards of Chalcedon, bathed in the warm light of evening, bolting across the flagstone pavement back to Constantinople, straight to the Imperial Palace. Straight to Caesar.

Chapter XLVI.

Sergius meandered his way through the massive walls of the Imperial Palace, his sandals creaking against the polished marble floors. Though he possessed a good sense of direction, even he could not navigate so vast and alien a structure as the Palace, doing his best to find his way to Julian's office, ignoring the disdainful looks of the Eastern soldiers or the disgust of the discharged servants as they huddled and whined like haughty peacocks, strutting their way out into the city, decadent belongings in hand. He dared not ask directions, inviting ridicule from the already resentful palace staff who regarded him as an interloper and rebel. He had, after all, served Julian in the civil war against Constantius, and though the Empire now bowed to Julian with minimal dissent, Sergius knew it would take more than a figurehead to extinguish the tensions between the armies of East and West.

After wandering the halls for what seemed like hours, Sergius at last recognized the bellowing moan of the exasperated Caesar.

Charging down the hall towards an open doorway, he strode past to Eastern Palatinae, paying them no mind as he burst into the room. There he discovered Oribasius clad in a new toga of linen dyed a majestic blue, reclining on a jasmine couch with silken upholstery. Julian, his diminutive body adorned in the Imperial robes of Caesar Augustus, watched as a pair of servants struggled to roll an enormous rug of ornate thread into a transportable cylinder that it, like most of the room's luxuries, could be removed.

"The rug, then the furniture," Julian commanded. "I want everything gilded in this room removed and sold immediately! I've an Empire to rebuild!"

"Julian!" Sergius blurted, wrought with anxious fury. The two butlers struggling with the rug dropped it to the tile floor with a loud and dusty *thunk*, shocked at a soldier's candor before Caesar.

"Sergius," Julian acknowledged with trepidation, casting a self-conscious look at the incredulous servants. The Emperor regarded his Philosopher Soldier with scrutiny, unaccustomed to seeing him behave with such abandon.

"Sergius!" Oribasius yelled, breaking the awkward tension in the room. "We have figs!" The round physician jumped up with giddy excitement, snatching a bronze tray from a table thereto unnoticed by Sergius, the platter stacked high with a pile of succulent figs just off the vine. The doctor stuffed one of the plump fruits into his mouth whole, gnawing away with glee. "You must try one!" Oribasius chewed.

"I've no taste for figs," Sergius replied, recoiling from the doctor's outstretched platter.

"Oh, the seeds, I know!" Oribasius blared with unusual volume. He shoved another fig in his mouth. "The seeds are horrid, but how can you resist?" Julian shot his doctor a sideways glare, even as he took a fig for himself from Oribasius's horde.

The Passion of Sergius & Bacchus

"The rug! Go!" Julian ordered to the servants, confounded by the scene unfolding before them. Caesar took a bite from his fig and stroked his goatish beard, his critical eye hovering over the butlers as they dragged the carpet from the room. As they exited, he turned to face Sergius, flinching with perplexity as he masticated.

"So my Philosopher, what has you so agitated?" Julian popped the remainder of the fig in his mouth and walked over to a plain wooden chair and table covered with the usual stack of maps, proclamations, letters and other papers that seemed to travel everywhere with the Emperor. He took a seat, leaning one arm across the paper stacks and propping his head with his fist. Julian took a deep breath and shut his eyes, rubbing his temples with the back of his free hand before opening his lids wide, forcing his attention to Sergius.

"Lord Caesar, I've come from the tribunal," Sergius explained. "Florentius has been sentenced to execution by incineration!"

"Welcome news," Julian scoffed, indifferent to his Primercius's angst. "Tell me, did you find him becoming in his feminine dress? You that so enjoys the flesh of men."

"One man," Sergius rebutted with venom. He gazed at Julian, stupefied by the Emperor's indifference. "What of the virtue of forgiveness, the kind you bestowed on Vadomar? Did not his allegiance benefit your rule and your spirit?"

"Spirit?" Julian hissed. He regarded Sergius, his teeth clenched. "You speak again as a fool Galilean would, Sergius. I've known you to be lofty in your mind, but never naïve."

Sergius could feel Julian's scrutinizing eyes burning into him past the flesh and into his soul. His heart thundered in his chest, sweat beading on his forehead, his blood going ice cold and curdling, clogging in his veins, suffocating him from within.

"I believed you of the same lofty mind as I," Sergius, speech enunciated and deliberate. "I thought you the Philosopher Emperor, the pragmatic, high-minded thinker who dreamed of a restored republic, of a just law for all Romans. What has changed? Have the laurels that so corrupted the minds of your predecessors poisoned yours as well?"

"I care not for your analogy to my cousin, or especially to my uncle, my Primercius," Julian quipped, demeanor cooling. "Killing Vadomar would have made him a martyr to a cause and invited only further war in the West. Sparing him showed wisdom." He twisted at the curls of his beard. "Florentius is a traitor and deserves torture and death, and so shall he have it. That is not only wise, it is just."

"I thought only courts could doll out justice," Sergius fired back.

"So it has," Julian reminded the Primercius.

"What I saw today at Chalcedon was not a court of justice, but a fixed tribunal designed to purge your enemies," Sergius insisted, eyes wide with passion.

"Your valiant devotion never ceases to amaze me," Julian laughed. He shrugged, casting his hands up in gesture of helplessness. "What higher authority is there than that of Caesar Augustus?"

"The laws of Rome govern all men, even those who wear a crown…" Sergius began.

"And so shall it be when my rule is unopposed!" Julian bellowed in interruption. "Pragmatist; was that not the word you used? How might I restore the republic if I find a dagger in my side?"

Sergius couldn't argue, for he knew that to wear the Imperial laurels meant Julian had placed an assassin's target atop his head, and to place the ideals for which they'd struggled for over the past years on the razor's edge. *What a heavy burden for one man to bear*, Sergius pondered. He watched Julian for a prolonged, quiet moment, until the abrupt noise of suckling wrestled both men from their stalemate. Both looked across the room at Oribasius, sprawled across the couch, platter in his lap, as he sucked and picked at a fig seed lodged between his molars. Julian scowled, prompting the doctor to leap to his feet, dumping the tray and scattering the fruit across the floor. Oribasius stood, his face red with embarrassment for a silent moment, before all three men erupted into relieving laughter.

The two servants, both their togas sopping with perspiration, rushed back into the room at the sound of the reverberating tray. Both froze at the sight of the cackling Emperor, unaccustomed to humanity in their leaders. Oribasius grabbed the tray from the floor and swatted at the air, motioning for the dumbstruck two to gather the mess of figs without question. Sergius and Julian watched the three men scurry about cleaning up after the doctor, the physician chasing the other two from the room, his plump body giggling as he followed.

Julian turned back to Sergius, their glad eyes meeting and alleviating the acrimony between the two. Caesar rose to his feet, arms outstretched and embraced Sergius at the Primercius's shoulders.

"You are truly my brother, Sergius," the Emperor said, "for no other man could possess so stubborn convictions but you and me." He sighed. "Florentius will die; on this my mind is set. However I will need your counsel in the next step in restoration of a true Roman republic."

"My lord?" Sergius asked in puzzlement.

"I've set forward an initiative," Julian began, placing his arms behind his back, moving back toward the cluttered table, glancing down at the strewn papers. "I shall restore the gods of Rome to their rightful temples, but I shall not force their worship as Constantine did with the Galilean, nor persecute those who would reject them as Caligula did. I've sent letters to Hillel, a chief Rabbi here in the city, as well as to a Galilean I knew in Athens with the hopes we can convene a counsel on religion and establish polices regarding practice and taxation across the Empire."

"Lord Caesar," Sergius stammered. "Julian…such a counsel has never happened in the history of Rome! You surely will preside over a new golden age of the republic!"

"I hope," Julian uttered with a sigh. "The Jews are a sensible and educated people, despite their absurd laws of Moses. The Galileans…" He raised both eyebrows in awed realization. "The Galileans are irrational, babbling hypocrites who take pride in ignorance and utter stupidity. Still, Basil is an educated man. That offers hope."

Sergius cocked his head to the side like a curious sparrow, observing Julian, excitement flickering in his chest.

"Basil?" Sergius asked, careful not to sound too anxious.

"Yes, the bishop," Julian elaborated. "Basil of Caesarea."

Chapter XLVII.

"Macrina's brother?" Bacchus gasped, tightening his grip around Sergius. The pair lay in bed, cool air from the sea drifting in through the house and into their bedchamber, seeping through their blankets and kissing their skin into gooseflesh. They held their naked bodies together for heat, and Sergius found himself grinning with satisfaction at the sensual battle of dry, frigid cold and the hot moisture emanating and reflecting off his and Bacchus's bodies. He nestled close to his beloved, relishing the tickle of Bacchus's soft, blond body hair as it caught on the coarse wisps of his own. He lay a kiss atop Bacchus's forehead and sighed.

"I'm certain," Sergius answered. "Basil of Caesarea now holds more influence over the Empire than any other Galilean. Pay he comes to Caesar's aid."

"No," Bacchus whispered. "There is one who holds more." He rolled over on top of Sergius, their legs weaving together, Bacchus's golden hair shimmering in the pale glow of the moon. Sergius smiled again, this time a full-blown toothy grin, looking away in flattered self-consciousness. Bacchus leaned down and nuzzled Sergius's cheek, his nose brushing the prickles of his Spaniard face, laying a peck at the crux of his jaw.

"Caesar holds my opinion in high regard, but I am still only a soldier," Sergius contended, his dark eyes gazing back into the purple of Bacchus's own.

"He trusts you," Bacchus insisted.

"This I know," Sergius ceded. "But his loathing and distrust of Galileans…he could not accept a Primercius of the faith. Not even me."

Bacchus sank his face down into the pillow beneath them, as Sergius reached up with his lips and suckled at Bacchus's ear lobe. The Secondarius giggled and writhed, his head popping back up; grimace so wide the socket of his lost molar came into view. Sergius thought it a flaw in an otherwise perfect gem, elevating it beyond the superlative into the only higher pantheon: the unique, a model crafted in the hands of the divine, unparalleled in the entire world.

"Julian trusts Basil, or at least respects him enough to invite his counsel," Sergius elaborated. "He knows him. That is worth something. It gives me hope." He ran his fingers up along Bacchus's spine letting his fingers web into an embrace. "Besides, I've greater concerns."

"What is greater than your faith?" Bacchus asked.

"My source of it," Sergius cooed. "You. My allegiance to Rome and to Caesar have not diminished, nor has my faith in Yeshu. But my heart desires greater riches."

"What?"

"Life with you. My beloved." Sergius shut his eyes a moment, scoffing. "And yet the word seems not enough to proclaim my affection for you. What should I call you? Brother? Husband? No title seems great enough for you."

"Call me what you will," Bacchus said, his body stiffening against Sergius's. "Say what you please, so long as it means you love me. I am yours."

"You could never belong to me, Bacchus. I love you too much; you are so much more. I hold you not in my heart, nor in my soul, for neither could encompass the vastness of my love for you. You are as my flesh, as my spirit itself, not one with it; but all of it."

"Then we are one, as Macrina has said," Bacchus whispered. "God has made it so."

Their lips met in a tender, gentle kiss, less an act of carnal lust than a very breath sustaining the life of the both of them.

"I worry for Rome, and I worry for our Brother and Sister Galileans," Bacchus said when at last their mouths parted. "You must do what you believe is right in your heart."

"Life with you: that is my now, my future, my always." Sergius reached up, pushing back Bacchus's tangled golden hair from his forehead. Bacchus leaned in and kissed him again, then rolled onto his side, arms wrapped about Sergius's waist, pulling him close and tight again. The two lay silent together a long moment, just staring up at the ceiling into the dim light, contemplative.

"I wish my Grandfather could have known you. And my mother." Bacchus words rippled into the quiet darkness. "What pride they would have that I should unite with you!"

"Would they not object to my sex?" Sergius asked, only half in jest.

"No," Bacchus purred. "Grandfather loved me despite my low birth and claimed me as his own. Mother loved me, though I served as a living reminder of her rape and torture by barbarians." He paused a moment in thought, then let out a deep sigh. "They would love me no matter what. And they would love you: a wise, handsome Roman." Sergius giggled at the flattery. The two fell silent again.

"Do you ever think of it Bacchus? Being a father? Raising Roman sons?"

Bacchus's head slowly levitated up to look down into Sergius's face, his arm propping up to hold his cranium in place over his beloved, eyes narrowed but glinting with a sparkle of pure enchantment.

"I have, many times," Bacchus admitted. "And I have thought what a great father you would make. But I fear that no approval from Caesar, no divine blessing from Yeshu could gift to either of us a womb."

Sergius concurred with a grim nod. His thoughts drifted to his father's razed estate, to the crushing loneliness and fear, the utter hopelessness of knowing he was alone in the world. Still, he had known his family. He had sat and learned the classics with his father. He had known the warmth and comfort of his mother's embrace. *What despair a child who never knew the love of a parent must feel!* he pondered. His thoughts lit on a man he'd not thought of in years: Justinian, raised in the Paris brothel, from all those years ago. Though he'd lusted for Justinian's body, though he felt a great passion for the young man, it was not love like he felt for Bacchus, not the yearning he'd known since he kissed his beloved for the first time on the battlefield of Strasburg, but a swelling of pity, the affection of compassion at the horrible acts the child Justinian must have submitted to for survival. *What an affront to Rome! What a disgrace in the eyes of God!*

"Rome births orphans every day," Sergius observed at last, his voice grave and coarse. "Why should we not offer them love and shelter? Why should they not know the love of a parent? Yeshu teaches that we must love one another, that we must do all we can to ease suffering in this world. And how could Julian object to a child provided with an education and a loyalty to the Empire? How could a childhood of death and plague and starvation and desperate torment be better than the love of two of his favorite Palatinae?"

Bacchus chuckled, watching Sergius's expression for some indication of jest. A moment, past, and finding no insincerity, Bacchus exploded into full, joyous laughter, cuddling Sergius tight in his arms. "Fathers!" he exclaimed, laying a kiss on Sergius's neck.

"Let us go to Macrina," Sergius declared. "Through the Galilean charities, she must certainly know of children needing parents."

"Sons!" Bacchus proclaimed at full volume. "Our sons!" He and Sergius kissed again, their bodies grinding together, hands probing every contour of each other's warm flesh. Bacchus pulled back aglow with delight, hands moving down around the sinew of Sergius's waist. "What a shame that we cannot enjoy the pleasures of conception!"

"Why shouldn't we?" Sergius grinned. "God will grace us with a child; why shouldn't we act as if it came from our seed?"

Bacchus leapt from the bed, flinging back the blanket and letting the cold night air pour over Sergius's naked flesh. Sergius yelped and contorted his body, clawing for the sidelined blanket to insulate himself from the cold. Bacchus seemed not to notice as he hopped to the vanity table, the cold tile of the floor stinging his feet. He rummaged around in the dark, then skipped back to the bed and jumping atop the mattress, burroughing under the covers next to Sergius, a bottle of oil in his hand. He removed the stopper from the bottle, and dripped the lubricant over his palm, rubbing it between his fingers, letting it warm with the friction.

He placed the open vial on the floor next to the bed and nestled close to Sergius.

"Then let us conceive this night," Bacchus whispered, reaching down with his oiled hand, rubbing it over Sergius's hardening organ. Sergius's body shuddered at the sensation of the warm oil on his body as Bacchus's hand moved from his body to his own, massaging the remainder of the oil between his legs. They kissed, Bacchus leaping atop Sergius with primal instinct, their two bodies sliding together into one, making love with total abandon until dawn.

Chapter XLVIII.

Sergius had never heard such wails, not even in the most butchering of combat. The flames rose higher and higher into the moonless sky, dwarfed only by the billowing ashen plumes of smoke cresting for miles over the land. From their base, eclipsing the dyne of crackling wood and a screaming crowd, an obelisk of charred mortar stood erect in the destruction, and bound to it, the mouth of the agony: Florentius, head shaved, adorned in a naphtha-soaked tunic, its fibers reddish-brown with the flammable liquid. Coiled rope held him to the stake, freezing his limbs and body to the slab, leaving only his head to writhe in turmoil.

From his vantage point, Sergius could see the tiny glint of tears rolling down Florentius's face as he twisted his head back and forth in futility, trying to escape the encroaching smoke and heat. The disgraced Prefect mewled and screamed like an infant, banging his head against the obelisk in frustration, leaving a crimson splattering against the blackened pillar. His cries for mercy had turned to primal sputtering and choking as the inky smoke poured into his lungs, bringing about slow asphyxiation as his face reddened and blistered from the heat.

This kind of death—this pitiful, helpless, mocked and loathed desecration of the body and the soul—had haunted Sergius for so many years, only to shrink in the light of Bacchus's love. Sergius hadn't pondered death in months, and now here stood the undiscriminating harbinger of oblivion again, ready as ever to consume anything it desired.

"Lord God of Yeshu," Florentius cried, his voice coarse as sand, "protect me!"

A tear brimmed in Sergius's eye, and the Primercius turned from the execution flames and strode back through the darkness toward the gates of the city. Julian felt no remorse or hesitation for his sentencing of Florentius, and Sergius understood why— the man had committed sedition. The question nagging at Sergius with sudden ferocity was *why* Florentius had done it. Out of simple loyalty to Constantius? Out of avarice and lust for power? Or did he suspect Julian's pagan leanings, and did he stand with Constantius in the name of Yeshu, out of faithful obligation to Constantine's version of the faith? That Constantine had altered the application of Yeshu's teachings didn't matter; the Apostle Paul had done the same, as had many other teachers in the three hundred years since Yeshu's time often out of necessity, adapting Yeshu's philosophy to new crises and situations. That the fundamental axiom of the faith—belief in Yeshu's commandment of love, and in life eternal—remained unrevised mattered above all else. Florentius, in some way, had chosen to die for his faith.

Sergius stopped along the path toward the Mese and looked back at the engorging blaze, sympathy bubbling in his chest for Florentius, a man he so despised—a traitor yes, but one of conviction. Starting along the path again, Sergius closed his eyes in silent prayer: *Yeshu, may all the tormented souls of this world find peace in your Kingdom. And please, for the sake of the faithful, send Basil to help me sway Caesar's wrath.*

Chapter XLIX.

"Thank you Rabbi, for your insight," Julian said, rising to his feet. "Constantius's slaughter and suppression of your people is an affront to common sense as well as Roman principle." He paused, clearing his throat. "But I look forward to ending that portion of history." Julian's eyes darted to the entry to his study, spying Sergius who had entered in quiet reverence.

"Ah, my Philosopher!" Julian welcomed, his arm outstretched in greeting to Sergius. "Rabbi Hillel, this is Sergius, son of Maximinius, one of my Palatinae from Hispania." The Rabbi, an ancient man with ashen, almost translucent skin, white hair sprouting from beneath a skullcap, small eyes, a round face, and dressed in traditional Semitic flowing, white robes stood to greet Sergius with a nod. Sergius nodded back, casting a glance, surveying the room. All of the opulent furniture, including Oribasius beloved couch, had been removed, replaced by simple furnishings of plain wood. Julian had cleared his worktable for his guest, leaving only a few documents, no doubt pertaining to the treatment of Jews in the Empire scattered across the tabletop, along with a few trays of well-prepared lamb, hummus, olives and matzos.

"Soldier," Hillel acknowledged through a thick accent. Sergius could tell that, while fluent in Greek by necessity, Hillel more often spoke Hebrew. The Rabbi turned back to Caesar. "Emperor, my people have too often in our history been fed platitudes of tolerance only to meet with the blade of suffering. How should I believe one more?"

"Because Rabbi," Julian oozed, speech dripping with all the aristocratic charm he could muster. "I am well educated in your history, and of Jewish tradition. I offered you hospitality by welcoming you into my home. I presented you with food prepared according to your Kosher laws. And..." Julian raised his right hand, index and middle finger extended to punctuate his words. "...In the first place, your people are my people as well."

"Than I can trust your word," Hillel said, eyes narrowed with thoughtful deliberation.

"Trust not my words, Rabbi, but my actions." Julian lifted a page from the table and handed it to Hillel for examination. "Henceforward no one will be able to oppress the Jewish people by the collection of disproportionate taxes, so that everywhere throughout my Kingdom you may be free Romans. And as the ultimate gesture of brotherhood between Jew and Roman Gentile I shall restore the Holy Temple of Jerusalem, and rebuild it at my own expense, as you have for so many years desired it restored."

Hillel gazed over the page which quaked between his nervous fingers, their joints swollen and inflamed. He squinted, raising his lip over his upper teeth, revealing them as gnarled with age, holding his breath in deliberation.

"Than so shall the Jews be Romans at last," Hillel said, handing the edict back to Julian. Caesar smiled and embraced the Rabbi, who returned the gesture with awkward discomfort.

"Brothers!" Julian proclaimed, firing off a playful glance at Sergius. He released Hillel, motioning him to the door. The Emperor called for a guard, and with a few last formalities, had him escorted from the palace. A triumphant Julian spun around with a look of frenzied excitement on his face, grinning ear to ear at Sergius.

"I've done it, Sergius!" the Emperor said, pounding his fists in the air before his chest. Sergius could see the tendons of his fingers bulging out from beneath the layers of skin. "I've ended the anti-Semitic practices of my predecessors! Jews will no longer suffer at the mercy of Rome!"

"I had no idea you possessed such affection for Jews, Julian," Sergius admitted, almost needing to stifle his own laughter.

"The Jews are a studied and thoughtful people, even if they cling to the absurdities of Mosaic Law, keeping pointless diets and hacking at the genitalsof their sons in honor a nameless deity" Julian explained. "They should be allies of a unified Rome even if the refuse to bend to Roman customs. I'll no longer need to send troops to quell riots at Passover, and they shall once again be allowed in Jerusalem without fear of revolt. No more Masadas."

"A bold exercise, my Caesar," Sergius chimed, his eyes widening at the thought of Jewish inclusion. "With alliances with Vadomar in the west, Euhemerus in Ethiopia to the south, and no need for constant military action along the Sinai, that leaves only the Eastern Campaign against the Persians."

"And with our armies focused there, Rome will retake the orient, and once again the Empire will stand united!" Julian laughed with giddy joy.

"But what of the lost revenue from the reduced taxation of the

Jewish people?" Sergius asked, stepping to Julian's side, glancing down at the proclamation in the Emperor's hand.

"The Galileans," Julian answered with curt diction. "Constantine gave the Galilean churches and clergy tax exemption when he converted the Empire. Now they shall pay their own fair share. It's the first step in extinguishing their preposterous and offensive faith for all time."

Sergius's stomach burned at Julian's words. The warmth of his blood drained from his face, replaced by frigid tingling as his jaw loosened in shock.

"But what of Basil?" Sergius pleaded, careful not to sound too desperate. "I thought you wished to make inroads with the Galilean clergy?"

"Basil," Julian spat, "refuses my invitation, calling me a heathen." He scoffed. "I knew him once, Sergius. His oration skills were matched only by my own. What a great Senator he could have made! But instead he preaches ignorance and treason, even as he lives off the tithing of his followers. I shall end him, and his religion, once and for all."

"You propose to massacre them, even as you condemn such action against the Jews?" Sergius uttered in panic.

"These are the robes of an Emperor, not a butcher!" Caesar yelled back in offense. "You should know that Primercius!"

Sergius froze in place at Julian's wrath as the Emperor approached him, pacing in a circle like a tiger to a hare.

"Your continued affection for the Galilean fools unnerves me, Sergius. Were you not my best friend, my brother, had you not struggled in battles along side me for the Roman cause, I might think you one of them." Sergius tried to conceal his frantic panting, averting his eyes from the securitizing glare of Caesar. "But you are too educated a man for that," Julian concluded.

The Passion of Sergius & Bacchus

"Still," Julian declared, striding across the room, his footsteps echoing against the bare walls, "you do know the Galilean belief. You have familiarized yourself with their customs. Do you know not of their prophecies?"

"You mean that Yeshu will return to lead a new order?" the Primercius stammered. He watched as Julian riffled through the papers on his table, finally producing a folded document, which he unfurled to cover the surface of the slab. The Emperor smoothed it with his hands, a glimmer in his dark eyes betraying thoughts of sadistic pleasure.

"The order of Yeshu will replace Rome," Julian reminded Sergius, hunched over the table, eyes darting up in a glare. "In Jerusalem of all places. If you need further evidence of the Galilean stupidity, look no further than the filth they would make their capitol, their Heaven on Earth."

"This is about Jerusalem?" Sergius questioned, his voice flat and grave.

"In a manner of speaking. It is said that Yeshu's return will be heralded by the rebuilt Jewish temple. It was, of course, destroyed in the Great Revolt under the Emperor Vespasian—against his wishes, mind you! The Zealots forced his hand."

"And what has this to do with the Galileans?" Sergius pressed. Julian smirked, beckoning that Sergius join him at the table.

"The Galileans believe that only their Messiah can rebuild the temple. Imagine their shock when it is not Yeshu that lays the first stone, but his great *satan* Caesar!"

Sergius looked down upon the creased page, the drafted architecture unmistakable: plans for the Holy Temple of Jerusalem, realized again upon the very broken stones which had once held the mortar of the most holy site in Judaism. Yeshu had predicted its destruction, and that only he could see it raised once again in glory to the One God. Julian hadn't just concocted a plan to rebuild some historical monument, or even to placate the Jews. He'd found a way to prove Yeshu as a false prophet and end the Galilean faith for all time!

Sergius stared at the plans, Julian's elaboration on the construction details falling deaf on his ears. He wished Bacchus was with him, just for simple comfort, but knew that even his beloved could offer no counsel, no solution to this crisis of faith. Only Macrina, the deaconess with all her spiritual insight, could do that, and even then, when she learned of this plan, what hope could she present for this crisis of faith, perhaps the greatest since Yeshu's execution?

Chapter L.

Sergius could not believe his ears. He and Bacchus had journeyed hundreds of miles, fought in countless battles and faced innumerable threats to their lives. But, as they sat opposite Macrina and Didymos, the four of them forming a rough circle on the floor in the middle of the shadowy room of the deaconess's insula, the Primercius couldn't help but grind his molars in frustration.

"Never before has a Brother held a position of such influence with the Emperor," Macrina observed, voice insistent, even desperate. "You must protect the Galilean faith from this Apostate at all costs. You have a duty to your Brothers and Sisters in Yeshu to uphold the faith and protect them from the Great Adversary. You are your Brother's keeper."

"And which version of the faith might that be?" Sergius asked, turning combative in his frustration. "Yours? Constantine's? And what of the other cults that follow the other gospels, of Peter or Thomas or Judas?"

"The fear permeates all communities of would-be Galileans," Macrina contended, her own impatience apparent. "They fear a pagan Emperor."

"Julian is not a man to fear," Sergius replied. He paused a moment in thought. "Or at least, he's not a man to fear over the question of religion. He desires peace above all things, the restoration of Rome to her former glory."

"He is rebuilding the Temple of Jerusalem!" Macrina exclaimed. "If he succeeds…"

"He can't," Sergius interrupted. "Or else our Lord Yeshu *is* the charlatan the Emperor believes him to be. You must understand his hostility," Sergius pleaded. "Julian lost his whole family in the name of Yeshu!"

"In the name of the Empire," Macrina corrected. "Those who kill in the name of Yeshu know not his teachings." Sergius nodded in deference, knowing the deaconess spoke the truth.

"I will do what I can," Sergius assured them. "I shall always speak my conscience; truth is a virtue espoused by Yeshu and one that Caesar Augustus treasures in my counsel."

"And at vat kossst?" Bacchus interjected, fury bubbling in his face. "Vat rizk must my hoozbant make?"

Macrina and Didymos stared at Bacchus a moment, trying to decipher his words buried under his Germanic accent.

"Sergius is not your husband," Macrina declared, bristling at the suggestion.

"He iz…" Bacchus stopped himself, forcing proper articulation into his speech. "He is my beloved. My husband. Brother. We are one by any name. And you ask him to risk his position, even his freedom to plead with Caesar over a *building*?"

"Yeshu preached self-sacrifice above all else," Didymos observed, his voice low, tone reflective.

"Love," Bacchus rebutted. "Yeshu preached love."

"And what would you sacrifice for your love of Sergius?" Macrina pressed, her face the same stone-mask it had been all those years before at their first meeting. A beat of silence passed between the four.

"You know," Bacchus said flatly.

"And what would you sacrifice for Yeshu?" Didymos added.

Sergius and Bacchus looked at one another, the latter taking his beloved's hand between his own callous fingers. They gazed into each other's eyes, amethyst meeting deep chestnut, looking beyond the sparkling pools of color into the soul within.

"Bacchus is my greatest gift," Sergius uttered. "And I would sacrifice my very life for him, for the Lord that brought us together. Any less would insult the blessing of his love, or the joy he brings to my life. Yeshu asked that of Judas." Sergius's eyes met those of the deaconess and his servant. "Judas did not betray Yeshu as some say, but helped him complete his plan of salvation, if we are to believe the Gospel. And while Judas and our Lord did not love each other in the nature Bacchus and I do, their bond of friendship was just as strong in its own way."

"You speak deep wisdom, Sergius," Macrina whispered, averting his gaze, somehow ashamed. "And I've no right to ask you to sacrifice more, or to speak on Yeshu's behalf." She rose to her feet, her plain toga draping limp and shapeless over her body. "Only you must decide what He would ask of you. I shall pray for you regardless."

"I will do all I can," Sergius agreed, rising to meet her. Bacchus stood up along side him. "Just as I'm sure we all will. And I shall pray for you too, deaconess."

"Let it be so," Macrina whispered, her dark eyes glittering with moisture and pride. Yeshu be with you."

"Let it be so," Sergius repeated, reaching for Bacchus's hand without breaking his gaze at Macrina. The two soldiers walked to the door, ready to take leave, when they noticed their servant still on the floor, slouched over, eyes distant.

"Didymos?" Bacchus said.

"Let it be so," Didymos whispered, eyes lost in oblivion, unwavered by the call of his master. He stared into the darkness, unmoving a moment, before jumping to his feet and opening the door for Sergius and Bacchus. The servant never met the gaze of his masters, nor that of Macrina; he just stared down at the tile floor, distant.

Chapter LI.

Sergius wriggled his toes at the irritating dust and gravel seeping up into his Caligulas, the laced hide of the sandals creaking with his flexing feet. The cool breeze of winter had intruded from midday sun blazing vivid in the spring heavens, lighting the bronze spires of the city with a warm glow, a gentle wind breathing life to the scenery. The perfect weather made Sergius long to lay beside Bacchus under a tree or on the shore, a bottle of wine split between them, the music of his lyre charming and arousing Sergius's sprits. Yet that afternoon, Sergius found himself called to other duties.

The high walls of the empty Hippodrome made the Primercius sigh with humility, dwarfed by so large and grandiose a building. What Roman splendor! What a testament to the glory of the Empire! Still, despite his wonder, as he paced laps around the racetrack median alongside his Caesar Augustus Sergius felt troubled by some ethereal dread, the source of which he could not ascertain. Moreover, Julian's eyes, sunken in darkened sockets encompassing his eyes and the sandy, deep set wrinkles on his temples and forehead betrayed the Emperor's own inner furor. He kept his right arm clutched about his abdomen, face muscles contracting with the rhythm of each step, taking regular sips from a goblet of runny, white fluid.

"Goat's milk," Julian grunted between gulps. "Oribasius says it will quell the burning stomach." He took another swig. "I fear my physician has lost his wits; the drink does nothing but offend my taste."

"And what is the cause of such sour digestion?" Sergius inquired with soothing tone. Julian shrugged.

"Perhaps the Gods just hate me," the Emperor scoffed. Sergius chuckled at the joke, unsure of the Emperor's sincerity. Julian looked at his Philosopher Soldier and gave a weary smile. "My physician blames the stomach pains on the burden of ruling," Caesar explained. "He says the same of the headaches and the sleeplessness. And the fits of melancholy. His recommendation is to drink goat's milk and take a daily jaunt to relieve my thoughts."

"And do you find the relief you seek?" Sergius asked. Julian gave a crooked smile.

"The weight of the laurels offers no reprieve, my brother," Julian uttered. "I fear I shall only know peace when at last I meet death, my soul relegated to oblivion." Julian revisited his goblet, frowning at the taste of the milk before casting it from the cup onto the dusty path. He grunted, clutching at his burning stomach again. "Tell me," the Emperor said, trying his best to raise his spirits, "what of Bacchus these days?"

"He takes on stable duty," Sergius purred with a grin. "My beloved finds Byzantium far more hospitable than his native lands of the West."

"What fool commander relegated him to stable duty again?"

Julian spat in anger. "He owns the strength of ten soldiers, and with greater wisdom!"

"He requested it, Julian," Sergius explained. "The soldiers of the East regard him as some barbarian intruder, even more so than the Western ranks. Besides, he's a love of animals and, I suppose, spending the day with Hylas is some substitute for my own presence."

"I hope not in all matters," Julian joked, a genuine smile crossing his face for only a moment before the pain of his stomach again soured his expression.

"No, no," Sergius laughed. "In the carnal regard, I believe I satisfy him more than enough."

"If only you could restrain your lusts," Julian mused. "What greater works you could accomplish!"

"You are not the first to suggest that," Sergius admitted. "But in my union with Bacchus, I believe I find a deeper wisdom." Sergius turned to Julian and smiled. The Emperor met his expression with rolling eyes and a shuddering grunt, shaking his head in disapproval.

The two rounded the end of the track, turning south around the median, pacing back toward the direction they had come. They walked in silence a few moments, as Sergius studied Julian's face, his gaze having detached into some far-off distraction. Sergius believed, though he would never utter such a thought, that in distant moments such as this, Julian's thoughts lit on Helena, and of the life he might have had as a husband and father. No doubt the love of a family could ease the pains of ruling and offer true reprieve from his angst, much as Bacchus's love had for Sergius. But Julian, Sergius realized, who had known only pain and fear from allowing himself to love would never again allow himself the joy of affection. Now, there was only Rome.

"Shapur, king of Persia, has made an advance on our front lines in the East and our time for offense has come," Julian declared, much to Sergius's alarm. "I've assigned Jovian to devise a plan of attack based from Antioch. We will soon have to march."

Sergius's blood flooded with adrenaline at the thought of returning to battle. He felt his palms wet and begin to tingle, his calf muscles spasming, heart pattering. Sergius realized that he had neither desire—nor anticipation—of returning to the battlefield; indeed, he thought that his days of killing lay behind him in the forests of Germania. No, Julian ruled supreme! He and Bacchus had united in the eyes of God and with the Anointed One's blessing! They desired children and domesticity! Why should Caesar force them to risk their lives and spill more blood!?

"My lord Caesar," Sergius pleaded, "please spare Bacchus and I this service. We've found tranquility and happiness here in Byzantium. Let us stay here as your deputies, enforcing your laws!"

Julian stopped in his tracks, regarding Sergius with his wary eyes, a flicker of sympathy lighting in the dark pools of his irises. He stroked his curly beard in a moment of consideration and sighed.

"Sergius," Julian enunciated. "I need your wisdom and Bacchus's strength. Many of these Eastern troops are still loyal to Constantius, or at least suspicious of my rule. I need loyal advisors with me on this campaign. It's certain to be as hard-fought as those against the Alemanni. I need you at my side."

Sergius stared at the Emperor, his diminutive figure wrapped in robes of wine with golden thread made even smaller by the great arena around them. He locked eyes with his friend, his Caesar, the one he would call brother, the man who he'd fought for, who he'd shared his dreams with, the most powerful human being in all the world for whom Sergius had felt no fear, only camaraderie. All at once, he could feel an overpowering sensation boiling, vibrating with furious magnitude deep in his chest; shapeless, Vesuvian anger that he'd never felt before, not even when laying eyes on his family's destroyed estate for the first time. He clenched his jaw, trying to resist the spillage of his resentment, but no amount of restraint could suppress his emotion.

"Why Julian!?" Sergius cried, balling his fists with rage. "How will conquest restore the republic? What threat is Shapur?" Sergius flailed his arms about his head and shoulders, as if fighting off an army of ravenous falcons. Julian's eyes froze at the sight. "Send emissaries to end the war! Take your battle to the senate and fight with wisdom, not swords! Has not enough blood washed over the world in the name of Rome?" Sergius clawed at the ebony curls of his hair, pulling at them in frustration, squinting his eyes closed with consternation. Julian stood motionless, awestruck.

"I believed in you," Sergius said, his voice lowering to a controlled growl. He heaved for breath, trying to control himself. "I believed in you because I thought we shared a vision for our Empire, one of peace and equality and prosperity for all men..."

"My Empire," Julian interrupted. "Rome is my responsibility, and the laurels do not sit light upon my head, nor would they weigh any lighter upon yours. You who has not even the stamina to wear a *helmet* in battle." The side of his lips curled with a subtle twitch, as if Caesar fought back a smile. "I must protect all we have suffered for; that is my passion, and my plight. When our boarders with Persia are inked with the blood of their soldiers, and when the Galilean folly meets the same oblivion as their crucified Jew..."

Sergius tossed his head back in annoyed exasperation.

"What is it about the Galilean issue that so excites you?" Julian asked, the pitch of his voice rising with irritation. "They are criminals, traitors. Their threat looms larger than even that of Persia and yet you, a man of wisdom and education, still have sympathy toward their bigoted and destructive religion." He stepped face to face with Sergius, the Emperor's tiny form staring up into the face of his towering Primercius. "Why?" Julian gasped.

"Yeshu is dead," Sergius mumbled, averting the stare of Caesar.

"But the Galileans believe he lives," Julian declared. "What's more, they believe that they too will live forever if they worship him. And a man that lives forever, Sergius, is an omnipresent, infinite threat. The Galileans will be shamed and eliminated, and the traitor Yeshu forgotten if Rome is to know life eternal. On that my mind is set."

Julian reached up and squeezed Sergius's left shoulder in a gesture of affectionate solidarity. Sergius felt his jaw muscles tighten as he fought back the urge to squirm and write away from the Emperor's grasp, his eyes dodging Caesar's, pointed at the dusty ground below.

"Go home to your Bacchus and inform him," the Emperor ordered. He released Sergius's shoulder with a gentle pat, and turned to exit the racetrack. He took a few paces, stopped, and turned back to Sergius, still frozen in place. "I hope you would call me brother, Sergius," Julian called back. "But never forget that you must also call me Caesar Augustus!"

Julian spun around and exited the arena, leaving Sergius alone, a minuscule figure in the great design of the Hippodrome. He stood motionless, contemplating his crushed hopes and the suddenly bleak future ahead, swept away by feelings of despair, anger and pain…physical pain.

For the first time in recent memory, his keloid earned at Strasburg throbbed with agonizing hurt.

Chapter LII.

Didymos had set the table with upmost care: greens and olives, vinegar, seared lamb and a loaf of fresh bread served with a decanting jug of local red wine, and though his masters joined him at either end of the dinner table, only Didymos could ate, the noise of his slurps and chewing the lone noise in a painful silence.

The amethyst gems of Bacchus's eyes glittered in the dim light of evening still creeping in through the windows, augmented by well-placed oil lamps around the room as he stared across the table Sergius, who could only stare down at his untouched meal. Didymos continued to eat in blissful obliviousness.

"I fear for his mind," Sergius declared at long last. Didymos looked up from his half-eaten plate and realized for the first time that neither of his companions had engaged their food. Choking a bit, he took a long swig of wine from his cup and wiped his mouth with the back of his hand, his attention bouncing from one master to the other, suddenly aware of the depressed mood around him.

"Have you spoken to Oribasius?" Bacchus asked.

"No, but I've a feeling the good doctor thinks as I do," Sergius answered. "He's expressed worry over Caesar's state of mind for some time. Besides, Oribasius seems transfixed by the urban luxuries here in Constantinople."

"You think the Emperor has gone mad?" Didymos blurted. Sergius and Bacchus looked at their servant as if realizing his presence for the first time.

"He has changed," Sergius lamented. "Power has changed him. Fear…and I dare say loneliness, the empty pain of abandonment and the isolating paranoia of the crown have distorted his spirit. He means to make war with Persia, not to mention extinguish the Galilean faith. I've pleaded with him, tried to appeal to his sense of reason but…" He closed his eyes and sighed. "He means for us to accompany him on this campaign." Sergius leaned back in his chair, rubbing his eyes in mental exhaustion. "And the killing will start again."

Sergius looked at Bacchus again, then let his gaze fall on the smooth wood of the tabletop. Didymos took another long drink of his wine, shifting in his seat, slouched over his place setting.

"Eat," Bacchus ordered Sergius.

"I've no appetite," Sergius countered in a tired moan.

"Does not Caesar still value your consul?" Didymos inquired, a hint of desperation in his voice.

"I'm certain he does," Sergius admitted, "though what more I can do to sway his mind…" His voice trailed off as he shook his head with doubt.

An agonizing quiet fell over the three men, none quite sure what to say or do to alleviate the impossible situation before them. Sergius propped his elbows against the table, bowing his head in his hands. Bacchus sat motionless, his eyes sparkling with empathy for his beloved. Didymos tapped at his cup with his index finger, brow furled, the weight of the conversation distancing him from the present. They sat and sat, hearts brimming with sorrow.

"Let's take a walk," Bacchus declared with uncharacteristic authority, rising from his chair. "The Nymphaeum…"

Sergius looked up into his beloved's face, an irrepressible smile crossing his face. Even in his darkest moment, the light of Bacchus's love could guide him to joy.

"Alright," Sergius agreed as he stood up.

Didymos gaze rebounded from Bacchus to Sergius again as the two donned their Palatinae regalia, Bacchus packing his lyre under his arm. As his masters readied themselves for a stroll through the city, he took one last morsel of bread, smearing it in the vinegar and juice of the meat and tossed it in his mouth, washing it down with a final sip of wine.

"I too, have an errand," Didymos announced to his masters' indifference.

"Do what you must," Sergius said as Bacchus took him by the hand, leading him downstairs to exit the manor.

The lively streets of Constantinople did offer some levity as Sergius and Bacchus walked hand in hand, the admiring citizens nodding with respect to the two decorated soldiers, each wearing his golden torque with pride. Bacchus squeezed at Sergius's hand every so often, each compression a reminder of his love.

The Nymphaeum, as usual, embodied all the urban charm that Sergius and Bacchus so enjoyed. Other citizens, dressed in fine togas mulled about in cheery conversations, sampling wine, reveling in the romantic nighttime beauty of the Nymphaeum fountain, the flowing water sparkling in the amber light of torches and cisterns. Sergius and Bacchus sat on a bench underneath a trellis of hanging greens which reminded Sergius of the gardens of his family estate. He smiled again, laying a soft kiss on Bacchus's stubbled cheek, as the Secondarius produced his lyre and began to pluck away at the strings in a sweet, soft tune. His playing attracted the attention of several other congregants, a small crowd forming a semi circle around the couple, listening to Bacchus play with wonder and admiration at the sight of a soldier-musician, and a skilled one at that. Sergius grinned again as his misfit Brother, his love and gratitude for Bacchus's entry into his life extinguishing any feeling of fear or sadness in his heart.

Bacchus finished his song, and the crowd thanked him with hearty applause. Sergius kissed him again, this time on the mouth, prompting the crowd to chuckle with glee and adulation. As their lips parted, the two lovers met eye-to-eye, adoring one another in silence, Sergius making a slight lean forward, brushing his nose against Bacchus's. The sound of children laughing jarred them from their loving moment, capturing their attention.

The soldier's gaze lit on two small boys splashing one another in the gushing water from the fountain. The oldest, aged no more than four years, scampered about dripping wet, his toga adhering to his body, messy blond hair tussled and wild. The younger child—the brother of the older, Sergius postulated—sat in a puddle, flailing his arms against the surface, flicking water everywhere, his chubby face putting forth a toddler's gummy smile, the first wisps of brown hair stuck to his otherwise bald head. Sergius giggled, motioning for Bacchus to look.

The lovers watched the two children play and laugh, captivated. Sergius and Bacchus both smiled wide in amusement as Sergius's hand found Bacchus's again, the two scooting closer together in a half-cuddle.

"When we return from Persia," Bacchus said without fanfare,

"when Caesar has at last relieved us of our service…" His voice trailed off.

"What?" Sergius asked with great interest. Bacchus paused a moment, thoughtful.

"When we return, what shall we name our sons?"

"*There!*"

The great yell shook Sergius and Bacchus from their bliss, both leaping to their feet. The crowd parted, making way for a group of six soldiers—among them, Minos and Tarasis, the disdainful guards the couple had met when they first arrived in Constantinople—who surrounded Sergius and Bacchus, their swords drawn, eyes narrowed with hatred. Bacchus let his lyre slip from his fingers and fall to the ground at the sight. The sound of the toddler's wail distracted Sergius just long enough for him to see a fretful mother gather the child from the ground and rush off into the shadows of the city streets. It was then, across the Nymphaeum, that he saw Jovian, the general's face a mask of anger and disgust. Behind him, cowering like a frightened street rat, Sergius recognized the cowering form of Didymos. The general nodded to the servant, and Didymos too ran off into the night.

"Sergius. Bacchus," Jovian declared, voice booming that the whole crowd could hear. "In the name of our Emperor Julian, Caesar Augustus, I hereby place you under arrest."

"On what charge?" Sergius demanded. Jovian scowled, letting out a grim sigh.

"Suspicion of sedition."

Chapter LIII.

Like every other room in the Imperial Palace, Caesar had ordered the consistorium stripped of all treasures and baubles. Yet nothing could dim the splendor of the round hall of polished marble with a great onion-dome of bronze held aloft by eight pillars of beige stone, octagonal chandeliers casting eerie light about the barren chamber. The sound of the night wind moaned low between the walls. To Sergius, it seemed more like a tomb than the Emperor's reception hall.

Julian awaited the arrest party, sitting only in a simple chair beneath an archway, opposite where Sergius, Bacchus and the soldiers entered. Despite the late hour, the Emperor showed no signs of sleepiness. Rather, he seemed agitated and fatigued, drumming his fingers at the arms of his chair as Jovian's troops stood back from the arrested two, the soldiers keeping their swords drawn and ready.

Julian, dressed in violet robes embroidered with golden leaves and vine, rose to greet his prisoners. Saying nothing, he folded his arms behind his back, looking them each in the eye, pondering the circumstance.

"Kneel," he ordered at last, turning his back to Sergius and Bacchus, taking his seat once more. The two Palatinae complied, exchanging a quick look of fear and helplessness. Bacchus reached for Sergius's hand, only to feel Jovian's boot collide with the back of his neck, throwing him to the stone floor with a pained grunt.

"Keep apart," Jovian commanded. Though he spared Bacchus no pain, the general sounded more like a reprimanding father than a torturer. Bacchus sat up on his heels, his face flushed with pain, dragging his hands back so that the edge of his left palm rested against Sergius's right; a touch so subtle, the couple could hide it from their judges.

Julian turned back to his captives, nostrils flaring with anger, pupils dilated, jaw clenched like a vice. He could only look at the two Palatinae whom had so trusted at first; words could not escape his mouth.

"Your fool servant Didymos has made accusations against you," Caesar said at last with rapid enunciation. "His charges come to me through Jovian and are so egregious I almost had him killed on the spot. But he offers evidence." Julian motioned to Jovian, who yanked at Sergius by the hair, tilting his head back to unfurl his neck and, thrusting a hand into the toga of the Primercius, produced a bloodstained wooden necklace concealed beneath the folds. Jovian tore it from Sergius's neck and tossed it to the floor before the Emperor. Julian looked down at it, quaking with rage, again saying nothing for a long moment.

"It appears," Caesar snarled at last, "that counting on my great friendship and kindness to you, you have deceived me and become enemies of Rome." He paused again. "Well, what have you to say?"

Neither accused spoke, averting their eyes from their infuriated ruler. Sergius didn't know what to do; Macrina had never offered any guidance for this, nor had he ever taken serious the possibility that Julian might one day learn of his religious convictions. A gentle nudge from Bacchus hand signaled to the Primercius to speak for the both of them. Sergius searched his soul for words.

"Lord Caesar," Sergius uttered with quaking words. "We are loyal to you, and always shall be. As subjects of the Empire, our bodies fall under your jurisdiction, and for that, we have pledged to serve you and all of Rome."

"Very clever, my Philosopher Soldier," Julian hissed. "You pledge loyalty with your defiled bodies. But what of your minds? What of your souls, if indeed you have souls?"

Sergius and Bacchus turned to each other, Bacchus's expression revealing terror and pain, but also resolve.

"We…" Sergius's heart pounded as he heaved for breath. He closed his eyes a moment in prayer: *Lord Yeshu, God of love, protect and rescue us in this, our hour of trial. For all you have blessed us with, let us stand for you with absolute resolve.* Sergius's breathing hastened as he pursed his lips, restraining his burning anger until he could face his Emperor. He raised his eyes to Julian, meeting his gaze across the bellowing room.

"We have pledged our souls to Yeshu, the Anointed One, and to the God of love who hath begotten him." Sergius did not blink, nor did Julian, their eyes locked with equal determination.

Caesar's jaw quivered with rage, until the Emperor howled with agonizing hatred. He clenched his fists, face red as he kicked his chair with enough force to launch it into the air and down the hall where it landed in a great, echoing calamity, shattering into splintered pieces.

"Do you not realize your Anointed One was an ignorant, bastard, peasant Jew who sought to overthrow and undermine the sovereignty of Rome and was executed by crucifixion?!" Julian screamed, his voice cracking with rage. "You would claim loyalty to Rome but devote your souls to one who would destroy it, replacing the Empire with his own Kingdom of folly?!? What madness has befallen you?"

"It is our lord Yeshu that has brought us together!" Bacchus exclaimed without hesitation. "It is he that has brought us love in a world of death! He is the divine Reason for all that is good, the light of hope in a world of pain and darkness!"

Julian rushed to face Bacchus and, grabbing the Secondarius by the chin, spat a great wad of phlegm into his face. Bacchus recoiled, falling backward and sliding across the floor, prompting the guards to rush toward his fallen body, swords ready to strike. Julian raised a hand, ordering them to stand down. The guards retreated, even as Sergius crawled to Bacchus's side, cradling his body in his arms, wiping the spittle from his face.

"You both disgust me," Julian raged. He turned away from his subjects, facing down the long, empty hall leading further into the Palace. He stood still a long while, arms locked together behind his back, his body quivering, shaking his head in revulsion. When at last he turned to his subjects again, the Caesar's eyes had grown as red and bloodshot as his ruddy completion.

"Renounce him," Julian whispered, his voice still echoing against the cavernous walls. "Renounce the Galilean now, and I shall concede to his espoused virtue and forgive you both."

Sergius and Bacchus did not even need to look at one another to agree on a response.

"No," Sergius declared. "We will not." He and Julian locked eyes again, still unblinking in the face of the other.

"Then follow his example you shall," Julian said without inflection, voice like an ominous bell. "Let your city know your choice. Follow the path of the Galilean. Suffer."

Chapter LIV.

A few hours of breathing the dank, moldy air of a prison cell held no humiliation when compared with the indignities suffered by Sergius and Bacchus at dawn. Claimed from their cells by the same malicious cadre of soldiers that had arrested them the night before, the lovers found themselves stripped of their clothes, their belts slashed, and their torques confiscated before their captors bound them each to a table in another dungeon beneath the palace. They lay naked, their screams their only means of resistance as Tarasis and Minos cleared the other soldiers from the room, both cackling with devious satisfaction.

"Caesar says you are not men of Rome," Minos hissed. "You emasculate yourselves with your treachery." He smiled a grimace of rotten teeth, as he produced a rusty pair of shears, snipping them in the air over Sergius face. The Primercius's stomach burned and his legs shook at the sound of the creaking metal. "Let your bodies reflect your deeds!"

Minos reached down and grabbed Sergius testicles with the

grip of a vice, forcing an agonized howl from the bound soldier, his stomach knotting in unbelievable pain.

"Stop it!" Bacchus screamed, twisting against his restraints in futility. Tarasis struck him across the face with the back of his hand, a spring of blood flowing forth from Bacchus's lips.

Minos laughed and twisted at Sergius's manhood, relishing his pain before pressing Sergius's scrotum between the blades, ready to cut.

"No!" Tarasis commanded, tedium in his voice. "Caesar wants their bodies unspoiled." He looked down at Sergius and grinned. "For now."

"Now," he went on, "he just wants all of Constantinople to see what treacherous bitches they are!" Tarasis grabbed the writhing Bacchus, shoving a rag dripping with lead paste into the Secondarius' eye, smearing the pitch-black cream all over the socket, laughing at his prisoner's screams of pain. Minos did the same, rubbing the Kohl into Sergius watering eyes, yanking his ebony curls for extra effect. When the two torturers at last relented, neither Sergius nor Bacchus could form words from their pain, only shuddering and crying in agony.

Minos and Tarasis then poured red powder into a rotting wooden bowl, each taking a turn urinating into it before smearing the foul rouge over the cheeks of their captives, then rotten-smelling henna paste over their lips.

Sergius and Bacchus spat and yelled, but could do nothing to deter Tarasis and Minos from their sadistic pleasure. With both prisoners weakened from their pain and humiliation, their captors called for the other guards to join them. Minos released Sergius and Bacchus from their restraints and forced them both to don rent stolas, so dirty that even the poorest, naked whore of the city would forsake dressing in them.

The Passion of Sergius & Bacchus

Sergius couldn't bear to look at Bacchus, nor could he stand the thought of his beloved seeing him in such humiliating attire. He only cowered and sobbed, even as the soldiers manacled his neck with a heavy iron chain, and led him out of the torture chamber into the morning light. Through his swollen, burning eyes, Sergius could make out the battered form of Bacchus, also chained about the neck, dragged along side him as the soldiers lead them onto the Mese.

Sergius recognized the sounds of the morning rush as they made their way though the city marketplace, the noise of mocking laughter and howls punctuated by the sting of stones flung from passers by. He could only hang his head in shame, bare feet staggering over streets. He hoped to himself that he would go blind and deaf, that somehow the God of Yeshu would intervene and protect him from parade of degradation if only by making him an invalid. More than even his own mockery, Sergius prayed that he would never see Bacchus in the same humiliating dress. How he loved him so! Sergius would have rather had his testicles crushed and cut and borne both chains than let Bacchus suffer the same tortures.

Amid the scorn, though, Sergius could also hear moans of pity from passers by: men yelling in offense, women shrieking in compassion, children weeping at the sight of something they knew deep inside was wrong. Their empathy gave Sergius hope that Julian would somehow relent and forgo his prideful chastisement of a man he would call his brother, whom he long considered an equal. Surely to a man who did not even believe in God the question of faith could not warrant so grave a punishment!

After what seemed like days walking up and down the length of the city, Sergius and Bacchus were taken back to prison, held captive in different cells, left wearing their rancid dress and cosmetics.

Sergius lay on the ground, numb from pain and exhaustion, stomach cramped with hunger and burning with fear. The thick wooden door of his cell creaked open, and the officious figure of Jovian appeared in the room, a bowl of water in one hand, a tray of fresh bread in the other. Sergius crawled back in fear in reflex to his visitor as the wooden door slammed behind him.

"No, Sergius. I do not come to torture," Jovian soothed, kneeling beside Sergius and taking a soft cloth from the bowl. The warm water calmed Sergius's nerves enough to restore his senses as Jovian cleaned the horrid make-up from his face. The Primercius's body quivered with a primal rush of terror coupled with overwhelming pain. It took all his strength just to raise his eyes to face Jovian.

"Bacchus?" Sergius uttered at last.

"I tended to him first," Jovian said. "I knew you would ask that of me. He'll be alright."

"You mean he's suffered no lasting injury," Sergius pressed.

"He has not," Jovian confirmed, "though Caesar's fury has not quelled."

"Then why does he send you?" Jovian rinsed the cloth in the bowl and lay it in Sergius's palm

"He did not," Jovian explained. "I came of my own will."

Sergius posture sprang erect and he began wiping his face as if nothing happened. He looked into the wary face of Jovian anew, seeing for the first time a light of charity hidden in his eyes.

"Why?" Sergius gasped. Jovian took a heavy breath, sliding the tray of bread to Sergius. He leaned in very close, putting his mouth to Sergius's ear.

"It is what Yeshu would do." Sergius's eyes welled at the words of the general, his head spinning in dismay.

"You're not alone, Sergius," Jovian whispered. "You never have been." The general rose to his feet with a subtle nod at Sergius. "Caesar will send for you soon. Decide now what you will say to him. I have told Bacchus the same."

"What of Caesar?"

"He moves though the palace screaming, throwing furniture, breaking pottery and fine glass. I have never known a man to spew such anger." Jovian sighed. "Not even Constantius when he learned of the rebellion, and he killed with far less discrimination than Emperor Julian."

"And Didymos?"

"Escaped for the moment. The Emperor sent guards to sack your estate looking for him, but we have yet to locate your traitor servant." Jovian lowered his head in thought. "If he's found, he'll suffer equal punishment to you." Sergius had to chuckle at the perverse humor of it all. He wiped his face with the damp cloth a final time and tossed it back into the bowl where it landed with a *plop*, sloshing the dirty water onto the floor of his cell.

"Why would he do this?" Sergius narrowed his eyes, confounded.

"Because he's a fool," Jovian retorted. "Because he thought he could do God's work by giving you up to Caesar, same as Judas gave up Yeshu. He thought he could serve the greater good."

"Men should not presume to act for God, or Yeshu," Sergius uttered.

"Is that not what you do this very moment?"

"No," Sergius replied. "I stand firm for what I love, and I refuse to lie or apologize for my beliefs. Caesar cares not what

Bacchus and I do; he cares what we believe, for it shows the limits of his power."

"And you will stand firm," Jovian said, rising again, "even at the cost of your lives?"

"I speak not for my beloved," Sergius answered. "But if I am to honor my ancestors, my Empire, my God, my love, and even my Caesar Augustus then yes." Sergius leaned back against the filthy wall of the cell, cocking his head back, gazing into oblivion. "To compromise my truth is to compromise all that I believe, and my love and render my life and soul worthless. Julian can take my life, but he cannot steal from me my love for Rome, for Bacchus, or for Yeshu."

"This is the difference between you and I, Primercius," Jovian declared through a sardonic grimace. "I believe a man can accomplish more alive than dead."

He pounded his fist against the cell door, and, escorted out by another guard, said nothing else, leaving Sergius to ponder the general's words. Jovian had a point, and Sergius agreed: keeping their faith secret, acting on conscience, he had no doubt that he and Bacchus could have accomplished more for Rome and the Galilean cause than by declaring open allegiance. But Didymos *had* forced the lovers to do just that, and given the choice between denial and honesty, a lie and integrity, Sergius could only in good ethics hold fast to his faith. Without it, he knew, his love would mean nothing.

Chapter LV.

Sergius and Bacchus threw themselves at one another, their filthy, scarred bodies meshing with one another, defiant and oblivious to the looming guards around them. The soldiers moved to separate the lovers, but Julian extended his palm, allowing the reunion to take place uninterrupted, the two Palatinae embracing and weeping in exhaustion and fear in each other's arms.

Daylight lit the bulbous consistorium as Caesar presided over his captives, the Emperor himself looking the product of insomnia, bruise-like circles around his eyes, darkening and expanding like wellsprings of pitch on his face. Cuts and scrapes on his hands betrayed this physical violence of smashing objects in anger about the palace, but his face showed no sign of pain, only seething fury.

"Have you tasted enough humiliation in the name of your disgraced Jew?" Julian prodded, locking his arms behind his back. "Or need you endure more?"

"All your torture and cruelty cannot change my beliefs,

Caesar!" Sergius roared back in unbridled defiance, his bellowing voice jarring the surrounding guards with shock. He cast a glance over at Jovian, who in silence watched the scene unfold from one of the great archways, his face obscured by the shadow of a pillar. Sergius's insolent gaze lit back on Julian, even as he held fast to Bacchus, both their hearts pounding.

"Oh, why?!" Julian raged in exhausted disgust. "Does condemning your false idol disgrace your love?"

"It disgraces my faith," Sergius replied, rising to his feet, holding on to Bacchus's hand, tethering his balance. "And if my faith is worth nothing, my love is worth nothing, and I'll not sacrifice that for you, or for Rome, or for anything!"

Sergius took a step forward, eyes locked with the sunken pupils of Julian, even as the guards drew their swords, edging forward, ready to strike. From across the room, Jovian motioned them to hold steady, letting Sergius approach the Emperor.

"Spare Sergius," Bacchus pleaded, making no effort to hide his desperation, pulling at his beloved's arm.

"No," Sergius insisted in a whisper.

"Yew pruvv yer lav…" Bacchus uttered in full Germanic accent. "Spare my husband," he said with slow, deliberate enunciation, "and I shall do what you ask."

"Even at the cost of your life, bastard?" Julian orated with icy flatness.

"Sergius is my life." Julian laughed in nervous frustration.

"Dying for the sake of others," the Emperor wretched. "Very Galilean, and just as foolish. Your sacrifice would only deepen his convictions. Such is the case with those observing martyrdom."

Julian paced a wide circle around the imprisoned couple, his eyes looking down in thought.

"Love," Caesar vomited in disgust. "I can think of no greater stupidity, no greater vanity or selfishness. You both endure torture and humiliation…why? To prove your love? To appease your empty God? Why does your resurrected Yeshu not rescue you now? Surely he must enjoy watching you suffer as he did, encouraging such masochism in his followers. This is the nature of a God of love?" The Emperor threw up his arms in exasperation, turning his back to the couple. "Damn you both," he growled. "And damn my foolishness at ever taking your counsel."

Julian turned around and gazed at them, one last time, the light of his eyes snuffed to emptiness. He then turned to the half-hidden figure of Jovian. "Put them back in manacles and let us see how long they cling to their convictions when Rome yolks them. Chain them to my chariot. We ride for Antioch."

Chapter LVI.

Julian had demanded a chariot. In true imperial fashion, he received one of the most decadent varieties: wood cased in gold, engraved and pressed with images of teams of horses and Roman soldiers in battle, spears raised, swords crossed, eagles flying overhead, marks of the gods tracing the rounded outline of the carriage. A team of four horses—Demosthenes conspicuous in his absence—assembled at the head of the chariot clad in golden armor and headdresses of white and lavender plumes, whinnied and stomped, eager to spring forth into a gallop. Sergius and Bacchus each had their hands bound with chord, the great iron chains once again manacled at their necks, this time tethered to the base of Caesar's chariot like a team of horses, but in the rear.

The sun overhead scorched at the stola-clad Palatinae, both kneeling close together in silence, awaiting their next punishment. The remnant of the foul cosmetics still stained both their faces, and both men wreaked of the abominable odors of sweat, filth, mold and all the disgusting scents of prison. They clung together nonetheless.

"I'm here," Sergius whispered, trying with futility to hide the tremble in his voice.

"I know," Bacchus whimpered back.

Minos and Tarasis, each atop a horse, looked down on the two lovers with scorn, spewing insults and taunts without feeling. Only the arrival of Jovian and Oribasius silenced the two sadists, and while showing Sergius and Bacchus no particular compassion, at least spared them further indignity at the words of their torturers.

At last Julian arrived, unescorted by palace staff, dressed in ornate golden armor, sword at his belt, enwrapped in a violet cloak and bearing the golden laurels atop his head. For the first time, Sergius saw the utter ridiculousness of his Emperor's attire, coupled with his hair, over plucked to the point of near-baldness to conceal his graying tresses, and the curls of his preposterous goat beard swirling together to a fine point about his chin. The commanding if diminutive figure Sergius first beheld at Strasburg had somehow vanished, replaced by ragged dwarf, with all the gravitas of a boy posing in his father's clothing. The thought gave Sergius reprieve, but no comfort from his plight.

Julian climbed aboard his chariot and turned to the two soldiers chained in tow.

"You've a long march ahead, and this one without the benefit of a horse to carry you. We make haste to my troops already positioned on the Eastern front. I do hope you can keep the pace."

Bacchus simply rose to his full height, proud and unflinching, staring Julian in the face without humility, his amethyst eyes glittering like precious stones in the sunlight. Sergius did the same, saying nothing, but declaring his defiant resolve in silence.

Julian scowled and spun around, taking the chariot reigns in his hands.

"Antioch!" Julian declared as the towering palace gates opened onto the Mese, a small compliment of cavalry already gathered outside, ready to follow their Emperor into battle. Julian snapped the reigns and the team of horses leapt into a stride, yanking Sergius and Bacchus into a full blown run as they charged down the city thoroughfare. Jovian, Tarasis and Minos joined formation with the cheering troops outside the gate riding behind their Caesar toward presumed victory.

The procession had not even exited the city before both Sergius and Bacchus lost their footing and fell to the rough streets, dragged behind the charging vehicle. Each rough patch, bump or divot in the road bruised and scraped away at their flesh, shredding their already ragged clothing down to almost nothing. Blood dripped from the chord binding their wrists as they struggled to hold slack the chain around their necks, lest it pull taught and snap their heads from their bodies.

After the first few miles, Sergius watched Bacchus hoist himself up the chain. Inverting himself over it, wrapping his legs over the tight links, rolling side to side over the jagged road, Sergius realized, it would insure the chain stay loose in its pull and to minimize the friction of his body across the ground. Sergius mustered all his strength to do the same and managed to climb up along his tether, threading his body over the links, still in horrendous pain, but at least able to breathe. Neither lover shouted words of affection, nor curses to their Emperor, nor prayers to their God, their only verbalizations their grunts and hollers of pain.

Julian never looked back at his prisoners, keeping his eyes only to the road ahead. When at last the procession stopped to make camp for the camp for the night, he stepped down avoiding the sight of the bound men with obvious purpose, refusing to acknowledge them at all. Tarasis and Minos unchained the Palatinae and bound their arms and feet together, placing them each in separate areas of the camp for the night. Neither were granted a sleeping mat or even a blanket to protect them from the elements, and Sergius found himself shuddering all through the night, less from temperature than physical shock, every cell of his body screaming with pain. Late into the night, when the roar of the camp had quieted and the campfires died, Jovian himself brought each captive some water and bread, cradling their heads in his lap, helping them to eat. Though he offered meager nourishment, the general offered no words of comfort, nor aid in escape.

The next morning Tarasis and Minos re-chained Sergius and Bacchus, and fearing to speak the two Palatinae again wrapped themselves around their chains of tether in a pre-emptive effort to protect themselves. Caesar, upon boarding his chariot, observed this defensive maneuver, scoffing at his prisoners, but making no effort to stop them. He said nothing to them as the chariot sped off onto the warpath, hauling his prisoners against the jagged ground. Neither did the Emperor address his captives again that night, leaving them again bound and separated, with Jovian sneaking to offer them mercies of food and drink.

And so it went, the cycle repeating every day for weeks, Bacchus and Sergius never speaking to one another out of shock and exhaustion, only able to exchange looks of affection and compassion in fleeting moments when their eyes met. Sergius prayed to the God of Yeshu for some deliverance, for some grace that might quell the hatred in Julian's heart or at least allow them the peace of death along the way. Death: nature's dark, inescapable spectre which Sergius had feared his whole life…on the road to

Antioch, Sergius would have welcomed so terrible a figure with a glad heart.

But no miracles came, no celestial deliverance, nor even the mercy of death. The God of Love and the Anointed Yeshu had left their servants in silence.

Sergius had lost all concept of time when the caravan arrived at Barbalissos, a Roman fortress along the Euphrates River with towering, plain walls of stone, its cubish buildings colliding and stacked in a utilitarian geometry sans any decorative adornments. As Julian's chariot skidded to a halt, Sergius and Bacchus coughing and heaving dirt from their lungs, their eyes burning with dust, bodies caked in filth, manure, and their own festering scabs, rolled once more to a merciful reprieve. The weathered Julian looked down at the almost-naked Palatine he had so loved, studying their bruised and torn bodies for a long moment as Sergius and Bacchus each released their grip on their chains, their arms and legs peeling from the iron links, leaving behind bloody craters tracing up their bodies.

"Minos! Tarasis!" Julian called, summoning the two soldiers before him. "Wash my Philosopher and bring him to my chamber. Take the bastard German to a cell."

Sergius cried out, to weak to even form words, in a primal scream of horror. Tarasis's boot met with his abdomen, eliciting a heaving wheeze from the chained Primercius. Minos unfastened the manacle around Bacchus's neck, just as the crumpled body of the Secondarius jolted to life. Splitting the rope binding his wrists and jumping to his feet, Bacchus swung a wild fist into Minos's teeth, knocking the captor to the ground, blood gushing from his mouth. Tarasis leapt for Bacchus, who caught him by the neck, hoisted him over his head, and tossed him to the ground atop Minos with a brutal slam.

Bacchus turned to Julian, his violet eyes dilated and red as a rabid wolf's as he strode for the Emperor. Julian jumped from his chariot to Sergius's stunned body, drew his sword from his belt, raised it, and thrust it down, holding it just shy of the fallen Primercius's windpipe.

"I'll split him open," Julian declared, meeting Bacchus's ferocious gaze with his own. Bacchus relented, and, giving into exhaustion, fell to his knees in a shapeless heap. Six other guards grabbed Bacchus's limp body, and dragged it into the winding passages of the hulking fortress followed by a limping Tarasis and Minos, both nursing their wounds. Julian yielded, sheathing his sword as Sergius watched the events before him with helpless despair.

The Emperor glared down at his prey, Sergius lifting his eyes to meet Julian's in silent pleading. Yet, in the darkness, his own vision obscured with dirt, he could not find the shine of his once-friend's irises; only dark craters like the empty sockets of a skull. Caesar nudged Sergius with the tip of his right foot, just looking down at him a long moment.

"Bring him," Julian called out, assured someone would comply but paying no attention to who as he stomped off into the shadows.

Chapter LVII.

As Sergius would have predicted, Julian's room had no decorative elements of consequence, just a mere table, two wooden chairs and a simple bed, with brown curtains of linen draped over an open window overlooking the rest of the Barbalissos fortress. A gentle wind flowed in through the window, rebuffing the curtains and pouring over Sergius's battered body; cool to the touch, but with a strange undercurrent of warmth, a reminder of the ever-growing heat of the daytime.

Sergius's hands and feet were bound together with fresh rope to prevent any chance of repeating Bacchus's earlier feat, forcing him into a posture like a hog ready for spiggoting over a fire. Nonetheless, the guards had positioned him at Julian's request in one of the chairs after having doused him in cold water and myrrh so as not to offend Caesar's olfactory sense.

Not that Julian cared. Sergius knew that, even at his most condescending, decadent vanities mattered not to the Emperor, despite concern over his own appearance. Neither man spoke, Julian shuffling around in the dim light of a single oil lamp suspended from the ceiling as he unfastened his Imperial cloak and armor, tossing them on the table, stripping down to only his loin cloth and the laurels. He dragged the open chair over in front of Sergius, and sat down, his face tight with fury in the flickering illumination. He paused a moment, just staring at his Philosopher Soldier, before taking the Golden Laurels from his head and tossing them across the room to the table as he would an old rag. The crown hit the edge of the tabletop and bounced, falling to the floor, wobbling around its edge until it came to a quiet rest on the upswept ground.

"I would have killed you, you know," Julian declared after a painful silence. "If Bacchus had come any closer, I would have split your throat."

"I do not doubt it," Sergius wheezed, his voice hoarse and polluted from weeks of nonuse and the dust in his throat. He reached for his throat in a reflex of pain, his restraints yanking his arms back down. He relaxed again, realizing the futility of his movements.

"There was a time I would have had a man thrown in prison for accusing you of what you now openly proclaim," Julian said, voice deep and cold as a gong. "Does that not matter to you?"

"It changes nothing."

"Your foolishness knows no bounds, Sergius!" Julian hissed. "Nor does your stubbornness! You endure this agony for…what? A dead Jew? Some matter of uncompromising principle?"

"How is your allegiance to Jupiter and the old gods any different?" Sergius asked in monotone.

"Zeus…Jupiter…the old gods by any name! They are part of our identity, part of being Roman!" Julian stressed. "But no amount of folly or proof could ever convince me they *exist*. I believe in what they stand for! Not that they live!"

"But you've no faith in them," Sergius observed.

"No!" Julian insisted. "I put my faith in Rome, in this world, in this life! Not some ethereal and preposterous eternal life! Not some afterlife in a Kingdom ruled by a criminal! This, this is all there is, Sergius! You know that! This is our chance to make the world what we would dream it to be!"

"A world of equality, of peace, of enlightenment," Sergius recited with dispassion.

"Yes!" Julian hissed in exasperation.

"You are right, Lord Caesar," Sergius declared, eliciting dumbfounded shock from Julian. "And I wish for that idealized, egalitarian world too. But it cannot be born of conquest and bloodshed. Only with love."

"LOVE!?" Julian bellowed, rising from his chair and spinning around in frustration.

"Yes, love!" Sergius pressed. "The nature of love is acceptance and forgiveness, and the conceit of those is trust. *And the essence of trust is faith.*"

"Ridiculous," Julian sneered. "And why should I or anyone have faith in love, for all the pain and misery and tears it breeds? What has love for my parents, or my brother Gallus, or my lost friends like Severus or Helena…" He paused, choking on his words. "Helena," he repeated, trying to sound assured. "Why love?"

"It's your choice, Julian." Sergius closed his eyes in exhaustion. "Choose to believe what you want."

"Love," the Emperor spat. "You love Bacchus? Enough that you would die for him?"

"A thousand times over," Sergius replied without hesitation. "I would die every moment of eternity for him."

Julian looked at him a long, ominous moment. "Would you?"

Before Sergius could reaffirm his conviction, Julian had thrown open the door to the room and charged down the hall, screaming for guards. Sergius looked down at the fallen golden laurels lying indifferent and discarded on the floor. How inconsequential and feeble they looked in the lamplight…

A pair of guards dragged Sergius, still bound, from Julian's bedchamber down several flights of stairs, through a labyrinth of halls, across the fortress courtyard and into another building. They descended another flight of chipped and worn stairs, unusual stains tracing the path downward. Sergius recognized a stench worse than prison: death, fresh and brutal, smelling of rancid meat tossed atop a blazing fire.

Indeed, for a moment Sergius had thought he'd entered Tartaurus itself at the sight of a roaring fire, barely contained within the subterranean fireplace, and the silhouette of a limp, bloody figure chained to the ceiling above. Alongside it, Minos and Tarasis strutted like roosters, each holding a whip of leather tassels, the pain of each strip augmented by jagged bits of metal and glass punched through the hide.

The guards dropped Sergius to the greasy floor, covered in a mix of blood, excrement and other unspeakable grime. He rolled around the grungy floor in revulsion, noticing the bulbous form of Oribasius cowered alongside Julian in a corner of the room. The flicker of firelight across Julian's wrinkled face made the Emperor look like a gorgon: his hair wild and uneven, enormous, dark eyes seeming to absorb any illumination into their black craters.

A slight nod from Caesar, and Tarasis and Minos went back to work, each striking their victim on his front and back, the nettles of their whips slicing into the delicate flesh of their prisoner with a wet *chock*, like the sound of a knife cutting through cabbage.

Even with his blurred vision in the dim light, Sergius could see the bits of flesh peel away from the chained man's body, the muscles and sinew beneath shredded and rent like the frayed edges of a threadbare rug. The captive writhed like an eel on a meat hook with each blow, screaming and shivering in pain.

Only at the sound of his cries did Sergius realize the man still lived. Only then did he recognize him as Bacchus.

"No, Caesar! Please!" Sergius yelled, pulling at his bonds in futility. Julian waved his palm across his neck, signaling a pause in the torture. He walked over to Sergius, his feet making a squishy peeling sound with each step against the filth of the chamber floor. He looked down at Sergius, saying nothing, leaving the bound Primercius to supply a reason.

"Let me take his place!" Sergius begged. "Kill me, do what you will! Only please spare him!"

Across the room, Bacchus's limp head quivered and raised, the Secondarius taking notice of the unfolding scene before him. The sweat and blood ran down his face, stained the blond curls of his head and sullied his countenance, but as his eyes fluttered open, his body seemed to erect with stamina anew at the sight of his beloved.

"I don't wish death on either of you, Sergius," Julian growled. "I want to hear you say it...I want you to renounce Yeshu as a false prophet and messiah and his God of Love as a fantasy. Deny the Galilean now, and I let Bacchus live!"

Sergius's eyes welled with tears of despair as he looked at the skinned, broken form of the man he so loved, so scarred that Sergius himself could not even recognize him at first. Bacchus made a slow pivot on his chains, straining his head to behold Sergius tied up on the ground. In the darkness, Sergius could feel the gaze of Bacchus's eyes, the two gems that had once restored life to him, that he looked to for comfort, guidance and love, and within their elegant color, the soul of his beloved, the source of his faith and love in the world.

"I.." Sergius gasped.

"Eyyyyyy laaaaaav yewwwww," Bacchus strained. "Always."

"Quiet!" Minos cracked his whip over Bacchus abdomen, the nettles burying in Bacchus's musculature like nails in sand. The torturer yanked the whip back, and as he did, Bacchus's stomach burst open with a geyser of blood and entrails, spewing forth, dousing Minos in the fluid and pouring oozing vicera over the floor. Bacchus yelled in pain, his cry stifled by the sound of blood and vomit flooding his throat, chocking from him the last breath of life. His body went limp again, his head dropping forward, blood, vomit and bile pouring forth from his lips, the light of his eyes lost in darkness.

Oribasius rushed forward in a panic, slipping in the gore as he did. The doctor pushed Minos back away from Bacchus, observing his emptied abdominal cavity in horrified futility.

"Fool!" Oribasius shouted in devastated alarm. "You ruptured his liver!"

"What he deserved," Minos spat back.

Sergius's body quivered, numb with shock. He prayed a long moment that Oribasius might find some way to save Bacchus, that Yeshu himself would appear and restore his beloved to life and carry the lovers away to safety that they might live forever in bliss, free from this Empire of slaughter.

But God was silent again.

"Throw him in a cell," Julian commanded, wiping sweat from his face with shaking hands. He did not dare look at Sergius as he exited the room. "Throw the body to the dogs," he called back, climbing the stairs.

The Passion of Sergius & Bacchus

Sergius burst into howling cries, tears pouring from his eyes, spittle and mucus running down his face. He curled himself into the shape of a fetus, trying to cradle his face in his hands, yanking at his bonds in anger and despair. Guards carried him from the room, and Sergius made no effort to resist as they placed him in a lightless cell, alone with his screams, praying his cries be heard.

His wails went unheralded that night, and no mercy came to him there, forsaken in the blackness.

Chapter LVIII.

Sergius did not sleep that first night, alternating between wailing and weeping in agony, pounding his head on the floor in anger and frustration, and laying with catatonic stillness, listening to the shuffling of guards outside his cell, and the creeping scurry of vermin in the darkness.

After several hours—three? Four?—his cell door creaked open, and Jovian entered carrying meager rations for his prisoner. He lay the food beside Sergius, who never acknowledged the presence of his visitor, only staring into the abyss, his mind and soul lost in search of Bacchus.

"I've protected his body," Jovian whispered. "There are men still loyal to the Galilean cause here in the East. They have concealed his remains, and will bury him in a cave with dignity. Just as the Lord was."

Sergius lay motionless, paying no heed to the general's words. Jovian laid a hand atop Sergius's greasy head, giving it a soft pat as a father would comfort a son.

"One day we will have a Holy Empire again," Jovian declared. "A Holy Father on the throne of Rome, and the Kingdom shall reign on Earth!"

Sergius again ignored Jovian's attempt at comfort, prompting the general to depart, leaving the Primercius alone in the dark again.

What has Yeshu bequeathed me? Sergius contemplated. *He has cost me my friends, my treasures, the only remaining keepsakes of my family. He has taken away my freedom, surrendered me to torture and humiliation, and now he takes from me Bacchus, for whom I would have given my own life. What God of Love is this?*

The next morning Minos and Tarasis cut Sergius's bonds and lead him from his cell back to the chains of Caesar's chariot. Neither guard spoke, treating Sergius with unusual reverence, even as they clamped the manacle around his neck again. As the procession of troops reassembled, preparing to leave Barbalissos, Julian appeared in full Emperor's regalia again, paying no mind to Sergius as he boarded his chariot.

"Why does he not wear the boots?" Julian asked without acknowledging anyone in particular.

"Lord Caesar, you'll drag a corpse down the road," Minos explained.

"Better to kill him now, here," Tarasis added.

"Give him the boots, or wear them yourself!" Julian yelled, taking the reigns in his hands, ready to charge his team of horses.

Tarasis disappeared back into the fortress chambers, returning a few moments later with a set of Caligulas, rusted, long nails protruding up through the soles. Tarasis exchanged a look of subdued pity with Sergius, as the former solicited help from Minos, the two torture masters fastening the boots to Sergius's feet, the nails cracking and puncturing the soles of his feet, jutting up through bone and sinew, blood spraying everywhere as they fastened them on.

Sergius wailed in pain again, but did not resist, all will and defiance lost with Bacchus. Julian snapped the reigns and the chariot darted off onto the road, Sergius plodding along behind, taking only a few steps before collapsing from the most intense pain his body had ever known. The chariot dragged his body a full nine miles that day, leaving a smearing line of blood tracing their path as Sergius's limp body rolled and writhed in pain.

That night, when the procession had stopped to make camp, Sergius again found himself alone in the desert far away from the revelries of the troops. This time his captors left him unbound, as no one feared his escape with such grave injuries. By that time his tears had run dry, body twitching, unable to process all the pain inflicted upon him. His feet had shredded like ground meat into bloody cakes held together only by the leather of the boots, the flesh searing and burning, already blackening and oozing from gangrenous infection. Jovian again visited him in the middle of the night, after the fires had died and the troops fallen asleep, bringing bread and water to the fallen Primercius.

Jovian placed the food before Sergius's limp head, sitting down next to him, wringing his hands with nervousness.

"They say that Tartaurus burns just beneath the ground here," Jovian said, trying to illicit a response from Sergius that would confirm the Philosopher Soldier still had his wits. "Some nights the Earth cracks open, and the flames of the inferno escape up to the world of the living." He paused, his eyes narrowing in thought as he let out a heavy sigh. "Julian will be there soon enough."

"Let me die," Sergius croaked, only half aware of Jovian's presence.

"Death will come soon, Sergius," Jovian answered. "May your soul then find peace."

With that the general withdrew to camp, leaving the broken Sergius alone in the cool dark of night. No moon shown overhead, and thick clouds obscured the starlight, making Sergius feel as though he had never left his cell. Indeed, the torment of his mind and body made Sergius question if he had even left the prison of Barbalissos, or for that matter, if he had not already died, and if this pain and torture would endure for all eternity.

"Yeshu, why have your forsaken me?" Sergius whispered into the dark. "Why?" His eyes welled again with the tears he thought had dried, burning his cheeks as they flooded down his face. "Bacchus!" he heaved. "Bacchus! You leave me alone and widowed without comfort! And why? What good can come from death?!"

As he laid his head upon the ground, a strange flicker of light and color appeared in the distance, blurred through the distortion of Sergius's tears. He thought at last his vision had failed him, eyes infected from the bombardment of the warpath. But the light did not dissipate, growing in luminosity as Sergius watched it flicker like the flame of a lamp in the night wind. Shapeless at first, it shifted and expanded, taking on vague form, colors separating from one another, growing ever brighter like the sunrise over shimmering water.

Why do you grieve, Brother?

The words seemed to have no origin, but Sergius knew that he heard them, clear as any other sound in the night. He raised his head a bit, blinking through the tears, looking around for some stranger in the darkness, transfixed by the intensifying light before him.

How good and holy it is to dwell together as one…

"Who torments me with this deceit?" Sergius hissed into the

dancing colors, contracting his body into a protective ball. The strange lumen exploded into beams of radiant light, stretching out like sunbeams over the landscape. Sergius clawed at the ground with fearful strength generated by adrenaline pounding through his veins.

The light contracted back into perfect shape and color, in the unmistakable form of a man.

"Bacchus?"

Why do you grieve, my beloved Brother?

The words seemed to come from all around him, sounding more like a choir in unison than the speech of one man. Sergius peered up at Bacchus's perfect face, his skin luminous as the sun, amethyst eyes shining like gems, his body perfect as the moment Sergius first beheld him at Strasburg. He wore robes of white and red over glittering golden armor, a variety Sergius had never seen before, and though Bacchus looked dressed as a soldier, he carried no sword at his side.

Bacchus moved closer to him, his feet touching the ground but never moving, gliding over the rough earth as if it were ice. He smiled and outstretched his palms to his lover, as Sergius felt a great wave of serenity consume his body, all the pain of his tortures evaporating into nothing.

"Are you alive?" Sergius asked in wonder.

Your love keeps me alive. Bacchus lips didn't move, but somehow, Sergius knew, these words came from his beloved. *Death may have consumed by body, but cannot consume my soul. I am with you now and always, for Yeshu and the God of Love have made us one for all eternity.*

"Hold me," Sergius begged. "Let me feel your touch once more! Stay with me this night, until death finds me at last!"

What is one on the inside is also one on the outside, though you may not see it with Earthly eyes. Though his lips still did not move, somehow Bacchus face intensified, emphasizing his words. *I am with you forever, my friend, my Brother, my love. Our soul is one. My justice is with you.*

The light of Bacchus's halo grew once more, consuming Sergius in a swell of blinding color. His body tingled with a strange sensation as he shut his eyes, reveling in the euphoria.

Chapter LIX.

When he opened his eyes again, daybreak had come as Minos and Tarasis approached to return Sergius to his chains. Much to the shock of the two Romans, Sergius rose to his full height, unfatigued, with no hint of pain, despite his mangled, still-bloody feet. Minos and Tarasis staggered backward in shock, as the former Primercius smiled with peace and serenity. Paying them no mind, Sergius walked without stumbling through the awestruck camp of soldiers, up to Julian's chariot where he fastened the manacle about his neck without aid.

He stood in patient waiting, until Caesar appeared once again, and, beholding the restored Sergius, staggered weak-kneed to his carriage, gazing at the Spaniard in sick fascination.

"Your torture is sweeter than honey, Caesar," Sergius declared. "Do as you will."

"How?" Julian gasped. "What trickery?"

"Bacchus lives, Emperor," Sergius affirmed. "He lives forever. He offers me comfort from the pain you would inflict."

"You have given your mind over to madness!" Julian bellowed, his face blushing with fury. "Let us see how long your insanity withholds your pain!"

Caesar climbed aboard his chariot, paying no mind to the cavalry amazed by Sergius's resolve. Whipping his horses to a full gallop, Sergius kept pace the entire day, traversing another full nine miles, never stumbling once, or showing the faintest hint of pain or fatigue.

As twilight fell, the setting sun blood red low in the sky, Julian halted his chariot and disembarked, again regarding Sergius with awe. They had stopped just outside the village of Resafa, another massive fortress designed as a bastion to hold off the advancing Persians which also provided an oasis for traders and travelers along the Syrian roads.

"Jovian! Oribasius!" Julian called. The general and the doctor rode their horses up along side the Emperor's chariot and began to climb down. Julian halted them, ordering them to lead the rest of the troops on into the village. He then sent for Tarasis and Minos to unyoke Sergius. The two soldiers, still reluctant with fear of Sergius's miraculous recovery, quickly complied then backed away from Sergius, ready to draw their swords.

"Imbeciles!" Caesar barked. "This ends here! And now!" Searching around, Julian discovered a nearby boulder with a rounded top, commanding Sergius to join him before it. Sergius complied without hesitation, grinning at the Emperor all the while.

The dark eyes of Julian met the shining chestnut of Sergius's irises as the Emperor began to quiver, turning away from his prisoner, shy in his emotion.

The Passion of Sergius & Bacchus

"I know not the source of your strength, my Philosopher…"

"Bacchus," Sergius simply answered. "And Yeshu."

Julian howled in frustration, hunching over, balling his fists, shaking them in the air. He turned to face Sergius, seething with hatred and anger, his face red and nostrils flared. He stomped over and grabbed Sergius by his ebony curls, pulling the taller man down to face him. Tarasis and Minos rushed to the Emperor.

"No!" Julian rebuffed, frightening the two soldiers away. "I'll do it myself!"

"I forgive you, my brother Julian," Sergius affirmed, voice serene. "Because I love you. Yeshu loves you. And he too will forgive."

Julian wailed in wretched frustration, his body crumpling with despair. He yanked hard at Sergius's head, tearing from it a fistful of dark tresses. Sergius didn't even blink. Julian stared at him, the Emperor's face awash in fear, his countenance transparent, revealing the churning toil in his soul.

"Sergius, please…" Julian whimpered. "Do not force my hand." Tears welled in his eyes, his body shaking, overcome with pain and anger.

"Your hand is yours to wield," Sergius answered without inflection. "Do as your conscience dictates." With that he lay face down and stretched his head across the boulder, neck extended and vulnerable. Julian looked down at him, his best friend in all the world, ready to meet execution without fear. His breathing hastened. His lips curled, trying to stifle a cry before falling to his knees to face Sergius in a final desperate plea.

"<u>Why</u> Sergius?" Julian whispered, shaking his head in confoundment. "Why choose this superstition? Why force yourself to endure this?" Sergius lifted his head to face his Emperor one final time.

"Because it's what I want to believe."

Julian roared with volcanic fury, staggering to his feet. With that, the Emperor drew forth his sword from his belt and planted his feet on the ground, positioning himself perpendicular to Sergius's body. Arms shaking, he raised his sword above Sergius's head, gritted his teeth, and prepared to do what he never thought possible…

Julian's eyes widened like a crazed beast as rage erected his sword a split second before bringing it down with the power of all his angry might. The blade cut into Sergius's spine with a wet chop, as the former Primercius gagged and choked in burning pain. Julian wiggled the sword, lodged midway though Sergius's neck. He pulled, trying to wrench the blade free as Sergius sputtered and clawed at the ground, his vision blurring, breath stifled. Julian lay a foot on Sergius's shoulder and finally wrested the sword, a wild gush of blood spraying out behind it. He raised the blade again and brought it down once more with equal fury, this time chopping all the way through Sergius's neck, metal clanging against the stone beneath, beheading Sergius, a sanguine fountain pouring forth from his decapitated body.

Julian stumbled and fell against the stone, plunging the sword into the Earth as he caught himself on the rock only to slip in the deluge of blood, the warm, flowing gelatin soaking the Imperial robes, splattering all over Julian's face.

The last thing Sergius saw was the Emperor, his once-friend, the man he thought could save the world, crying and wailing like a frightened infant on his knees. Julian clawed at his own face, trying to smear the blood from his eyes just as the world fell silent and Sergius's pain dissolved, along with his vision, into nothingness.

* * *

The Passion of Sergius & Bacchus

Julian had rushed off into the city, leaving Tarasis and Minos to tend to his chariot and the bloody remains of Sergius themselves. Too afraid to approach the body, they lead the team of horses into the walls of Resafa, meeting with Jovian along the way. Ordering them to tend to the horses, Jovian himself wandered outside the city gates to the sight of Sergius's execution where his remains lay in a crimson stain on the ground, still unmolested by scavenging beasts. Alongside his body, the Emperor's sword, sullied with blood, driven indifferent into the ground. Jovian approached and yanked forth the sword, taking a step back to regard Sergius's body one final time, contemplating his burial.

As Jovian looked down in pity at the body, there came a great rumbling like thunder, knocking the general backward to the ground. As he fell, the Earth trembled and shook like the shock of an earthquake. Before he could climb to his feet, Jovian gasped as the bloodied soil under Sergius's body cracked and sank, replaced by a massive pillar of fire spiraling upward from the ground in a churning vortex, cremating Sergius's body as the flames burned up into the heavens.

The heat of the column of flame searing into Jovian's face, sweat beading about his brow, the general rushed back into the city where a group of soldiers watched in awe, questioning what man had fallen beneath Caesar's blade.

And they were afraid.

Epilogue:
Alive

Only three months after departing for Antioch, the Emperor Julian lay in his tent upon a bed of straw, his troops in retreat, the Persian forces under Shapur pursuing them back into Roman territory. Caesar's troops, though numerous and valiant in battle, could not withstand the Persian onslaught, nor could they protect Julian from the enemy blade which pierced his side, cutting open his liver and intestines.

Oribasius did all he could to treat the wound, pouring wine over the gaping cut, trying his best to suture the gaping hole shut as Julian writhed in pain, having imbibed no anesthetic. The Emperor's pulse had slowed as cold sweat soaked his body, his vision blurred, as he heaved as if to vomit, but could produce no fluids from his stomach.

As he laid there, life draining from him, Julian cursed himself. Everything he'd hoped for…a restored Rome, equality and tolerance for all peoples, a united Empire, peace with foreigners and an end to the Galilean menace had failed. Wealthy aristocrats around the Empire fought his decrees. The military would, without a doubt, coronate the next Caesar as an autocrat destined to bring civil war and unrest to the fragile peace. Even his aspiration to restore the old gods and eliminate the Galilean menace lay crumbled: the fool architects of the new Temple in Jerusalem had attempted to build atop the foundation of the old; the new Temple walls caved in within days of their erection.

So much he strode for, all in vain.

Weeping and shivering in pain and shock, Julian looked out into the daylight beyond the flapping curtain of his tent, the sun low in the sky over the empty plain. As he clutched at his abdomen in futility, he felt a strange light-headedness, gazing out into the sun. His vision blurred and filled with dark spots, all moving and scattering around his field of sight save one which seemed to pour forth from the sun itself, shapeless at first, then forming the faint outline of a man. Julian watched in fascination as the darkened silhouette seemed to swell and part, forming two separate outlines, oddly joined where their head should be. A schism in the shadow formed, marking the distinct form of two men, the darkness still touching at a single point.

"I think I die now," Julian uttered, watching as color bled into the two silhouettes, the familiar sight of Sergius and Bacchus emerging from the light, the couple locked in a passionate kiss. Both seemed to glow with divine light, their bodies perfect, showing no signs of the tortures they had endured, dressed in heavenly uniform and, without question, *alive*.

The couple's lips parted, eyes shimmering with happiness as they joined hands and faced the fallen Emperor. Julian gasped with wonder, his tears flowing, pain fading away. Sergius and Bacchus reached out their free hands to Julian, as if greeting a friend after a long and arduous journey.

"The Galilean has won," Julian whispered as his body went limp, breath escaping his lungs for a final time, his soul rising to meet his beaconing friends, peace in his heart as they welcomed him home.

Afterword:
Traditional Novena to Saint Sergius and Saint Bacchus

Oh glorious Martyrs,
St. Sergius and St. Bacchus,
your courage and love
are an inspiration and joy to me.
I call upon you now
and beseech you
to intercede for me to our Lord,
God, Christ Almighty.

You are the two servants of our Lord,
whose trust in the One God,
and Holy Trinity,
was so great,

that neither public humiliation,
nor torture,
nor even the threat of death
could sway you from publicly
proclaiming your faith
in the Son of the Father, Jesus.
Our God showed how proud He was
of your love and courage,
when after the death of Bacchus,
when Sergius,
being at his lowest and loneliest,
began to lose heart,
and so the Lord sent
the spirit of Bacchus to Sergius
to allow him to console Sergius
with the promise that the two of you
would again be together in Heaven.

I beseech you now
to implore the Lord our God
and pray

(State your intention here...)

and that I may at the end of this life's journey
join you and all of the saints
and angels and the elect in Heaven
to behold the face of God
and to praise God throughout eternity.
In return for your help and intercession,
I promise to spread the word

of your love and courage and devotion
to God our Lord.

And one final thing,
I pray that you be at my side
along with my guardian angel
to guide and guard and encourage me
throughout all the days of my life,
but especially at those times
when life seems to be most difficult
and my sufferings seem to be greatest.
Pray for me and watch over me
St. Sergius and St. Bacchus.

Amen.

Acknowledgements:

I could not have written this novel without the profound insight of a few individuals stated herein:

Adrian Murdoch, for his definitive and rich biography of Emperor Julian I which offered me great insight into the Last Pagan's character and the times in which he lived;

David Woods and John Boswell, for their thorough research into the cult of Sergius & Bacchus and the rite of Adelphopoesis performed in their name;

Elaine Pagels, Gary Whills, Bart Ehrman, Helmut Koester, Morton Smith, Plato, Aristotle and Marcus Arelius for their research, theories, philosophies and acumen into the anals of overlooked history;

Tony Kushner, Nikos Kazantzakis and Olvier Stone for their courage and example in finding historical truth in historical fiction;

Rasheed, Tyler, Jim, Derek & Jody for their continued encouragement and coercion in, by turns, validating my ego or kicking me in the ass to push my limits, grow as a writer and as a man to create the best work I can;

Vaunceil Strassenburg-Kruse for her gifts I continue to employ;

And to you, for sticking around this long.

About the Author

SELF PROCLAIMED UBER-GEEK DAVID REDDISH is the award-winning author of *Sex, Drugs & Superheroes: A Savage Journey into a Wretched Hive of Scum & Supervillainy*, as well as *The Passion of St. Sergius & St. Bacchus*. A prolific screenwriter as well as a novelist, Mr. Reddish has also written the as-yet unproduced *Sycophant, Embellishment, Algonquin Hills and Leopard Messiah*, as well as the television sitcom *The Temps*.

A native of Chicago, Illinois, Mr. Reddish demonstrated early verbal gifts, first speaking in complete sentences at nine months old, and an ability to read by age one and a half. By age five, he was already writing short stories and plays which he would often produce in his living room for family and friends. His talent with words lead him to work as a child stage actor and classical vocalist before turning to his focus to writing in his college years. A decorated scholar, Reddish graduated with a degree in Film from the University of Central Florida.

Always known for his brash, outspoken manner and eccentric behavior, David Reddish has won awards for his political activism with the Stonewall Young Democrats, as well as pop culture acclaim for his fashion design work, his style ranging from grunge rock to Cyberpunk chic. Working on occasion as a model and go-go dancer gained Reddish notoriety as a Los Angeles socialite, his circle of friends ranging from poverty row to the Hollywood A-List-his persona, like his written works, always versatile and original. He currently resides in Studio City, California.

Made in the USA
San Bernardino, CA
12 July 2016